JACK HARKAWAY

AMONG THE BRIGANDS

EDWIN J. BRETT,

"BOYS OF ENGLAND" OFFICE,

173, FLEET STREET,

AND ALL BOOKSELLERS.

VOL. .]   (1)   [PRICE ONE SHILLING [.

JACK HARKAWAY

AMONG THE BRIGANDS

"BOYS OF ENGLAND" OFFICE,
173, FLEET STREET.

HARKAWAY SERIES NO.

JACK HARKAWAY

AMONG THE BRIGANDS.

BEAUTIFULLY ILLUSTRATED.

VOLUME I.

LONDON:
"BOYS OF ENGLAND" OFFICE, 173, FLEET STREET, E.C.,
AND ALL BOOKSELLERS.

DE FUST KNOCK DOWN.

"HIM GOT IT DAT TIME."

EDWIN J. BRETT'S.

JACK HARKAWAY
AMONG THE BRIGANDS.

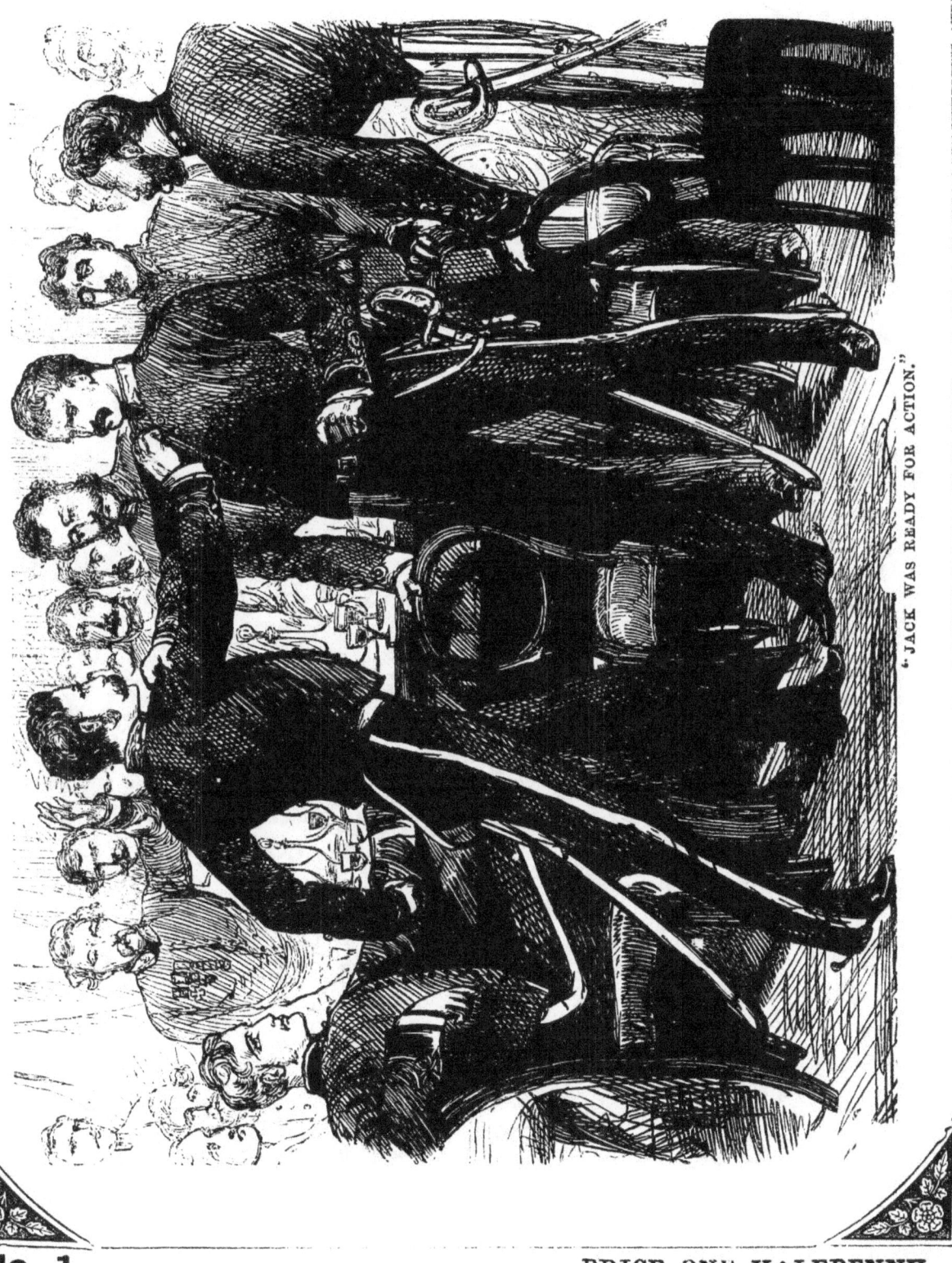

"JACK WAS READY FOR ACTION."

No. 1.

PRICE ONE HALFPENNY.
[PUBLISHED EVERY TUESDAY].

"THE BULLET, AIMED WITH UNERRING PRECISION, STRUCK JACK."

JACK HARKAWAY

AMONG THE BRIGANDS.

CHAPTER I.

A ROW IN THE OFFICERS' QUARTERS.

HARKAWAY, old fellow, I've got some news for you, which I don't think you will like any more than I do."

"What's that?"

"A man is gazetted into 'ours,' *vice* Annesley, who retired, you know, when he got spliced."

The officer who had just spoken to Jack was Major Tremlet.

He had seen service in the Crimea, and during the Indian Mutiny.

"Well," said Jack, "we are not too strong in officers. I've been orderly officer three times in the last fortnight."

"But the fellow's a cad."

Jack whistled.

"That's a different thing altogether," he said. "How did you find that out?"

"Darrel told me. Darrel knows everything about everybody. By Jove! here he is; ask him yourself."

A tall, thick-set man lounged into Jack's room at the cavalry barracks at Canterbury.

He was not a handsome man, but there was an insolent air about him, which either denoted great self-confidence, or the possession of rank and wealth.

In fact it was a mixture of both.

His name was Augustus, Lord Darrel, a wealthy nobleman and a captain in the —th Dragoon Guards, which celebrated regiment was, for the time being quartered at Canterbury.

Lord Augustus Darrel was usually called in the regiment Gus Darrel and he was regarded with fear rather than love.

Jack Harkaway had been in the —th Dragoon Guards for about two years.

His brother officers liked him very much.

The new regulations abolishing the purchase of commissions in the army, had just come into force.

Some of those who had bought their commissions did not like the men who were to come in by examinations.

Lord Augustus Darrel was one of those.

Harkaway, however, was far too liberal in his ideas to entertain any such petty prejudices.

He was sure that the new system would procure the best officers for the army.

Mr. Cardwell, the Secretary of State for War, was the author of the scheme.

Therefore, the new officers who came in without purchase were called "Cardwell's cads," or "non-purchase cads."

As if a man became a gentleman simply because he had more money at his command than those less fortunate.

Jack's room in the cavalry barracks at Canterbury was plainly furnished.

He had hung a few pictures on the walls, and put some flowers on the window-sill.

But he did not take much trouble over it, because he expected to leave it soon.

Emily, his wife, had been very ill, after

the birth of a son, the only issue of their marriage.

An attack of fever had made her extremely weak, and she had been recommended by her physicians to go to the south of France.

Mr. and Mrs. Harvey had accompanied her.

Lately Jack had received reassuring accounts of his wife's health, and he expected her back every day.

He had taken a house for her in Canterbury, and when she arrived, he would, of course leave barracks and live with her.

It was a great grief to him not to be able to be with her, but he could not get away from his regiment.

His first idea had been to go into the Blues, but his father persuaded him to go into a working regiment.

The —th Dragoons had seen plenty of fighting.

They had gained credit long before the Peninsular campaign, and India and the Crimea testified to their courage and dash.

It was an honour to belong to such a famous regiment.

When Gus Darrel entered the room with a cigar in his mouth and his hands in his pockets, he caught Major Tremlet's concluding remark.

"Talking about that non-purchase cad are you?" he said.

"Yes," replied Jack; "Tremlet's been telling me about him. Who is he?"

"Son of a man who makes snuff wholesale"

"Sells it wholesale, I suppose you mean," said Jack.

"I don't want you to tell me what I mean," replied Captain Lord Augustus Darrel.

This was spoken with his usual insolence.

Jack's face flushed.

"What is the new man's name?" asked Major Tremlet, wishing to avoid an explosion between Harkaway and Gus Darrel.

"The fellow rejoices in the name of Samuel Cockles," replied Darrel. "Lovely name isn't it?"

"And his father is a snuff maker?"

"Yes; beautiful combination! The

—th Dragoons is coming to something."

"Perhaps he may be a very decent fellow, after all," hazarded Jack.

"So might you be, but you're not," said Gus Darrel.

"I say, Darrel," cried Major Tremlet, "what's the matter with you this morning? Do you want to have a row with Harkaway?"

"I'm not at all particular."

"His lordship can have as much row with me as he likes," said Jack calmly, "though it is none of my seeking."

"Fact is," replied Darrel, "that this War Secretary riles me. What does he want to pitchfork a snuff man into 'ours' for?"

I don't see any objection to the new system of giving commissions and promotion by merit," said Jack.

"Don't you? Sorry for you," sneered Gus Darrel.

"I can understand your grief," answered Jack.

"Why?"

"Because if merit is the test of promotion, you're not likely to get any."

"Capital! bravo!" laughed Major Tremlet; "you've given it him back, Harkaway."

Lord Augustus Darrel bit his thick, ugly lips with vexation.

He shrugged his elephantine shoulders in a manner expressive of disgust,

"If you like the cad," he said, "you may make as much fuss with him as you please."

"I shan't ask your permission," replied Jack.

"Don't suppose you will."

"You fellows are quarrelling like a couple of schoolboys," remarked the major.

"Is that any business of yours?" asked Darrel.

"He likes to snarl," replied Jack; "let him alone."

"All I know is," said Darrel, "that I object to the introduction of this man Cockles into the regiment, and I shall lead him such a life that he will be glad to get out of it."

"That won't be fair," said Jack.

"Why not? Are we to have anybody in the —th Dragoons?"

"Wait till you see the man. He may not be a bad so

"I'll lay six to four he is ; his name's enough."

"If I see the fellow bullied without any cause, I shall take his part," replied Jack.

Turning to Major Tremlet, Darrel said—

"You see Harkaway is bustling himself to have a row with me."

"Well," said Jack, "just get out of my quarters, will you? I can say what I like in my own place, can't I?"

"No," replied Gus Darrel; "my commission is much older than yours, and I'm not going to be dictated to by a sub-lieutenant."

"Sell out then."

"Come with me, Darrel," said Major Tremlet. "We will have a game of billiards somewhere."

"I want to settle this matter with Harkaway," replied Darrel, obstinately. "He has taken the cad under his protection."

"I don't see that he has done that," answered Tremlet.

"Oh, yes, he has."

"You want to organise a conspiracy against the poor beggar, and make his life a misery and a burden to him," exclaimed Jack; "and I say I won't lend myself to it."

"Then we are to be cad-ridden out of our lives. We shall be the laughing stock of the service," replied Darrel.

"Go and talk to the colonel about it; don't bother me," said Jack.

"I don't like being ordered out of a man's room."

"If you don't go——" began Jack, while his eyes flashed threateningly.

"Well!" ejaculated Gus Darrel, staring at him rudely.

"You shall come with me," exclaimed Major Tremlet, taking hold of his arm.

"Please, don't pull me about," replied Darrel.

"What on earth do you want?" continued the major. "Is it a row in quarters? A court-martial would be a great deal worse than half-a-dozen non-purchase men in the regiment."

Jack walked to the window and began to pluck the dead leaves off a geranium.

There was a knock at the door.

"Just see who that is for me, Tremlet, will you; there's a good fellow?" exclaimed Jack.

Going to the door, the major opened it and said—

"It is your bow-man."*

"What is it?" exclaimed Jack.

"Telegram for you, sir," replied the bat-man.

"Put it on the table,"

Again taking Gus Darrel's arm, the major said—

"Come with me, and leave Harkaway to read his electricity."

Reluctantly the quarrelsome Lord Augustus Darrel, captain in the —th Dragoon Guards, accompanied Major Tremlet into the passage.

"Glad he's gone," muttered Jack, breaking open the telegraph message.

As he retired Jack heard him saying—

"I hate a cad. Can't think how a man like Harkaway can stick up for the snuffy beast with the ugly name."

CHAPTER II.

THE NON-PURCHASE CAD.

DURING the two years Harkaway had been in the army, he had improved very much.

Everyone said he was a remarkably smart officer.

There was not a better rider in the regiment.

He had grown a long moustache and whiskers, though he did not patronise the beard movement.

If it had not been for Emily's illness and her enforced absence from him, he would have been perfectly happy.

Army life pleased him.

* Spelt "bat-man. An officer's regimental servant.

He longed, however, for a war, and an opportunity of distinguishing himself in the field.

The telegram he had received was from Harvey.

"To Sub-Lieutenant Harkaway, —th Dragoon Guards, Cavalry Barracks, Canterbury."

It came rrom Naples, and stated that the sender was coming to England at once.

Mrs. Harvey and Emily were to come with him to an estate he had bought, about three miles from Canterbury, called Burton Beeches.

Emily sent her love to Jack, and said she was much better and stronger.

In a few days he might expect to see his loved wife, from whom he had been separated nearly three months.

This news delighted Jack, who had been very anxious about the state of Emily's health.

His son, a boy twelve months old, was a fine, hearty, boy, the image of his father.

Jack forgot all about his row with Gus Darrel about the non-purchase cad.

Strolling into the barrack yard, he saw Monday in conversation with a slim, fair-haired, delicate looking youth.

Monday was still Jack's valet.

He and his wife had lodgings in the town and lived very happily together.

"Yes, sare," replied Monday, "me show you to Mr. Harkaway's quarters, sare'"

"Thank you, very much," replied the slim, fair man. "Will it be asking you too great a favour, if you will kindly see after my luggage, which is outside in a fly?"

"No, sare, cert'ny not," answered Monday; "me very glad."

Jack advanced to the stranger as Monday went to the gate of the barrack yard.

"My name is Harkaway," he said. "Can I be of any service to you?"

"Sub-Lieutenant Harkaway?" inquired the stranger, looking at a card upon which something was written.

"Yes."

"Of the —th Dragoon Guards?"

"Yes."

"Then you will recognise this card."

Jack took the card and read—

"Mr. Richard Harvey."

Underneath was written—

"Naples. Dear Jack,—The bearer of this, Mr. Samuel Cockles, is going to join your regiment. We have met him and his people over here, and, if you can do him any good, I shall take it as a personal favour.—R.H."

"I am very glad to make your acquaintance, Mr. Cockles," said Jack.

"Thank you," replied the little man, who was extremely meek and deferential in his manner.

"Mr. Harvey is a very great and old friend of mine."

"So he told me."

"You met him in Naples, I believe."

"Yes; my father and mother, and my sister Lily and I have been over there for a little while, and it was owing to my father that Mr. Harvey has just bought an estate at Canterbury."

"Indeed."

"We have a place adjoining it, called Motcombe Hall."

"I saw your gazette in the paper," said Jack.

"Did you?"

"More strictly speaking, I heard of it. But now let us see what can be done for you. My servant will show you the colonel's quarters. Go and report yourself, and then come up and see me."

Sub-Lieutenant Cockles thanked Jack again, and when Monday had seen his luggage safely stowed, he went with the black to report himself.

Jack returned to his room and waited until Mr. Cockles came with Monday.

"Here you are," said Jack, gaily. "I hope you begin to feel yourself one of 'ours' already."

"The colonel seemed a little stiff and formal," answered Sub-Lieutenant Cockles.

"It's a way colonel's have," replied Jack, laughing.

"I'm afraid my name is against me, Mr. Harkaway. Samuel Cockles don't sound very pretty, does it?"

"What's in a name?"

"Oh, I don't know. There was a man named Bugg, and he changed his name to Norfolk Howard, which is much prettier,"

"Have you ever done anything to be ashamed of your name, Mr. Cockles?" asked Jack, a little sternly.

" No, never ?"

" Then stick to it. There are many jwells I can tell you, who would be glad to be the sons of honest men, or honest themselves."

" I am pleased to hear you say that," said Cockles, " because I thought I should be dreadfully snubbed in a crack regiment like this for having such a name."

" What made you enter it then?"

" Well, you know, my father has made a lot of money in trade."

" Snuff?" said Jack.

" Exactly," replied Cockles, with a half sigh ; " you have heard that. I thought it would travel about."

" Never mind."

" But I can't help minding. My father has determined that I shall be a gentleman and cut a shine, as he calls it, and that's why I have come into a swell cavalry regiment."

" I will do all I can to put you on your legs," said Jack, " owing to my friend Harvey's introduction."

" Shall I have a very hard time of it ?" asked Cockles.

" I hope not."

" What is the routine ?"

" Well, you will have to dine at mess to-night ; that's the worst. I hope fellows will not chaff you ; if they do, you and I must lay our heads together, and see what is to be done."

" Is it a very dreadful thing, Mr. Harkaway, for a man's father to have made his money by selling snuff ?" asked Cockles, mildly.

" No ; why should it be ?"

Seeing Monday waiting at the door, Jack continued—

" You will take something after your journey, will you not ?"

" A glass of wine, thanks."

" Monday," exclaimed Jack, " go to the mess, and get a pint of sherry and order lunch."

" Yes, sare," replied Monday.

Some cold chicken and ham was brought up and placed before the young officer, who ate sparingly.

" You, of course, saw my wife," Jack took occasion to observe.

" Oh, yes, frequently at Naples. Mrs. Harkaway is stronger and better. Mr. and Mrs. Harvey are very kind to her,

but she seems to miss you," replied Cockles.

The afternoon passed quickly, and Jack did all he could to put the fresh arrival straight ; settling his things in his quarters, and chatting pleasantly with him to put him at his ease.

To a shy and nervous man like Cockles it was very agreeable, on his new arrival amongst strangers, and his introduction to a new kind of life, to find a friend.

At last it was time to dress for mess.

When Mr. Cockles entered the room with Jack, the colonel gave him a stiff bow, and the other officers stared at him rudely.

Gus Darrel put his glass in his eye and regarded him very offensively.

Then he turned to some one and made a remark, at which there was a subdued laugh.

Cockles coloured up to the eyes, and felt hot and uncomfortable.

He guessed he was the subject of his brother officers' mirth.

" Who is that gentleman ?" he asked of Jack.

" Captain Lord Augustus Darrel, the bully of the regiment. You will find him a teaser, but don't be afraid of him. I'll stand by you."

" Will you really ?" replied Cockles, gratefully.

" Sit down here," said Jack. " I have to go a little higher up the table."

Presently the dinner began, the band playing agreeably in an ante-room.

The —th Dragoon Guards prided themselves upon their excellent band.

It was unrivalled in the service.

Sub-Lieutenant Cockles looked at the fine handsome gentlemen who were in future to be his brother officers.

He admired the graceful ease of their manner, the tone of their conversation, and their bearing generally.

He was surprised at the splendid service of plate, the excellence of the dinner, and the style in which everything was done.

But his astonishment was not to be wondered at.

It was the first time he had ever dined at the mess of a crack cavalry regiment in the British army.

No one spoke to him, however, except

Harkaway, who once or twice addressed a remark to him.

It seemed as if by common consent the officers of the —th had resolved to have nothing to do with the non-purchase cad.

When the band ceased for a moment, an event happened which proved to Jack that the officers did not mean to lose time in insulting Sub-Lieutenant Cockles.

Looking straight at the young man, Gus Darrel sneezed loudly.

There was a subdued laugh all round the table.

Presently another officer, and then another, and a fourth sneezed in the same marked manner.

It seemed as if a sudden attack of influenza had seized the whole of the gallant —th.

Jack's face flushed with annoyance.

As for Sub-Lieutenant Cockles, he became purple with rage and indignation.

The insult was unmistakable.

It was evidently known that his father had made his fortune by manufacturing snuff, which fact, in conjuction with his common name, had made him obnoxious to his brother officers.

This was, though, no fault of his own.

He was the victim of aristocratic prejudice.

The sneezing went on all dinner-time at intervals.

When the cloth was removed, the sneezing became more frequent.

The colonel could not help noticing it.

"Really," he said, "some of you fellows seem to have very bad colds. I wish you would try to get them cured before you come to mess again."

Gus Darrel had a violent fit of sneezing which caused all the younger officers to laugh immoderately, while the older ones could not help smiling.

Suddenly Sub-Lieutenant Cockles rose to his feet.

Jack wondered what on earth he was going to do.

He was very pale, and the corners of his mouth twitched with nervous agitation.

But there was an expression of resolution about his face which showed that he meant to go through with some purpose.

Every one regarded him with silent wonder.

"Gentlemen," he said, "I have come among you to-day as a stranger, but still on an equality with you by virtue of the Queen's commission which I hold."

Loud murmurs arose.

"Listen to me," he continued, raising his voice. "I am the son of Cockles, the snuff maker, and I am not ashamed of it."

He placed a handsome snuff-box on the table.

"In that box," he went on, "is some of my father's snuff. You will find it very good, and I beg leave to state that if any gentleman sneezes again, without first taking a pinch of that snuff, I shall consider it a personal insult, and resent it as I think fit."

"Very well put. He's got some pluck in him," remarked Major Tremlet, to a neighbour.

The colonel of the regiment had listened attentively to this speech.

He felt himself called upon to say something.

"I think," he observed, "that what has fallen from Mr. Cockles is well worthy of your attention."

The officers were silent.

No more sneezing was heard.

Even Gus Darrel, the bully of the regiment, was for the moment cowed by the resolute bearing of the young man.

CHAPTER III.

HOW SUB-LIEUTENANT COCKLES THOUGHT FIT TO ACT.

COLONEL PRENDERGAST was essentially a weak man, and he felt glad to think that the prospect of a disturbance at mess was over.

He knew that the Horse Guards had determined to carry out the new regulations of the government to the letter.

The army was to be reformed.

Money and position were to be no longer the means of obtaining commissions and promotion.

A poor man of obscure birth was to have the same chance as an earl.

The colonel was particularly anxious to avoid any scandal in his regiment.

He knew that the press and the public would take the matter up.

There would be an official inquiry, and very likely the Duke of Cambridge, as commander-in-chief, would, by way of punishment, send the —th Dragoons on foreign service.

They hoped, when they left Canterbury, to be quartered at Brighton.

This was a much more pleasant prospect than going to India.

An oppressive silence fell upon everyone after the colonel spoke.

Gus Darrel was the first to recover himself.

Reaching over the table, he took up the snuff-box, and threw it some distance from him without opening it.

Then, taking out his scented cambric handkerchief, he sneezed again in the most pointed manner.

Sub-Lieutenant Cockles rose.

Jack left his seat, and taking his arm, begged him to be quiet.

"It is infamous," he said, "but for God's sake be calm."

"Leave me alone, Mr. Harkaway; I will not disgrace myself," he answered, with a smile which denoted perfect self-possession.

"Gentlemen," he exclaimed, with a sarcastic emphasis on the word, "you have all witnessed the unmistakable insult I have just received from one whom I am informed is Captain Lord Augustus Darrel?"

"Yes, yes!" cried several.

"I have too much respect for myself and for you, though your treatment to me this evening has been anything but kind or friendly, to create a disturbance at mess."

"He's a rank cur; I told you so," whispered Gus Darrel to Captain Sinclair.

"Of course," replied Sinclair. "Those fellows have no blood in their veins, only ditch water."

Sub-Lieutenant Samuel Cockles spoke again.

"I shall find an opportunity, however, of punishing the man, who, though an officer, is certainly not a gentleman."

This was what he said.

"My good fellow," said Gus Darrel, "how can you possibly know anything about gentlemen? You have had no opportunity of judging."

Taking no notice of this remark, Sub-Lieutenant Cockles said, addressing the colonel.

"Have I your permission, Colonel Prendergast to retire to my quarters?"

"Certainly, Mr. Cockles," replied the colonel.

Bowing to the head of the regiment, the lieutenant slowly left the room.

A heavy silence again fell upon the officers.

Colonel Prendergast was the first to break it in a tone of vexation.

"You certainly have got a knack, Darrel of making things deucedly unpleasant," he said.

"Why not?" answered his lordship. "I'm not going to stand the cad. He's some counter jumper or other. Why couldn't he be satisfied with the line?"

"You know that they are putting Cardwell's men in everywhere."

"So much the worse for the non-purchase cads. I'll bet this Snuffles or

Cockles, whatever his name is, will wish he'd never been born."

"If he were to pull your nose," said Jack, "it wouldn't surprise me."

"Look here, Harkaway," exclaimed Gus Darrel, colouring with anger, "I have told you to be careful what you say to me."

"And I choose to say what I like, that's all the difference."

"Why don't you go and comfort your cad? We know he is a pet of yours," sneered Darrel.

"I declare," said the colonel, "that this mess is becoming a bear garden. I'm ashamed of some of you men."

Gus Darrel was evidently in a quarrelsome mood that evening.

There had never been any friendship lost between him and Jack, who on this occasion felt that he had been violent and unjust to the new comer, Cockles, who had been insulted through no fault of his own.

All the chivalrous feeling which had led Jack to take the part of the weak and persecuted at school, rose in his mind.

There only required a spark to flash in order to create an open rupture between him and the insolent young lord.

But a mess table is very different from a playground or a schoolroom.

It was only when Darrel said, "We have more than one cad amongst us," that Jack rose and approached him.

"Do you mean that sneer for me, my lord?" he asked, with white lips.

"If you like, you can appropriate it to yourself," was the off-hand answer of Darrel.

"Then all I can say is," exclaimed Jack, "that it is you who are a disgrace to the regiment."

"I?" repeated Darrel.

"Yes. You have shown more of the instinct of a thoroughbred blackguard than any one else."

At these words, Darrel sprang forward and seized Jack in a rude grasp.

He was regardless of consequences.

His evil countenance glared with passion, and was fiery red.

Jack pushed him away with one hand, which he held against his breast, while the other was ready for action.

"By Heaven! this is too much!" he cried.

"I'll let you know," said Darrel, "that I am not to be insulted for nothing."

Half a dozen officers sprang to their feet, and with some difficulty separated the combatants.

They stood glaring at one another.

"Pretty behaviour this, gentlemen!" said the colonel, angrily. "I insist upon an immediate reconciliation."

Gus Darrel laughed heartily.

"I didn't mean anything," he said. "Harkaway and I are not going to annihilate each other this time; it is all over for the present."

He was afraid of the colonel's displeasure, and resumed his seat.

Jack also sat down at his part of the table, after bestowing a significant glance at Darrel.

He wrote on a slip of paper, "The time *will* come,' and passed it on to his late opponent.

Lord Darrel read it, and nodded his head in token of assent.

"'Pon honour," cried Colonel Prendergast, who had noticed this, "I will put the first man who begins a row under arrest. I will indeed. I give you my word."

This was a threat not to be despised.

Although the colonel was known to be easy-going and tolerant, he could act harshly if provoked too far.

After mess, the orderly officer went his rounds. It was Captain Sinclair.

As he was leaving the room, the colonel called him on one side.

"If there is any riot, Sinclair," he said, "let me know at once, and put both under arrest."

Jack left the mess room, went straight to Cockles' room, and found him making an entry in his diary.

"Writing home?" asked Jack.

"No. I keep a diary, and am merely putting down what took place. Did I behave well?" asked the sub-lieutenant.

"Capitally. I think you had the majority of the mess with you."

"I want you to do me a favour, Harkaway, if you will?"

"What is that?"

"To take a challenge from me to Lord Darrel."

"Absurd, my dear fellow," said Jack; "you cannot fight a duel.

"What can I do then?"

"Demand a court-martial, to see who is wrong, or write to the Horse Guards for a commission of inquiry."

Cockles shook his head.

"No," he said. "Whatever is done, must be done by my hand."

"Don't be rash, that's all," said Jack. Then changing the conversation he asked—

"Do you smoke?"

"Only cigarettes."

"Come to my diggings then, and blow a peaceful cloud. I want to talk to you about my dear little wife, bless her."

Sub-Lieutenant Cockles gladly accepted the invitation, and they passed a couple of hours very agreeably together with the aid of coffee, tobacco, and chess.

Meanwhile the lieutenant's enemies had not been idle.

Gus Darrel, during a walk he had taken in the afternoon, had remarked the arrival in a field outside the town of a travelling waxwork caravan, containing portrait models of celebrated people.

After mess, he sought the veterinary surgeon. His name was Potts.

Darrel talked to him for five minutes in a low tone, and ended by saying—

"Can you do it, Potts?"

"Yes, my lord, I'll do it," replied the vet.

"Look alive then, and I'll send you two boxes of the best cigars Carreras has in his shop."

"Ha! ha! ha!" grinned the vet, "your lordship's the boy for a joke."

"You grinning old jackal, be off."

"Yes, my lord. Ha! ha! I'm off, my lord," answered Potts.

Half an hour passed.

Then the vet. entered Captain Lord Angustus Darrel's quarters and found five or six officers assembled.

He looked round cautiously.

"Speak out; these gentlemen are all in it," said Darrel.

"I've got a beauty, my lord," said Potts.

"Where is it?"

"In his bed, lying as natural as life."

"And the owner of the show?"

"I've got him below, only waiting for a signal to come up and kick up a row. He fell in with the joke beautifully."

"All right," said Darrel; "when you hear me whistling 'Garry Owen,' let the beggar loose, and tell him not to be afraid of giving tongue."

"Yes, my lord."

"And I say, Potts, take a couple of bottles of whisky off my table. You must moisten his clay, and I know you are no enemy to a stiff grog yourself."

"There's no word of a lie about that," replied Potts, putting a bottle of L.L. under each arm.

A little later the colonel sought Darrel, and was delighted to hear that no disturbance had taken place.

"That's all right," he answered. "I feel that I can trust to your good sense, Darrel; I'm going to play a rubber with Tremlet against Forbes and Deering. Keep things as quiet as you can, there's a good fellow."

"But we mean to get rid of the snuff man, colonel," said Darrel.

"Well, well, time will show. He will see the wisdom of exchanging, perhaps. It is a great bore to be afflicted with such fellows, but don't make a row about it."

While the easy-going colonel of the —th Dragoon Guards was, in an indirect manner, aiding and abetting the conspiracy against Sub-Lieutenant Cockles, the latter came out of Jack's quarters.

It was his intention to go to his own and retire to rest early.

He was tired with travelling and the excitement of the scene at the mess.

By the light of the gas in the passage he distinctly saw his tormentor, surrounded by his friends.

"Now's my time," he said to himself.

He set his lips firmly together.

Advancing towards Darrel, he did not stop till he got close to him.

Then he took his snuff-box from his pocket, opened it, and prepared to throw the contents in his lordship's face.

"This is how I treat a ruffian," he said, moving his hand.

CHAPTER IV.

THE "DOOK" IN BED.

ONE of those trifling occurrences which a man can never guard against took place.

It changed what might have been a serious affair into a scene of confusion and laughter.

Captain Sinclair, who was a devoted friend of Darrel's, saw Cockles' intention.

Just as he moved his hand to throw the snuff into Darrel's face, he jerked his elbow.

Instead of going in the direction he intended, it went the other way.

The full contents of the box were cast straight in the colonel's face.

He was in the act of speaking.

His mouth was filled, and, as he gasped for breath, he drew it up his nose.

It went into his eyes and nearly blinded him.

The colonel uttered a fierce yell.

He coughed and sneezed, and the more he sneezed the more he coughed.

Very improper remarks came from the colonel's lips.

His language would have made a clergyman's hair stand on end.

"Confound it!" he said, clearing his throat; "who has done this? Perdition! I am half blinded! Pah! pish!"

No one could help laughing.

"What's the shindy?" inquired Jack, coming out on hearing the noise.

"Cockles has made a bad shot," replied Captain Sinclair.

"How?"

"He wanted to shy his snuff at Darrel, but it went wrong."

Darrel brought the colonel a wet towel, with which he wiped the snuff out of his eyes.

Still he continued to cough and stutter.

"I am very sorry, sir; it was an accident," exclaimed Cockles, crimson with vexation.

"Sorry, sir! Pah!" said the colonel, furiously. "You ought to be cashiered, sir—pah! I've a good mind to order you under arrest, sir. Pish! bah! pish!"

"The snuff wasn't intended for you sir."

"Hang it all, sir! it's too bad. Take the snuff away from him, someone. He'll commit some dreadful mischief with it. Pish! bah!"

Jack touched Cockles on the arm.

"Come with me," he whispered, "and explain in the morning. The colonel's frantic, and no wonder."

"Take his snuff away!" roared the colonel, stamping his foot.

"All right, sir," said Jack; "I'll see to it."

By main force he dragged Sub-Lieutenant Cockles away along the passage.

"Take a better shot next time," replied Darrel, with a provoking smile.

"Let me get at him," said Cockles. "I'll strangle him."

"Are you mad?" said Jack. "You've made shine enough for one night. Come along."

He got him into his quarters, and shut the door.

Meanwhile, the colonel was getting a little better.

"Deuce take that man," he said; "what made him do it?"

"He meant it for Darrel, sir," said Sinclair; "but, being nervous, he missed his aim."

"You don't think he did it on purpose?"

"I shouldn't think so," replied Darrel, "I'm the fellow's mark, not you, sir."

"Well, well, well. He must not be allowed to carry snuff. How on earth shall I be able to play at whist? Confounded nuisance! Monstrous bore this. I do wish the government would keep its manufacturing division in its place."

"Or at all events, not allow them to bring their manufactures with them," said Darrel.

"We shall have the son of a washerwoman bringing a patent mangle with him," suggested an officer.

"Or some fellow whose father makes quack pills, coming to physic the whole regiment," said another.

"I do believe I shall shudder all my life at the sight of snuff," said the colonel, shuffling away.

When the officers were alone again, they retired into Darrel's quarters.

Cockles did not stay long with Harkaway.

He was more bitter than before against Captain Lord Augustus Darrel.

Luck seemed to have deserted him.

"Best to keep still," said Jack, "at least in barracks. If you meet Darrel outside, punch his head and have done with it."

"But his insult to me was public, and so ought my retaliation to be," said Cockles.

"My dear fellow, please yourself. I believe in a quiet set-to with fists."

"He's too big for me and too strong at that game. I'm consumptive."

Jack shrugged his shoulders.

"Good-night," continued Sub-Lieutenant Cockles.

"Going to roost? Ta, ta; don't forget parade at seven to-morrow morning."

Sub-Lieutenant Cockles went to his rooms, baulked of his revenge that night.

He shut the door, placed the candle—a very dim rushlight from the quartermaster's stores—on the table, and looked round at his belongings, which the servant had put in order.

"I had hoped to be so happy in the army," he sighed. He turned to the bed.

Starting back with a cry of astonishment, he exclaimed—"This is too bad!"

In the bed, cosily tucked up, was a man.

He appeared to be in a deep sleep.

Probably he had drunk too much, and mistaken the room.

"By Jupiter!" said Sub-Lieutenant Cockles, whom a sense of wrongs was beginning to rouse, "I won't have this."

He went nearer to the bed.

This outrage was the last straw to break the back of the much-enduring camel.

That long-suffering animal can bear a good deal. But there is a limit to the patience of camels, and so there is to that of sub-lieutenants in crack cavalry regiments.

"Dear me!" continued the lieutenant; "it's very funny, but he's got a face like the late Duke of Wellington."

He took a closer look.

"Yes, he is indeed what my poor father would call the 'dook.' But how the dickens did the duke get into my bed?"

This was the problem.

CHAPTER V.

A STRANGE INTRUDER.

SUB-LIEUTENANT SAMUEL COCKLES could not remember having seen the face at mess.

But there were so many faces.

Perhaps the gentleman had obtained leave, and had been dining out.

That must be it.

"How sound asleep he is," mused the lieutenant

His anger increased.

"I will not have it!" he said; as sure as my name is Cockles, I will not put up with it."

Raising his voice, he continued—

"You, sir, come out of my bed!"

There was no answer.

Not even the least movement.

"Do you hear me, you villain—you drunken wretch?"

Still no reply.

"I'll shake him," he said, "and see if that will have any effect upon him."

He put his hand on his arm, and pushed him backwards and forwards.

"He's very light," said the lieutenant; "quite a bag of bones."

Hesitating a moment, he wondered how he ought to act with regard to the strange intruder upon his privacy.

"He must go away; he ought to—he shall!" replied Cockles, at last.

Opening the door, he returned to the bed, and lifting the body in his arms, propped it up in the passage.

"How stiffly he stands! Is he—can he be dead?" said Cockles.

Deering had been watching him.

"Come along, you fellows," exclaimed Deering, looking into Darrel's room.

They were all in the passage in a moment.

Cockles was rather short-sighted.

When anything embarrassed him he put on a pair of spectacles.

These he was adjusting over his nose to look more closely at the intruder.

"Go up to him," said Darrel to Deering.

The latter strolled up with his hands in his pockets.

"What's the matter now?" he said to Cockles.

"I have turned a man out of my bed. His conduct was disgraceful, but I fear there is something the matter with him," replied Cockles.

"Good Heaven! You've killed him!" exclaimed Deering.

"Nonsense! It cannot be true."

"The man is, dead. You've done a nice thing for yourself and the regiment too."

"Dear me. He seemed very stiff and cold," said Sub-Lieutenant Cockles, in an agony of apprehension, "But I declare solemnly I did not hurt him."

"It's your snuff, perhaps, that did the trick."

"Do you know him?"

"Of course. He is one of ours, poor fellow!"

Gus Darrel walked up the passage, whistling "Garry Owen" as loud as he could.

Suddenly voices were heard.

They came nearer.

"You can't go upstairs, I tell you," Potts, the veterinary surgeon, was heard to say.

"But I say I will; and when I say I will, I will, and no error," replied the waxwork showman.

The whole affair had been arranged, and they were to divide a ten-pound note between them, given by Captain Lord Augustus Darrel.

It was a very neat little bit of acting.

"Well, at least you can tell me what you want," continued Potts.

"Some of you hossifer gents have been and broke into my show."

"What show?"

"I'm the proprietor of a waxwork."

"Well?"

"They've been and gone and stole the dook."

"What duke?" asked Potts.

"The Duke of Vellington, the finestest life-like himage as I've got in the whole show."

"I don't believe it," said the vet.; "all the officers in the —th Dragoons are gentlemen. They would be incapable of such a thing."

"Gammon! I know my book," said the showman, "and I've had the straight tip given me."

He winked his eye knowingly.

"You'd better see the colonel."

"Kernal be bothered. You don't kid me," said the showman. "Look there."

"Where?"

"Up against that wall. That's the dook. Think I can't tell my own dook ven I sees him?"

He ran along the passage, closely followed by the vet.

Grasping Sub-Lieutenant Cockles by the arm, he said—

"I ax your pardon, Mr. Hossifer, but is it you as 'as been a-having larks with the dook?"

"I—I put the unfortunate man here; but if he is dead, I am not to blame," replied Cockles, mildly.

The showman burst into a loud laugh.

All the officers who were in the secret of the joke, and some who were not, crowded round.

"Unfortnit man!—dead! What does he mean?" he asked.

"What do you mean by laughing at me?" demanded Cockles, facing him angrily.

"Come that's a good un. You mean to say as how you didn't steal him?" said the showman.

"Steal—a—man?" gasped the lieutenant.

"Yes, he's what I get my livin' out on. He's a wax un. Tell me next that you don't know that."

The truth flashed across Cockles all at once; with a groan he sank back against the wall.

Loud laughter rang in his ears.

"Give him a pinch of snuff, that will wake him up," said a voice.

Cockles had closed his eyes, but he knew it was Gus Darrel who spoke.

Afraid to trust himself to answer him just then, he made a rush to his room and shut himself in.

"Bolted," said Deering.

"You'll have to square this 'ere job, sir. I shall come up in the morning. If it ain't put rosy, I shall speak to the colonel. People can't have their wax dooks stole like this, not by no manner of means," said the showman.

Sub-Lieutenant Cockles made no answer.

"Sold, by Jove!" he said to himself. "What an infernal ass I must be."

The vet. led away the showman, who had picked up his waxwork "dook" with great care, and the officers retired to laugh at the joke they had played the non-purchase cad. Jack had been an amused spectator of the scene.

For Cockles he felt sorry, but he couldn't openly interfere.

If personal violence had been used it would have been different.

But he had seen too many jokes played, and played them himself, to take much notice of such a trifle.

"I'm afraid they'll kill him, or make him exchange," he said to himself.

CHAPTER VI.

IN THE WOOD.

AT breakfast next morning Monday burst into Jack's room, full of excitement.

"Oh, sare!" he cried, "um brought um good news, sare."

"What is it, you wild Indian?" asked Jack.

"Mast' Harvey, him downstairs, sare, talking to the colonel."

"Have they all come over?"

"Yes, sare, all come in the night. Missy Emily and all," answered Monday

While Monday was speaking, Harvey made his appearance.

He and Jack were soon shaking hands as only old friends can, displaying a heartiness which showed the affection that existed between them.

If Jack had become manly, so had Harvey.

He was a little bronzed by the sun of Italy, and his whiskers and moustache were nearly as long as his friend's.

"Delighted to see you, Dick," said Jack. "It seems an age since we parted."

"Only a few months," replied Harvey.

"Where is Emily?"

"She and Lily Cockles and Hilda are getting up a pic-nic in Boughton Wood, to which I am to bring you and Sam Cockles at once."

"All right. I'll soon be ready."

"By the way, how does Sam get on?"

"So, so. The men of the —th don't like him, but I daresay he'll settle down, when he's rubbed off the rough edges, and fellows have forgotten the chaff about the snuff. Tell me about Emily."

"She is much stronger, and the babe is a regular young tyrant. I find my new estate, Burton Beeches, is close to Cockles' place, Motcombe Hall. We are near neighbours, and that is very jolly, isn't it, because our wives have taken quite a fancy to Miss Lily Cockles."

"It is a lovely summer day," said Jack. "Let us walk up the London Road to the wood."

"As you like."

"Have you got your trap here?"

"Yes. It is at the 'Rose.'"

"Well, send Monday to tell your man to go back and let them know we shall be up in an hour or so."

"Certainly," said Harvey.

Monday was dispatched to the hotel with the message, and Sub-Lieutenant Cockles was apprised of the invitation to the pic-nic.

In a short time they were all in readiness, and left the barracks, walking down the Military Road, and up the London Road to Bonghton Wood.

The pic-nic was to take place at a romantic spot known as Five Oaks, or the Gipsies' Glade.

Before Harvey's man servant started on the homeward journey, he gave Monday a note.

"It's for one of your officers," he said; "give it him, but on no account let him know where it came from. Twig?"

"Yes," replied Monday, "um twig, 'ight 'nuff."

Going back to the barracks, he looked at the envelope, and saw it was directed to Captain Augustus Darrel.

He put it on the table in the captain's quarters, thinking that was the best way to avoid questioning.

Ten minutes afterwards, when Darrel entered, he saw the note.

It was in a lady's delicate hand-writing.

Breaking it open, he read—

"You will remember meeting a young lady several times last autumn. She is anxious to meet you again. Come to the Gipsies' Glade this afternoon in Boughton Wood, and you shall know who the lady is, that is to say, if you are desirous of renewing your acquaintance with Lily of the Valley."

"By Jove!" said Darrel, "this is an adventure. I remember the girl well. She would not tell me who she was, and seemed as virtuous as she was pretty. I'll go like a shot."

Six months before, he had accidentally met a pretty, fair-haired girl, evidently a lady from her dress, manner, and conversation.

They used to walk together, but she would not tell him anything more about herself than that her name was Lily of the Valley.

Suddenly she left the neighbourhood.

Darrel was delighted to renew the romantic friendship that had begun to spring up between them.

Accordingly he too prepared to go to Boughton Wood.

The letter was destined to have important results to all the personages in our story.

Jack, Harvey, and Cockles walked along together in the pleasant sunshine, perfectly happy and light-hearted.

"Did you see the news in the paper about old Mole?" asked Harvey.

"No. What was it?" answered Jack, eagerly.

His curiosity was aroused.

Anything relating to so old a friend as Mole could not fail to be interesting.

"There was a ship called the 'Tarpidon' wrecked in the Bay of Biscay the other day," said Harvey.

"And was Mole on board?"

"Yes, the account describes him as late Governor of the Island of Limbi, which he had quitted on the ground of ill health."

"Was he drowned?"

"No. His wife and family are reported to have been lost, but it was hoped that he had escaped to the shore of Spain with some sailors in a boat."

"I'm glad of that. Poor old Mole!" said Jack, "it would be a great grief if he were to die."

"We may see him again," said Harvey.

"I hope so. What sort of a crowd did you have in Naples?"

"Very jolly. There were several Oxford men there, notably Tom Carden and Sir Sydney Dawson, who is mad about an actress," replied Harvey.

"Does Emily think of going back again?"

"I fancy so. Hilda has bought a villa there, and she declares she must run over to see an eruption of Mount Vesuvius, which is predicted for this month."

"If my wife thinks the place agrees with her better than England," said Jack, "I shall get leave, and we can all go together."

"Nothing could be jollier," answered Harvey.

Sub-Lieutenant Cockles was unusually grave, and so much so that Jack rallied him upon his silence.

"I don't feel in the humour for talking," replied Cockles, sadly.

"Why not, Sam?" asked Harvey.

"If I could only have it out with Darrel, I shouldn't care."

"If I were you," said Jack, "I wouldn't think any more of the matter. Take things quietly, and the fellows will soon get tired of persecuting you."

"I'm upset. Let me wander about the wood. I know every inch of it, because we have lived at Motcombe Hall for some years."

"Won't you come to the pic-nic? Your governor and mater and sister will be there."

"Later on," answered the lieutenant. "I want to quiet my nerves."

"STARTING BACK, HE EXCLAIMED, 'THIS IS TOO BAD.'"

"All serene," said Jack, "you stroll about. We shall expect you at the Gipsies' Glade in an hour."

They had entered the wood, which was full of wild flowers and honeysuckle.

Nuts were beginning to show on the hazels, butterflies flew lazily about, and the song birds made the trees resound with their sweet melody.

It was a lovely scene.

Sitting down on the moss-grown trunk of a tree, Cockles gave himself up to reflection.

Jack had not gone far before a cobweb caught his face.

He felt in his pocket for his handkerchief, and could not find it.

"What a bore," said Jack.

"What's a bore?" asked Harvey.

"I've lost my rag. Lend me yours, Dick. I've got a cobweb in the eye."

Harvey gave him his, but if Jack had gone back a few yards, he would have found his own lying near the trunk on which the lieutenant was sitting. An hour glided away.

Lieutenant Cockles had not moved from the position he had taken up.

Suddenly a noise as of some one pushing his way through the branches, fell upon his ears.

There was somebody coming that way.

His mind was full of bitter thoughts.

He sprang to his feet as a tall, athletic form appeared before him.

It was Captain Lord Augustus Darrel, who was going towards the Gipsies' Glade to keep the appointment given him by the mysterious Lily.

"At last," cried the lieutenant, while his eyes sparkled with joy.

"Hullo, my young and intelligent snuff merchant!" exclaimed Darrel. "What's your little game?"

"Fortune has thrown you in my way," replied Cockles, eagerly.

Captain Darrel stared at him as if he was at a loss to understand his meaning.

CHAPTER VII.

A COWARDLY BLOW.

THE two men were facing one another now.

Lieutenant Cockles' eyes blazed with a hatred which he did not care to conceal.

"You have insulted me!" he exclaimed. "Made fun of my father, and got me laughed at."

"Well, yes; that's about true," replied Darrel.

"What do you mean by it?"

"When we get a man like you in the regiment, we very naturally try to persuade him that he has made a mistake."

"It is you who have made a mistake, you insolent ruffian!" cried Cockles.

"Don't be violent, my little man," said Darrel. "It might hurt you."

"Will you apologise?"

"What's that?"

"Beg my pardon publicly."

"Oh, yes, certainly; very likely to do that," replied Darrel, with a provoking smile."

"You won't, eh?" screamed Cockles.

"Take a pinch of your own snuff, and be quiet. You're only making an ass of yourself."

"Am I? What do you think I'm made of to stand your tricks and taunts?"

"You look remarkably putty-faced just now," said Darrel.

"Villain," cried Cockles, clenching his fists.

"Run away and play, little man," said Darrel, who was inclined to laugh.

"I'll have my revenge."

"Don't be stupid. I shouldn't like to spoil your beauty," said Darrel.

"Not that he's got much to spoil though," he added, in a low voice.

The young lieutenant had been brooding over his wrongs until he was half mad.

Disregarding the size and strength of his opponent, he rushed upon him, and struck him on the breast.

"Don't do that again," said Darrel, flushing.

Cockles struggled madly to get at him.

"You're out of your mind. I must put

a stopper on your performances," exclaimed Darrel.

He was beginning to lose his temper in his turn.

Raising his sledge-hammer fist, Darrel dealt the young man a tremendous blow under the ear.

Then, as Cockles reeled, he repeated the blow with even greater force than before.

The young sub-lieutenant fell like an ox in the shambles.

A deep groan escaped him, and he lay still and motionless.

Captain Lord Augustus Darrel watched him for a little while curiously.

Seeing he did not come to, he knelt down upon the greensward.

Putting his ear to his breast he listened.

There was no sound.

The heart had ceased to beat.

" Good God!" cried Darrel, " I can't have killed him."

He listened again, and this time conjecture deepened into certainty.

Sub-Lieutenant Samuel Cockles was dead.

With the utmost dismay upon his pallid countenance, Darrel looked round to see if anyone had witnessed the cowardly blow.

Not a soul was to be seen.

The insects hummed in the long grass.

The sun cast slanting shadows through the waving branches of the trees, and the merry birds sang.

Nature did not seem to know that a young man had been brutally done to death.

All at once Darrel perceived a handkerchief.

Taking it up, he looked for the mark.

In a corner was written—

" J. Harkaway, 12."

Letting it fall again, he smiled grimly.

" When the body is found," he murmured, " this will tell a tale."

Giving one more shrinking, shuddering glance at the corpse, he strode away.

CHAPTER VIII.

" ARE YOU HIS SISTER?"

THE expression of the dead man's features was serene and calm.

He must have died instantly.

But who could suspect Captain Lord Darrel of such a dreadful crime as murder?

No one, as he thought, had seen the deed done.

Pushing his way through the wood, he hastened to the Gipsies' Glade.

Scarcely had he quitted the spot when a stalwart gamekeeper emerged from behind a tree.

He advanced to the body and examined it.

" As I thought," he said. " Dead! What a fist that fellow has ; he knows how to floor his man. But I shall recognise him again."

Then he gazed sadly at the pale, still face.

" Poor young man! he has died before his time," he added.

A tear of pity stole down the rough weather-beaten cheek

He had seen death before.

But never in so melancholy a form.

Gus Darrel strode on, pushing his way through the wood, his mind ill at ease.

But in spite of what had happened, he determined to meet the young lady who had written to him.

He thought he should not be found out.

If he had the misfortune to have the crime brought home to him he could fly.

" At all events," he said to himself with his usual aristocratic insolence, " I have only killed a cad, an unsufferable beast whom nobody will regret."

He had not gone far before he saw two ladies strolling along a bye path.

" Lily of the Valley," he exclaimed.

They stopped at the sound of his voice.

He approached them, taking off his felt deerstalker, and making a polite bow.

" Ah!" exclaimed one lady, who was fair and fragile in appearance. " You are a faithful knight."

" What praise can I claim," asked

·Darrel, " when I have such an agreeable end in view as an interview with your fair self ? "

Turning to her companion, the young lady said—

" Allow me to introduce an admirer of mine to you,"

" With pleasure," was the reply.

" Lord Augustus Darrel, Captain in the —th Dragoon Guards."

" Jack's regiment."

" Yes, I told you I would give you a surprise. This lady, my lord, is Mrs. Harkaway."

Darrel looked astonished.

" Delighted, I'm sure, to make your acquaintance, Mrs. Harkaway," he said.

" I have heard my husband talk of you, my lord," answered Emily.

" And now," continued Darrel, " for pity's sake let me know who you are."

" You know already. I am Lily of the Valley."

" But your real name——"

" Is Lily Cockles."

Lord Augustus Darrel started back as if a shell had burst under his feet.

He gasped for breath.

His eyes started from his head, and he trembled like a leaf.

In a voice that shook with emotion he said—

" Are you his sister ?"

The unknown girl, whom he had loved in a wild, romantic sort of way, was the sister of the young man whom he had murdered.

He was face to face with the sister of his victim.

How lovely she was.

How mild and gentle—how fascinating —how like a little blue violet raising its pretty and odorous head amid a bed of moss.

Alarmed at the sudden change in his manner, Lily said—

" Are you ill, my lord ?"

" No ; a faintness, that is all. It will soon go off," he replied.

" The heat of the weather, perhaps ?"

" My little friend has surprised you," said Emily. " I have no doubt you thought it very wrong of Miss Cockles to talk to you last autumn, when you used to meet out of doors.

" Oh, no."

" Yes, you must have thought so.

What did you take her for ? Some little milliner ?"

" One couldn't take Miss Cockles for anything but what she is," said he.

" And what's that ?"

" A lady."

" Now you are paying me compliment," said Lily, smiling.

He had not known until now how much he cared for her.

Love was awakening in his heart.

Yes ; he loved the pretty sister of the " non-purchase cad " whom he had slain, as Cain slew Abel, but half an hour before.

What would he not have given now to recall him to life ?

But, alas ! regrets were useless.

He was sleeping his last sleep on the flower-strewn sward of the wood.

" I can tell you that Lily was quite ashamed of herself, and she would not have made herself known to you if I had not persuaded her," said Emily.

" Why, may, I ask ?" said Darrel.

" Because we have heard you are a dreadful tease."

" Indeed !"

" And terribly aristocratic."

" Really !"

" Lily's brother joined your regiment yesterday, and we thought, if we could gain you over to our cause, you would not torment him."

" Why should I ?"

" His father made his money in trade, you know," continued Emily.

" Will you promise to protect him for —for my safe ?" asked Lily.

She looked up imploringly into his face.

" Certainly," he answered, in a sepulchral, stony voice.

The poor boy wanted no protection now.

He, unfortunate lad, was with the angels.

" Will you join our pic-nic, my lord ?" continued Emily.

" Kindly excuse me ; I must get on," he answered.

" Oh, how unfortunate !"

" Another time, thank you."

" At all events," said Lily, " I may consider it settled that you will look after my brother ?"

" Yes," he gasped.

"Thanks, very much. I shall be so grateful," said Lily, gushingly.

Raising his deerstalker again, he said something incoherently, and rushed away.

"How strange he is in his manner to day, so different to what he used to be," remarked Lily.

"Perhaps knowing who you are, and seeing two ladies instead of one, frightened him," said Emily.

"Very likely. Men are strange creatures. The bigger they are the more shy they are of little women."

"Well," said Emily, "we will just stroll on a little further, and then work our way round to the Gipsies' Glade, or we shall be missed."

"As you like, dear. Is he not handsome?" answered Lily, in an abstracted manner.

"Why," said Emily, laughing, "I do believe you are in love with Captain Darrel!"

"I never saw anyone I liked so much, and yet——"

She broke off abruptly.

"What?"

"There is something about him which terrifies me at times."

The ladies walked on in silence for some minutes.

When they arrived at the glade, they found everyone waiting for them.

The lunch was spread out upon the grass.

Pigeon pies, chickens, hams, tongues, jellies, and tarts were flanked by bottles of champagne, sherry, lemonade, brandy, soda water, and beer.

In a moment, Emily was clasped in Jack's manly embrace.

"My darling!" he cried.

Their lips met in a sweet caress.

The jovial party enjoyed themselves, until the sun sank to rest in the burning west.

Old Cockles, as everyone called him, was in his best humour.

He proposed everybody's health.

There was only one drawback to the general hilarity.

Sub-Lieutenant Cockles did not appear.

Jack and Harvey said they had left him in the wood, rather silent and moody.

It was generally supposed that he could not find his way.

"Never mind," said the snuff maker. "He was always a queer lad. He'll turn up somewhere."

"Perhaps he has gone back to the barracks," observed Jack.

"Let him be," said old Cockles, "you take a pinch of my snuff."

He handed his box round.

"It is Prince's Mixture," said old Cockles. Shall I tell you how it get the name?"

"If you please," said Jack.

"When I was young, I was poor. I kept a little shop, and tried to save, by squeezing out a little snuff from each paper after I'd weighed it. All this I mixed together. One day I tried the mixture, and it was uncommon good.

"I sent a sample to the Prince of Wales, afterwards George the fourth. He liked it too.

"He gave me an order for a lot, and I called it Prince's Mixture by permission. That made my fortune. Ha! ha! Success hangs on trifles, eh?"

As old Cockles finished speaking, a tiny shriek broke from Lily.

"What is the matter?" asked Jack. "Wasps?"

She made no answer.

"Snakes?" he continued. "Don't say it's snakes."

She pointed with her hand, and all followed with their eyes the direction she indicated.

An oppression, as of death, fell upon everyone.

Each voice was hushed.

CHAPTER IX.

FINDING THE BODY.

Four men, looking like labourers going home from their work, appeared.

They carried between them a body.

From the listless way in which the head, arms and legs hung down, it was easy to see it was a corpse.

"What's this?" asked old Cockles, rising hurriedly.

He advanced to the men.

Jack and Harvey followed him.

When Mr. Cockles' eyes fell upon the countenance of the dead man, his knees seemed to give way under him.

He took another look.

Then a great cry broke from him, such as comes from a strong man in the prime of his health and strength, when some astounding grief overwhelms him.

"My boy!" he cried. "My boy!"

Jack was equally affected.

But he was more calm and collected.

"Put down the body," he said, "and tell us where and how you found it.

The men told their simple tale plainly.

They were returning from work, and cut through the wood, as it was their shortest way home.

When two-thirds through they came upon the body, and thought they ought to take it to the nearest police-station.

"Who has done this?" screamed Mr. Cockles, fiercely. "I will have blood for blood! Oh, my poor boy! my darling! the support and comfort of my age!"

He sank on his knees by the side of the body.

It was now cold and rigid.

"We found this handkerchief near the place, sir," said one of the working men.

Old Cockles seized the handkerchief, and looked at it.

"There be a name in the corner," continued the man.

Springing up, the bereaved father grasped Jack by the collar.

"This is your doing!" he said.

"Mine! What do you mean?" asked Jack, indignantly.

"Look! Your name is here. This is your property. You must have dropped it on the spot."

"Harvey will tell you that I have not been out of his sight."

"Yes," said Harvey; "I and Harkaway have been together all day."

"Never mind. This shall be investigated. I will have blood for blood!" cried the old man, doggedly.

He kept the handkerchief tightly clutched in his hand.

Instead of fainting or going into hysterics, Lily was wonderfully calm and self-possessed.

She had become pale as the flower from which she took her name.

Her slender from shivered and shook with the tremulous motion of a leaf agitated by the wind.

Walking towards the spot she said—

"Mr Harkaway is not guilty."

"Back, girl!" cried her father. "What can you know about it?"

"I see as with a second sight, and the murderer of my brother is not here."

Then she fell forward insensible.

Emily at once threw herself on her knees, and tried to restore her.

She too received a terrible shock.

Her mind recalled the interview they had had with Captain Darrel.

She remembered his agitation and abrupt departure.

Nor did she forget the peculiar tone in which he said—

"Are you *his* sister?"

"Jack, dear," she said, looking up from her recumbent position.

"Yes, Emily," he answered.

"Go back to Canterbury with these men. Do not mind Mr. Cockles; he is not master of himself now. All will be clear soon."

"God grant it!" answered Jack.

"Look after him," said Mr. Cockles, pointing to Jack. "He is a prisoner; I give him in charge. Were he ten times my friend, I would not forget it. The slayer of my son shall be judged, and I will have blood for blood."

"Take him up again," said Jack! "we will all go to Canterbury. Harvey, come with me. Tell the servants to see to my wife and Lily."

Harvey gave the necessary directions.

The rustics took up the corpse again, and began to wind their melancholy way through the wood.

Jack followed more as a mourner than anything else.

Behind him walked, with lynx-like watchful eye, the father, who, in his turn, was followed by Harvey.

He had only known the young man four-and-twenty hours.

Yet he was deeply shocked at his fate.

When they got into the London Road, Harvey put himself by Jack's side.

"Awfully sad thing this," he said.

"Isn't it?" replied Jack, thoughtfully.

"Old Cockles has gone mad."

"Clean off his head," answered Jack.

"I wonder who did it."

"Can't imagine. It seems to have been done by a blow on the head, though I can see no blood."

"A doctor will settle that."

"Awkward for the regiment," said Jack.

"Deucedly awkward."

"I began to like the young fellow; there was a lot of stuff in him."

"So I thought," replied Harvey. "Sorry for his poor sister."

They relapsed into silence.

A crowd began to follow them, which increased to a mob when they reached the town.

"Shall we take him into the barrack-yard?" said Jack.

"Yes, yes," cried Mr. Cockles, who overheard the question. "Go to head-quarters first."

The sentry saluted his officer and allowed them to pass.

Then the gate was shut and the mob kept outside.

"Send for the colonel," shouted Mr. Cockles. "My son has been murdered."

A knot of soldiery gathered round curiously.

"Stand back!" exclaimed Jack.

The men respectfully retired to a distance.

In a short time Colonel Prendergast was in attendance.

"What is this?" he asked. "God bless me! Sub-Lieutenant Cockles dead?"

"Yes," replied the father, whose madness increased every moment.

"How did it happen?"

"He has been murdered in Boughton Wood. I was a fool to put him in your regiment. I might have known he was not good enough for your empty-headed fops who call themselves swells. But I will have blood for blood."

"Do you suspect anybody?"

"I do. I charge Lieutenant Harkaway with the crime."

"But, if I recollect right, Mr. Harkaway was the friend of the deceased gentleman," said Colonel Prendergast.

"Friend or no friend, I charge him. His handkerchief was found on the spot. Lock him up."

"I cannot act without further information; let the police be sent for."

"Do you mean to let him escape?" screamed Mr. Cockles.

He foamed at the mouth.

His eyes rolled in his head.

Staggering for a moment like a drunken man, he fell down in the barrack yard in a fit.

Turning to Jack, the colonel said—

"What is the meaning of all this?"

"I know no more than a baby sir," answered Jack, "except that Lieutenant Cockles was found in the wood by these men."

"But you all went out together?"

"Yes, we left Mr. Cockles in the wood; but I and my friend here, Mr. Harvey, have never been out of one another's sight."

"Dear me, this is most perplexing. We must put the body in the guard house, and send for the police. Perhaps a doctor will do this old gentleman some good Who is he?" said the colonel.

"Lieutenant Cockles' father."

"Oh, that accounts for his violence. Sad affair! What can we do for the best?"

The colonel was terribly upset.

He foresaw a dreadful scandal for the regiment, and he was powerless to prevent it.

It was a sad state of affairs altogether Who could tell how it would end!

CHAPTER X.

FLIGHT.

WHEN Captain Lord Augustus Darrel left the two ladies in the wood, he made his way as quickly as he could to the high road.

Here he saw a man, dressed as a gamekeeper, leaning thoughtfully upon the knob of a hazel stick.

The man happened to be in his path.

Pushing him rudely on one side, he said—

"Get out of my way."

The man started and looked up.

His eyes lighted up with a brilliant flash.

"Your way!" he said insolently. "Why should I?"

Gus Darrel raised his fist.

He was in an angry mood, and did not feel in the humour to be thwarted or to stick at trifles.

"Drop it, sir," said the man; "you may strike a cove once too often."

"What do you mean?" asked Gus Darrel, while his face went as white as a sheet.

"I saw you kill one man to-day. Isn't that enough for you?"

"Liar!" cried Darrel, seizing him by the throat.

"Let go, or else I'll split," gasped the gamekeeper. "Let go, I say; it ain't safe to kill two men in one day."

The grip tightened on his throat.

"L-let g-go!" said the gamekeeper, with difficulty.

A sound of oxen approaching caused Gus Darrel to pause.

"Who-a, there! who-a!" cried a voice.

"Curse it!" muttered Darrel; "someone is coming up the road—some drover fellow or other."

His grip on the gamekeeper's throat relaxed.

"That's better," said the man, drawing a deep breath and arranging his disordered necktie.

"Come on one side," said Darrel, anxiously. "What do you want? We must not have a vulgar scene."

"Vulgar, you call it!" replied the man. "as sure as my name's Newby, I'll back you don't see such things as I've seen to-day in any low quarters in Canterbury."

He shook himself like a Newfoundland dog just coming out of the water.

The cattle drover came by with his beasts.

"I say, mate!" he cried.

"What's up?" asked the drover.

"I'll give you half-a-dollar if you'll bide here a few minutes."

"Right you are."

The drover halted his cattle, and looked curiously at Gus Darrel and Newby the gamekeeper, while he smoked a short clay pipe, which had evidently seen some service.

Newby went close up to Darrel.

"My eyes and limbs!" he said, "ain't you a caution?"

"I suppose that you want money?" answered Captain Darrel, in a low voice.

"If you mean me to hold my tongue, I must be paid for it."

Darrel saw that there was no means of escaping from the witness of his crime.

In vain he reflected, bit his lips, frowned, and fidgeted with his hands.

He was in the power of the gamekeeper.

"I can be as silent as the grave," continued Newby, "if needs be. My old dad used to read me that text about putting a bridle on the tongue.

"'Ben,' he'd say, when I was going on a bit, 'bridle, my lad, bridle.'

"This pulled me up short. He'd only got to say 'bridle,' and I was mum as a mouse."

Captain Darrel took a card from his pocket.

Handing it to Newby, he said—

"Here's my card. Come to the cavalry barracks at Canterbury to-night, and I will settle with you."

"Thank you, sir."

"Don't open your mouth too wide," continued Darrel, "and perhaps we can come to terms."

"All right, sir—bridle," said Newby, putting his finger by the side of his nose in a knowing manner.

Darrel walked away, leaving the gamekeeper in a state of delight.

The drover received his half-crown, and the two adjourned to the nearest public house, where they indulged in beer.

That afternoon passed miserably enough for Darrel.

He scarcely ate anything at mess.

When Mr. Cockles, Jack, and Harvey entered the yard with the dead body of the sub-lieutenant, he heard the commotion.

His ears were sensitively alert to the slightest sound.

He was quickly on the scene.

Almost at the same time Newby was admitted to the barrack-yard by showing Captain Darrel's card.

Colonel Prendergast had just turned to Jack.

"Mr Harkaway," he exclaimed, "you are in mufti, and therefore cannot give up your sword, but I think it will be best that you should consider yourself under arrest in your own quarter's until this unfortunate affair is cleared up."

Jack bowed his head.

He was too good an officer to dispute the commands of his colonel.

Newby pressed forward.

"What's that?" he asked. "Mr. Harkaway accused of murdering the gent?"

"Yes," replied a soldier.

"What are they a-going to do with him?"

"Put him under arrest."

"No, they don't," said Newby, with some feeling. "Mr. Harkaway saved me and mine from the workhouse last winter, when I was laid up with the rheumatics, nd paid the brokers out of my bit of a ottage. No they don't."

He pressed his way to the front.

"Mr. Harkaway," he cried.

Jack looked round.

"Don't you know me, sir? I'm Newby the gamekeeper, and I'm not a brute beast to have no gratitude."

"I am afraid you cannot be of any service to me now," replied Jack, with a sad smile.

"That's where you're wrong. Bridle up, sir; let me talk. Where's the colonel?"

"I am Colonel Prendergast," was the answer.

"Then I tell you Mr. Harkaway didn't do it, sir."

"Who did, then?"

"Captain Lord Augustus Darrel; here's his card," replied Newby.

There was a sensation in the crowd.

A form stole to the gate, which the sentry opened for him, and the person passed into the street.

"I saw him strike the poor lad down, sir," continued Newby, "and he told me to come here to-night and he'd give me money. If it hadn't been that my good friend and preserver, Mr. Harkaway— God bless him!—was in trouble, perhaps I should have bridled and said nothing."

"This alters the case," said the colonel. "Where is Captain Lord Darrel?"

Inquiries were instantly made.

Gus Darrel was nowhere to be found.

He had sought safety in flight.

Jack was told that he might consider himself at liberty, and Colonel Prendergast at once walked up to the police-station to consult with the authorities.

Mr. Cockles was taken to the infirmary, where he continued in a dangerous state.

The body of his son was placed in a room to await an inquest.

Thanks to Newby's evidence, there was no doubt that it would result in a verdict against Captain Lord Augustus Darrel.

All the officers of the —th Dragoon Guards were greatly shocked at what had happened.

But they felt some relief to think that their companion had fled.

If he could not be found, the scandal would not be so great.

CHAPTER XI.

THE PRINCE OF VILLANOVA.

A FEW days slipped by, and the jury, directed by the coroner, brought in a verdict of murder against Lord Darrel, for killing Sub-Lieutenant Cockles.

Great was the scandal.

So great, indeed, that the authorities at the Horse Guards ordered the ——th Dragoons to go to India in a fortnight.

Jack scarcely knew how to act.

The shock of the murder had affected Emily greatly, and Jack was told by her doctor that her health would never stand a hot climate.

So he used all his interest, and exchanged into another regiment, obtaining leave of absence for some time.

Emily expressed a wish to go to Naples.

Harvey and his wife willingly consented to accompany them, and the little party started at once for this charming Italian city.

The Neapolitans have a saying, "See Naples and die," and authors, poets, and travellers all agree in calling it the most lovely spot in the world.

They took lodgings in the Strada di Toledo, and Emily began rapidly to recover her health.

Nothing had been heard of Lord Darrel.

Mr Cockles and his daughter lived a life of seclusion, and buried their grief in their hearts.

The famous Contessa di Malafedi, who occupied a palazzo in the Toledo, near Harkaway's lodgings, was a great friend of Emily's.

Twice a week the splendid saloons of the contessa opened to receive all the fashionables of Naples.

It was said that gambling was carried on to a great extent in the palazzo, and indeed some strange characters were admitted.

But society abroad is not so difficult of entry as in London.

A fortnight after their arrival, Harvey and Jack were at the contessa's.

The heat was so oppressive, that Hilda and Emily did not accompany them.

Thousands of wax lights shone in immense candelabras, and lit up the gilded, mirrored saloons.

Jack was standing in the refreshment room, eating fruits buried in snow, and drinking iced water.

By his side was a tall, handsome man, whose features were unmistakably Italian, though he spoke English very well.

This was the Prince of Villanova.

No one knew much about him.

He constantly appeared in Naples, and as constantly disappeared, going no one knew whither.

His residence was at an hotel, and he was reported to be enormously wealthy.

No one played higher than he, and his contempt for money was shown by the coolness with which he lost heavy sums.

At times his brow grew dark and contracted, and a savage scowl stole over his face, which became cruel and murderous in it's expression.

But when the storm passed off, he was again the calm and princely gentleman.

"Good evening, prince," exclaimed Jack. "How does the heat suit you?"

"What is the heat or cold to me?" replied Villanova. "You Inglize are so sensitive to changes of climate. As for me, I take my iced wine at the Cafe d'Europa; I walk under the trees in the Villa Reale, when the Acacia Avenue is snowy white with perfumed clusters. Cospetto! life is to be enjoyed, if you are only in earnest."

Suddenly a hand slapped Jack on the back.

"I say, don't do that again," said Jack, with a gasp, "you've taken all my——. Hallo! Tom Carden, by all that's odd and singular."

"Yes. Here we are again. Glad to see you, old fellow. I've just come from Rome, where I've left Sir Sydney Dawson spooning a flower girl."

They shook hands heartily,

"Allow me to introduce you," said Jack, "the Prince of Villanova."

The prince and Carden bowed stiffly to

one another, and the former walked slowly away.

"Do you know one another?" asked Jack.

"We have met," replied Carden.

"Is there anything seedy about him, or have you had a row?"

"Not exactly. Fact is, I saw him at Civita Vecchia—he's always cutting about somewhere—and I was advised by an Italian friend of mine to shy him."

"Why?"

Carden lowered his voice.

"They say he has something to do with the brigands," he whispered.

Jack laughed loudly.

"Come, I say." he answered, "you don't mean that you allow yourself to be frightened by such an old Bogey tale as that."

"Well, as for that, there are brigands in this part of Italy—and murderous ones —or rumour lies."

Surely there are no brigands in the large towns and cities," said Jack.

"You can't tell where the chiefs go, or what disguises they put on. We know that the king's soldiers can't put them down, and we hear of the atrocities and crimes they commit."

"But the prince is a thorough gentleman," said Jack.

"Possibly. However, I'm not going to cotton to him. I don't like him, and you know my blunt way," replied Carden, sturdily.

"You're the same dear old Tom Carden that you were at Oxford," said Jack.

"And I hope I shall never alter. Come out and stroll up the Strada. We can come back in half an hour."

"With pleasure."

"I want to talk to you. Of course I saw the Canterbury affair in the paper. Darrel's a scoundrel."

"Do you know him too?" asked Jack, in surprise.

"Considering we come from the same county, there will not be anything extraordinary if I do, will there?" replied Carden.

"Hang it! I shall have to give up the honour of your acquaintance," said Jack, with a laugh; "you're becoming quite a private detective."

"I've got good eyes, and I keep my ears open."

They walked down the marble staircase, threw their light coats over their arms, and passed into the street, and turned into a well-known promenade on the Chiaja.

"How long have you been in Naples?" asked Jack.

"Since yesterday. If I'd known you were here, I'd have found you out before. Luckily a friend procured me an invitation to the contessa's this evening. She's a queer fish."

"They're all queer fish according to you."

"You'll find them out in time, but here's a cafe. What do you say to some iced lemonade?"

Going upstairs, they sat at an open window, from which, looking over the Chiaja, they could see a streak of blue water silvered by the moon, which was just visible over the trees of the Villa Reale.

"What a heavenly place this is!" exclaimed Carden, rapturously.

"Yes, it would be bearable," replied Jack, "if it was not for the heat, and the dirt, and beggars, and the fleas."

"Don't you knock all the sentiment out of a fellow; it is not often I go in for poetry and romance, but I think I could live and die in Naples."

"When you have got over the fit, will you tell me what you were going to about Darrel?" said Jack.

"Darrel! Oh! ah! cad Darrel, certainly. Bully Darrel, we used to call him; it's a tale."

"What is?"

"Why his family history. Have a cigaritto, as they call them," replied Carden.

He offered his case, and Jack helped himself.

The soft and balmy breeze entering at the window fanned their cheeks with its perfumed wings, and the gentle strains of a guitar, coming from below, lulled their senses.

Tom Carden was right, for Naples is an earthly paradise.

CHAPTER XII.

JACK HEARS DARREL'S HISTORY.

"AUGUSTUS LORD DARREL," began Carden, "is only the second peer of that name."

"Indeed!" remarked Jack. "It's quite a new title then?"

"Quite. His father was a diplomatist attached to a foreign court, and was raised to the peerage for his services. His estate adjoins my father's"

"Has the first lord been dead long?"

"About three and twenty years. He was murdered when Darrel was a baby."

"Murdered!" repeated Jack, astonished. "By whom?"

"An Italian steward, named Dominico; at least, so it was supposed at the time. Dominico lived with a young wife in the house. Lady Darrel had just been confined with her first child, a son, who was christened Augustus. Dominico's wife was in the same interesting condition, but she died a few weeks afterwards."

"Was there a quarrel between old Lord Darrel and Dominico?"

"So the servants declared. At all events, one morning the old lord was found dead in his bed with a stiletto sticking in his heart."

"And the Italian steward?" asked Jack, who was deeply interested,

"Had vanished,

"Poor Lady Darrel! How she must have suffered!"

"No one could tell that, for she, too, was missing. Dominico, Lady Darrel, and the Italian's child were all gone when the murder was discovered."

"Perhaps," hazarded Jack, "Dominico carried her off."

"It might be so," answered Carden. "People went the length of saying so; and they said more."

"What?"

"That the baby that was left was more like Dominico's baby than the little Augustus Lord Darrel. But these things were whispered under the breath, and, being merely local conjectures, did not get into the papers. Guardians were appointed for the child, who was sent to school, and afterwards put in the army. He always showed a headstrong, violent disposition, and you know what he has come to."

"What a strange story!" ejaculated Harkaway.

"Yes. You might almost expect a man to go to the bad under such circumstances."

"The actual facts amount to this," continued Jack. "Gus Darrel's father was murdered by the Italian steward, and he never knew his mother"

"Exactly. Supposition goes farther. Lady Darrel is supposed to have been taken away by the steward, Dominico, who also took the real heir, leaving his own child in its place."

"So that Lord Darrel isn't Lord Darrel?" said Jack. "But that can't be the case, as he has enjoyed the title and estates since he came of age. Well, as I said before, it's a strange story, anyhow."

"So it is. Have another liquor?"

"Don't mind if I do. Wonder where Gus Darrel is now? By the way, does he know all this scandal?"

"No. I think it has all been kept from him. He was told his mother and father died when he was a baby," replied Carden.

"Shall we go back to the contessa's?" said Jack, throwing away the end of his cigarette.

"As you please. I could ' take the moon,' as they call strolling by moonlight, all the evening, it is so lovely," answered Carden.

They left the cafe, Jack carelessly tossing a ducat to the waiter for what they had drunk, and telling him to keep the change.

This paid him very well, as about six ducats go to the English pound.

Some beggars, or lazaroni, with whom the streets of Naples always swarm, saw this extravagant act on the part of our Ingleze.

So they crowded round them, begging,

and were rewarded with a few small coins, for which they scrambled on the pavement.

The Neapolitans, like most foreigners, believe that every Englishman is a "lord," and is made of money.

Getting back to the gorgeous palazzo of the Contessa Di Malafedi, they found dancing going on in spite of the heat.

But it was a professional *danseuse* from the San Carlo Theatre who was amusing the company.

She was dancing that most graceful and fascinating of all dances, the Tarantella.

Her every movement was full of grace and expressed the poetry of motion.

As she finished her performance, and glided away like a fairy, even the most *blasé* inmate of those gilded saloons feebly clapped his gloved hands together, and murmured—

"*Brava, bravissima!*"

"By Jove! can't these foreign women do it?" remarked Jack.

"Some small few," answered Carden. "Where are Harvey and the ladies? I want to renew my acquaintance with them."

"Hilda and Emily have stopped at home; they may turn up later—I don't know. Harvey is here somewhere," replied Jack.

Before they had completed the circuit of the saloons, they found Harvey in search of Jack.

He greeted Tom Carden very cordially.

"Are you going to stop in Naples?" he asked.

"Think I shall, now I have met you fellows," he replied. "You know, I suppose, that my poor old dad has popped off the hooks."

"No, indeed; very sorry to hear it."

"So was I, for he was very fond of me; but he's left me five thousand a year—bless the old boy—though I'd rather he'd been spared me than have the coin."

He was honest in what he said, and his hearers respected him for it.

"I was looking for you, Jack," said Harvey.

"What for?"

"You know the Prince of Villanova?"

"Yes."

"He's playing hazard with another fellow, and they are going for a cool thou. at each cast of the dice. Wouldn't you like to come and look on?—it's awfully exciting, I can tell you."

"By all means," replied Jack.

The three young men passed through a corridor, and pushing aside some green baize curtains, found themselves in the card room.

It was the custom of the contessa to allow gambling to any extent in her house.

But it was fully understood that the winners should pay her ten per cent. of what they won.

Thus, if a player won a thousand pounds, he would give her one hundred out of it.

She trusted to the honour of her guests and, strange to say, she was seldom cheated by them out of any part of the black mail she claimed.

When they entered the room, they discovered that the Prince of Villanova had been unlucky, and gone away.

Harvey made a few inquiries, and, returning to his companions said—

"The prince lost five thousand pounds and paid it like a bird, after which he hooked it."

"Best thing he could do," answered Carden. "I'm not a gambler, but I've played at Baden and Monaco for small sums, and I'd never follow up a run of bad luck."

"What's the game now?" asked Jack. "The night's young yet; my wife won't expect me till the small hours."

"Nor mine," said Harvey. "Hilda knows we are together, and are not likely to get into any mischief."

"Let's get into a barca in the bay, and be rowed to some trattoria," said Jack.

"What's that?" inquired Carden.

"A sort of tavern by the sea, where you have fish suppers—fish fried in oil, you know—and then there are people with guitars, and some sing."

"All right," said Carden and Harvey, in a breath, "we will take our leave of the contessa."

"And promise to bring our wives," added Harvey, "the next time she receives."

"That will be Saturday," said Jack.

They pushed their way through the gay

and brilliant crowd to the Contessa Di Malafedi, who received their adieux with her accustomed well-bred politeness.

Then they walked to the bay, and hired a boat to take them to a respectable trattoria.

Harvey and Jack being well acquainted with Latin, did not find it difficult to speak Italian, and they were both picking it up rapidly.

The row along the blue waters of the lovely bay was delightful in the extreme.

A gentle breeze blew across the sea, and softened the force of the heat.

In the distance, a luminous haze hung over the famous volcano called Mount Vesuvius, and ever and anon, bright vivid flashes, like sheets of lightning, shot into the torrid air.

"Per Baccho !" said the boatman, resting on his oars, "Vesuvius will kick up a pretty noise before long."

" Is there going to be an eruption," asked Jack.

"It is feared so. The people from Terra del Greco—that's a village at the base of the mountain—have been coming in all day, signor."

" Have you had a dust up lately ?" inquired Harvey.

"No, signor, about two years ago was the last of any importance, and then, celenza"—this was short for excelenza, or your excellency, a title the poor of Italy are fond of bestowing upon Englishmen— " it was fearful !"

" It was a fine sight I suppose ?"

"Fine ! Santissime Virgine ! it was as if Hell had boiled over, and all the fires were coming up to burn the earth, celenza," replied the boatman.

Jack watched the intermittent flashes, and occasionally heard the deep rumbling of distant thunder.

The barca, or boat, glided swiftly over the waters, and the lights of the trattoria glittered round an angle of the bay.

CHAPTER XIII.

A STRANGE LIKENESS.

RUNNING the barca against a landing stage, the boatman jumped out and held it for his passengers to alight.

He was told to wait, and the three walked along a path to the tavern, where a small crowd of people were enjoying themselves.

The Neapolitans are cheerful, light-hearted, animated, and talkative.

A smell of garlic pervaded the place, which was relieved by an odour of fried fish.

One of the waiters, with a snowy white napkin over his arm, asked for orders, detailing his bill of fare.

There were oysters from Lake Fusaro, but the weather was voted too hot for these.

Eventually some fish fried in oil was ordered, and Jack looked around him.

A man played the guitar, and a woman sang a sweet song, afterwards going round with a shell, and smiling modestly when she received the smallest contribution.

Jack noticed a man in a retired part of the room, who wore a slouched hat and a long cloak.

Whenever his eye wandered in his direction, he turned his head as if to avoid his gaze.

Something in his appearance reminded him of a face he knew, and suddenly he said to himself—

"Darrel !"

" What's that ?" said Harvey.

"Nothing," answered Jack, "only that man over there reminded me strangely of Gus Darrel. It's just his phiz and the cut of him altogether."

" One does see those strange likenesses occasionally," said Harvey, "but it is easy to tell that garlic-smelling brute is an Italian. Look at his heavy black eyebrows and moustache."

Jack said nothing more, but a little later another man in a slouched hat and a long cloak, peeped into the room.

This man had but one arm.

He beckoned to the first one of whom we have spoken, and they went out together.

Ten minutes afterwards, Jack, who had finished his supper, strolled to the doorway.

Just outside he saw the Prince of Villanova talking earnestly to the two men.

"Ah, prince," he exclaimed, "have you too come to try the delights of fried fish?"

The prince addressed a few hasty words to his two companions, who quickly disappeared in the darkness.

Then he turned to Jack.

"My dear Mr. Harkaway," he said, in his blandest tones, "this is indeed a pleasure. You will have a bottle of wine with me? We Neapolitans love the night so much that we prefer it to the day."

"Thanks," replied Jack; "my friend and I must think of getting home. I am a married man you know."

"Bah! what is that? A wife's place is at home. I love to flit about the bay in my torchlight bark, with Vesuvius gleaming red in the distance," answered the prince.

Villanova took Jack's arm in a friendly manner, and they entered the tavern together.

Carden looked annoyed at this.

"Ah," said the prince, "there is your friend. What are you doing here, Signor Carden?"

"I've got nothing to do, and I'm doing it," replied Tom Carden, in his blunt way, as he turned his back upon him.

The prince grew fiery red.

But he was a man who had an admirable command over his temper when he chose.

Addressing Harkaway, he said—

"If a Frenchman or one of my own countrymen had treated me in this manner I should have felt myself insulted."

"Don't you now?" asked Jack, who was rather annoyed at Carden's behaviour.

"Oh, dear no. I have lived in England and am accustomed to the peculiarities of your insular nature."

"Well," began Jack, "I'm very sorry——"

"Don't apologise on my account," replied Carden, turning round again quickly.

"Ah, you Ingleze," laughed the prince; "you have always your fists made up for a row. We use the——"

"Knife," put in Carden. "I know it, and for that reason always carry a pistol; and mind this, if I see a knife I shoot."

"How droll!" said the prince. "Here is an Oxford man and a gentleman, who has a large income, and he treats me as if I was a——"

"Brigand," interrupted Carden, who was in an ill temper that night, and seemed bent upon making a quarrel.

"Ha, ha!" laughed the prince; "you English are so—what do you say?—eccentric. Mr. Harkaway, I am grieved, but I have come here to have supper, and you will pardon me if I go to another table, and quit the most agreeable society of yourself and your friend."

The prince of Villanova bowed, and went to an unoccupied table, where he sat down and ordered what he wanted.

Jack was annoyed.

He had not taken the dislike to the prince that Carden had, and did not believe a word of the insinuations that were directed at him.

His idea was that Carden had behaved in a rude and unpolished manner, which was unjustifiable.

He led the way out of the room, and Harvey and Carden followed him, getting into the boat which was waiting, with many others hard by.

The oars splashed and coruscated in the water, but Jack did not speak.

"What are you sulking at, old bear?" exclaimed Tom Carden at length.

"I don't think you have behaved properly, if you must have it," said Jack.

"Look here, Harkaway," said Tom Carden, "you and I are not acquaintances of yesterday, are we?"

"No."

"Then why do you put me behind a fellow who calls himself prince, and of whom you know nothing, except that you have met him at the contessa's?"

"I don't dislike him," replied Jack. "He seems a very jolly sort of fellow, for a foreigner."

"All right, stick to your opinion. Your great fault, Jack, is chumming up with anybody. I'm very careful how I make friends," said Carden.

"Never mind, old boy, we won't quarrel over it; only don't insult my friend again, if you can help it."

"FOUR MEN CARRIED THE BODY BETWEEN THEM."

"Do you call him a friend ?"

"An acquaintance, if you like ; it's all the same."

"No, it isn't," replied Tom Carden, in his dogged manner. "I hope I am your friend, but I shouldn't like you to place me in the same light as that Villanova."

"Don't talk about him," said Harvey, "and then you can't fall out."

"Very well ; drop him," replied Carden.

It was evident that Tom Carden had taken a strong dislike to the prince, and his name was not mentioned any more.

Perhaps he had his reasons for his dislike.

Whether he was right or wrong will be soon seen.

They returned to Naples and separated Jack wanted Carden to come in and see the ladies, whom he expected would be sitting up, but he excused himself, owing to the lateness of the hour.

CHAPTER XIV.

WHAT HAPPENED AT THE BALL.

EMILY and Hilda were delighted to hear that so old a friend as Tom Carden was in Naples.

He called the next day, and they all agreed that they would go to the next reception of the contessa.

This, however, was a grand ball, an extravagance which the Malafedi indulged in occasionally.

It only involved more ices, more wines, and more musicians.

The assemblage was very large, and everybody in Naples, who was anybody, was present.

Two such attractive young ladies as Emily and Hilda, who were splendidly dressed and adorned with jewels of price, were of course the observed of all observers.

Jack and Harvey liked to see their wives noticed, and let them dance to their hearts' content.

Tom Carden had as many dances as he liked with each of them.

The Prince of Villanova was there, and made himself especially agreeable to Harkaway and his wife.

Emily was pleased with the Italian's fascinating manners, and danced with him twice.

This Tom Carden did not like.

He sought Jack, and found him talking to a very pretty Neapolitan girl, with whom he had been walking through a quadrille.

"I say, Harkaway, old fellow, may I have a word with you ?" he said.

"Certainly. Half-a-dozen, if you like, replied Jack.

"Well, if I were you, I wouldn't allow the prince to dance with your wife."

"What prince ? Villanova ?"

"Yes."

"Why not ?"

Carden shrugged his shoulders.

"I dance with whom I like, and I don't interfere with Emily. We understand one another," said Jack

"By George!" exclaimed Carden, "here's your wife coming towards you, and she don't look very well pleased."

Jack in his best Italian, made some apology to the lady with whom he had been dancing, for quitting her so abruptly, and advanced to meet Emily.

She was evidently put out, for her cheek was flushed, and she had bitten her lips.

"What's the matter, my darling ?" he asked.

"I have been grossly insulted !" she replied.

"Who by ?"

"The Prince of Villanova. Do you know him ? That was the name by which the contessa introduced him to me. He claimed acquaintance with you."

"Oh, yes, I know him," replied Jack.

Tom Carden laughed as if this pleased him.

"What has he done ?" asked Jack.

"He told me that you were in love with that girl you have been dancing with, and that you were with her the other night at a trattoria, when you stopped out late."

"The lying thief!" said Jack. "Why Carden was with me all the time."

"But you did not tell me you had been to one of those low places they call a trattoria," replied Emily, in a tone of reproach.

"I didn't think of it"

"Were you with that—that lady you have just left?"

"No; on my word, I wasn't, Emily," replied Jack, earnestly.

"I believe you, dear," she answered, grasping his arm, tenderly.

"But look here," said Jack, "I must hear something more about the insult. What else did he say?"

"You will not quarrel with him if I tell you," asked Emily, hesitatingly.

"That depends."

"I don't want to get you stabbed, Jack dear, and if you won't promise me, I won't tell you," said Emily.

"I promise, then."

"You won't have a row with him?"

"No."

This came very reluctantly from Jack, and as Tom Carden heard it, he said to himself—

"I'll lay odds he don't keep his promise."

"He told me that he had a friend in the country who loved me, oh! ever so much more than you did," said Emily, "and if I'd only come——"

"Did you listen to him, the scoundrel?" asked Jack, indignantly.

"No; I came over at once to tell you," answered Emily.

"Where is Hilda?" asked Jack.

"Not far off; with Harvey I think."

"Come with me and stay with her for a minute or two will you?"

"You are not going to fight? Oh Jack, if you were to be killed by one of these foreign people!"

"Not I. Carden is coming with me to play a game at whist. We have had the engagement this long while."

"Really?"

"Haven't we Carden?" asked Jack.

"Yes, indeed, we have," replied Carden. "You'll believe me Mrs. Harkaway, won't you?"

"Keep him out of mischief, Mr. Carden," said Emily. "You are an old Oxford man, and know what my husband is."

"I know he's every inch a man," replied Carden.

"How long will your game take?" asked Emily.

"About half an hour, that's all."

"I will let you go, then. In half an hour I shall expect you," she said, with a smile.

Jack and Carden walked away together, both looking pale and determined.

"Have you thought of the consequences of what you are going to do?" asked Tom Carden.

"How do you know what I mean to do?" replied Jack.

"Of course you are going to chastise the Neapolitan ruffian for insulting your wife."

"Yes," said Jack, through his clenched teeth,

"I knew it; a gentleman could not do less."

"What his object in being insolent to Emily is, I cannot imagine. He said some one in the country loved her; who could be mean? That face at the trattoria— the man with one arm—your suspicions— a thousand thoughts flash through my mind," exclaimed Jack, hurriedly.

He spoke in short jerks, his voice being thick and husky.

"If you strike him," remarked Carden, "you will have to fight him."

"It matters little," answered Jack; "the chance of receiving a bullet will not deter me from doing my duty."

They approached a servant who was carrying a silver salver laden with ices across the room.

Of him they inquired where the Prince of Villanova was, and the domestic replied that he saw him a moment ago on the top of the grand staircase.

Thither they hurried.

The prince was already half way down the marble stairs.

"Hi!" said Jack, by way of attracting his attention.

Villanova turned round, and became a shade paler as he saw Jack.

"I must have a word or two with you, if you please," said Harkaway.

"I am engaged," replied the prince, "and regret that I am obliged to ask you to call at my hotel to-morrow morning, if you will be so good."

"You shall not escape me!" cried Jack, furiously. "I will expose you, brigand!"

At these words the prince uttered a shrill and piercing whistle, which came wildly and weirdly from between his teeth.

Was it a signal.

It appeared to be so, for in an instant a dozen rough, savage-looking men sprang from behind doors and statues in the hall.

They had evidently been hiding.

With knives and pistols displayed, they hurried to the prince's assistance.

Jack was about to throw himself upon Villanova, but seeing the state of affairs, Carden attempted to restrain him.

"To-morrow. Wait!" he said.

"No," cried Jack, "let me get at the villain! I will strike him publicly."

He struggled fiercely to get away.

"Brigand," cried Jack again, "I know you now. It is your life or mine!"

He succeeded in throwing off the impeding grasp of Tom Carden.

Villanova, however, drew himself up to his full height, and with a commanding gesture, waved him back.

"Mr. Harkaway," he exclaimed, in a clear, shrill voice, "you have behaved in a rash and foolish manner. Stand back, as you value your life."

Jack stood his ground.

"To teach you that a Villanova is not to be trifled with," cried the prince, "I am about to lodge a ball in your shoulder."

He deliberately raised his pistol.

The trigger was pulled, and a loud report awoke the echoes of the marble hall.

The ball, aimed with unerring precision, struck Jack full in the right shoulder.

With a groan, he fell back in Tom Carden's arms.

A cry of horror arose from the ladies, and the gentlemen were petrified with amazement.

Apparently satisfied with the result of his shot, the prince lowered his weapon.

"Beware of Villanova!" he said, in a terrible voice.

Then he slowly stepped down the staircase, the wild-looking men closing in behind him, and forming as it were a body-guard.

In a few moments he had passed into the street and was lost to sight.

Jack, bleeding profusely from his wound, and in a half fainting state, was carried by Carden into an ante-room.

Almost as soon as he had laid Harkaway upon a sofa, Emily rushed in.

She pushed her way through the trembling crowd.

Falling on her knees by the side of the wounded man, she sobbed out—

"Oh, God! is he dead? Speak to me, Jack. For the love of Heaven, speak to me, dearest."

But his eyes had closed, and his arms hung powerless by his side.

CHAPTER XV.

THE LITTLE COXSWAIN.

FORTUNATELY among the guests of the contessa that evening was the surgeon of a British man-of-war lying in the bay.

Attracted by the cries of the crowd, he pushed his way into the room where Tom Carden had carried Harkaway.

Addressing the contessa, he asked what was the cause of the noise and disorder.

"Oh," she replied, with a shrug of the shoulders, "it is only an Englishman who has been shot."

"Shot? What for?" inquired the surgeon.

"For insulting an Italian prince," said the contessa. "Our countrymen, signor, are very high-spirited, and I am sure the Prince of Villanova would not have shot Mr. Harkaway had he not been grossly provoked."

"Did the Englishman strike the prince?"

"No, I have not heard that; but, depend upon it, the poor prince would not have fired had not his honour been attacked. We all feel very deeply for him."

"For whom—Mr. Harkaway?"

"Oh, dear no! santissima Virgine!" exclaimed the contessa, with a little laugh. "It is for the prince we feel. As for Mr. Harkaway, why, really, he deserves it all."

The surgeon looked angrily at the cool unsympathetic Neapolitan lady.

"I don't know what you and your countrymen, madam, may be pleased to think of such a scandalous affair," he exclaimed, "but I have no hesitation in calling it an assassination. Where is the sufferer?"

"On the sofa, where the crowd is. Someone said he was dead. I hope not. How very awkward for *mio caro* Villaneva; he will have to go away for a time. Ah, let me see, you are a doctor. Will you try to save him and not let him die, for—for the poor prince's sake?"

"Devil take the prince!" answered the Englishman, bluntly, as he made his way through the crowd.

"Stand back there; give the man air!" he cried, loudly.

No one seemed inclined to obey these instructions, and the people kept on flocking into the room.

"Has he any friends here?" cried the surgeon.

Harvey and Carden came up and joined him, saying they were friends of Jack's.

"That's all right," replied the doctor. "I am a medical man attached to H.M.S. 'Warspite.' Clear the room, will you? Turn all the macaroni, garlic-eating beggars out at any price."

"I can't do it at the point of the bayonet," replied Tom Carden, "but I will at the point of the poker."

He took up that useful domestic article from the fender, and Harvey imitated his example with the tongs.

By dint of great exertion, and not a little swearing, they succeeded in clearing the room, and Harvey shut the door and put his back against it.

Carden opened a window.

Emily and Hilda, who had joined her at the first alarm, were kneeling by the lounge, trying bravely to staunch the blood as it flowed from the wound.

The doctor, who was a practical man, slit up the coat sleeve with a knife, and laid bare the shoulder.

"Ah!" he exclaimed, "queer shot wound; bone not broken, as well as I can judge. No; ball has glanced off and lodged in the flesh. Ring the bell, please, for cold water and a sponge, and some linen for bandages. You are related to the gentleman, I presume?" he added.

"I am his wife, sir," answered Emily. "Oh, do tell me, will he live?"

"Live? I should think he would. Why, my dear lady, he is worth a dozen dead men yet. The ball has lodged in as comfortable a place as it well could."

"I feel so thankful," cried Emily, joyfully.

Hilda and she looked at one another, and smiled through their tears.

"If you ladies will kindly fall back," said the doctor, "I'll have the bullet out before he comes to, and then we'll bandage him up and take him home."

He was as good as his word.

With a skill and quickness which he had learnt during the Crimean War, he extracted the ball, bound up the injured part, brought Jack, who was very weak and ill, to himself, and then with Carden's help, he carried him to the carriage, which took him to his own house at a gentle walk.

"Keep him quiet," said the doctor to Harvey. "I'll look him up to-morrow. You'll know my name if I call; it is Halsey."

"Is he much knocked about?" asked Harvey.

"Not more than he can stand. He'll lay up for a few weeks, and then keep his arm in a sling for a few more, to prevent a strain on the joint."

"Then it's nothing serious?"

"It might have been a long sight worse," said Halsey, shaking his head.

"Well, we are all very deeply indebted to you for your kindness, Mr. Halsey," remarked Carden.

"You will let us see as much of you as you can, I hope," said Harvey.

"With pleasure, so long as my ship stays. Tell your friend, if he asks any questions, that I've got the lead pill out, and that he needn't flurry himself, though, mind you—although I don't want to praise myself—he might have lost his arm if any of those foreign doctors had got messing him about."

The good-natured doctor accepted a glass of wine and a cigar.

Then he shook hands and departed, leaving all Jack's friends highly pleased at what he had said.

Late in the following day the Contessa Di Malafedi took the trouble to send a servant to inquire after Harkaway.

There were also a few cards left at the house in the Strada di Toledo, where he was lying.

But all the inquiries were made in a half-hearted sort or manner.

Tom Carden took a stroll in the afternoon, and heard various accounts of the affair, which made quite a stir in Naples.

All agreed in one point.

The Prince of Villanova had been infamously treated by the Englishman, and not a lady or gentleman, Italian bred and born, seemed to think that the slightest blame attached to him for shooting.

Everyone said that Harkaway was wrong, and the prince perfectly in the right.

This made Carden indignant.

"Wait till he gets well," he said, "and if this prince shows his ugly nose in Naples again, I'll bet that Harkaway pulls it, and if he can't, I will."

Harvey also went about breathing vengeance against the cowardly Italian.

The authorities made no efforts to find the prince or bring him to justice.

But his highness showed his sense in keeping away from the scene of his late exploit.

Harvey inquired of a score of people where the fiery nobleman lived.

No one in Naples seemed to know exactly.

He could not meet one who had ever been to his house.

He was said to have a castle, about forty or fifty miles from Naples, east of Capua, on the banks of the rapid little river Volturno.

When in retirement at his castle, he never received any visitors, and allowed no stranger to enter.

"I'll find out the villain when Jack gets well," said Harvey to Carden, "and when I have I'll go to the King of Italy at Florence, and demand justice, if I can't get it here."

"And I'll back you up through thick and thin, old cock," replied Carden, smiling at his enthusiasm.

The time did not pass so slowly during Jack's illness as they had all expected.

He was soon able to sit up and talk.

Then he walked a little and drove in the country, rapidly regaining his strength.

His rage against the mysterious prince was fully as great as that of his friends.

"Wait till I can use my right arm again," he exclaimed, "and I'll——"

"Oh, Jack," interrupted Emily, who overheard this remark, "what will you do?"

"Eat him, my dear," he replied, with a smile, not wishing to alarm her.

"You must not provoke such a dangerous man," she said, gravely. "He deserves to be punished, if you can find him, but I should leave the law to deal with him. You will, will you not?"

"Yes, darling," replied Jack, kissing his pretty wife.

He thought there was no great harm in telling her a little fib to prevent her from alarming herself.

When he grew strong enough Monday used to drive him out with Emily in a handsome "Victoria," which had been brought from London.

It happened one day that he was being driven along the road leading to the ruins to Pompeii.

Suddenly they heard the sounds of wheels approaching rapidly.

Looking up, Monday saw a man in a one-horse sort of gig coming along at a gallop.

The horse had evidently got the bit between his teeth and was too much for his driver.

"Hi, hi! yah!" cried Monday. "Where you coming to? Look out, you sare! What you up to? Yah, yah!"

His warning was not attended to.

On came the gig at the same headlong pace, though the driver a young Englishman, tugged away at the reins with all his might.

The next moment there was a collision.

The gig caught the "Victoria," taking off a wheel, and then toppling over on its side.

Its driver was thrown out, and fell in the middle of the road, where he lay for a time as if stunned.

Neither Emily nor Jack was hurt.

though the shock had made them a little nervous.

"Confound the fellow!" exclaimed Jack, stepping out. "He ought to be horsewhipped for driving in that manner.

The young fellow, for he was not more than nineteen, jumped up, shook himself, winced a little as if hurt, took a look at the ruins of the trap, and saw the horse disappearing in the distance, with the harness and the broken shafts rattling behind him.

Then he turned his attention to Jack.

"Pardon me," he said, in a gentlemanly tone, "but, if I am not mistaken, you thought fit to make a disagreeable remark just now."

"I only said that——" began Jack.

"I heard what you said," interrupted the young man. "Possibly you thought you could take advantage of my apparent insensibility."

"Hang it all!" said Jack; "you run into a man and take his wheel off, and then you are riled if he grumbles."

"Certainly I am."

"You ought not to be trusted out with a horse."

"That may be your opinion," replied the young stranger. "We will not talk about that. You have insulted me by saying I ought to be horsewhipped; I heard you."

"Well?"

"Are you going to apologise?"

Jack burst out laughing.

"It's no laughing matter, let me tell you that. Will you apologise?"

"No, I distinctly refuse to do anything of the sort.

"Then mind your eye, for I'm going to take it out of you," said the reckless driver.

"My good fellow," said Jack, "it isn't two months since I was shot in the shoulder, and you may perceive, if you use your eyes, that I still wear my arm in a sling."

"What's the odds? I've broken my right arm, and I don't howl over it."

"Your arm broken?" asked Jack, in surprise.

"What is there wonderful in that?" said the young man. "What a child you must be."

"Why?"

"You don't suppose a man can get chucked out of a trap when the horse is bolting like mad, and not hurt himself, do you?"

"Well, on consideration, no," answered Jack.

"It's a puzzler to me how I didn't break my neck. But, look here, we're evenly matched; your arm's slung up, and mine's broken somewhere—I don't know where, though it hurts like old boots."

"I'm sorry for that," put in Jack.

"Blow your sorrow!" said the youngster. "I want an apology, if not, I shall punch your head."

"You forget I have a lady with me," said Jack. "My wife it not well. Under any other circumstances, I should be glad to oblige you."

"Don't let a petticoat stand in the way. Send her home."

"Can't."

"Then you won't fight? I shall have to give you the coward's blow," said the young man.

"Monday!" said Jack.

"Coming, sare," said the black, getting down off the box.

"Secure this lunatic," cried Jack. "Don't hurt him; his arm is broken. I only want to keep him quiet."

"No, by George, you don't!" said the youngster, rushing up to Jack. "I'll have a cut in after an insult, if I die for it."

Seeing he was determined, Jack drew back, and saying to Emily, "Sit still, dear," faced the little bantam cock.

"If you will have it, you must," he added.

A fight began between them, and was all the more severe while it lasted because it was one-handed.

Their was less chance of guarding the blows which each aimed at the other.

Jack, however, was the stronger and bigger.

His blows were like those from a sledge hammer, and in five minutes the stranger was sitting down in the middle of the road, with one eye closed up and his nose very liberally distilling the claret.

"Have you had enough?" asked Jack.

"Yes; you've licked," replied the stranger. "But I don't bear any animosity because a fellow has given me a hiding. Shake hands."

"Willingly," replied Jack.

Their hands, which had lately been engaged in hitting one another's faces, met in a friendly grasp.

"That's English, isn't it?" said the young one, with a smile.

His face was convulsed with a spasm of pain as he spoke.

"You're hurt?" said Jack, kindly.

"Yes; it's my arm. I told you it was broken, and that last knock-down shove on the left peeper you gave me sent me on to it again. Never mind; I've kept up the honour of Cambridge."

"Are you a Cambridge man?" asked Jack, in surprise.

"I have the honour to belong to that university, my pippin,"

"And I'm Oxford."

"The deuce you are. What's your name?"

"Jack Harkaway."

"By jingo! this is funny. I'm Walter Campbell. Don't you remember I steered the Cambridge eight in the 'varsity race at Putney the year you rowed so well for Oxford?"

"Of course I do. Were you the little coxswain who got so cracked up by everybody for his steering?"

"I'm the infant," answered Walter Campbell, with another grimace, caused by the pain he was suffering.

"By Jove!" said Jack; "what a rum go that we should meet like this."

"It is rum," answered the coxswain; "but it's a rum world—everything's rum. Bother my arm!—don't it just hurt?"

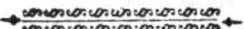

CHAPTER XVI.

BRIGANDS AT WORK.

MONDAY and Emily had watched this singular fight with more interest than fear.

Emily did not think that Jack was in any danger, and was only anxious that Walter Campbell should not be more punished than could be helped.

"It all over, mum," said Monday, grinning. "Mast' Jack lick; knew um would. One arm make no difference to him when fight fair and not use pistol. Any way, him plucky little man. I say that for him."

"Go Monday," replied Emily, "and ask your master what we are to do. The wheel is broken."

Monday left the carriage, and went to the middle of the road.

"Please, sare," he said, "missus wants to know what um to do."

"Blest if I know," answered Jack.

"It's a case of stump, isn't it?" said the little coxswain.

"Stump and no mistake," replied Jack. "Can you walk?"

"Don't think I can. I'm as weak as a rat, and could do a good yell or two, the pain's so great. Besides, I can't see very well; you've bunged one eye up quite, and t'other's closing fast."

"It was your fault."

"Oh, yes, I admit that; but if I'd known you were Jack Harkaway, I don't think I'd have had a mill with you."

"You showed your pluck, anyhow."

"So did you," answered Walter Campbell. "But Oxford and Cambridge are bound to do it everywhere. I licked a lot of brigands the other night."

At the word "brigands," Jack pricked his ears up.

"Brigands!" he repeated, eagerly. "Where?"

"Out Portici way. I haven't been here long, and I always make a point of whacking myself about a bit in a new place."

"Yes."

"I'm a midshipman, mate, odd man, anything you like on board my governor's yatch, the 'Samphire,' you know."

"Is that pretty little schooner your governor's? The one that came into the bay on Saturday?" asked Jack.

"That's her. Isn't she a beauty?"

"Every inch of her."

"Well," continued Walter Campbell, "I got out walking up Portici way, and five coves in long cloaks and slouched hats stopped me."

"What did you do?"

"Shot two of them, slipped into two more like the Tipton Slasher, and kicked the starn of the fifth.

"That's what it all came to, but how I did it I don't know any more than a baby. It was all done in a few minutes, and I put it down as a big fluke."

"But I say, what are we to do?"

"That's just what I am bustling myself about.

"I can't stay here; my arm does hurt a ripper and no mistake," said the little coxswain.

"Shall I send Monday on for another carriage?"

"Do something, there's a good fellow. I'd give the world for a doctor to put me in splints."

Jack was just about to tell Monday to ride one of the horses into Naples, when he heard something coming.

"What's that?" he said.

Monday looked up the road.

"It all right now, sare," he cried.

"What's all right?"

"That Mast' Harvey's drag coming, sare."

"Oh, by Jove! that's lucky," said Jack, joyfully.

It must be mentioned that Harvey, having plenty of money and nothing much to do with it, had ordered a handsome drag to be sent out from England.

This had cost, including the sending-out expenses, £450, and the four blood bays that drew it had cost £550, so that altogether it came to the very respectable total of £1,000.

The drag had only just arrived.

It was the first time Harvey had driven it, and, as may be imagined, it created a great sensation, such a thing as a four-in-hand coach, fitted up in London style, being unknown there.

"What does Monday say?" asked Emily.

"His eyes are better than mine answered Jack, "and he says he can see Dick Harvey's new drag coming along."

"Oh, that's awfully jolly," said Emily.

"He'll pick us all up," continued Jack.

"I'm so glad," said Emily. "Because your new friend, Mr. Campbell, really ought to be attended to. I wish I could do something for him.

"Thank you," replied the little cox-swain, pluckily. "I'm all right bar the arm; don't bother about me, please. It is I who ought to be sorry for knocking your wheel off, and I really am."

"Your horse ran away with you. It was not your fault."

"No, it was not; you're right there. The jibbing beast took fright and shied. I lammed into him with the whip, and then he showed his nasty temper."

The four-in-hand approached at a steady pace.

Harvey was driving, and considering that he'd never driven anything more than a pair or a tandem, he got on very well.

By his side was Tom Carden, an experienced whip, who was giving him instructions.

"Gently, mare," said Tom; wo-a there, ease the off-side wheeler a bit That's your sort, whip up the near-side leader. Soh! gently all; mind the mare. What a nasty knack she's got of bearing on the pole."

"We must cure her of that," answered Harvey.

"Hulloa. Thithorth, as a man with a lisp I know says, what's up in front?" said Tom.

"A smash up, I think."

"Why, there is Jack. By the hookey, it's Emily's Victoria that's come to grief. I hope to goodness that Harkaway isn't hurt again."

"Lucky we came up," said Harvey. "Jack seems to be all serene. Who's that sitting in the road?"

"Not knowing, can't say."

Harvey whipped up his team and stopped within a few paces of the Victoria.

He and Carden bowed to Emily, and Harvey, throwing the reins to one of the grooms, of whom there were two behind, got down.

"Are you hurt, Jack?" he asked nervously.

"No, thank God," replied Jack; "a fellow ran into me."

"The lubber. Where is the clumsy beggar?" cried Harvey.

The little coxswain got up.

"Look here," he said. "I can't afford to be called lubbers and clumsy beggars, you're worse than Harkaway."

"Is this the man?" asked Harvey.

"Yes, that's the child," replied Jack.

"If you want a row, you can be accomodated," continued the little coxswain.

"I am not ambitious of anything of the sort," said Harvey.

"Then don't call people names; take the tip from me, old fellow."

"Oh, if you're on for a row, I daresay I can oblige you," cried Harvey.

"Hold your row, both of you," said Jack. "This is my friend, Mr. Harvey of St. Aldate's, Oxford. And this is, I hope I may also say, my friend——"

The little coxswain bowed.

"My friend, Mr. Walter Campbell, who steered the Cambridge eight in my year."

"Proud to meet Mr. Campbell, I'm sure," replied Harvey. "But, I say, how did this spill happen?"

"My horse bolted," said the coxswain. "I suppose he thought I was taking it in too free and easy a manner."

"Are you hurt?"

"I've broken one arm, and am doubtful about a rib."

"And here are we, keeping you chattering here. By jove! it's too bad," said Harvey; "let me help you inside the drag."

"I'll go with him," said Jack; "take Emily on the roof, the air does her good."

They were soon placed, and leaving Monday to look after the horses and the Victoria, until they could send him assistance, they returned to Naples.

Jack insisted upon the coxswain coming to his lodgings, where his arm was set.

Here he stayed for some time, as his father was obliged to go back in the yacht a day or two afterwards.

He was young and healthy, so that there was nothing to retard his recovery which took place as rapidly as Jack's.

Young bones set together easily.

Meanwhile the Prince of Villanova kept in his castle, at least people supposed so, as he did not make his appearance in Naples.

As he had been very popular with the fashionable Neapolitans, he was much missed.

They one and all blamed Jack, and scouted the idea that he was a brigand.

Some went so far as to declare that his highness ought to have killed Jack outright for saying such a thing.

But Jack did not care a rush for the Italians.

He kept his own counsel.

Only Harvey and Carden knew that he was determined to sift the matter to the bottom, and if the prince was what he suspected him to be, to tear the mask from his face and show him up in his true colours.

The Contessa Di Malafedi constantly regretted her dear prince.

He had, by his high play, been a source of income to her.

She showed her displeasure so much as to cease to invite Jack or any of his companions to her house.

This did not break their heart.

Reports of brigandage continued to come in from all sides.

That the brigands were at work, there could not be any doubt.

Travellers were stopped and plundered, while sometimes a whole village was robbed of provisions.

General Cialdini, who was in command of the troops at Naples, received orders from the Italian Government at Turin, to put a stop to these depredations.

He sent parties of troops to scour the country.

This they did without success.

All the people in the villages could tell him was that the ravages were committed by Barboni.

This Barboni, according to them, was a terrible miscreant, who was in league with the devil.

In their superstitious minds, no bullet could harm him.

Sometimes he took a rich merchant captive, and sent to his friends to say, that if a certain sum of money was not paid within forty-eight hours, they would receive the ears, or the tongue, or the nose of the poor wretch.

And, so sure as there was any failure in paying the ransom, the ears, tongue, or nose came in a basket.

When released by payment, the captives all agreed that they were taken blindfolded some distance and placed in a dungeon.

They were also blindfolded when set at liberty.

No one could describe the place of

captivity, or the features of the brigand chief Barboni.

He always wore a black mask, his eyes flashed fire, he had a long beard, and he spoke in a terrible voice.

His men who were very numerous, and well armed, obeyed him blindly.

There was one peculiarity about the accounts of those captured travellers who were lucky enough to be liberated on ransom.

They one and all said that Barboni's lieutenant, who was more cruel and blood-thirsty even than his master, had but one arm.

It was impossible to arrange a plan to surprise the brigands, when they agreed to liberate a captive, for this reason.

We will suppose a rich man captured. In the morning his friends receive a letter demanding a certain sum of money which, if refused, will subject their relative to torture and death.

The money must be brought to a certain spot, by one person only.

If any treachery is attempted, the captive will die, and that most cruelly.

When the money is paid, the prisoner is let loose in some unfrequented part of the country, where no one thinks of looking for him, and told to make his way home as best he can.

No precaution that the brigand chief could take was neglected.

Barboni became a name of terror in the vicinity of Naples, for upwards of sixty miles round.

This was especially the case on the northern side, or that of the river Volturno.

General Cialdini offered, in the name of the Government, a reward of six thousand ducats for him, which was about a thousand pounds sterling.

This was to be paid for him, alive or dead.

It was fully three months after Jack's "accident," as it was called, that he was able to pronounce himself well.

The coxswain still went about with his arm in a sling.

He had taken an immense fancy to Jack.

In fact, Harkaway's character was just the sort to captivate the mind of a young and chivalrous youth emerging from his teens.

Jack's exploits while at the university were almost as well known at Cambridge as Oxford.

To the young coxswain Harkaway was a hero of romance.

One day, while strolling in the shady groves of the public park called the Villa Reale, Walter Campbell said to Jack—

"I'm going to put a fishing question to you."

"Fish away," answered Jack, cheerily.

"Do you like me?"

"Well, I don't care about paying a fellow compliments, but I do like you," said Jack.

"And so do I you," said the little coxswain. "Now, look here, Harkaway, I'm not a rich sort of bloke, like you and Dick Harvey."

"I'm not rich," said Jack. "My means are moderate and I depend on the dear old gov. for my screw. It's Harvey who is the man with the coin."

"Never mind. You are comfortable. Harvey married an immensely rich heiress, didn't he?"

"Yes, a sort of female Bank of England."

"Perhaps I shall do the same some day; at present I've only a humbugging hundred a year, which my pater allows me."

Jack wondered whether he wanted to borrow a five pound note.

He began rather to sink in his opinion.

Men generally begin in this way when they want to borrow.

The young coxswain was as quick as a needle.

He saw the flush come over Jack's face; for Jack was too honest to be able to hide what was passing in his mind.

You could read Jack like a book.

"I don't want to put my hand in your pocket; no fear," said the young coxswain. "I'm hurt, Harkaway, that——"

"My dear fellow——" began Jack.

"It's all right," interrupted Walter. "I suppose I laid myself open to it. I'm such a blundering fool."

"What is he driving at?" thought Jack.

"Look here," said the little coxswain, "I've got a little income settled on myself, and the governor wants me to see something of Continental life."

"Well?"

"Well, I'll give it all to you, if you'll let me stop with you and be your friend until——"

"Until what?" asked Jack, smiling curiously.

"Until you've had your revenge on that brigand cove. I've heard you talking to Harvey and Carden. What friends you three fellows seem to be. I wish you'd let me into your friendship, all of you."

"Have you thought of the danger of the task we have set before ourselves?" asked Jack, becoming grave.

"I don't care for danger; and you said yourself, when we first met, I was plucky, and being a Boy of England the brigands will find you are not mistaken."

"I shouldn't like you if you weren't so plucky," said Jack to the young coxswain.

"And you do like me?" asked he.

"Very much," answered Jack.

"By Jove! if you only knew how happy you have made me by saying that," cried Walter Campbell. "It's the dream of my life to join you three fellows and hunt down the brigand chief. Will you let me?"

"Nobody knows who he is, or where he hangs out," said Jack.

He was determined to put as many objections in the young man's way as possible, because the vengeance that Jack had promised himself was not to be easily obtained.

Danger, perhaps death, would bar the way.

"Bother all that," said the little coxswain. "We'll find him. We're bound to do it, man alive, if four such fellows as we are make up our minds."

Jack smiled again.

"You are right in supposing that Carden, and Harvey, and I have made up our minds about this matter," he said, "and we mean to work together; but I cannot agree to take you in until I have spoken to them."

"Will you try for me?"

"Certainly I will."

"Hurrah! it's as good as done, then," said the little coxswain, gleefully. "Won't we warm up the jolly old brigands that's all."

"Don't forget one thing," said Jack; "that is, you must not let a word fall before Emily and Hilda. It would only make them ill and nervous. But I mean to stay here until——"

"Look out," interrupted Walter; "here they are."

Jack turned round and perceived Mrs. Harvey and his wife walking together.

"Oh, here you are, Jack dear," exclaimed Emily. "Monday told me you had left word with him that you had gone to stroll here."

"And so you thought you would follow us?" said Jack.

"I hope there is no harm in that," replied Hilda.

"Not at all. What would the world do without the ladies? But I feel sure of one thing, and that is, you had an object in coming."

"You're a magician, I do believe," replied Hilda. "We did come to ask you to do us a favour."

"I am sure," said Walter Campbell, "that you only have to ask to obtain it."

"Oh, I don't know, Mr. Campbell; husbands are great tyrants," replied Emily. "But what we want is a box at the San Carlo to-night.

"I'll go and secure one—the best in the house," said Jack. "What's the attraction?"

"They are going to play a new opera of Verdi's."

"Oh, all right. Consider that done," said Jack.

"Will you come with us?" asked Emily.

"If you will kindly excuse me, I shall be glad," answered Jack, "because I have promised to dine with Carden; but we will all look in at your box after dinner. Won't that do as well?"

"Quite; and now you can continue your stroll. Be good boys," said Emily, with a smile.

The ladies returned to the Strada, while Jack and the coxswain went on to the San Carlo theatre, where they were lucky enough to secure a box nearly opposite that of General Cialdini.

"They will be well fixed up there," remarked Jack; "and women are never pleased if you put them where no one can see them."

Having arranged this, they went home to dress for dinner, and were told by Monday that the ladies were going to wear their best jewellery, as Ada, Monday's wife, who was Emily's maid, had told him.

Emily's jewellery was not nearly so valuable as Hilda's, though she had received many handsome presents on her marriage.

Hilda's diamonds were worth twenty thousand pounds at least, to say nothing of pearls and other precious stones; so that when Hilda said she was going to wear her best jewellery, it meant that she intended to carry about her person what most people would call a fortune.

The ladies were both beautifully dressed, and when they entered the opera house, all eyes were directed towards them.

Never had the San Carlo been more brilliantly and fashionably attended.

The overture was listened to in rapt attention, and the curtain fell on the first act amidst loud applause.

Verdi himself, the great composer, was present, as were General Cialdini, the contessa, and others of note in the city.

When the curtain fell, Hilda and Emily drew back in order to avoid impertinent observation.

Suddenly they heard a slight tapping at the door.

"It is Jack," said Emily, "dear, good fellow he said he would come early."

She got up to open the door.

Scarcely had she done so when a man in evening dress entered, but as he passed the threshold, he put on a black mask.

The girls were too frightened to speak, and sat riveted to their chairs, which were at the further end of the box, and removed from the notice of the visitors to the theatre.

It was easy to see anyone in the front of the box, but not at the rear.

"Ladies," said the stranger, with an air of good breeding, which was strangely at variance with his mask. "If you scream, move, or make the least noise, I shall be under the painful necessity of putting you to death with this dagger."

He displayed a stiletto, which flashed before their eyes in the gas light.

"I am a man of my word, though I wish you no harm," he continued, as Hilda made a slight movement.

Emily was so frightened that she fainted away, and fell like a log on the floor of the box.

Hilda seemed scarcely to breathe.

"Give me those jewels you wear, and collect those of your friend, or——"

"What if I refuse?" asked Hilda, her dark eyes flashing fire.

"Simply you will sign your own death warrant. I mean to have them, and if I don't take them from a living body, I shall from a corpse; it is all the same to me," said the mask.

"Who and what are you?" she demanded.

"Shall I answer your questions one by one?" he said.

"Yes."

"First, I am Barboni."

"The brigand!" gasped Hilda, turning ashy pale.

"You have saved me the trouble of replying," he said; "but, cospetto, you might have added the compliment of famous, for I have made a stir lately. Come, come, I am an admirer of beauty, yet the time presses; the diamonds, quick!"

"Wretch!" exclaimed Hilda. "If you have them at all, you must take them. Dare to touch me, and I will call for aid."

"He advanced a step and then stood irresolute.

Hilda raised her voice and cried out, but at the same moment the orchestra broke out with a burst of music which completely drowned it.

Seeing his advantage, Barboni grasped her by the wrist, and threw her to the ground.

She fell by the side of Emily, and, like her friend, lost her senses by the force of the shock and fright.

Barboni now lost no time in stripping the two ladies of their jewellery.

This he stowed away in a bag which he seemed to carry for that purpose.

"Per Baccho! this is a prize worth having. It's even better than I expected; my information was correct."

When he had taken everything, he looked at his watch.

"Diavolo!" he exclaimed. "Time flies. I shall be caught red-handed if I linger."

Concealing the bag with its precious load about his person, he carefully removed his mask, let himself out of the box, and, closing the door after him, was soon lost in the many winding galleries in the San Carlo theatre.

This audacious robbery, the most daring and impudent which the dreaded Barboni had yet committed, had not occupied more than five minutes in its execution.

CHAPTER XVII

BIGAMINI.

A SHORT time afterwards Jack and Harvey entered the theatre and went to the box where the ladies were.

Carden and the coxswain were promenading on the Chiaja, smoking their cigars, having promised to join them later.

Jack knocked at the door, and was surprised at getting no answer.

He could only suppose they had not yet arrived, and went in search of the box-keeper, who opened the door of the *loge* with a key.

The young men started back in alarm when they beheld their wives stretched on the floor insensible.

Cold water and smelling salts were applied to revive them, and successfully.

The girls, looking deathly pale and shuddering, sat up.

"What is the meaning of this?" asked Jack. "You will drive me mad if you do not tell me."

"Oh, Jack," answered Emily, "we have had such a fright."

"From what?"

"A man in a mask came into our box and told us we must give up our jewellery. We must have both fainted, for I remember nothing more."

"Do you recollect, Hilda?" asked Jack.

"Only that the man showed a dagger and threatened to kill me, and then I fainted."

"What was the man like?"

"Tall and thin. The mask hid his face," replied Hilda.

"The villain! Did he say anything?"

"Yes; he said he was Barboni, the chief of the brigands."

"Had you on your diamonds?" inquired Harvey, anxiously,

"Unluckily I had."

"By the living jingo!" cried Harvey, "the fellow has got a splendid booty.

Look. He hasn't left them even a ring."

"Stay here, Dick," replied Jack. "I will go to Cialdini the general, who is in his box, and raise an alarm. The robber may not be out of the theatre."

Harvey nodded, and Jack hurried away.

The general readily admitted him to his box, and listened to his tale with evident consternation.

An alarm was given, and all the entrances to the theatre watched, while the interior was thoroughly searched.

But no one answering the description of the robber could be found.

He had made off.

The general sympathised very deeply with the ladies upon their heavy loss, and declared it was the most daring outrage that he had ever heard of.

"These brigands," he said, "puzzle me altogether; but both the police and the military shall be set to work immediately. All that I can do shall be done."

"Thank you," replied Jack. "Will you send soldiers to the castle of the Prince Di Villanova?"

"With what end in view?"

"I suspect him to be either the chief of the brigands, or connected with them in some way."

The general smiled incredulously.

"My dear young sir," he replied, "you insult one of the representatives of our old nobility. The idea is ridiculous. I could not insult the prince by suspecting him."

"Then I shall have to do it myself,"

"Do what?"

"Expose this fellow, and bring him to justice, if he is what I suppose him to be," said Jack.

"You feel strongly against the man," replied the general, "because you had a quarrel with him, and he shot you in the arm. That's it, eh?"

"Not at all," answered Jack; "of course I don't like him any better for his cowardice."

"No—no," cried Cialdini. "These brigands are common fellows after all, though they are getting very daring, and you must really dismiss from your mind any connection between Barboni and the Prince Di Villanova."

Jack, with disgust, saw that it was useless to try to make any impression upon the general at present.

So, thanking him for his promises and courtesy, he returned to Harvey.

Emily and Hilda recovered themselves, now they had their protectors with them, though they trembled whenever the dreaded name of Barboni was mentioned.

Harvey was furious at being robbed of the valuable jewellery worn by Hilda.

Long before the performance was over, it was known all through Naples that Barboni had robbed two English ladies in their box at the San Carlo.

The value of the diamonds amounted to a sum fabulous in the eyes of the Neapolitans.

Nothing else was talked of but this audacious act of brigandage.

Barboni became at once a great man, and as the victims were English, the people did not sympathise much with them.

The Neapolitans are rigid Catholics, and they hate the Protestant Inglese for being what they term heretics.

On the following day, the walls of the city were covered with huge posters doubling the reward for the capture of Barboni.

Jack, Harvey, and Tom Carden, laid their heads together, to devise a plan by which they could solve the mystery which surrounded the famous brigand.

That the authorities were on the wrong track they did not doubt.

"The key of the riddle," remarked Carden, "lies in establishing the identity of Barboni with the Prince Di Villanova."

"I think so too," replied Jack

"You know I was the first to start the idea of the prince's being a brigand."

"Yes, you were, and you think the prince and Barboni are one and the same person," observed Harvey.

"I wish I was as sure of a thousand pounds as I am of it," answered Tom Carden, confidently.

"The mystery is only to be solved in the prince's castle; what do you call it?" said Jack.

"Castel Inferno. There is some horrible legend connected with it, which accounts for the name."

"I told you that the little coxswain wants to join us," said Jack.

"Yes," replied Harvey and Carden.

"Shall we admit him into our fraternity? He is a very decent fellow, and brave as a lion, or he would not have milled me with his arm broken."

"As far as I am concerned, I should like him to be one of us," exclaimed Harvey.

"And I also," replied Carden.

"That is settled then. I will tell him to-day, and as soon as his arm is quite well we will admit him, and then we will, in this room, swear, all of us, never to leave Naples until we have exterminated this nest of brigands."

This proposal was well received.

The idea of forming a society, and binding themselves by a solemn oath was quite romantic.

Jack was sitting near the open window, throwing cigars to a crowd of beggars in the street.

The lazzaroni lazily picked them up, but looked as if they considered it almost too much trouble to do so.

While he was thus occupied, Monday entered.

"Please, sir," he exclaimed," "there is um rum sort of chap downstairs; him want to see you.'

"What about?" asked Jack,

"Him not say."

"Show him up."

Presently Monday ushered in an Englishman, about five feet nothing in height, very thin, with a sharp, hatchet-like face, having a comical expression about the mouth and eyes. He appeared to have a nervous affliction, which made him inclined to smile when he had no real intention of doing so.

His dress was shabby and dusty, his boots and clothes belonged to the "have beens," that is, they had been good once, but it was so long ago, that one was tempted to doubt that they ever were new at all.

"HAVE YOU HAD ENOUGH? ASKED JACK."

The continual grin on the man's face was rather amusing, and his sharp grey eyes twinkled like a ferret's.

He looked round nervously, as he glided cautiously into the room, then he peeped under the table, and took the liberty of shaking the curtains to see if there was any one behind them.

"Excuse me, sir," he answered, in a shrill treble, which was an apology for a voice. "It's a way I've got."

"Who are you?" asked Jack.

"I've come from England, sir, and changed my name. Here I'm Bigamini."

"That's a funny name too."

"So it is, sir. At home I was Smiffins; you won't repeat it, sir."

"No."

"Yes," continued the little man, with a deep sigh, though the smile was all the time visible. "I was once a happy Smiffins."

"And now?"

"Now, sir, I'm a miserable Bigamini."

"How did that happen?" inquired Jack, who could not make the fellow out at all.

"I didn't like my wife, sir. She led me such a life, so I—I left her and married another."

"That's bigamy."

"I know it, sir, to my cost. I'm a tailor by trade, sir, and my first wife found me out, and threatened to prosecute me, so I got on board a ship and it brought me here. I was afraid of the police, sir, and that's why I looked under the table and shook the curtains, and as I've always got bigamy on the brain, sir, I called myself Bigamini. It's Italian, sir, and they can't twig it over here."

"The fact of the matter is, I suppose, that you are too lazy to work at your trade, and you have come to beg of me," replied Jack, testily.

"No, sir," said the little man, drawing himself up proudly; "a Bigamin—I mean a Smiffins couldn't so far bemean himself as to beg."

"Oh, you don't want money?"

"No, sir."

"That's lucky, for I shouldn't have given you any," replied Jack. "I hate encouraging idleness."

"Begging your pardon, sir," said Bigamini. "I'm in employ as a snip here,

getting good wages. Oh, yes, I could always earn good money."

"Well, what in the name of goodness, do you want with me?" demanded Jack, impatiently.

"You won't betray me to the police, sir?"

"What have the Naples police to do with a charge in England?"

"But I always fancy there is a detective after me."

Here the little man took another look under the table.

"My first wife's an awful woman, sir," continued Bigamini. "She'll never leave me. She swore she'd have me some day, and I believe she will; that's what's making me so thin and redoocing of me to a shadder."

"I won't split on you. Go on," said Jack.

"Thank you, kindly, Mr. Harkaway, sir; I've heard of you in England, sir."

"The deuce you have?"

"Yes, sir. I ain't a cockney bred and born," said Bigamini. "I was raised in Iffley, near Oxford, and that led me to take an interest in the university boat race."

"Oh, I see," said Jack.

"Yes, sir, I used to bet on Oxford, sir, but that was when I was a happy Smiffins, and now I'm a miserable Bigamini."

The little man drew a deep sigh, which shook his feeble frame.

"Yes, Mr. Harkaway, sir, the day you rowed and won, I got on Oxford at threes to one, sir, and pulled off a pot of coin. Ah, well do I remember it, for I got on the spree for a week with the money, and my wife beat me shameful with the carpet-broom when I came back."

"I wish you'd postpone your private history and come to the point," said Jack, still more impatiently.

"Don't interrupt him," whispered Carden, nudging Jack's elbow. "He's a gift."

"Yes," said Harvey, in the same tone. "He's a character. I never heard anything so amusing, except old Mole, in my life."

"I'm a-coming to the point, sir," replied Bigamini, "and that reminds me this is a thirsty place, and when I was a happy Smiffins, I used to take my pint regular."

"You shall have some bottled beer when you have told me what you want, and not before."

"Right, sir. You have recalled me to my miserable self. I have heard of your loss, sir, and that of Mr. Harvey's lady. I presoom that is Mr. Harvey?"

"Yes," replied Harvey. "you've made a good shot."

"Thank you kindly, sir. I hope you don't find me forward. I try to be as 'umble as I can in the presence of my superiors."

"I never saw such a fellow," said Jack. "can't you speak out?"

He began to lose all patience.

"Well, sir, there wasn't a better man of business once than me, though I say it who shouldn't, but that was when I was a happy Smiffins."

He wiped away a tear.

"But now I'm a miserable Bigamini," he continued, in a doleful tone, adding— "I say, sir."

"What the d——"

"Don't swear, sir. It comes 'arsh against the ears to hear a gentleman a-cussin'."

"What *is* it you want?" asked Jack, in despair.

"Are you quite sure, sir," there ain't no one a-'iding under the table?"

Jack groaned in anguish of spirit.

Harvey and Carden laughed and enjoyed the scene immensely.

"I tell you," roared Jack, angrily, "that there is no one in the room but ourselves. "Can't you understand that, you idiot?"

"Thank you kindly, sir," replied Bigamini. "It's only my nervous way. I fancy my wife's come over after me with a D. sometimes. I can't bear a detective, sir, and never dreamt of no such thing when I was a happy Smiffins. But now I'm a——"

He began to cough violently.

Jack could not bear it any longer, and getting up, seized him by the collar and shook him roughly.

"A miserable Bigamini," said the little man, concluding his sentence. "I thank you, sir, for shaking the words out. My cough came on. It does sometimes."

"Do you see that window?" shouted Jack.

"Yes, sir. Pleasing prospect. You can gaze upon the blue waters of the bay."

"Hang the prospect. I'll throw you out of the window, if you don't speak."

"Anything to oblige, you, sir," said Bigamini, shrinking back.

"And stop that infernal grin, will you?"

"Can't sir; that's the effects of bigamy. It makes me feel all overish. But I came to-day, sir, thinking you'd like to hear something about the brigands."

Tom Carden and Harvey left off laughing.

Jack's face displayed at once a keen interest.

"What do you know about them?" he asked.

"I was captured by them, sir, and kept a prisoner, having only escaped yesterday morning."

"By Jove! you're the very man we want," exclaimed Jack; "and you've come just in the nick of time. Sit down and tell me all you know."

"Yes, sir; but touching that beer?"

"Ring the bell, Dick, for Monday," said Jack.

Bigamini went up to the curtains, and gave them another nervous shake.

Then he glanced timidly at the table, saying—

"You're quite sure there's no one under that table, sir?"

"No, no, it's all right," replied Jack.

Monday brought some beer, which he poured into a silver tankard.

The young men stood round Bigamini and anxiously waited to hear what he had to say.

CHAPTER XVIII.

THE SOLEMN OATH.

WHEN Bigamini withdrew his face from the tankard he seemed refreshed, and smiled benignantly upon his audience.

"There's nothing like good malt and 'ops," he remarked; "'op picking in Kent's a 'ealthy ockipation, they tell me."

"Never mind that; go on with your story. How were you captured by the brigands?" said Jack.

"I was going to Capua, sir, on a job."

"Yes."

"I crossed the Volturno by the ferry and hadn't gone far before a lot of fellows in masks came up, knocked me down, bound my arms, and blindfolded me."

"Did you see their faces?"

"Never a one."

"Well, they captured you; what then?" said Carden.

"They wouldn't ha' done it, sir, if I'd been a happy Smiffins instead of a miserable Bigamini."

"I dare say not. Go on."

"No, sir," replied the little man. "I'm what you call crushed now. I'm a kind of worm, and when I'm trod on, I don't turn."

"I have always heard that a tailor is only the ninth part of a man," observed Harvey.

"Tain't true, sir. You should have seen me when I was a happy——"

"That will do; forge ahead," interrupted Jack.

Bigamini looked suspiciously at the table.

"Ain't it funny?" he said; "I can't get it out of my 'ed that there's some one under that table."

He laughed a low, chuckling sort of laugh.

"Of course," he added, "I know there ain't but I fancies it."

"What did the brigands do with you?" asked Jack, biting his nails with impatience.

"Ah! the brigands. Yes, sir. What with bigamy and brigands, I ain't the man I use to was to be."

"Confound you! Will you get on?" cried Jack.

"There's one question I should like to ask, Mr. Harkaway."

"What is it?"

"I hope you find me 'umble, sir; I don't want to take any liberties with my betters, and it isn't becos you're treating me as a friend, and standing me bottled beer in a foreign country, that I should presoom upon it," said Bigamini.

"You're all right. Go on."

"Where was I?"

"Bound and blindfolded."

"Oh, yes. Well, sir, I was taken over a rough country, as well as I could judge, for three miles. Then we crossed a bit of water, went down some steps, and I was put in a dark dungeon."

"Was there no light?"

"Very little; what there was came through a narrow grating. Bread and water was my fare, and the next day a tall man came and asked me if I had any friends with money. I told him no. He told me to think it over. Who did I know in Naples? I mentioned my employer the tailor.

"'Write him a letter,' he said, 'demanding a thousand ducats ransom, and if it is not sent, I shall cut off one of your ears, and forward to him—nose to follow, ditto tongue and big toes.'"

"Pleasant," ejaculated Harvey.

"I didn't think so, sir, and turned sulky," replied Bigamini, "and he left me. During the night, I tried the bars of the window; they were rusty and rotten. I pulled them out, and crept through, and fell into the moat."

"How do you know it was a moat?" asked Jack, a little suspiciously.

"Because, when I swam across it and got to the bank, I took a look at the place I had escaped from, and saw by the light of the moon that I had been in a castle."

"Surrounded by water?"

"Yes, sir."

"Whose castle was it?"

"That I did not stop to inquire," answered Bigamini, with a touch of dry humour. "I took to my heels, and ran for miles without stopping."

"Fool!" said Jack. "What is the use of your information? Why did you not ask who the castle belonged to?—you must have seen some cottages along the road."

"You see, sir," replied Bigamini, "I didn't like the idea of having one of my ears sent to Naples, nose to follow, ditto tongue and big toes, which would have been the case if I had been recaptured."

"Could you give us any means of finding the castle?" inquired Carden.

"Yes, I think I could, sir."

"You could guide us to it?"

"I don't say that for I wouldn't go within a mile of it for the Bank of England, nor ought you unless you have a regiment of soldiers with you," said the little man.

"I don't want you to tell me what we ought to do. Just answer my questions," said Tom Carden.

"Ain't I a-answering of them?—begging your pardon for being so bold as to say so," replied Bigamini.

"You know the spot where you were captured?"

"Yes, sir; well. It was near the ferry across the river Volturno."

"Very good; the march to the castle, you say, was about three miles."

"Not more, sir."

"There can't be many castles about there," said Carden, triumphantly. "And I think this man can give us a clue to the brigands."

"So do I," replied Jack.

"Harvey concurred in this opinion.

"One more question," said Carden, after a moment's pause. "Did you hear any name mentioned while you were with the brigands?"

"Any names?" repeated Bigamini.

He seemed to be taxing his memory.

"Yes, any name?"

"I think I did, sir. There was a man the robbers called Barb—Barbarous. No that wasn't it, though it was Bar something."

"Was it Barboni?" asked Jack.

"That's it, sir. Barboni was the name," cried Bigamini.

The three young men considered the information given them of the utmost importance, as it fixed the locality of the brigand's home.

Jack and his friends now felt certain they were on the track of Barboni, the brigand chief.

Bigamini had spoken of a castle and a moat within three miles of the ferry across the Volturno, east of Capua, as the brigand's home.

It was useless for Jack and his friends to go to General Cialdini and tell him what they had heard, for he would scarcely dare to attack a castle without stronger proofs.

So they advised Bigamini to say nothing to any one, and to keep very quiet at his lodgings in Naples until they had decided how to act. The little man received a couple of pounds for his information and thanked them all very much for their kindness.

"You can go now," said Jack. "But leave your address so that my servant may know where to find you when you are wanted.

Bigamini wrote it down on a piece of paper.

"That'll find me, sir. It's only a rough sort of a home, on a third-floor facing back," he said. "I ain't got the comforts I had when I was a happy Smffiins."

"Serve us well," replied Jack, "and we will see if we can't arrange things for you in England."

"Never sir," answered Bigamina emphatically; "you may square a bobby or even a beak, but my missus—never. I'm doomed to be a miserable Bigamini."

"You needn't be afraid. No one is likely to find you so far away."

"She might. Sarah Anne Smiffins ain't a common sort of woman, and the fear of being took back and tried for bigamy is a'most more than I can stand. Was that the wind, sir, a-rustling of them curtains or was it some one behind?"

"The wind," replied Jack. "Now mind what I have said to you. In a day or two you will be sent for."

"Thank you for me, sir. You won't think me forward in asking you to accept the thanks of a miserable Bigamini."

"Not at all."

"That takes a weight off my mind. Good-day, gentlemen," replied the little man.

He took one look under the table, and shuffled to the door, which he opened cautiously, and glided ghostlike down the stairs.

In the street he displayed the same nervous apprehension, and the three friends saw him look over his shoulder several times before he got out of sight.

He had not been long gone before Monday ushered in Walter Campbell.

The little coxswain had his arm out of a sling for the first time.

Slapping Jack on the back, he exclaimed—

"What cheer, my hearty ! My wing is mended at last, you see."

"Glad to hear it," answered Jack. "How are you ?"

"Nicely, thanks. What's up ! You look as grave as a judge on a trial for murder."

"We have received information about the brigands, which gives us a pretty good general idea of their whereabouts," said Jack.

"Come, that's news worth having."

"You asked the other day if you might join us, Walter. Are you still of the same mind ?"

"Of course I am. May I ?"

"Yes. I have spoken to my friends, and they have no objection to your being added to our number," answered Jack.

The little coxswain threw his cap in the air joyfully.

"Hurrah," he exclaimed. "We will capture the brigands or die in the attempt. Who's afraid ?"

"In order," said Jack, " that there may be no flinching or drawing back on the part of any of us, I propose that we bind ourselves by a solemn oath."

"Very proper," observed Carden.

"I mean to have Hilda's jewels back," replied Harvey. "Jack has to avenge the shot in the shoulder, and you, Carden —what is your object ?"

"My object in joining this brigand extermination society," replied Carden, "is a wish to help you two and a love of adventure."

"And yours, Campbell ?"

"Oh, I go in for the fun of the thing, and—and because I like Harkaway," answered the little coxswain.

Jack took a pen and a piece of paper, with which he occupied himself for a minute or two. Looking up, he said—

"I have sketched the form of an oath. Shall I read it to you ?"

"No necessity," answered Carden. "Eh, lads ?"

"I think not," replied Harvey. "Let Jack say it out, and we'll say it after him."

"I'm agreeable," said Walter Campbell.

"I, Jack Harkaway," began Jack— "you must put in your own names you know—solemnly swear that I will not rest until I have discovered and either killed or brought to justice Barboni, the chief of the brigands of Naples, and I promise to act loyally and faithfully to the three friends ? who have associated themselves with me in this enterprise ; and this I pledge myself to, by my sworn oath and word of honour, our motto being ' Death to the brigands, wherever they may be, on earth or water.' And I humbly pray for the aid of Heaven in this my sworn enterprise."

"Cross hands," said Tom Carden.

He took Jack's outstretched hand, and Harvey took the little coxswain's across Jack's and Carden's.

In a deep tone, each exclaimed—

"I swear !"

Thus was the oath solemnly taken, and they were pledged as men of honour to destroy the brigand chief and break up his gang.

"You all know," said Jack, "that I have been grossly insulted by the Prince of Villanova. First of all through my wife, and secondly by being shot in a cowardly manner."

"Certainly," said Harvey.

"Thirdly," continued Jack, "there is the robbery of the jewellery. We suspect the prince of being the chief of the brigands."

"And we have strong cause for doing so," remarked Carden.

"If I could have met the prince, who has kept out of the way, instead of offering me the satisfaction I had a right to expect, such as a duel with sword or pistols, this crusade might have been avoided," Jack went on.

"As it is," said Harvey, "this course we have adopted is the only one left open to us."

"Yes," said the little coxswain, "we have nothing to be ashamed of, and what we have to do is to go in and win "

"And what's more," said Tom Carden,

lighting a fresh cigarette, "we mean to win."

A sound as of mocking laughter was heard in the corridor through the half open door.

The four young men looked strangely at one another.

"Did you hear that?" asked Jack.

"Yes," answered Harvey. "What the deuce could it be?"

"It sounded like a devil's laugh," said the coxswain.

Jack rushed out on the landing.

"Monday, Monday!" he cried loudly.

The black came running up the stairs.

"Have you seen anyone in the house," asked his master.

"No, sare. Um not see a soul," replied Monday.

At this moment, Emily came from the top of the house in a great state of alarm.

"Oh, dear Jack!" she cried. "Ask Harvey to come upstairs."

"Why?"

"Hilda has been nearly frightened out of her life."

"By whom?"

"The same man in the mask who robbed us at the San Carlo.

"Barboni?"

"Yes, the brigand chief. She was in her bedroom; he walked in and helped himself to her purse and everything of value lying about," replied Emily.

The three young men had crowded round Emily, and heard her statement.

Harvey sprang upstairs at a bound to his wife.

Tom Carden and the little coxswain ran down to the hall to search the house.

"By Jove," said Jack putting his hands in his pockets, "this is getting serious."

It seemed as if Barboni laughed at locks, defied the law, and mocked every one who stood in his way.

This entrance of a house and robbery by broad daylight was more daring than the outrage at the theatre.

Clearly the chief of the brigands was no ordinary man.

The four friends had perhaps set themselves a task more difficult to accomplish than they had imagined.

Barboni was no common thief to be easily captured.

He could plan.

He could dare.

He was able to execute his undertakings with success.

CHAPTER XIX.

THE TEMPTER.

As it was at San Carlo, so it happened at Harkaway's house in the Strada di Toledo.

Not the slightest trace could be found of the robber.

Carden and Campbell rejoined Jack, who was pacing the room in an agitated manner.

"Can't see a soul," said the little Cambridge man.

"Tell you what it is, coxswain," exclaimed Carden, "I don't like that buffer Bigamini."

"Oh, he's right enough," replied Walter Campbell.

"I don't know so much about that. It seems to me that while he was taking an hour to tell what he might have told in five minutes, the house was being robbed."

"You're wrong to suspect him, Tom," said Jack. "He is a harmless fool."

"He may be, but I have my doubts about him," answered Carden.

Harvey having seen his wife and calmed her, came down to the drawing-room.

"We'd better send what valuables we have to the bank after this," remarked Jack.

"Too late, my boy," replied Harvey. "You're like the man who lost his darned old fiddle."

"Why?"

"It's locking the stable door after the horse has been stolen; we've nothing left."

"Nothing," echoed Jack.

"No; the scamp has made a clean sweep this time, and I should think the things he's collared will set him up for life. Neither Emily nor Hilda has any jewellery left," replied Harvey.

"Well, hang my sister's cats!" exclaimed the little coxswain, "we're not going to stand this, are we?"

"Not much," answered Jack, "but we

must bide our time. It's no good running our heads against a brick wall."

They talked the matter over for some time, and then Jack went to the chief of the police, and afterwards to General Cialdini.

Fresh placards were posted about the city, and the reward for the brigand increased.

The people of Naples laughed.

"When they catch Barboni," they said, "the sky will fall and we shall catch larks."

"Yes," said others, "we shall lie on our back's, and sucking-pigs, ready roasted, will fall into our mouths.

The Neapolitans were again rather amused than otherwise that the Inglesi should have been once more robbed.

The same day Bigamini made his way very cautiously along the Strada di Toledo, until he arrived at the Palazzo Malafedi.

A servant who seemed to know him, ushered him promptly into the presence of the contessa.

"Ha!" she exclaimed. "Is the master in Naples?"

"No, 'celenza," replied Bigamini, "but I am the bearer of a message and a letter."

"Proceed," said the contessa, eagerly.

"The master wishes you, 'celenza to give this letter to Mrs. Harkaway, and he will expect you both this evening at the grotto of the sybil."

"It shall be done. The master's will is law. Tell him I kiss his hand," answered the contessa.

Feeling for her purse, she gave the messenger a piece of gold.

Bigamini's nervous manner deserted him while with the contessa, and he seemed to be thoroughly self-possessed and to know what he was about.

He bowed to the ground, and when the contessa dismissed him with a wave of the hand, he expressed his thanks, and retired.

The contessa dressed herself after his departure, and ordered her carriage to drive her to the Villa Reale, where the fashionables of Naples were airing themselves, and displaying their charms and attractive dresses to their acquaintances.

Emily was also there, attended by her maid, Ada, who, as Monday's wife had accompanied her to Naples.

It was somewhat difficult for the con-tessa to approach Emily, after what had occurred at her palace.

In conjunction with most other notables of Naples, she had openly espoused the cause of Prince Villanova.

Since the memorable night when the prince shot Jack in the shoulder, no invitations had been issued to any member of Harkaway's party.

They had been practically cut by the higher classes of society in Naples.

It was rumoured that Villanova had been seen at more than one grand house since the affair. But neither Jack nor any of his friends had seen him.

The gay crowd was promenading up and down under the shade of the trees.

In the distance was the serene and beautiful Bay of Naples, reflecting the azure of the fleecy clouds.

Meeting Emily in the grand walk, she stopped, smiled, and held out her hand, which Emily took rather coldly.

"Ah!" said the contessa, "how glad I am to meet you again! This is a delight to me which I had not expected. Why have you not been to see me? I feared you were offended."

"Thank you," replied Emily; "but you know I could scarcely come without an invitation, nor should I have felt inclined to enjoy your hospitality after what has happened."

"Don't blame the poor prince," said the contessa, in a tone of entreaty. "Our nobles are so proud and so impulsive."

"Rather too much so."

"You are thinking of your husband, but it was nothing after all. He is well now. The prince might have killed him. See how Mr. Harkaway insulted him by calling him a brigand.

"The poor prince told him he would hit him in the shoulder. That was all he did. After the insult it was but a slight chastisement."

Emily shrugged her shoulders, and parted her pretty lips disdainfully.

"What would many another have done? Shall I tell you?" continued the contessa,

"If you please," said Emily, in a tone of indifference.

"He would have hired a bravo to kill him with a stiletto after dark, and no one would have known anything about it, except that an Inglese had been found dead in the street.

Emily shuddered.

"We don't do things in that way in England," she replied.

"Perhaps not. We are Neapolitan, and so different from you, But say, shall we be friends?"

The contessa spoke in a winning manner.

"I have no particular wish to be on anything but distant terms with you," answered Emily.

"Stupidezza!" replied the contessa, tapping her playfully with her fan.

"No; indeed I have not. While we remain in Naples, I have no wish for the society of any one but those of my own circle."

"Ah; you are resentful. Well, I will not be cross. It is my wish to save you."

"Save me?" repeated Emily.

"Yes. Your husband is very unpopular here. I fear there is a plot against him."

"Of what nature?"

"Will you promise to say nothing to anyone, but to act as I advise you, if I tell you all I know?"

"Oh, yes," said Emily, trembling.

She loved Jack so, and feared so much for his precious life, that she was weak and yielding when she heard that he was in any danger.

"Just now," said the contessa, "a rough-looking man pushed by me, and handing me a letter, told me to give it to Mrs. Harkaway, who was a friend of mine."

"Where is it?" demanded Emily.

"I have it in my pocket, but hear me out. I am concerned in this. The man declared that if any eye but yours saw the letter, both you and I would be in danger of death. Oh, promise me to be cautious. You do not know the power of the dagger in Italy."

"I promise. Give me the letter," said Emily, impatiently.

"No eye save yours shall behold it."

"None."

"Stay, your maid is behind you. Tell her to wait for you on that seat near the statue of Mercury. We can retire under the trees, where we shall be free from observation."

Emily nodded.

She spoke a few words to Ada, who obediently sat down in the spot pointed out, and her mistress walked away with the contessa.

When they had reached a shady place, they retired from the throng.

The contessa handed Emily the letter which she had received from Bigamini.

It was written in a delicate Italian hand, and was to the following effect—

"Madame, if you love your husband, whose life is in extreme danger, you will meet the writer of this note as soon as possible at the grotto of the sybil. I pledge my word that you shall run no risk."

That was all.

"What can this mean?" asked Emily.

The contessa took the letter from her hands, which shook with emotion.

"It is in English," she said, "though written by an Italian. Depend upon it that it is meant as a warning."

"Against what and whom?"

"How can we tell unless we go?"

"We!" said Emily.

"Yes, my child, I will incur any danger for your sake. It will show you that you have mistaken my character, and though I sympathise with my countrymen, I yet have affection for you."

Emily was deceived by the manner of the contessa.

"Dear friend," she exclaimed, "I will put my trust in you. What shall I do?"

"Keep this appointment. You will then know the extent of the danger."

"But should it be a trap?"

"Oh! you can trust to the honour of the Neapolitan. The letter expressly says, 'you shall run no risk,'" said the contessa.

"Where is this grotto?"

"Not far from Naples, scarcely ten miles. In it resides an aged sorceress, who can pry into the secrets of the future. She is called the Cumœan sybil and many people of high rank go to consult her. I have been myself."

"May I not tell my husband?"

"Certainly not; that would spoil all," said the contessa. "Send your maid home. Tell her you are going to my house, and I will drive you in my carriage without delay to the grotto of the sybil."

"I have never had a secret from Jack," sighed Emily.

"That don't matter," the contessa urged; "we shall be home in three hours. It is now four; you don't dine till eight. No one dines till the heat has passed."

"It must be as you say, though I have sad misgivings."

"Am I not with you?"

"Yes, that comforts me."

"Besides, your maid will be able to say you are with me, if she is questioned. Surely the Contessa Di Malafedi should be a fit companion for Mrs. Harkaway."

This was said with some pride, and Emily, seeing the point and admitting it, made no further opposition.

She leant on the contessa's arm and they sought the maid, who had followed them with her eyes.

"Ada," said Emily, "you will go home, please, and if I am inquired for, say I have gone for a drive with the contessa."

"Yes, ma'am," replied Ada.

"Say nothing, girl, unless you are asked," said the contessa.

The two ladies passed on, but as Emily sought to put the letter which she had held in her hand into her pocket, she was so nervous that she let it drop on the path without perceiving it.

Ada, however, saw it.

She darted forward in an instant, and picking it up, held it tightly.

"It's odd, mistress going off with the contessa," she murmured. "Perhaps this letter will throw some light on it. I will show it to Monday, and if he thinks there is anything wrong, he shall give it to master."

Utterly unconscious of having dropped the letter, Emily accompanied the Contessa Di Malafedi to the entrance of the Villa Reale.

There the contessa's carriage was waiting.

They entered, and the Malafedi said in Italian to her footman—

"Drive to the sybil's cave. Go slowly through the streets, but outside Naples increase your pace. I am impatient. You understand?"

"*Si, 'celenza*," replied the man, who mounted the box, and the carriage drove off.

CHAPTER XX.

THE CAVE OF THE SYBIL.

THE Cumæan sybil, as she was called, was a fortune-teller of considerable reputation.

She lived in a cave or grotto, which she never quitted, and subsisted on the sums of money she received from those who came to consult her.

Her only attendant was a dwarf, named Bomba, who was as much like the popular idea of an imp of darkness as he could be.

Misshapen, ungainly, hideous, cruel and mischievous, Bomba was supposed by the ignorant to be the familiar spirit of the witch.

As the carriage neared the cave, the dwarf, who was perched on a rock like a toad on the edge of a precipice, jumped from crag to crag with incredible rapidity, and gaining the ground, ran into the cavern.

He had evidently been on the watch.

The cave of the sybil was situated at the extremity of a narrow rocky defile, the sides of which were covered with stunted shrubs, pine trees, and long grass.

This defile was capable of being defended by a handful of men against an army.

A small entrance admitted the visitor to a spacious cavern dimly lighted from a fissure in the rock.

By the imperfect light could be seen the arrangement of the interior.

Ghastly skeletons from Pompeii, horrid mummies from the East, grinned from the sides, where they had been placed, piles of bones were seen in the corners, hideous bats were nailed to the roof, and strange birds and animals, stuffed, seemed preparing to spring upon the intruder.

A brood of tame snakes crawled all over the floor, gliding into holes, reappearing in other parts, and keeping up a constant hissing.

On a ledge sat an owl, while at the old hag's feet lay a savage wolf, who had for his mistress the fidelity of a dog.

The sybil herself was an aged crone, with bent back and wrinkled face.

She wore a short black serge skirt, and over her shoulders was thrown a blood red cloak, while her grey and tangled hair hung in matted ringlets down her back.

In spite of age and growing infirmities, there was a fire in her eyes which showed that her mind was active enough.

When Bomba bounded into the cave, he exclaimed—" They come."

" Go, child," replied the sybil, " and guide them to me. Stay! Is the curtain securely drawn round the entrance to the secret cavern ?"

" Yes, mother," answered the dwarf.

" Then all is well. Let them approach."

From this conversation it will be seen that the visit of the contessa and Emily was not unexpected by the witch and her goblin attendant.

A moment afterwards the carriage had drawn up at the end of the defile, and in front of the rock, at the base of which the sybil had her home.

" Is this our destination ?" asked Emily, regarding the gloomy-looking place with an involuntary shudder.

" Yes ; lean on my arm. You tremble, mia cara," replied the contessa, in a reassuring tone.

Together they passed through the narrow aperture and entered the cave.

The snakes ran about hissing, and raised their spiral coils defiantly.

The owl flapped its wings, the wolf's back bristled as it bared its glistening teeth.

The skeletons seemed to rattle their bones, and even the mummies appeared to gibe and mock the visitors to the gloomy abode of witchcraft.

Bomba, having indicated the way to the ladies, retired to the doorway, and again posted himself on the look-out.

" What would you with me ?" asked the witch.

" Give her the letter," said the contessa, in a whisper.

Emily searched her pockets for it, but in vain.

" I have lost it," she answered. " Perhaps it is in the carriage."

" No matter," said the contessa, " I will speak to her. Have you no one here, mother, who expects an English lady ?"

There was a slight rustling at the darkest portion of the cave.

A curtain veiling an aperture was thrown aside, and a tall man stepped forth.

" I will answer that question in person," he exclaimed.

When he came into the light, his features remained unseen, owing to a black mask, which concealed the upper part of his face.

" Barboni !" exclaimed Emily, uttering a cry of terror.

" The same," he replied. " We have met but once, and that under unpleasant circumstances, and yet you do me the honour to remember me."

" What is the meaning of this ?" cried Emily. " Have you dared to bring me here under the false pretence that my husband is in danger ?"

" I stated nothing but the truth," replied the bandit, boldly. " Your husband has sworn, in conjunction with three companions, that he will capture me or die."

" Ha ! has he sworn that ?"

" My information may be relied upon. Now I wish you to tell Mr Harkaway that his insane determination must end in death for him and his friends."

" I will try to dissuade him," said Emily.

" He underrates my power and my resources ; he thinks me a simple robber, when I am a chief. Follow me, lady, to the outside of this cave."

" For what reason ?" asked Emily, who feared some foul play was intended her.

" Nay, you have nothing to fear," said Barboni. " In my letter I pledged my word you should be free to come and go as you pleased."

Emily followed him to the outside.

" Look, lady," continued the bandit. " you behold the two sides of the ravine ?"

" I do," she answered.

" What do you see ?"

" Nothing but stunted shrubs, black-looking pines, and tall, reed-like grass."

The bandit smiled significantly.

His lips parted, and from them came that weird, wild, mysterious whistle, so piercing and so shrill, to which we have had occasion to allude before.

In a moment, as if by magic, both sides of the ravine were alive with men, attired in the picturesque costume of the brigands.

Their rifles were displayed, and in

their belts were to be seen knives and pistols.

The feathers in their hats waved in the wind, but they neither moved nor spoke, standing like machines, awaiting the word of command.

"Ha, ha!" laughed Barboni, "am I to be despised, signora, when I can make men spring out of the earth like that?"

"*Madre di Dios!* what would an army be against my fellows, posted as they are now?"

"Perhaps you are right," answered Emily. "It may be that Jack is no fit match for you, but why cannot you let him alone?"

"It is he who will not permit me. I am willing to allow him to leave Naples, if he will do so at once."

"No, he will not do that," replied Emily, with a shake of the head. "You don't know my husband.

"If he says he will do a thing, no power on earth can turn him from his purpose."

"Not even your influence?"

"Not even mine."

"That's a pity. It will be best for him to go. What can four young men effect against me?" said the brigand.

"Perhaps more than you think," replied Emily. "But I am deeply grieved to hear that my husband has sworn to kill you, though——"

She hesitated.

"Speak fearlessly, lady," said Barboni.

"Though I am sure he will keep his word, in spite of your power," she concluded, becoming bolder, as her first alarm passed off.

"*Santa Maria!*" cried the brigand, angrily. "Am I to be frightened by four boys, whose beards have scarce begun to grow?

"You are deceived in your husband. He it neither so brave nor so faithful as you imagine."

"For shame!" exclaimed Emily. "You would not dare to abuse him before his face as you do behind his back."

"Come to the sybil," said Barboni; "she cannot lie. Let us consult her art."

"For what purpose?"

"She will tell you that you are deceived."

"In what way?"

"Mr. Harkaway loves another woman. You shall hear it from the lips of the sybil."

"I'll not believe her!" cried Emily.

She drew her breath in quick, short gasps, more from indignation at the shameful accusation, than because her jealousy was really excited.

She had too much faith in Jack to listen to such idle stories.

"Then you shall read it in the crystal globe," said Barboni. "Come, come!"

Again he uttered his peculiar whistle, and the brigands sank back into concealment, as magically as they had risen from it.

As if by enchantment they vanished, and not a rifle, not a feather, not a form was to be seen on the rocky sides, which a moment before had been alive with them.

"Come to the sybil, come!" cried the brigand, taking her by the hand.

He led her unwillingly into the cave, and spoke a few words rapidly in Italian, to the aged crone.

The sybil rose from the rock on which she had been sitting, and approached a small and roughly-made table, upon which reposed a large globe of crystal.

"Look steadily at this," she said, "and you will behold your husband as he is engaged at this minute."

Emily bent her gaze curiously, but doubtingly, upon the surface of the shining crystal.

For some time she saw nothing.

At length two figures appeared before her eyes.

One was Jack, the other that of a dark-haired, beautiful woman, to whom he was talking earnestly.

She uttered a cry and started back.

"Are you satisfied?" said Barboni, in an exulting voice.

"There is some jugglery in this," she replied.

"As you please. I will undertake, in a short time, to show you the reality. Will you believe then?"

"What I see with my own eyes, in flesh and blood, I will believe, and nothing else," she answered.

"So be it."

There was a momentary pause.

All this time the contessa had been a passive observer of the scene.

She stood by herself, leaning against the rough and rocky wall, seeing all and saying nothing.

"Oh, *donna bella!*" cried the brigand at length, "fly from Naples! It would spare you many perils. You have enemies."

"I fear them not."

"I can see what will happen to you, though I see as through a glass—darkly," continued Barboni, in a tone of deep sympathy, whether real or affected.

"My place is by my husband's side," answered Emily, bravely.

"His life is threatened, and your liberty. Persuade him to leave this land of intrigue and mystery."

"You fear him already," said Emily.

"I? No; Barboni never yet felt fear," rejoined the brigand, drawing himself up proudly.

"All I will say is this," Emily continued. "My husband and I have seen something of life in various parts of the world, and you will find him no ordinary man to deal with."

"*Corpo di Christo!*" cried Barboni. "I am as sure of grinding him to powder, as if I had him under my heel."

"Don't make so sure of that."

"I have taken an interest in you, why I know not," said the brigand, more mildly. "But I would save you from the perils that threaten you."

"If my husband has sworn to kill you," said Emily, "he will do it, in spite of the apparent odds in your favour, which make me think that you have all the strength on your side."

Barboni laughed defiantly.

"This is the last time we meet as friends," he said.

"That is not my fault," replied Emily.

"Pardon me, signora, you are to blame. Leave Naples; take your husband and his friends with you."

"At the bidding of a bandit!"

Emily laughed scornfully as she uttered these words.

"No matter! We are enemies from this day forth.

"You call me bandit and brigand," he added bitterly. "But I have the authority of the church for what I do."

"The church!"

"Yes, I have a dispensation from Rome, for I am in reality fighting the battle of the exiled King of Naples—the battle of the Bourbon against the excommunicated King of Italy.

"But you do not understand our politics. Go, signora, and remember in time to come that Barboni offered you his friendship."

"Which I rejected as became me," answered Emily.

"Adieu," he said. "But stay. We meet again soon in Naples. I have promised to expose the infidelity of your husband. You shall see in reality what you beheld in the globe of crystal."

"Am I at liberty to go now?" asked Emily, taking no notice of his remarks about Jack's inconstancy, and firmly believing them to be a tissue of inventions.

"Certainly. Shall I have the honour to conduct you to your carriage?" replied the brigand, with the finished politeness which he could assume when he chose.

Emily slipped a coin into the sybil's hand, and prepared to follow him to the carriage, which was in waiting a short distance from the grotto where they had left it.

At this moment the dwarf came running into the cave in a state of alarm and excitement.

"The soldiers! the soldiers!" he exclaimed.

Barboni turned back directly, and seemed to share the dwarf's agitation.

"Where?" he asked.

"Coming towards the defile."

"How many of them?"

"Two companies," said the dwarf.

"That can't be much less than three hundred men," replied Barboni. "I am betrayed, but woe to my enemies."

He cast a withering, vindictive glance at Emily.

"We part. Adieu once more," he continued. "You have rejected all my advances. The war has begun."

With these words he quitted the cavern, and ascended the steep sides of the ravine, clambering from rock to rock with the agility of a wild cat.

"What shall we do?" asked Emily clinging to the contessa.

"Stay here for the present," replied the contessa; "we have nothing to fear."

The dwarf danced about the floor, panting with delight.

"Blood in the air!" he cried. "I can

smell it! Blood on the trees. I have seen it hanging on the leaves all day—blood in the dusty road—blood everywhere. Cospetto! we shall have some fun presently."

And the little demon rubbed his hands and chuckled with glee.

The snakes ran quickly about, and the wolf licked his chaps as if he too sniffed the coming banquet.

"Ha, Remus!" said the dwarf, patting the neck of the wolf, "you too can smell it. What a feast we shall have, eh, my beauty? Blood—blood!—oh, I love to see it run!"

Emily shrank horror stricken from the little savage.

The contessa, meanwhile, was calm and collected, and awaited what was to happen with indifference.

CHAPTER XXI.

THE DEADLY AMBUSH.

BARBONI had let fall before Emily some hints to the effect that he was encouraged in his brigandage by persons in high quarters.

Nor was this improbable.

Only a few years had passed since Ferdinand II. had been driven from the throne of Naples by Garibaldi.

Naples then became a part of united Italy, under the sanction of Napoleon III., who was then, as the Emperor of Prussia is now, the arbiter of the destinies of Continental Europe.

But Victor Emanuel, the King of Italy, was the avowed enemy of the Pope, while the ex-king of Naples was the ally and friend of Pio Nono.

Therefore Rome encouraged all internal dissensions in Naples, and smiled upon the brigands.

The ex-king of Naples hoped some day to come back to his throne.

Barboni made no secret of his being aided by Rome and the exiled Bourbon.

But we must quit the brigand chief for a while, and return to the Villa Reale, where we left Ada, who had just picked up the note which Emily, in her agitation, had let fall.

"I will take it at once to Monday," she muttered.

Accordingly she hurried home, and found her husband lazily smoking a cigarette in a room which he had selected as his own on the ground floor.

The heat of Naples suited him.

It was so much like that of his native land.

"Come in, Ada," he exclaimed. "Bless um heart. Give um old man um kiss then."

"Don't be stupid, Matabella," replied Ada. "Missis has just gone off in the Contessa di Malafedi's carriage, and she let fall this note in the Villa Reale."

"Give him here—um letter, I mean," said Monday.

He took it from the girl's hand and his face grew grave.

"Better show this to Mast' Jack upstairs; I go show him," replied Monday.

Ada had great confidence in Monday's judgment, and she felt that she had done her duty.

The four friends were together, and looked up as Monday entered.

"What's in the wind now?" asked Jack.

Monday related what Ada had told him, and handed Jack the letter, which he read aloud.

"This is a plant," said Jack. "What is your opinion, Carden?"

"I have no doubt of it," replied Tom getting up and opening a case of pistols which lay on a side table.

"What are you going to do?" sked Harvey.

"We're going to fight, aren't we? I am only making ready."

"By Jove!" exclaimed the little coxswain, "I'm on like a naval ram."

There was the sound of wheels at the door, which caused Monday to run down.

Presently he returned, saying—

"His excellency the general commanding in chief."

"General Cialdini," answered Jack; "that is fortunate. Show him in."

The general entered and bowed very politely to the Englishmen.

The object of his visit was to express his regret that nothing had yet been heard of the robbers.

An account of the audacious robbery at the San Carlo Theatre by Barboni had appeared in all the Italian papers.

It had attracted the attention of the king and his ministers, who had sent a strong dispatch to the general commanding at Naples, reprimanding him for not having captured the bandits.

"I have this day," he exclaimed, "sent two companies of infantry, who are those excellent riflemen we call Bersaglieri, and their instructions are to scour the country."

"In what direction, may I ask?" said Jack.

"Between Naples and the grotto of the Cumæan sybil," he answered.

"By George, the very quarter!" exclaimed Jack. "Read this, general."

Cialdini gravely perused the note and listened to such particulars as Jack could give him.

"This is very extraordinary," he said; "more especially as the chief of the secret police has to-day told me he has reasons for suspecting the contessa."

"Of what?"

"Of some connection with this Barboni."

"Indeed!"

"At present," continued the general, "we are certain about nothing. Vague suspicions fill our minds; at any moment something may happen which will clear up the mystery."

"Pardon me, general, if I cut short the discussion," remarked Jack.

"Ah, certainly; your wife is in danger."

"May I prefer one request?"

"By all means," replied Cialdini.

"If I can meet your Bersaglieri near the cave of the sybil, will you authorize me to lead them to the rescue of my wife, and the capture of Barboni?"

"Willingly. Give me pen, ink, and paper. I will write a line to the officer in command, giving him instructions to search the cavern," answered Cialdini.

"Thank you, general; that is all I ask," said Jack.

The authority was hastily written, and the general took his leave, exacting a promise that he should hear the result of their expedition as soon as possible.

He further expressed a hope that Mrs. Harkaway might be in no danger from the trap which the brigand had laid for her.

Monday was sent to the stables to order four horses to be saddled and brought round to the Strada Di Toledo in the shortest possible space of time.

In the course of his excursions into the country, Carden had visited the cave of the sybil.

Consequently he knew the way, and the four companions started at a hand gallop.

When within a mile of the cavern, they met the two companies of soldiers, of whom the general commanding in chief had spoken.

Jack at once dismounted, and saluting the officer in command, handed him the letter written by the general.

The officer read it, and said that he and his men were at Mr. Harkaway's disposal.

He gave the order "Quick march!" and the soldiers set forward.

They were a serviceable body of men, well equipped, and had seen service at Custozza against the Austrians.

The officer recommended the four friends to ride behind, as they were civilians, and the soldiers would not like them in front.

This request was fortunate in the result for Jack and his companions.

On marched the Bersaglieri, unconscious of danger, and least of all were they suspicious of a deadly ambuscade.

Half-an-hour brought them to the defile, which they entered, four abreast.

Jack and his friends were the last to come within its sombre and forbidding shades.

Suddenly a terrible fire was opened upon them from both sides of the defile.

White wreaths of smoke arose, and were followed by flashes of fire, which in their turn gave place to loud reports.

Half their number bit the dust.

In vain did the survivors look for their concealed enemies.

No one was to be seen.

The brigands fired from their sheltering places of concealment, and presented no mark to the Italian soldiers, who discharged their pieces at random.

Panic-stricken, they turned and fled,

"BARBONI THE BRIGAND CHIEF GEASPED HER WRIST."

PRICE ONE HALFPENNY.
[PUBLISHED EVERY TUESDAY].

falling in increased numbers at each step. Their officers were all killed, and a mere handful of men huddled together at the mouth of the pass.

The four friends, horror-stricken at this massacre, dismounted.

Jack tried to rally them.

"Follow me!" he cried, snatching a sword from the dead body of an officer. "Follow me up the cliff. If we can only gain the summit, we can dislodge the rabble."

The soldiers were brave, and burned to avenge the death of their comrades.

Jack and Harvey, followed by Tom Carden and the little coxswain, climbed up the rocks.

The Bersaglieri followed them valiantly.

This movement, being at the entrance to the pass, was unperceived by the brigands, who fancied the soldiers had fled routed.

The first intimation they had of their being surprised in rear and flank was a discharge as deadly as that they had poured into the companies.

About a hundred brigands had descended the sides, emerging from their places of concealment to plunder the dead and put an end to the wounded.

Only seventy soldiers had escaped from the massacre.

But these were armed with breech-loaders, and well supplied with ammunition.

The brigands were all leaving, or had left, their shelter.

Consequently they presented as easy a mark as the Bersaglieri had done when they marched unsuspectingly into the defile.

Volley after volley was sent down upon them under Jack's instructions.

The little coxswain had seized a rifle, and was as coolly potting the brigands as if he had been in his father's park in England, shooting rooks.

"Here's a lark," he said. "Down goes another, flop."

"Same here," remarked Harvey; "that makes seven."

The brigands found they were caught in their own trap, and had been too hasty.

Above the sharp crack of the rifles, and the ping—thud of the bullets, arose the well-known whistle of Barboni.

He was calling his men off.

The next minute the pass was clear, and not a brigand was to be seen.

They had lost heavily, however.

Not so heavily as the soldiers, but nevertheless, their bodies lay thickly piled upon those of their enemies.

"We must go to the cave," said Jack. "Will you, Carden, stay here with Campbell, while Harvey and I go and look after Emily?"

"What shall I do?" asked Carden.

"Keep the pass. Stay, I forgot you know nothing about soldiering. I will throw the men out as skirmishers."

Turning to the Bersaglieri, he added in Italian—

"My lads, your officers are all dead. I am an English officer; will you be led by me?"

An affirmative shout arose.

The men saw he had so far saved them, given them their revenge, and scattered the enemy.

Giving the necessary words of command, he threw them out in a double line of skirmishers, telling them to take advantage of the rocks and shrubs for shelter, and to shoot any brigand they might see.

"Though," he said, "I don't think the dastardly miscreants will dare to show their faces again."

Having disposed of the men to the best of his ability, and to his satisfaction, he descended the rocky slope with Harvey at his heels.

Running along the road, his pace was quickened by hearing the cries of a woman.

Surely it was Emily's voice.

This thought lent wings to him, and he reached the grotto in an incredibly short space of time, trampling rudely over the heaps of dead and dying in his headlong haste.

It was as he supposed.

Outside the cavern he saw Emily struggling in the arms of Barboni.

"Help, help!" she cried. "Oh, Jack, Jack, where are you?"

"Not far off, my darling," he replied. "Hold on!"

The contessa was standing by the side of the carriage and waved her servants back, for they seemed to evince an inclination to help Emily.

The main body of the brigands were

already in full retreat, so that the robber chief was alone.

Enraged at the unexpected loss his men had sustained, he seemed to have forgotten his pledged word, for he had seized Emily just as she was about to enter the contessa's carriage.

"You're my prisoner," he had said, "and must come with me. In open warfare there is no friendship, and no faith. It must have been so sooner or later."

Jack rushed upon him like an avalanche.

He was afraid to use his sword, and Harvey did not like to fire, as the brigand held Emily in front of him as a sort of shield.

"Duck, Jack! duck your head!" cried Harvey.

The warning did not come a moment too soon.

Barboni discharged a pistol, which sent a ball harmlessly over Jack's head.

Clenching his sledge-hammer fist, Jack struck him in the mouth.

His teeth were loosened, and his lips cut, which prevented him from whistling for aid.

"How do you like that, old fellow?" asked Jack, giving it him right and left, straight from the shoulder.

A shower of blows rained in the brigand's face.

Each blow, as Harvey said afterwards, was like the kick from a horse.

Barboni dropped Emily, who fell senseless in the roadway.

His pistol also fell from his grasp, and he in vain tried to cover his face with his hands, to protect himself from the furious attack.

"Now you've got it," said Jack. "I've been living for this day, and you'll know after this what an Englishman can do with his bunch of fives, my gay moss-trooper."

Seeing that Emily was safe, and conscious of having well punished the brigand, his spirits rose.

"That's a return for the bullet you gave me," he went on chaffingly, "for I believe you and the Prince of Villanova are one and the same; only you have no beard and the prince has one. That's for stealing my wife's jewels. That's for telling lies. That's for writing letters, and setting traps. That's——"

He left off speaking, for Barboni turned tail and fled away after his men as fast as his feet would carry him, muttering indistinct threats of vengeance as he went.

"Shall I drop him?" asked Harvey.

"Yes; fire! fire!" exclaimed Jack. "Why should you show him any mercy? Fire, I tell you!"

Harvey levelled his revolver, and fired several shots without effect.

"Hang the fellow! he's out of range," he said, in a tone of vexation.

Jack turned round to attend to Emily, and saw the Contessa Di Malafedi bending over her.

"Oh, the poor, dear creature!" she exclaimed. "What we have suffered, Mr. Harkaway, no one can imagine?"

"I should think, madam," replied Jack, "that you have been perfectly at your ease."

"I! How can you suppose so?"

"It is chiefly owing to you that this has happened."

"Pray do not think so harshly of me," said the contessa, feelingly. "What is there—what can there be in common between me and that dreadful man?"

"That is a question for your own conscience to answer," rejoined Jack, drily.

"I declare to you, before the Holy Virgin, that I am not to blame; dear Emily will tell you the same."

"It matters little to me. I shall be on my guard against you in future, and I daresay the Neapolitan police will pay you a little delicate attention."

The contessa drew herself up proudly —haughtily almost.

"You are insolent, sir!" she said, while her dark eyes flashed angrily.

"Possibly," replied Jack. "I can't tell lies; it's not my form."

"Is it worth your while to make an enemy of me?"

"I don't care a rush for all the harm you can do me, now I have found you out," said Jack.

"Very well, sir," she replied. "You have insulted me quite enough. We understand one another."

"Oh, perfectly!" said Jack, carelessly. "As you brought my wife here, I shall take the liberty of using your carriage to convey her back again, though it will be the last time she will ride in it."

"She shall not ride in it now, since

you demand it as a right and not as a favour," said the contessa.

"I am sorry to be obliged to contradict a lady in your position," answered Jack, "but she shall, and to show you I am not to be trifled with, I shall leave you to get back to Naples as well as you can."

"My servants will——"

"Dick," said Jack, interrupting the contessa.

"What is it, old man?" asked Harvey, who was supporting Emily, she having just come to herself.

"Is your popgun loaded?"

"Yes."

"Jump up ·on the box by the side of the coachman. Show him the pistol; let the footman stop to attend upon his mistress. This carriage is ours. Carden will tell the soldiers to bring our horses back. Twig?"

"Rather!" replied Harvey. "I like the idea much."

In spite of the contessa's protestations, Jack lifted Emily into the carriage and got in by her side.

"You can stay with your friend the sybil," he exclaimed, "or perhaps Barboni will come and comfort you. I'm not going to be made a fool of any more by you. It is not good enough by a long way."

The contessa gnashed her teeth with rage, while the dwarf danced wildly about, and made a score of grimaces, as if to show that he enjoyed her discomfiture.

"You will repent this," said the contessa, her dark eyes full of an intense passion.

"Make the cove drive on, Dick,' said Jack, by way of an answer.

"Right," replied Harvey.

"Shoot the beggar like a rat if he turns nasty."

"No fear."

They drove to the extremity of the defile, and then Jack called the troops down.

He made a little speech complimenting them on their bravery, and assuring them that they had done their duty under very trying circumstances.

Then he ordered them to bivouac where they were and attend to the wounded, while he would report to the general and make arrangements for sending reinforcements and provisions without delay.

The men gave him a hearty cheer.

Tom Carden and the little coxswain mounted their horses, leaving the other two in charge of the soldiers, and Tom went on in front, while Campbell brought up the rear, after the fashion of outriders.

Emily was very weak and hysterical during the journey, for the whole affair had given her a fright and upset her nervous system.

Jack was very kind to her, and by degrees she recovered herself, leaning her head upon his shoulder, and pressing his hand lovingly, while she related all that had passed between her and the hated Barboni.

CHAPTER XXII.

THE SPY OF THE BRIGANDS.

WHEN the news of the fight between the soldiers and the brigands reached Naples, it created a profound sensation.

General Cialdini was furious.

It had been a sharp affair while it lasted, and his men had suffered very heavy losses.

The central Italian government would call him to a severe account for it, and his credit was concerned in exterminating Barboni and his band without delay.

This, however, was more easily talked about than done.

Barboni was one of those mysterious beings who could never be found when he was wanted.

But when he was not wanted, he was everywhere, as many travellers, stopped and robbed, could testify.

Jack had a long interview with the general, in which he tried to impress upon him the belief that Barboni and Prince Villanova were one and the same person.

But, as before, he failed in forcing this conviction on his mind.

He spoke of Bigamini, and related all that the little man had told him about being captured by brigands and escaping from a castle.

The general heard him attentively, and said—

"You may be right, Mr. Harkaway, though I regret that I cannot agree with you. Nor should I hold myself justified in arresting the prince without further evidence. I must have proof, solid proof."

"It shall be my business to obtain it for you," answered Jack.

"Do that, and I will act immediately."

"I propose," continued Jack, "to visit Castel Inferno, where the prince lives."

"If you are right in your conjectures, will it be safe for you to do so?" asked the general.

"Not unattended."

"Well, you shall have an escort of soldiers, though I trust my poor followers will not fall into another cowardly ambush."

"Give me twenty men," said Jack. "That will be quite enough. I only want them to see me enter the castle, and if I do not come out again, they will know where to look for me."

"Shall you go unattended by your friends?"

"I shall only take Bigamini with me, for this is simply an exploring journey. I want to form my own opinion, and I can act afterwards."

"Precisely. When do you want the escort?"

"To-morrow morning."

"It shall be ready."

Jack thanked the general for his courtesy, and, going home, sent Monday to the address given by Bigamini, ordering that worthy to call upon him at once.

When Bigamini was announced, Jack was in the drawing-room with his friends.

Dinner was over, and they were sitting in a flower-bedecked balcony, listening to Emily's graphic description of the horrors of the sybil's cave.

He apologised for his temporary absence, and went to see his visitor in another room, as he did not wish his wife to know anything about his proposed exploring expedition on the morrow.

Bigamini looked more nervous and frightened than he had done on a former occasion.

"Well, my little man," said Jack, "how goes it? Sit down and have a glass of wine."

Bigamini took a seat and drank some of the wine which was poured out for him.

"I'm a poor creature, sir," he remarked; "what little nerve I ever had when I was a happy Smiffins, is quite gone."

"If you haven't got any courage, you must manage to get along without it," said Jack, cheerily.

"It isn't that, sir. I've got courage, only when I want it, it goes out—oozes out, I may say, at my fingers' ends, and out of my toes, and even through my hair."

"What has upset you now?"

"I've heard about your brush with the brigands, sir. Very fine! The Italians say you rallied and handled them splendidly."

"I did the best I could," answered Jack, modestly.

"Won't old Thingamyjig be in a way over it?"

"Who's he?"

"Why, Barboni. I don't like to speak his name out loud, so I call him old Thingamyjig."

"You don't suppose he's here, do you?" asked Jack, laughing.

"I don't know, sir; couldn't say for certain," replied Bigamini. "He's a wonderful man. Would you kindly permit me to look under that table?"

"Rot! Sit where you are and have some more wine. Get up some Dutch courage. You can't be allowed to live in such a state of mortal funk."

"Of course, sir. Your word's law to me in your own house—and anywhere else, for that matter. But may I be a stiff un if I didn't think I saw——"

"It's all bosh, I tell you!" interrupted Jack.

"Very well, sir. Since you're so determined, bosh it shall be! though if Barboni—old Thingamy, I mean—were to catch me here, he'd think I was splitting on him, and there would be the deuce and all to pay."

"He shan't touch you. Are you not under my protection?"

Bigamini laughed one of his favourite artificial chuckles as he said—

"I'm afraid, Mr. Harkaway, the brigand will be one too many for you.

"Lor' bless your innocent soul, sir!" exclaimed Bigamini. "If Barboni said he'd have me, not you, nor all the soldiers, nor all the priests in Naples, could save me. He's an awful man, and he gives me the cold shivers to think of him. Ever had the cold shivers, sir?"

"No, nor don't want to," said Jack.

"It's just like having icy water out of a well in winter poured down your backbone, sir."

"Is it? Then I don't envy you the sensation."

"Excuse me, sir, if I trouble you with my symptoms. I'm a miserable Bigamini, but I oughtn't to murmur at my lot."

"If you've done talking, perhaps you will listen to me."

"Certainly, sir—only don't talk too loud. Old Thingamy's got spies everywhere, and my doom would be settled if he knew I was here with you, betraying of him."

"My house is private; he can't get in here," answered Jack.

"Didn't he come and steal the jewels, sir, from the ladies?" asked Bigamini.

This question rather staggered Jack.

"Yes," he answered, "and I wish I'd caught him at it. But what I want to tell you is that I shall want you as a guide to-morrow."

"Where to go, sir?"

"To the castle from which you escaped."

"Suppose I can't find it?" asked Bigamini, who seemed considerably taken aback.

"You'll have to do your best, and I shall pay you well for your trouble."

"Do you and I go alone, sir?"

"No. I shall have a military escort."

"Soldiers!"

"Yes; why not?"

"I wouldn't, sir. I'd go quite alone," answered Bigamini. "The sight of soldiers angers old Thingamy. He don't like 'em. It may cost us our lives."

"You seem to know a good deal about this Barboni," said Jack, eyeing him suspiciously, as what Carden had suggested to him came into his mind.

"I couldn't be among them without knowing something," replied Bigamini.

Jack made no answer as he paced the room impatiently.

"If you think I'm deceiving of you, sir, I'll go away, and there's no harm done," pursued Bigamini.

"No, no, I'm satisfied," said Jack.

"Perhaps you think I'm a spy, sir?"

And Bigamini laughed heartily at the transparent absurdity of such an insane idea.

"Ah!" he added, "it all comes of making a false step. He knows I've done a little bigamy, and he thinks I must be a duffer all over."

Jack stopped in his walk before Bigamini, and observed that a tear was trickling down the tallowy cheek of the worthy man, as if he felt much hurt.

"Forgive me, my good fellow, if I spoke hastily," he exclaimed.

"It's hard to be suspected," replied Bigamini, with a whimper.

Bigamini at all times was comical, but Bigamini with a whimper was irresistible.

Jack laughed in spite of himself.

"You won't think hardly of me any more, sir?" said Bigamini.

"No."

"Nor be down upon me for having had two wives, and been and done a little bit of bigamy."

"What has that to do with it? You be faithful to me, and you shall be rewarded. Help me in every way you can to find out this brigand stronghold, and I'm your friend for life."

Bigamini's face cleared.

"Oh, what a sweet and lovely thing it is, Mr. Harkaway, to be trusted," he said, rapturously.

"Try and deserve my confidence."

"I will, sir, I will. Oh, if old Thingamy was only to hear me, he'd collar me off, and send you my ears, likewise nose, ditto big toes in a basket. What should I be without my big toes?"

This idea seemed to strike Bigamini very forcibly, and he contemplated his boots with affection for some moments.

"I am much more likely to have his head than he is to cut off any part of you, my man," replied Jack.

"I hope so, sir. I should like to see his head stuck on a pole and chuck oranges at it, or rotten eggs, or 'taters. I shouldn't be particular," said Bigamini.

"Well, you can go now. Come again to-morrow, about the afternoon. On second thoughts, I shan't start till the heat of the day is over. The soldiers can be sent on to the ferry over the Volturno, and I will drive you to the spot."

"Thank you, Mr. Harkaway, sir. I feel as if I wasn't quite such a miserable Bigamini when I'm with you, sir."

"That's all right," said Jack.

"Yes, sir; I'm more like a happy Smiffins."

"Indeed!"

"I don't seem to have the cold shivers so bad."

"Get along," said Jack. "When you come into the place, there's no knowing when one is going to get rid of you."

"I'm off, sir. Going, going, as the auctioneers say, and I shall be gone soon, knocked down to the highest bidder. But——"

"What?"

"I *should* like to have one peep under that there table, sir. Old Thingamy might be there, or some detective from London to have me up for bigamy."

Jack's only answer to this was to take Bigamini by the elbow, after the fashion of a policeman when he has a man in custody.

He gave his arm a twist, and very dexterously ran him out of the room.

"The fellow gets to be a nuisance," he muttered, as he slammed the door.

A sepulchral voice sounded through the keyhole.

"Good day, sir. Pardon the thoughtless words of a miserable Bigamini."

"There is no end to him," muttered Jack.

But he heard footsteps descend the stairs, and looking out of the window, he saw the little man creeping along the street in his usual nervous manner.

But Bigamini did not go home, if his dingy lodging could be dignified with such a name.

He went to a place where they let out horses, and putting down some gold, he hired a horse for two days.

At first they looked suspiciously at him, and it was only when he produced more gold as a deposit or security that they let him have the animal.

Bigamini seemed to have a great deal of gold money for so poor-looking a man, yet it was no business of theirs to ask him how he came by it.

Jumping on the horse, and riding it very fairly, he took the road to Capua, and once out of the city, he rode as if a legion of fiends were after him.

The fact was, he had some distance to go—nearly forty miles, and time was an object to him.

He reached the river Volturno in three hours and a half, crossed over in the ferry, left his horse with the ferryman, and proceeded on his journey on foot.

The way was evidently well known to him, for he did not pause or falter once.

It was growing dark after he had gone about three miles, and the lofty towers of an ancient castle could only be made out dimly in the deepening twilight.

Striking boldly into a thicket of trees at the foot almost of the aged castle, he pursued a tangled path.

Then he stopped and whistled three times.

A man in a slouched hat and green cloak emerged from behind a tree.

He lowered his carbine at seeing Bigamini, and motioned him to pass.

A little further on rose a pile of rocks, neither very high nor very extensive, but in the middle of which was a yawning hole.

In front of this stood another man, who also allowed him to pass.

Stooping a little, for the hole was not large, Bigamini entered what was a spacious cavern.

Inside he met two more guards, who demanded a password, and, on his saying "Gaeta," he met with no opposition.

The outer cavern led into another, which was larger, and from which numerous passages branched off, showing that the rocks were honeycombed in various directions.

In one corner a lamp swung by an iron chain from the ceiling, and revealed at least fifty men who were lounging about, some engaged in card-playing, others smoking, drinking, sleeping, others again amusing themselves with hazard, as the rattle of the dice testified.

"Ha!" exclaimed one, jumping up, "here is our little Bigamini, the prince of spies."

"Good evening, Florio," replied Biga-mini.

"The chief has been expecting you. *Buon giorno.*"

"You have had hot work, I'm told," said Bigamini.

"Hotter than we cared for," answered Florio. "Santo Dio! I thought at one time we should none of us come back alive. It was that cursed Englishman who rallied the Bersaglieri."

"Did you lose many men?"

"Per Baccho! More than enough. We left forty dead in the roadway," growled the brigand.

"Will you let his highness know that I am here? Time is valuable," said Bigamini.

"I don't know that you won't get the blame of that ambush," said Florio. "Cospetto! Why did you not send us word that the soldiers were coming?"

"Because I did not know it myself. They did not leave the town purposely. But send for the lieutenant as quickly as possible, and give me some drink. I've ridden at speed from Naples," exclaimed Bigamini.

He seemed quite at home with those fierce, wild-looking men, many of whom crowded round and asked him a variety of questions.

Florio set wine before him, and despatched a messenger along one of the winding galleries in the rear.

All Bigamini's nervousness disappeared now that he was with the brigands, into whose cave he had penetrated as fear-lessly as if he had known them all his life.

He strutted about like a little bantam cock, and evidently knew that they thought highly of him.

In fact, he was the chief spy of the brigand chief, Barboni.

Like many other Englishmen who had fled to Naples in desperate circumstances, he had joined the robbers.

His cringing manner, and his sly nature, eminently qualified him for the part he had assumed.

We have seen how easily he imposed upon Jack.

Nor was Harkaway the only one taken in by his cleverness.

Still, when he was ushered into the presence of the lieutenant of the band, he put aside the free and easy manner he had used among the inferior members, and was once more subservient and crawling.

The lieutenant was a man of middle height, thin, with a dark skin, as if he had been exposed to the sun of the torrid zone, and he was the more remarkable for having only one arm.

He sat at a small table in a cavern of moderate dimensions, which was approached by a winding passage.

Bigamini stood before him, and his examination was carried on in English.

"Wait outside, Florio, and be prepared with a file of men to shoot this rascal if I find him a traitor," said the lieutenant.

Florio retired to the doorway, and Biga-mini once more trembled in every limb.

CHAPTER XXIII.

THE REPORT.

"Good Signor Hunstoni," exclaimed the wretched man, "I have ever been faithful. Once when I was a happy Sniffins, I was unfaithful to my wife, but——"

"Silence. We know that we have the power to send you to England in charge of the police to be tried for bigamy; that we shall do probably when we no longer want you," interrupted the lieutenant, who had been addressed as Hunstoni.

"No, no! do not deliver me to my countrymen. You will see that I have been faithful. I have, indeed, on the honour of a miserable Bigamini."

"Why, then, had we no notice of soldiers approaching the sybil's cave?"

"They did not leave the city for that purpose."

"Harkaway knew it."

"Yes; but he did not tell me. It appears he went to the general, because Emily—that is, Mrs. Harkaway—dropped the master's letter, and her maid picked it up, and gave it to her husband, a black man, who handed it to Mr. Harkaway."

"Well," said Hunstoni, stolidly.

"Harkaway took it to the general and asked for troops to capture the master, Barboni, and the two companies of Bersaglieri were exercising in the neighbourhood. He received from the general a letter placing them at his disposal."

"And then?"

"Then the attack, signor. On the word of a wretched Bigamini, it is the truth."

"You should manage better than this," said Hunstoni. "We suffered a very heavy loss yesterday owing to your carelessness and the bravery of that infernal Harkaway."

"Is the master angry with me?" asked Bigamini.

"He is. Harkaway fought him in a way he didn't understand."

"How was that, signor?"

"With his fists. Regular old English fashion," replied the lieutenant, who, though he had become a brigand, did not forget the manners and customs of his native land.

"What a lark!" said Bigamini, forgetting himself.

"Silence!" roared the lieutenant.

"Yes, signor. I forgot I was a wretched Bigamini, and thought I was once again a happy——"

A blow from Hunstoni's fist made him stagger, and effectually closed his mouth.

"Perhaps *that* will stop your jaw," he said.

The little man wiped the blood from his lips and glared from under his brows at the lieutenant.

"Now tell me what you have to tell. What's your report?"

The latter continued—

"Mr. Harkaway is coming to the castle to-morrow to visit Prince Villanova," replied Bigamini.

"Who accompanies him?"

"Twenty soldiers, and myself as guide."

"What time will he reach the castle?"

"Evening."

"Good!" exclaimed Hunstoni. "What else?"

"The chief of the police in Naples——"

"Sforza?"

"Yes, signor. Sforza has despatched one of his cleverest detective officers to search out the cave."

"The devil he has!" exclaimed Hunstoni.

"The detective's name is Steffano. I know him well, and was concealed under the table in the police office when he received his instructions."

"How is he going to do it?" asked Hunstoni, raising his eyebrows incredulously.

"Steffano can assume as many disguises as Proteus," replied Bigamini.

"What's his plan?"

"To-night he will pass by the ferry, where there have been several stoppages of travellers lately, and he expects to fall into your excellency's hands."

"Not at all unlikely. We have Ludovico there, with ten men, at this very moment."

"He will be dressed as a respectable tradesman, and pretend to be very deaf and stupid."

"You are sure of this?"

"On the honour of a miserable——"

"I thought I had knocked that humbug out of you," interrupted Hunstoni, fiercely. "Don't try it on with me. When I'm engaged in business, I like things short and sweet."

Bigamini apologised, and said it should not occur again.

"I will see Barboni," continued Hunstoni, "and make your report. His face is much better, but he will not be able to see anyone yet awhile. Harkaway's punches leave marks."

"Tell him that I was not to blame in the matter of yesterday," pleaded Bigamini.

"I will. Rest yourself in the cave for a few hours. You shall have your instructions by daybreak, when you must return to Naples."

"Thank you, signor," said Bigamini.

"Florio," said the lieutenant.

"Si, signor," answered the brigand.

"If any prisoners are brought in to-night, let me know at once."

Florio nodded, and then turning to the passage, exclaimed—

"Ho there! torches at once for the lieutenant."

Two men instantly appeared, bearing torches, and Hunstoni disappeared, with one before and one behind him, along the narrow passage, which seemed to lead into the bosom of the solid rock.

Bigamini returned to the brigands' cave, where he found plenty to amuse him.

The men were accustomed to face death, and they knew that if found out and captured by the police or the government troops, they would either be hung or shot.

Most of them were criminals who had fled from justice.

When a man's life, or at least his liberty, hangs upon a slender thread, he is apt to get reckless.

Many of their friends and companions had fallen the day before; the wounded they had carried off, and they were being attended to by a fraudulent doctor, who had joined the band, in a secret cavern.

The fate of their comrades did not weigh upon the spirits of the desperadoes.

Drink circulated freely, and many indulged in singing and dancing.

Bigamini lighted his pipe, which he preferred to the Italian cigaritto, and applauded vigorously at each effort.

It was nearly daybreak when he rolled off a wine cask, intoxicated, amidst the laughter of the brigands.

At this juncture, a noise was heard at the entrance to the cavern. The merriment was hushed in a moment.

"It is the night watch," cried Florio. "They have brought in a captive."

CHAPTER XXIV.

THE DEAF PRISONER.

THIS exclamation partly roused Bigamini, who raised himself upon his elbow, and regarded the entrance to the cave curiously.

The brigands, who savoured very strongly of oil, garlic, and stale tobacco smoke, also craned their necks in expectation, for as they all took their turn of duty, they all shared alike in any booty or ransom money.

For instance, the chief took a tenth part, the lieutenant a twentieth, and the rest was equally divided.

Thus, if one thousand pounds were extracted from the friends of a captive, Barboni would have one hundred pounds, Hunstoni fifty pounds, and what remained would be given in equal shares to the members of the band.

The prisoner was led in blindfolded, and appeared to be a highly respectable citizen of Naples.

His rings, watch and chain, and saddle bag, taken in conjunction with his clothes, denoted that he was well to do.

Florio took possession of him in the outer cavern, where Bigamini had made his report to the lieutenant.

Here the bandage was removed from his eyes, but the strong rope which had fastened his wrists together remained.

"You can sit down," said Florio, pointing to a seat roughly cut in the rock.

"Where am I, and what is the meaning of this outrage?" said the captive, not appearing to hear the remark addressed to him, as he still continued standing.

"You are in the power of Barboni," replied Florio.

"I didn't ask you what the hour was," answered the captive, testily.

Bigamini appeared in the doorway, and making a sign to Florio, remarked—

"The gentleman must be deaf."

"Per Baccho!" cried Florio. "His ears are big enough."

"What is that?" said the prisoner. "Did you speak of death? You will not take my life?"

"Confound the fool," replied Florio; "he's more trouble than he is worth. Have they gone for the captain?"

"Yes," answered Bigamini: "we shall have him here soon with Lieutenant Hunston and his friend Darrelli."

"Ah!" exclaimed Florio, "they are two splendid brigands, Hunstoni and Darrelli. They fear nothing. They can flay and torture, and never shudder at the groans of the victims."

"Why should they?"

"Oh, I scarcely know, but I have a soft heart, especially for women."

"And I haven't," said Bigamini. "I wish my old woman would come over here and fall into Barboni's hands. I could see her roasted at the stake. She drove me to be a miserable Bigamini."

The prisoner moved uneasily.

"Kind gentlemen," he said, "I am nothing more than a tradesman of Naples. Take what I have and let me go."

"You'll know your lot soon," answered Florio, carelessly,

"What! be shot soon!" repeated the prisoner.

"You deaf old fool, I didn't say that."

"Pardon me, I'm a little deaf. You must speak loudly if you want me to understand you. Every one in Naples knows that Andrea Parazzi has been deaf since the last eruption of Mount Vesuvius."

"Hit him in the mouth if he won't be quiet," exclaimed Florio.

Bigamini took up a piece of wood, and struck the prisoner in the face, covering it with blood.

"That's a gentle hint," he said, laughing.

A deep flush of anger overspread the face of the man who called himself Andrea Parazzi.

Fierce words seemed to come unbidden to his lips, but he choked them back, and cast his eyes on the ground.

"Don't be afraid to look at me, old boy," continued Bigamini; "you are not likely to get out of this alive, so there is no fear of your identifying me."

The captive showed no sign of hearing this speech, though his heart beat quicker, and a heightened flush mantled his cheek.

In a short time three men entered the cave, one being Barboni, whose face was bruised from the blows Jack had rained upon it.

The second was the lieutenant, Hunstoni, and the third was a man with a dark moustache, addressed as Darrelli.

They took three chairs which Florio placed for them at a table, and proceeded to examine the prisoner, to whose capture great importance was evidently attached.

"Who have you here?" asked Barboni.

"He calls himself Andrea Parazzi, signor, a tradesman of Naples, whom our men captured an hour ago," replied Florio.

"And he's as deaf as a post," put in Bigamini.

"We will soon see about that," said Barboni, who, with his companions, had been evidently drinking far into the night.

The prisoner stepped forward in obedience to a sign from Florio.

"What ransom do you want?" he asked. "My friends will pay you handsomely."

"Ten thousand ducats," replied Barboni.

"What does he say? A thousand ducats; that will be paid," exclaimed the prisoner.

"Ten thousand," roared Florio.

The prisoner put his hand to his ear.

"I'm very deaf," he replied; "speak louder."

"It is time to put an end to this farce," said Barboni. "Florio, do your duty."

Florio, who was a strong, powerful man, threw himself upon the prisoner, and bore him roughly to the ground, causing him to become nearly insensible, as his head came in contact with the rocky floor.

Seizing him by the throat with one hand, he, with a sharp knife, which he held in the other, cut off his ears, cropping him close to the head, as coolly as if he had been slicing a cucumber.

He then raised up the disfigured victim, and dragged him to the table.

"Steffano," said Barboni, "you are guilty of assuming a disguise, and you have purposely thrown yourself into our hands, in order that you might have an opportunity of describing and betraying us."

The wretched man fell on his knees before the three brigands.

"I confess—I confess!" he cried. "Spare my life, illustrious chief; for what I have done was by the orders of my superiors."

"You admit that you are Steffano?"

"Si, signor; as much as you are the terror of Naples, so much am I the terror of the evil doers in the city."

"You are not deaf, neither are you a tradesman."

"No; pardon the deception."

"You see that I know all things," said Barboni, calmly. "But do you not deserve death for trying to spy upon and betray me?"

"Alas! yes, signor. I should despair of my life, did I not know that you were as generous as you are brave."

Turning to his lieutenant, the brigand chief said—

"Can we afford to spare this man's life?"

"No," replied Hunstoni, decisively.

"Yet I should like to send him back with his ears cropped, as a defiance to Sforza."

"You forget one thing," said the man with the dark moustache.

"What is that, Darrelli?"

"*He has seen us without our masks.*"

"True," replied Barboni; "for the moment I had forgotten that. He must die."

At these words Steffano, the unlucky police agent, prostrated himself again at the feet of his judges.

"Spare my life, signor," he cried, piteously. "Not a word shall ever pass my lips—on my honour, I swear."

"What," said Barboni, "the honour of a police agent, a spy!"

"Hear me, for the love of God!"

"Hear me first," replied Barboni. "Was not your intention in coming here to drag us all to the scaffold?"

Steffano made no answer.

"You sought our lives, and felt no remorse. What's the life of a rascally police agent to us?" cried Darrelli.

"Nothing at all," said Hunstoni. "Waste no more time with him. Florio, kill him at once."

The brigand looked at Barboni to see if he wished this command to be carried out.

"Stay!" exclaimed Barboni; "let Bigamini kill him. I have never seen the little tailor let blood."

"I—I don't like the look of it, signor," replied Bigamini, shrinking back.

The police spy grovelled on the ground in the most abject manner.

He besought, he swore, he cried, raved, and cajoled in a manner piteous to behold, while the blood streamed from his wounds, and his bloodshot eyes almost started from their sockets.

"Oh, signor," he exclaimed, "for the sake of the Holy Virgin, spare me. Santa Maria! you will not let me die thus. I must see a priest. Curses on you! Oh, Santissima Virgine, will you allow this?"

"Silence the bleating fool," said Hunstoni. "Have you no dagger, Bigamini?"

"Ye-es, signor," replied Bigamini, fumbling in his waistcoat, and at length producing a dagger. "But I don't like the look of it."

"Make haste. You have shed blood before."

"Spare me, mighty signor," said the writhing victim. "Your time may come and you may have to plead for mercy."

"When it does come, I shall know how to die," answered Barboni, folding his arms proudly and sternly.

Bigamini sank on one knee, and, with a dexterous stroke, plunged the dagger into the heart of the defenceless police agent. Steffano gave one convulsive movement, and all was over.

"Cut off his head," said Barboni.

This was done, and Bigamini, after considerable hacking, held up the ghastly trophy.

Barboni called for a hammer and some nails, with which he fastened the ears on to the top of the head.

Gazing for a moment at the hideous spectacle, the convulsed features, the starting eyes, and the falling jaw, he turned to Bigamini.

"You will take that to Sforza, the chief of the police of Naples," he said.

"Si, 'celenza," replied the spy.

"It will be a warning to him how he tries to catch us napping again."

"Have you any further commands, signor?" asked Bigamini.

"No; depart at once, and report yourself again in three days."

Bigamini bowed, and, taking up the head, all gory as it was, carried it away.

The next day, Sforza, the chief of the police, found a parcel on the table in his private office.

On unwrapping it, he started back with horror on beholding the mutilated head of his faithful Steffano. Pasted on the forehead was a piece of paper.

On this was scrawled the single word—

"Barboni."

Some one had entered his office in the night, and presented him with the dreadful gift.

"Santa Maria!" he said. "This is not a man; he is a fiend."

Again Naples was thrilled with horror as the story circulated, and many prayed to the Virgin that they might not fall into the power of Barboni, the brigand.

CHAPTER XXV.

THE VISIT TO CASTEL INFERNO.

JACK was not deterred from his purpose of going in search of the brigands.

Many men would have given up the chase, after the shocking fate of the police agent.

But he had confidence in himself, and knew no fear.

Bigamini was his guide, and led him to the Volturno, which they crossed, attended by the soldiers.

At length they descried a castle, which Bigamini declared was, to the best of his belief, the one in which he had been confined by the brigands until his escape.

Inquiring whose it was of some peasants, they replied to Jack that the Prince of Villanova lived there.

It was the famous Castel Inferno, reputed to be haunted.

Many dreadful murders had occurred here years ago, and its history was as sad and bloody as could well be imagined.

Jack approached the castle.

The drawbridge was down, and he walked boldly into the courtyard.

Jack was intensely surprised when he found himself fairly within the castle.

There were no ferocious-looking armed brigands ; in fact, nothing whatever to indicate that it was the abode of a savage bandit.

Only an old man was visible, and he, in reply to our hero's question, said that the prince was absent, but no doubt the steward would attend to the signor.

Asking for the prince, the answer was that he had been at Rome for three weeks, and would not be home for four days.

The steward invited him to enter and take refreshments, which Jack refused to do, saying he would call again.

He returned to Naples and waited patiently for a week, when he again visited Castel Inferno.

The same absence of precautions against surprise struck him, and leaving his soldiers outside, he prepared to cross the drawbridge as before.

" Let me stop here, signor," said Bigamini ; " I may be in danger. You know I am nobody, and they would not hesitate to kill me."

" It does not look such a very ferocious place," answered Jack, regarding the goats running about in the yard, and the pigeons feeding peacefully with the fowls.

Bigamini's teeth began to chatter.

" You should never go by appearances," he said.

" Are you sure you have not made a mistake ?" asked Jack.

" I can't be quite sure ; it was dark when I ran away. Let me stay here, sir ; I daren't come in with you."

" If you are such a coward, remain with the soldiers," replied Jack, in great disgust.

" Thank you, sir," returned Bigamini, with relief. " Once, when I was a happy Smiffins, I shouldn't have minded, but now——"

Jack did not stay to hear him out.

He stalked across the drawbridge and through the court yard as before.

An aged servant, patting the neck of a pet lamb, looked up.

" Is the prince at home ?" Jack asked.

" Si, signor ; you will find him inside. Do not be afraid to enter. His highness lives so plainly and simply that we have few servants, and he dispenses with all state."

Jack wondered more than ever at this.

But seeing there was no one to guide him, he entered the house and looked into several rooms, all plainly furnished and empty.

At length he pushed open the door of a library, and beheld the prince seated in a chair, engaged in reading a volume of Tasso.

" Not much like a brigand," thought Jack.

His entrance aroused the prince, who instantly arose.

" Ah ! Mr. Harkaway, if I do not mistake," he exclaimed.

" Pray pardon me for intruding upon your privacy unannounced," said Jack, " but I could find no servants to introduce me."

The Prince Di Villanova smiled.

" That surprises you ?" he said.

" I confess it does."

"My habits are so simple. I keep but three servants, and the poorest peasant on my estate has permission to approach me when he pleases. All can enter here."

"You are doubtless astonished to see me," said Jack, feeling rather puzzled how to proceed.

"No. You have come to ask me for an apology for shooting you in the shoulder; you shall have it."

This was frank, and Jack could not but accept it.

He now saw the prince face to face, as the other day he had seen and fought with the brigand outside the sybil's cave.

But Barboni was fierce and truculent in his expression, while the prince was soft and mild, with a long beard, like a sage who is fond of peace, books, and retirement.

"You will admit that you provoked me," continued the prince; "your expressions were not complimentary. You called me a brigand—ha! ha! I a brigand! It is very amusing."

"You insulted my wife," said Jack, "and——"

"Tut, tut! Pazzi, amico mio," interrupted the prince. "Your English ladies do not understand the high-flown compliments of us Neapolitans. Let it all be forgotten. You will take some refreshment?"

Jack thought of wine poisoned and drugged, and respectfully declined.

"Come, you are my guest," continued the prince. "I will show you a lovely view of the valley of the Volturno from my terrace."

He leant gently on Jack's arm and led him through an open window to the terrace.

The first thing his eyes fell upon was the soldiers gathered together in a little knot outside the moat.

"What!" he cried, with a laugh. "Have you brought with you an escort of soldiers? Mr. Harkaway, I thought you a brave man."

Jack began to feel ashamed of himself.

How could he have mistrusted this amiable personage, who was so simple and inoffensive?

"You must have the goodness, prince, to excuse me," said Jack. "I have heard about—about brigands."

"And you thought I was connected with them, eh?"

"I did."

"You see how absurd the idea is. Why should I, a man of ample means and simple tastes, associate myself with such miscreants?"

Jack did not know.

"I shall go away with different ideas," he answered.

"If you will do me justice, I shall be satisfied," said the prince. "That I am a man of violent passions when insulted, I am willing to admit."

"You have heard of Barboni?" asked Jack.

"Who has not?"

"What do you think of him?"

"Simply that he is a desperate ruffian, best avoided."

"I have sworn to kill him or hand him over to justice," said Jack.

A peculiar smile crossed the handsome features of the prince.

"A rash vow, which may recoil upon yourself, caro mio," he said. "Let the government do its own dirty work. Return to England and forget all about this brigand."

"Never!" said Dick emphatically.

"Well," said the Prince Di Villanova, "you will do as you please. Pray come and see me again, Mr. Harkaway, if you will not stay now. Always make my poor house your own."

"Thank you," answered Jack.

"Now we are happily reconciled, and you have accepted my apology, I may expect no action on the part of the authorities for the unlucky shot I sent at you in a moment of anger?"

"Certainly not."

"We shall meet as friends?"

"By all means," replied Jack, who could not quarrel with this man—"though I should like to have a shot at you in return."

The prince laughed loudly.

"You are like all your countrymen," he said. "But here we consider an insult as good as a shot or a stab. You insulted me by calling me a brigand; that was your shot."

"Well," replied Jack, good-naturedly, "I will look at it in that way."

Perfectly confounded by the prince's treatment, and taken off his guard, he found himself saying adieu in a friendly manner.

Villanova saw him outside the moat, shook his hand, thanked him for his visit, and pressed him to come again.

He told the soldiers to march on, and ordered Bigamini to precede him, as he wished to be alone and think.

His interview had been so different with the prince to what he had expected.

He had pictured himself entering a castle bristling with cannon and armed men; the prince himself in armour, perhaps, and he hurling defiance at him.

"I can't make it out," said Jack to himself; "I'm in a fog."

The soldiers and Bigamini were a quarter of a mile ahead, and their arms could be seen glancing in the sun.

Cattle lowed in the meadows, the peasantry went on with their daily labour, and all seemed peace and contentment.

Suddenly he heard someone running behind him.

Turning sharply, he saw a thin, ragged youth, who might have been eighteen or four-and-twenty.

There was a meek, broken-spirited look about him which bespoke ill-treatment, and a vacant expression in the eyes which showed that the mind was not so strong as it might have been.

"Who are you?" asked Jack, sharply.

"Inglesi," was the reply.

"What is your name?"

"Luni, they call me. It's Lunatico in full. I'm not all right here."

The youth tapped his forehead.

"Well, Luni," said Jack, more kindly, "what do you want with me?"

"She sent me?"

"Who?"

"She of the vaults. Il Spirito—the spirit. I mustn't say any more, or they'll beat me," said Luni, with a start of affright.

Extending his hand, he held out a dirty strip of paper, on which something was written.

"She wrote it. Il spirito wrote it, and told me to run after a signor, and I suppose it's meant for you."

Jack took the paper, and gave him a piece of money.

"What's this?" he asked, looking at it curiously.

"Money?"

"No use to Luni," said the youth, shaking his head sadly and handing it back.

Then with a "Buon giorno, signor," he took to his heels, and darting into a thicket, was lost to sight.

Jack held the paper up to the light, and with difficulty read what was scrawled on it in pencil.

"Believe nothing you have heard or seen in the castle. Above all things be on your guard. Your life and the lives of those dear to you are in danger. Villanova is—another time—interrupted."

This scrawl did not amount to much.

It said too little, and it was with a feeling of annoyance that Jack put it in his pocket.

Mystery was accumulating upon mystery.

"I wonder what this means?" thought Jack. "Hanged if I don't feel like an old knight in a story book going to take an enchanted castle."

He walked on to the river, crossed over, mounted his horse, which was waiting for him, and left Bigamini to return with the soldiers, to whom he distributed some money, while he rode back to Naples.

On his arrival in the Strada Di Toled he called a council of war.

It was attended by Harvey, Tom Carden, and the little coxswain, who were all anxious to know the result of his journey.

He told them exactly everything that had happened, and showed them the mysterious scrap of paper.

"Now, gentlemen," he exclaimed, "you are as wise as I am. What is your opinion?"

"It's all kid," replied the coxswain.

"Rank humbug," said Carden.

"What do you think, Dick?" asked Jack.

"I was thinking," replied Harvey, "of the wolf who put on sheep's clothing. You know the fable."

"Bravo," said Tom Carden, "Harvey has hit it. Your prince has been trying to make a fool of you, Harkaway."

"He was quiet and civil enough," answered Jack.

"Yes, because you had soldiers, and did not go alone."

"What are we to do?"

"'WHO ARE YOU?' ASKED JACK, SHARPLY."

"Do? Why, be as foxy he is," said Carden.

"But," said Jack, "how are we to connect Prince Villanova with Barboni? The prince is polished and wears a beard. Barboni has very little hair, but is wild and savage."

"It's got to be done," replied Carden, in his dogged way.

"I have come to the conclusion," exclaimed Jack, "that the prince and Barboni are two different persons."

"Then we differ," remarked Harvey. "The mysterious scrap of paper ought to open your eyes."

"I've got a brilliant idea," said the little coxswain.

"What's that?" asked all.

"Let's capture the prince, and hide him away somewhere and torture him till he confesses."

Jack laughed.

"You've got to catch him first," he said. "The question is, who will bell the cat?"

Tom Carden nodded his head gravely.

"That's the best dodge I've heard of for a long time," he said. "It must be thought over."

Emily and Hilda here put their heads in at the door.

"Are you privy councillors coming to dinner?" said Emily.

"Shan't be ten minutes dressing, dear," replied Jack.

"We know what you are chatting about," remarked Hilda.

"You're very clever if you do," answered Harvey. "Because we were discussing the best way of cooking macaroni, and whether it was good without cheese."

"Nonsense," replied Hilda, "you were talking about catching your brigands. We have been listening at the door."

"Then you ought to be ashamed of yourself," said Harvey, pretending to be angry.

Hilda went up and kissed him.

"Don't be cross, dearest," she said, coaxingly.

"Cross with you, darling," he answered. "Not I. It was only fun."

At this moment there was a loud noise outside the door.

Bump, smash, bump, bump.

It was as if somebody's head was being knocked against the old oak panelling.

"What the deuce is that?" asked Jack, getting up.

"Somebody's tooth falling out," said Harvey, with a laugh.

Tom Carden rose and opened the door.

He disclosed to view Monday, who was struggling with someone.

"What's the row, Monday?" he said.

"It um rascal Bigami, sare," answered Monday. "Um thief always listening at um door. Um bump his head to teach him."

"Bigamini!" cried Jack. "Bring him in!"

The little man was dragged into the room, looking very crestfallen.

"How did you get back to Naples so soon?" asked Jack.

"I caught the mail cart and got a lift," replied Bigamini.

"What brought you here?"

"I came to see if you wanted me again, sir, and I wasn't listening. It's all his—but I suppose you won't believe me—once when I was a happy Smiffins, my word was good enough, but now I'm a miserable Bigamini——"

"Go about your business," said Jack, shortly; "I shan't want you any more."

"Will you take me into your service, sir?"

"No. I have as many servants as I want. You've humbugged me about the brigand's castle somehow. Don't let me catch you on these premises again."

"That all comes of being a miserable Bigamini," whined the spy.

"Run him out, Monday."

"Yes, sare."

He pushed him towards the door again, employing his knee with rather more force than was pleasant.

"Never mind, Mr. Harkaway; I'll watch over you, sir," said Bigamini.

"You come out this," replied Monday; "me teach you to listen at um door."

Bigamini was hurried ignominiously down the stairs, and thrust out into the street with a vigorous kick.

The little man shook himself and turned round savagely.

"I'll remember you for this, my dark beauty," he exclaimed viciously.

"What um do?" asked Monday, with a derisive sneer.

" I'll have your ears."

" They used to say in Pisang, ' I'll have your head,' " he muttered. " It um new thing to say ' I'll have your ears.' "

But there was something savage and bloodthirsty about Bigamini, which made Monday feel his ears affectionately as if to see if they were safe.

CHAPTER XXVI.

THE MYSTERIOUS ARTIST.

THE more Jack thought over the question, how to catch the brigand chief, the more he became perplexed.

He did not know how to begin.

Castel Inferno, the abode of Prince Villanova, did not look like a robber's stronghold, nor did the prince himself resemble a brigand.

Where was Barboni to be found ?

Neither of the four friends could suggest any means of commencing the campaign.

It was one thing to fight a man you can see, but to search for a hidden enemy was a totally different matter.

After dinner on the day of Bigamini's expulsion by Monday, he was thoughtful and preoccupied.

He had scarcely eaten anything.

Emily observed this with alarm, and tried to cheer him up, but without success.

The little coxswain dropped in with Carden, and proposed a four-handed game at billiards, but Jack was not in the humour for games.

" I wish," said Emily, " you would go home, Jack. Something dreadful will happen, I'm sure, if we stay here much longer."

" I can't help being quiet sometimes, my dear," replied Jack.

" Yes; but you are always grave now. I know what you are thinking of; it is that dreadful brigand chief."

" They are all thinking of the same person," said Hilda. " Dick has been a different man lately."

Harvey tried to laugh.

" And Mr. Carden and Mr. Campbell are quite changed," continued Hilda ; " they all talk in whispers, and shut themselves up in a room to hold councils of war, as they call it."

Jack frowned as if he did not like the turn the conversation was taking.

" I shall go out for a stroll, I think," he said, getting up and stretching himself.

" Don't go out, dear," said Emily.

" Why not?"

" I don't want you to."

" But why ? I like a reason for everything," he persisted.

" You may think me very foolish, but I feel as if something would happen tonight, if you left me."

" Nonsense," said Jack, lighting a cigar.

He went to a side table, and took up his hat and a small stick which he carried.

" Don't go, Jack—don't go, to oblige me," cried Emily.

" Very sorry," he answered. " But I like to have a will of my own sometimes ; I shan't be long."

Emily sighed deeply and resumed her seat.

She knew it was no use urging Jack further, if he had made up his mind to do a particular thing.

Going up to her, he kissed her forehead, saying—

" You stupid little pet. What are you afraid of—shadows ?"

Emily shuddered.

" Something more substantial than shadows—brigands," she replied.

He laughed, and exclaimed—

" Walter, will you go with me ?"

The coxswain quickly responded in the affirmative, in spite of a cross look Emily gave him.

" You must not be angry with me, Mrs. Harkaway," said Campbell ; " it is not I who take your husband out; he takes me."

Emily made no answer.

The two friends went away together, and enjoyed the fresh evening air, the night being the most delightful part of the day in Naples, for it is then that the fierce heat of the sun passes away as the cool breeze from the sea sweeps over the shore.

They wandered up the Strada Di Toledo, and entered the Corso, which had a fair sprinkling of people, who were taking the air.

By chance, a girl neatly but poorly dressed, though of ladylike appearance, pushed up against Jack, and something she carried under her arm fell on the pavement.

" Oh!" she cried, " my new picture. What shall I do ? It was scarcely dry."

The little coxswain stooped down and politely picked up the picture, which was a portrait in oils.

Unfortunately the dust had stuck to the fresh varnish, it having fallen on its face.

" Dear me, how troublesome," continued the girl. " I shall have to take it home and touch it up again, when I had expected to have received the money for it."

" Don't let that worry you," exclaimed Jack. " It was confoundedly clumsy of me to knock it from under your arm. I will buy it. What is the price ?"

" It is not for sale," replied the artist. " I am a portrait painter, signor, and this was ordered by a lady, who is impatient to receive it."

" Never mind," said Jack, " you shall paint me, and I will give you some money on account."

" And mine too," replied the little coxswain.

He turned to Jack and whispered—

" I never saw such a pretty girl in my life. Isn't she a beauty? Look at her dark glossy hair and sparkling black eyes."

" Thank you very much," said the girl. " My name is Bianca, and I live at the first house in the Strada D'Italia, which runs out of the Corso. I am nearly always at home. Good night."

" Will you have some money now ?" said the little coxswain.

" Signor !" exclaimed the Italian girl, drawing herself up proudly.

" I—I beg your pardon. I——"

" It is my custom only to receive money when I have earned it," she replied.

" But we have spoilt your picture."

" I ought to have taken more care of it."

" May we come and see you ?" asked the little coxswain.

" Any person who wishes to employ me as an artist will always be welcome. Good night once more."

" You said the first house in the Strada D'It——"

The little woman with the black hair and dark eyes had vanished.

" Hang it all!" exclaimed Walter, " she's gone."

" Don't cry," said Jack, smiling.

" I can't cry because I have nothing to sell," answered the little coxswain.

" Tell you what I'll do," said Jack; " there is a café open on the Corso; I'll fly you for two drinks."

" No, you won't," replied Walter; " you will come with me to the first house in the Strada D'Italia."

" What for ?"

" I want to be carved and gilded— portrait painted, you know. Have my phiz done in oils on canvas, and set in a gold frame."

" What rot !"

" It isn't rot. Come with me. You have nothing to do, and it will be a diversion from thinking of brigands."

" I want to get back to Emily. She seemed so cross at my going out. Poor little thing ! it does not take much to break her heart."

" You will come with me, I tell you," continued the little coxswain.

At this moment a thin, shuffling figure passed them, and, looking in their faces, turned back.

" I hope you'll excuse a miserable Bigamini, sir," he said, addressing Jack.

" What !" exclaimed Jack; " is it you ?"

" Yes, sir; and what may your little game be—as I used to say when I was a happy Smiffins—if I may make so bold ?"

" Stagging," replied the little coxswain.

" What, sir ?"

" The fact is," said Jack, " my friend has taken an interest in a little Neapolitan girl who paints portraits."

" Paints portraits. Yes, sir; go on."

" And lives in the Strada D'Italia," replied Jack.

" First house round the corner," put in the little coxswain.

" First house round the corner. Yes, sir ; go on," repeated Bigamini.

" And has glossy black hair and dark eyes," said the coxswain.

" Glossy black hair and dark eyes," said Bigamini, with his accustomed chuckle.

" Do you know her ?" asked Walter.

" Don't I? Ha, ha! This *is* funny. Excuse me, gents—I should say signors."

" Well, what do you know of her? Nothing bad, I'll bet," said the little coxswain, angrily.

" Don't you put up your feathers, sir. You're for all the world like a little bantam cock," said Bigamini.

The little coxswain let out strongly with his left.

Bigamini rolled over into the gutter, and lay there groaning.

" Don't you call me bantam or any other cocks," said Walter; " I don't allow such familiarity."

Jack had to pick him up.

" There was once a spirit in the heart of Smiffins," he said, shaking himself, " which would have washed out this hinsult in ber-lood."

Walter laughed heartily at his tragic manner.

" But," he added, " a time will come. No matter."

" Come," said the coxswain, " what do you know about Signora Bianca ?"

" She's a hartist," said Bigamini, sulkily.

" That's stale news."

" She lives in the house where I lodge."

" Is she square ?" asked the coxswain. " I mean, could we go and get our portraits painted ?"

" You couldn't get a cleverer hartist, as far as that goes," answered Bigamini.

" Why couldn't you have told us all that before, you old pumpkin ?" said the coxswain.

" You needn't have punched me **half** silly to get it out of me."

" You'll be all right presently. There is a ducat for you to go and get something to drink. Slope !"

Bigamini took the coin, mumbled his thanks, and pretended to go away, but he carefully watched the young men.

He saw them walk along the Corso, until they came to the Strada D'Italia.

They entered the corner house, and were evidently going to pay the artist a visit.

" Booked," he muttered. " I must lose no time in seeing the chief. Bianca played her part well, and I didn't work it badly, though I wish these university men weren't so jolly handy with their fists."

He set off at his best pace for the palazzo of the Contessa Di Malafedi.

Her ladyship had been obliged to walk all the weary way home from the grotto of the sybil, when Jack took her carriage for Emily.

Enraged as she was at this insult, she did not make any complaint, for she knew that her conduct in taking Emily to the cave where the brigand met her had laid her open to suspicion.

She feared also that the police might watch her movements, and hang about her house.

To avoid this she called upon the chief of the police the next day, and made him a very handsome present of diamonds, worth several thousand pounds.

Such was the corruption among high officials in Naples that, if she had committed a crime, this act would have shut the eyes of the authorities.

Bigamini passed freely in and out of the contessa's palace.

The domestics all knew him, and regarded him as a privileged person, high in the favour of their mistress.

In a delightful little boudoir, furnished in the first style of Parisian elegance, he found the contessa with the chief of the brigands.

" Well," cried Barboni, " has the fish swallowed the bait ?"

" Yes," replied Bigamini, with a grin; " hook and all. He only wants landing "

" Where is he now ?"

" At the apartments I have taken for Bianca, and she will keep him in play till your arrival."

" Good !" exclaimed Barboni. " Go t Mrs. Harkaway, and bring her into the strada."

Bigamini scratched his head.

" That's easier said than done," he replied.

" What !" cried Barboni, fiercely " Am I to have my commands questioned ? What value do you set on your life ?"

Bigamini ran from the room with a startled air.

He had a salutary dread of Monday,

but, of the two, he feared the bloodthirsty Barboni most.

"The black villain," he said to himself, "will make his shoemaker acquainted with my tailor again, if I don't watch it. But I shall be an out-and-out duffer if I can't get in without his seeing me."

The distance from one house to the other was not far, and he speedily traversed it.

On the ground floor of the house was a little conservatory, in which Emily spent much of her time.

It was her delight to attend to the flowers in the cool of the evening, water them, pick off the dead bloom and leaves, and inhale their delicious fragrance.

Perhaps the spy had remarked this habit of hers during one of his visits.

At all events, he crept in through a side door with a noiseless step, and glided at once to the conservatory without being seen.

"Good again," he murmured. "I've sold that jolly old black cove. Who says I can't do it?"

As Emily's eyes fell upon the grotesque figure of the little London tailor, she was inclined to cry out.

"Don't scream, mum," cried Bigamini. "It's only me. You know me, mum— Mr. Harkaway's friend, mum."

"Oh, yes," replied Emily; "I know you now. What do you want?"

"There's a gentleman outside, mum. I don't remember to have seen him before, though I may have, for all those furriner chaps is very much alike."

"What does he want?"

"He give me a ducat, mum—here it is —to tell you that he had a message for you, either about Mr. Harkaway, or from him, I can't remember which."

"Who is he?" asked Emily.

She was always agitated when Jack was out, and anybody came to tell her anything about him.

"Now I'm beat," replied Bigamini. "How can I tell you who he is, when he's a stranger?"

"I forgot that. Go on."

"He just wants you to slip your mantle or shawl over your head, mum, and come out and have two words with him."

"Why can't he come in here?"

"That's what I asked him, mum," said Bigamini, "but he shook his head,

and said it did not much matter to him whether you came or not, though——"

"What?" ejaculated Emily.

"*Though it might make a deal of difference to Mr. Harkaway*, he said, mum, for people do take other's lives very suddenly in this country."

"That is a threat," said Emily; "but it seems that everybody and everything in this city is surrounded by intrigue and mystery. No one can do anything in a straightforward manner."

"You'd best go, mum, I think," said Bigamini. "It's only just outside in the street."

"Just outside?" repeated Emily, abstractedly.

"You wasn't to say a word to nobody."

"More mystery."

"Well mum, no harm can come of it. The street's full of people, and the stranger will be close to the first lamp."

"Are you sure the stranger said that I should do my husband good by going?"

"Certain sure, mum."

"I will go. There is nothing I would not risk for Jack's sake. He may be in danger."

"Ah, mum," said Bigamini, "if my first wife had spoken like that, I might yet have been a happy Smiffins."

He wiped away a tear, real or imaginary, which he supposed had gathered in the corner of his left eye.

"Now," he added, "I am left all alone, to be a miserable Bigamini."

Emily paid no further attention to him.

She gathered a lace shawl she wore over her shoulders into a fold, and put it over her head.

Then she quitted the conservatory, apparently regardless of the little man's presence.

"That's all right," said he. "I'm getting quite a swell at dodges. My first wife used to say I wasn't worth my salt. But I'm wiring in strong, and getting my name up.

"The chief ought to part a lump of money for this wheeze."

It occurred to him, in the midst of this jubilation, that it was not safe for him to remain there.

Accordingly he retreated, performing what the French in the late war called a "strategical movement."

As he went through the passage, he

passed an open door leading into what in England is the butler's pantry.

This was Monday's head-quarters.

An easy chair invited repose.

Bottles of all sorts, sizes, and descriptions stood on shelves.

There was no one in the little room, and Bigamini felt thirsty.

It was a frequent complaint of his.

He looked at the paradise, and the sight of the bottles, together with a crystal vase full of ice, was more than he could withstand.

He yielded to the temptation.

"The black beast's out," he said. "I'll go in and lush myself up on the cheap."

Filling a tumbler with wine and ice, he threw himself in the armchair and sipped the pleasing mixture.

"That black brute hasn't got half a bad berth. I wish it was mine," he muttered.

A box of cigars was placed invitingly at his elbow, and he lighted one, a genuine Partaga.

"Come," he said, "this isn't half bad. I rather like this crib. Wonder where the black demon is."

The thought of Monday gave him a cold shiver which necessitated another tumbler of wine.

Bigamini's head wasn't very strong, and the wine soon mounted into it.

He nearly forgot all about Monday, and crossing his legs, began to sing a song.

"Blow the black," he exclaimed, as the thought of Monday once more intruded itself into his mind. "I mean to have a jolly. Strike up, governor; fiddle up, that's your sort."

At this moment Hilda began to play on the harp in the drawing-room.

The door was open, and the sound penetrated to Bigamini, who thought that some nigger minstrels had responded to his call.

"That's stunning," he said. "Now for a song. Nice sort of a crib this. Here goes.

"Massa's gone to sea—oh, golly !
No one here but me—be jolly.
I'll laugh and sing,
And have my fling,
And spend the time in folly."

Scarcely had he finished the last line of the stave, when a dark shadow filled the doorway.

"Massa's gone to sea——" began Bigamini, commencing the second verse.

His eye caught the dark shadow.

"Hullo!" he exclaimed, breaking off suddenly.

The dark shadow advanced a step or two.

"Bless um eyes and limbs ; him got the cheek ob um devil," exclaimed the shadow.

Bigamini's countenance fell.

He was still sober enough to recognise in the dark shadow his inveterate enemy Monday.

CHAPTER XXVII.

THE BRIGAND'S PROMISE.

"You come out that," exclaimed Monday, angrily.

"Not by no means," replied Bigamini, with a hiccup; "the governor sent me here on private business."

"Pack of lies," said Monday. "You come to steal um drink."

"Not bad tipple," answered Bigamini. "But I know where to get better. Sit down, old cock, and make your miserable life happy."

"You come out that, I tell you," was Monday's only reply.

Bigamini did not move, he swayed his head backwards and forwards to the sound of the music, and sipped his wine as before.

This was more than Monday could bear.

He rushed upon Bigamini and dragged him off the chair, and a struggle ensued.

The little man clung on to chairs, tables, anything he could grasp with his fingers, and stuck to it with the tenacity of a cat.

When he was near the door, for Monday gradually dragged him from one stand point to another, he desperately grasped an empty plate chest.

The key was in the lock, but it was not fastened, and the lid came up.

Bigamini struggled more fiercely than ever, for he did not like to leave such pleasant quarters, and resented Monday's attack upon him as a personal grievance of the liveliest kind.

With a clever twist of his leg, he caused the black to stumble.

Seeing his advantage, he threw himself upon him, and Monday, losing his balance, fell backwards.

The plate chest stood invitingly before him, and he dropped into it.

Only his legs stuck up in the air.

He was completely boxed up, and with a shout of triumph Bigamini gave the legs a push, shut down the lid, turned the key, and sat on the chest.

"Gone under," he exclaimed. "Hurrah! this child can do it. Why didn't he make himself jolly?

"Massa's gone to sea—oh, golly!"

"I'll have some more grape juice. Never say die."

He resumed his old seat in the armchair, filled himself another tumbler of the insidious Lachrymæ Christi, and lighted a fresh cigar.

"Now this is what I call spiff," he said, "awfully spiff; I've shunted the negro, and given him a body blow in the chest."

He laughed at his own wit, in his usual chuckling manner.

Just as he had finished his seventh tumbler, a fleecy cloud of muslin appeared, coming trippingly into the room, which was now growing rather dark in the twilight.

"Monday," exclaimed a gentle voice.

"No, my dear, it's Bigamini," answered the little tailor, "hoping I'm not intruding. You don't know me, I suppose, my dear?"

"Are you a friend of my husband, sir?" asked Ada, who was the person in the cloud of muslin.

"Oh, yes, great friends; like brothers we are. Sit down, my dear."

"Thank you, sir," answered Ada. "Mr. Matabella went out for a stroll. I expected him back before now."

"So did I, my dear."

A deep groan came from the chest.

"Oh, Lor'!" exclaimed Ada, "whatever on earth was that?"

"Nothing, my dear," replied Bigamini. "Ain't you a little pet, eh?" he said, chucking her under the chin.

"Don't you do that again," replied Ada, indignantly.

"No offence, my dear," he replied; "my only weakness is a petticoat. If I had been firm in the matter of petticoats, I might still have been a happy Smiffins."

"If you are unhappy," said Ada, "I daresay it is your own fault."

"You don't know my history, my dear," replied the little man. "If you heard all, you would weep to see me a miserable Bigamini. You'd do more than that—you'd give me a—a kiss."

"A kiss!" repeated Ada, blushing.

"Yes, my dear, a kiss of sympathy."

Again the groaning noise came from the chest.

This time more profound than before.

"Oh, that dreadful noise. There it is again," cried Ada, in alarm; "I wish Matabella would come in."

"Touching this kiss of sympathy, my angel," said Bigamini.

"You must be intoxicated," replied Ada, "or you would never talk to me like this."

"I am—I am. You've hit the nail on the head—that's the tip. That's the correct card. I am tight, and I mean to have a kiss. Come on, old girl."

Ada looked at him inquiringly for a moment, and then retired to the doorway, feeling rather afraid of the little tailor.

The groans which proceeded from the chest became more frequent and louder.

There was also a scratching noise inside, suggestive of a colony of rats.

"There is somebody in this chest," she exclaimed, tremulously.

Bigamini tried to stagger towards her, but was too tipsy to be able to keep his balance, and he rolled up against the wall.

"It's orright, my dear," he said, "on'y the wind—cur'us thing the wind."

But Ada wouldn't believe him.

She fell on her knees, and turning the key, unlocked the big chest just in time.

There was no air to be inhaled from the outside, and Monday was nearly suffocated.

A little time longer would have settled him altogether.

As it was, he could scarcely breathe, and gasped like a fish out of water.

The fresh air poured in and Monday drank it up as it were in gulps.

"My poor, dear Mat," cried Ada. "How did this happen?"

"Gulp, gasp, gulp!" was all Monday could reply.

"What you can see in that black lump of humanity beats me hollow—hic!" exclaimed Bigamini.

He tried to reach her, but his legs gave way, and he could only crawl on his hands and knees.

"Doosid funny room this—hic," he continued. "Got a slanting floor—hic—walls seem to go round."

Monday gradually revived, and with a plunge, got up.

"Ha, ha!" he said, with a hysterical laugh. "Man Bigamy shut um in chest, will he? Me see 'bout that."

He got out of the box and stretched himself, feeling rather cramped by his long confinement in such an unpleasant position.

Paying no attention to him, Bigamni had succeeded in crawling to Ada.

"I'll have that kiss, if I die for it," he cried.

"Oh, Mat, help me!" screamed Ada.

"Never mind him, replied Bigamini. "I don't want to hurt him; but if he comes near me, I'll muzzle him. Ain't you a duck? Kiss her own pet man, who loves her, a darling."

His amorous speeches were soon cut short by Monday, who fell upon him like a battering ram.

"Pancaked, by Jove!" exclaimed Bigamini, almost out of breath, as he lay flat on his stomach, with Monday on his back.

Monday kicked and hit him to his heart's content, scarcely leaving a spot in his body untouched.

"Here, I say, get up," roared Bigamini. "This won't do. I say, turn it up. I don't want mangling. Drop it. Oh, Lord, he'll squash me flat."

At last he contrived to wriggle from under his tormentor, and, his beating having partially sobered him, he ran into the street, being helped along in his flight by the toe of Monday's boot, which made frequent acquaintance with his back.

"That teach you your book, sare," said Monday, whose hair bristled angrily. "You not come here again to drink um wine and kiss um wife while um husband in chest."

Bigamini turned round at a safe distance.

"I'll cock a snooks at him," he muttered.

Accordingly he put his fingers to his nose and danced a war dance in token of derision.

"Yah, yah!" he cried. "Go home. Put your boots on, you black smeller. Who kissed your wife? Yah!"

Monday foamed at the mouth with rage, and he would have darted after Bigamini if his wife had not seized his arm and dragged him inside.

Bigamini meanwhile looked round for Barboni or Emily, but he could discover no trace of either of them.

He thought it advisable to make his way at once to the house in the Strada D'Italia.

Barboni might want him.

As we know, he was a spy in the pay of the brigand chief, and he could not afford to offend his master.

Though far from sober, he managed to walk tolerably straight, and did not cannon against more than one out of ten persons as he walked along.

"Cuss that wine," he said to himself; "I don't feel half up to Dick."

While he is making his way to the corner house, we must return to Emily.

She had left Bigamini without saying a word to either Hilda, Harvey, or Tom Carden.

Consequently they remained in ignorance of her departure.

Before she had gone more than a dozen paces, she was confronted by a tall man, whose face was partially shrouded by a slouched hat, and whose form was enveloped in the folds of a capacious cloak.

"I am he you seek," he said, in a full, deep-chested voice.

Emily started, for she knew the tones.

She had heard them in the box at the San Carlo, and again in the grotto of the sybil.

"Barboni!" she cried in affright.

"The same. Do not fear. I am here simply to fulfil my promise," he said.

"Promise!" she repeated, while the blood seemed to curdle in her veins, such was her horror of this man.

"When last we met, the sybil showed you the form of your husband talking to another woman."

"She did; but it was a juggle."

"You thought so at the time, and I promised to show you the reality."

"That you will never be able to do."

"You said that seeing was believing. To-night you shall see with your own eyes."

"To-night?"

"This instant—now. I come to fulfil my promise. Hear me."

"I will."

"At this moment Mr. Harkaway is in sweet converse with a Neapolitan girl of rare beauty. They are fondling one another; their arms twine round each other, his around her waist, hers about his neck."

All the outraged nature of a woman rose up in Emily.

"What is your object in telling me this?" she asked.

"I have a regard for you, and wish you to return to England to your friends, where you will be happier than with such a man."

"Ha!" cried Emily, "you are afraid of Harkaway and his friends. You think, if I went to England, they would all follow me. No matter; I will accompany you to see this sight."

"If I show you what I have promised, will you believe?" said the brigand, gnashing his teeth.

"If! But I cannot think Jack false to me."

"Other wives have thought the same, and yet their husbands have slyly kissed other lips. But come; time presses."

"I will follow you," she said.

"'Tis well," answered Barboni. "Fear nothing. The streets are crowded. I mean you no harm."

He led the way fearlessly, and several cloaked forms seemed to glide after him on each side of the way, mingling with the people, as if they were ordinary wayfarers.

If Emily had noticed them, she might have fancied they were bandits in disguise.

And such indeed they were.

Those sombre forms, silently threading the streets, and turning wherever Barboni turned, were the brigand's bodyguard.

Underneath their shrouding cloaks might have been seen cruel two-edged daggers, many-chambered revolvers, the sharp-pointed stiletto, and the Venetian poignard, of glass, so that the handle may be snapped off at the mouth of the wound.

The shrill whistle which Barboni knew so well how to sound, and which would have puzzled the cleverest schoolboy to imitate, would suffice to bring them all to his side.

No wonder he walked fearlessly when he knew how well he was guarded.

Besides, he had nothing to fear from Emily, who was thinking of the information he had given her.

Her heart was beating wildly, and her head was in a whirl.

One thing she was sure of, and that was, Barboni wanted her and Jack, with all his friends, out of Naples.

He feared them more than the police and the military forces which the general had under his command.

But that Jack was false she could not bring herself to believe.

She suspected some trick, and she was brave enough to wish to expose it.

When the corner house in the Strada D'Italia was reached, the brigand halted.

So did the spectral forms which followed him, hiding in shaded spots and doorways, so as to be within call, though out of observation.

"We have arrived, signora," said Barboni.

"What am I to do?" asked Emily.

"On the ground floor of this house there is a room; the door is open, but the entry is protected by a screen. When I wave my hand, you will come behind this screen."

"I understand."

"Having seen all that I have promised you, come away silently, and join me again outside."

"Join you?" said Emily.

"Yes; you must not reproach your husband here. I have more to say to you."

"Very well. I will join you," she answered.

Barboni stole noiselessly along the passage, and she saw him enter a room, the door of which stood open.

The seconds passed very slowly.

Each second seemed to her tortured mind a minute, and she waited impatiently for the signal.

CHAPTER XXVIII.

IN THE STUDIO.

WE left Jack and the little coxswain going into the house in which the artist said she lived.

The fact was that Walter Campbell had overruled Jack's objections, and prevailed upon him to give Bianca an order to paint his portrait.

"I've got quite spooney all in a minute on that little woman," said Walter.

"Better mind what you are about," replied Jack.

"Why?"

"She may have a sweetheart, and these Neapolitans are ugly beggars to rile. They think nothing of sticking a knife under the fifth rib."

"I'll chance that," answered Walter. "It's all very well for you married fellows to be so stuck up, but I like a quiet spoon sometimes, and don't often get it."

"Well," replied Jack, "I'll humour you this once."

They entered the house and experienced no difficulty in finding the artist's apartments, to which they were conducted by the porteress.

The rooms consisted only of a bedchamber and a studio.

Into the latter they were ushered; and when they had passed a screen, they saw Bianca sitting before her easel, brush in hand, and palette before her.

Various pictures, finished and unfinished, were scattered about the room, with plaster of Paris casts and statues, all in admirable disorder.

Bianca looked up in surprise as she saw her visitors, and asked them in Italian what the object of their intrusion might be.

"You must speak to her, Jack," said the coxswain "I can't patter Italian."

"All right," replied Jack.

Turning to the fair artist, he added—

"My friend and myself, signora, are desirous of availing ourselves of your undoubted talent, and we shall esteem it a favour if you will paint our portraits."

"Oh, certainly," she replied. "Shall I make a sketch of you to-night?"

"If you please."

Bianca turned the lamp which stood on the table so as to let it throw all its light upon Jack's face.

"How do you want to be taken?" she asked.

"Here is a photograph of my wife," he answered, showing her one he happened to have in his pocket.

"Do you want to be painted together?"

"Yes."

"A pretty face," said the artist, contemplating the portrait.

"My wife is considered a beauty in England," said Jack, proudly.

"And in Naples too, I should think. We cannot boast of those blue eyes and that fair hair here."

"If you will kindly stand up," said Jack, "I will show you the attitude I should like."

"With pleasure."

Bianca rose smilingly and approached Jack.

The little coxswain never removed his eyes from her face.

He was badly hit in that quarter.

"Look here," continued Jack; "put your arm round my shoulder, and I will put mine round your waist, if you will allow me."

She obeyed his instructions.

"So?" she asked.

"That will do. Look up in my face."

"Like that?"

"Capital? You are supposed to be my wife, you know, and you look up lovingly. I gaze down upon you in the same way."

"I see," replied Bianca, showing her pearly teeth.

"Do you think you can do it?"

"Certainly I can."

At this moment the little coxswain started.

"There is someone behind the screen," he said.

The next minute he had dashed towards it and pulled it down.

To his astonishment he saw Emily.

"Mrs. Harkaway!" he exclaimed.

Jack looked dumbfounded.

"My wife!" he cried. "Why, my darling, what, in the name of wonder brought you here?"

Bianca still kept her arm on Jack's shoulder.

"You can remove your arm now, signora," said Emily, quietly. "Your part is played."

"What does this mean, Emmy?" asked Jack.

"I have heard all," replied Emily. "Perhaps I arrived sooner than I was expected, and you would have known nothing about my visit had not Mr. Campbell pulled the screen down."

"Do explain."

"I was brought here to witness your infidelity, Jack, dear."

"Nonsense!"

"It is true. I was to see you making love to another woman; but I heard all that passed between you—at least, all that was important."

"But this lady is an artist," said Jack, pointing to Bianca.

"She is an accomplice," replied Emily, giving her a searching look.

"Of whom?"

"Barboni."

Jack and the little coxswain started.

"Did *he* bring you here?" demanded Jack.

"Yes. I will explain all presently. He is waiting for me now."

"What for?"

"To conduct me home again," she answered.

Bianca quietly returned to her chair, and toyed with her palette and brush.

"Confound it!" cried Jack. "Barboni so near, and I am unarmed. Have you a pistol, Walter?"

"Not even a pocket-knife," replied the little coxswain in despair. "But——"

"What?"

"We've got our fists, and can maul him a bit."

"No good. He would not venture into Naples alone and unarmed. Curse the luck!"

Emily turned to the signora with a low bow.

"You have played your part well," she exclaimed. "The portrait my husband wanted will not be required. Good evening."

Bianca simply lowered her head.

"Come along," said Jack. "Let's get out of this. We may succeed in bringing the police down on the beggar yet."

Emily took his arm, and, accompanied by the coxswain, they hastily quitted the studio.

As they went along, Emily explained how Bigamini had brought her word that a stranger wanted to see her.

She added that the stranger was Barboni, and that he had tried to make her jealous.

Further, that she had accompanied him to the Strada D'Italia, but had gone behind the screen a little too soon.

Instead of feeling jealous, she was pleased to think that Jack thought so much of her as to wish to have her portrait painted in such a loving position.

"I can't exactly see his game," said Jack. "But it is very evident he wanted to disgust you with me."

"He wouldn't do that for nothing," remarked Walter Campbell.

"Not he."

"There he is," said Emily, pointing to a man within a few yards of them.

Jack looked straight ahead.

Yes; there was the brigand chief, calm and motionless, as if a price was not set on his head.

He might have been in the midst of his rocky fastnesses, for all the emotion he showed.

Many people were passing to and fro in the busy Corso, though the side street was comparatively deserted.

"That's the cove; I twig him," said the little coxswain.

"Hi! hi! hi!" shouted Jack, at the top of his voice. "Barboni! Barboni the brigand!"

The people in the Corso stopped, and stared strangely down the dark, dingy little street.

Had someone gone suddenly mad?

That was what they thought at first.

"Go in a buster, Walter," continued Jack. "Back me up. Howl away a good un."

Joining their voices together they continued to shout—"Barboni! Barboni!"

Still the brigand chief did not move a step or appear to stir a muscle.

But all at once that terrible whistle was heard issuing from his lips.

It rose louder and louder.

It filled all the corners, and brought back an echo from the houses.

Silently, slowly, like ghosts coming from their graves at midnight, dark forms seemed to spring out of the earth.

They came from houses, from doorways, from corners, and even appeared to rise up out of the street, where, like lazaroni, they had been lazily lying.

These men, fifty or more in number, glided towards the brigand.

Fearlessly they flung back their cloaks, and their arms glistened in the feeble, flickering rays of imperfect light.

It was a strange sight; like that of an opera.

Only music was wanting to make it resemble a set scene on a large stage.

A couple of police agents were attracted to the spot by the loud exclamations of Jack and the little coxswain.

The crowd, which increased every moment, followed them down the street from the Corso.

At this juncture the state of affairs became critical.

Barboni saw that something had happened to interfere with his plans.

His idea was that Emily had betrayed him to her husband.

It was necessary to retreat.

Speaking a few words to his followers in a low but self-possessed voice, he advanced quickly towards Jack.

His men followed him in a semicircle.

Jack seized Emily by the arm and went into the middle of the street, still crying out very loudly—

"Barboni! Barboni!"

"Knock that noisy fool on the head," said the brigand. "But do not provoke a riot. We shall have the military upon us before we can get out of the city."

A dozen men ran towards Jack and the little coxswain.

Emily began to scream, and her voice added to the clamour.

"To the wall, quick," exclaimed Jack.

They retreated to a doorway and placed Emily behind them.

Then, with their backs to her, they awaited the onset. They were not long kept in expectation.

On came the brigands with a rush; but there happened to be an old iron railing close by their side.

Jack seized a rail in his strong grasp and tore it out of its bed.

He handed it to the little coxswain.

"Swipe away," he said; "keep them off. I'll soon have another."

Walter Campbell took the rail with both hands, and the foremost brigand fell with a broken skull.

The next shared the same fate.

By this time Jack was armed, and he laid about him with a will.

Several brigands went down before his sweeping strokes, and they could not reach him with the butts of their pistols or their daggers.

They were so enraged at seeing their companions fall, that some of the desperadoes fired.

Fortunately, in the half light, their aim was uncertain.

At the sound of the first shot, Barboni himself rushed up with the remainder of the brigands.

"No firing," he said; "you will kill the lady."

An unmistakable rush was made upon Jack and Campbell, who were pushed out of their position.

But they still fought valiantly.

At length a blow from a bandit stretched the little coxswain senseless on the ground.

"Help! help!" cried Jack. "Do you call yourselves men, and will you let us be murdered in the heart of Naples by brigands?"

The police agents and the crowd now came to the rescue, though in a half-hearted manner.

Barboni's name had frightened them.

Jack was dealing blows right and left.

But he was soon obliged to discontinue the conflict, because citizens and bandits became so mingled together that he did not know friend from foe.

Suddenly the brigands withdrew in a body down the street, carrying off their wounded with them.

At least a dozen men had fallen before Jack and the coxswain.

But each man was singled out and picked up.

The people did not seem to care to follow the brigands, nor did the police agents show any alacrity in the pursuit.

Jack's first thought was of Emily. He went to the spot where he had left her.

She was not to be seen. With a heart-broken cry he sank against the wall.

"Good God!" he said, in a moaning tone. "She is gone."

Rousing himself, he looked about in every direction, but could discover no sign of his beloved wife.

Emily was in the power of Barboni.

Walter Campbell was only stunned, and he quickly got on his legs, rubbing his head and looking about him.

"Jack," he said, "where are you?"

"Here," replied Jack, pushing his way through the crowd.

"Gad, how pale you look!" said the coxswain. "Did you get a topper, like me?"

"Emily's gone," answered Jack.

"Gone!"

"Yes, the brigands have carried her off."

"By Jove, that's bad news, and I'd rather they'd have smashed me into bits than that should have happened; but cheer up, old fellow, we'll soon have her back again."

"I can't cheer up," said Jack, gloomily, and leaning upon his iron bar, a tear fell from his eye.

"What curs those fellows are," said Walter; "they might have done something."

"Not they," replied Jack. "Neapolitans won't help an Inglesi; they hate us too much. But for God's sake, let's do something."

"Do what?"

"Go after Emily. See the general, and get him to send out the soldiers; a troop of cavalry might hold the roads."

"Of course," said Walter. "Come on; buckle to."

They joined arms, and pushing their way through the stupid, gazing, chattering crowd, they gained the Corso.

Here they saw a carriage, jumped in, and were driven to General Cialdini's.

Jack was mad with rage and grief, but he did his best to keep calm.

Barboni had dealt him a terrible blow.

It was like losing his life to have Emily torn from him by such a miscreant.

CHAPTER XXIX.

IN THE POWER OF BARBONI.

As Harkaway had imagined, Emily had been seized by the brigands in the confusion.

A cloak was thrown over her head, which effectively smothered her cries.

Lifted up by strong arms, she was half-carried, half-dragged along.

At the end of the Strada a carriage with two horses was in waiting.

Lifting her into this, Barboni took a place by her side. Two men stood at the door awaiting instructions.

They were the lieutenants of the band.

"You, Hunstoni," said the chief to one who had lost an arm, "will at once lead the men out of the city."

The man saluted in military fashion and fell back.

"To you, Darrelli," continued Barboni, "I assign the task of protecting and bringing up the rear. Retire across country. Leave the wounded at the Sybil's cave. The dead you must abandon."

Darrelli also saluted, and the carriage drove off at a rapid pace.

It was not until the last lamp of the city had disappeared in the distance that the stifling cloak was removed from Emily's face.

She saw Barboni seated opposite her, regarding her respectfully, and smoking a cigarette.

"For Heaven's sake, release me," she said, in a broken voice.

"That is impossible," replied Barboni, calmly.

"What do you mean to do with me?"

"Your treatment will depend upon circumstances. For the present it is enough for you to know that you are my prisoner."

"Jack will have a terrible revenge for this."

"He is at liberty to try."

"I have seen danger before," continued Emily, "and I have been a captive amongst cannibals and savages, from whom I received consideration and attention. May I hope for the same from you and your men?"

"I trust," replied Barboni, "that though we are brigands, you will find us gentlemen."

"That is all I ask."

"We are always weak and yielding when a lady is in the case."

"So long as my captivity does not subject me to insult and ill-usage, I can bear it; though if you want money, I am sure you can obtain a heavy ransom for me."

"Money at present is not my object," he answered.

"You will not accept a ransom?"

"No."

The light of hope which had momentarily illumined her eyes died out.

"I warned you," continued Barboni, "that by staying in Naples you and yours would incur danger. You would not go away, and you are reaping the consequences."

"I cannot help it," said Emily, with a sigh of resignation. "There is one in Heaven mightier than you, and He will protect me."

Barboni bowed as if he was not prepared to enter into a discussion on this point.

Though not in good health, Emily behaved with a calm courage that was admirable.

She did not go into hysterics and beg wildly for mercy that she knew would not be shown her.

Her faith was in Heaven.

Her trust was in her husband.

She felt confident that Jack would move heaven and earth, and leave no stone unturned to effect her release.

Barboni had told her that she should meet with respectful treatment, and she could expect no more.

At the river Volturno she alighted and crossed in a small boat.

Here an escort awaited her, and strongly guarded, she was conducted the remainder of the distance to the robber's cave on foot.

It was dark, and there was no necessity to blindfold her, as she could make no observations on the road.

At length the entrance to the cavern was reached, and she was conducted through winding galleries to a vaulted chamber, which was illuminated by an oil lamp, suspended by a chain from the ceiling.

It was roughly, but not uncomfortably furnished, being provided with a couch, table, and chairs.

A doorway communicated with an inner room, which was fitted up with a bed, looking-glass, washstand, and other things appertaining to a bedchamber.

This was also lighted up by an oil lamp, whose reflected rays showed that, like the sitting-room, the sandstone floor was destitute of a carpet.

"Signora," said the brigand, as he ushered her in, "these are your apartments. I regret that they are not handsomer and larger."

"Thank you; they are better than I expected," she replied.

"You will be attended by a boy we call Luni. I shall not lock the door leading into the gallery, as you will have no chance of escape, the outlets being guarded day and night by sentinels."

"If you give me an opportunity, I shall use my wings and fly away," said Emily, smiling for the first time.

The brigand's manner and treatment served to inspire her with happier thoughts.

"Breakfast, dinner, and tea will be brought you by Luni," continued the chief. "And on that table you will find English books and papers to while away the time."

Again Emily expressed her thanks to him.

"*Buon notte*, signora," said Barboni, raising his plumed hat respectfully. "I trust you will give us poor devils the praise of doing our best for our lady prisoners."

"Certainly. I have much to be grateful for," replied Emily.

The next moment she was alone.

Fatigued and exhausted by the stirring events of the evening, she drank some water that stood in a carafe on a shelf, and entering the second chamber, placed the washstand in the doorway as a barrier to impertinent intrusion.

Then, dressed as she was, she threw herself on the bed, and soon fell into a fitful slumber.

She woke early in the morning, it

"ON THEY CAME WITH A RUSH."

being half-past six by her watch, and went into her sitting-room.

The lamp seemed to have been trimmed, for it burned as brightly as ever.

She had not been long alone before the boy Luni entered, carrying a tray of breakfast things.

"I'm told off to wait on you," he said.

"Are you Luni?" asked Emily.

"That's what they call me, though she says I've got another."

"Who's she?"

"Why, don't you know? They're all afraid of her. Some say she's soft in her upper story like me. Anyhow, she does go on fearful if they knock her about."

"Does Barboni ill-treat her?" asked Emily, interested.

"Sometimes, though not often. When she's very bad he has her shut up in the caves for weeks, and that tames her."

"Have you ever been shut up in the caves?"

"Yes, more than once."

"Where are they?" continued Emily.

"Under the—but I mustn't talk too much, or else I shall get a beating," said the boy, breaking off in alarm.

"Do they beat you, poor child?"

"Oh, yes; everybody beats Luni. It's a kick here and a curse there."

"Why do you stay?"

"Stay! Where could I go to? Who'd have poor Luni? I've grown up here. They feed me, and I don't know anyone else; besides, I've got to like her."

"Come here, Luni; I want to talk to you," said Emily.

"But you mustn't talk loud, else they'll hear," replied the lad, timidly.

"What is this woman like? Is she a lady?"

"What's a lady?"

"Why, a person well and neatly dressed, quiet in her manner, well educated, and all that."

"Her dress isn't much. They give her some stuff to make up at times, and she goes on dreadfully, I tell you, when she's put out," said Luni.

"Can I see her?"

"I daresay you will. She's always wandering about when she isn't shut up in the caves."

"Is she fond of you?"

"Yes; she kisses me, and calls me her darling. No one else ever did that," replied Luni.

"Then she loves you. She must have a good heart. Bring her to see me, Luni, there's a good boy," replied Emily.

"I'll tell her. When will you have your breakfast?"

"Presently."

Luni went away, evidently fearful that he had stayed too long.

Emily was much surprised to hear of this fellow captive, for she could be nothing else, and hoped, by seeing her, to get at some of the secrets of the brigand's stronghold.

That there was some terrible history attached to her, she did not doubt.

Perhaps she had been carried off from home and friends, and was forced to pine away in captivity, until reason itself tottered on its throne before the assaults of her brutal captors.

Luni proved an excellent attendant, and she obtained everything she asked for, from a pockethandkerchief to a hairbrush and comb.

She did not fret much, for she had confidence in Jack.

It will be recollected that Emily was always a jolly, plucky sort of girl, not given to fainting and crying.

She was like Jack in one respect—if she got into a scrape, through no fault of her own, she tried to get out of it again as soon and as well as possible.

It was one comfort to reflect that Jack must know that she was in the hands of the brigands.

Her disappearance was not mysterious.

After breakfast she took up a book, and throwing herself on the couch, began to read a book.

The light of the lamp fell upon the paper, and she read without difficulty.

She had not been long engaged in this manner when footsteps were heard, and a man appeared before her.

Emily looked at him, and almost hesitated to believe the evidence of her senses.

"Can it be you?" she exclaimed. "I thought you were dead or hiding somewhere."

"Perhaps you wished me dead, and as for hiding, what do you call being here?" was the reply.

"Well, you have astonished me," she

said; "I should never have dreamt of meeting such an old enemy as Hunston in this place."

"It's a strange transformation," said the man, bitterly, "but so it is."

"Jack doesn't know this."

"He will sooner than he expects. In Hunstoni, the lieutenant of the brigand band, he will recognise Hunston, his old schoolfellow."

"How you have changed since those days, Hunston," said Emily.

Her mind went back to the time when she knew the boys as playmates at Pomona House.

"Who made me what I am?" cried Hunston, fiercely.

"Well?" she ejaculated, calmly.

"Your husband."

"I deny that!" said Emily, her eyes flashing.

"I tell you Harkaway made me what I am—a thief, a murderer, a brigand, a wretch flying from justice, for whom the scaffold waits; a mutilated being, an outcast!"

"No, no," answered Emily, "you wrong him, indeed you do. Jack has always tried to be your friend."

Hunston laughed scornfully.

"What's the use of talking such bosh to me?" he exclaimed.

"It isn't bosh," persisted Emily. "Didn't he spare your life when he might have shot you, as you were crossing the stream at the place near the river."

"His nerve failed him, I expect."

"No, it was his generosity of heart. He wouldn't take an advantage of an old friend."

"Pity he didn't; my career would have been ended then, and I should have had something to thank him for."

Hunston sank into a chair, overcome by the vehemence of his feelings.

The sight of Emily made all his past life rise up in judgment, as it were, against him.

"Are you so miserable, then?" said Emily, kindly.

"I'm never happy when I'm sober," answered Hunston.

Emily shuddered at this revelation.

It was indeed a confession of utter and complete heart-desolation and soul-deadness.

"How different your career might have been," she said.

"Might!"

"Yes, if you had been a better man. You and I, Hunston, have known one another for a long time, have we not?"

Hunston growled assent.

"During the whole time, have I ever known any good of you? Have you ever done a kind action or said a kind word to anyone? Have you got a friend in the world?"

"No," he said fiercely.

"And your worst enemy is yourself."

"Don't madden me," he exclaimed. "It is too late to think of that now."

"It is never too late to mend."

"That is what the preaching fellows say. No; I shall die as I have lived, a villain."

Again Emily shuddered.

"But," she said, "you admit you are not happy. Why not leave these evil companions, quit this dangerous life, and retire to some quiet spot in Italy or Spain, and work honestly for a living?"

"Harkaway has stopped that."

"How?"

"Didn't he shoot at me," said Hunston, "and make me lose my arm? How can a one-armed chap get a living?"

"It was your fault; you brought it all on yourself."

"Did I," said Hunston with a sneer. "Wait till I get hold of Mr. Harkaway. I'll break both his arms, and see how he likes to go about with none at all."

"Keep your threats until you do meet him. Don't insult me," said Emily, boldly. "I won't say you're no gentleman, but you are not a man to say such things to a wife in the position I am."

"Forgive me," replied Hunston. "At times I believe I'm half mad, what with the drink, and one thing and another."

"How did you come here?" she asked, wishing to turn the conversation.

"I escaped to Naples, and hearing of Barboni, the chief of the brigands, I resolved to join him."

"Do you like him?"

"I admire him; he's the cleverest and most unscrupulous scoundrel unhung."

"And that is a recommendation in your eyes?"

"Rather; he's a beauty in his way," said Hunston.

"What does he intend to do with me?" inquired Emily, hiding her anxiety for his reply under a calm exterior.

"He brought you here for me."

"For you?"

"Yes. You must know by this time that I love you."

Their eyes met.

His fell beneath her look of indignant scorn.

"And you must know by this time," she replied, "that if I do not hate you, I can only despise you and pity you."

"Perhaps you'll alter your mind some day," he said.

"Not I; you forget I am a married woman now, and I would rather die than listen to any words I ought not to hear from you."

"You are in my power."

"So I have been before. You have carried me off more than once, and that sort of thing becomes monotonous by repetition."

She laughed a little sarcastic, defiant laugh.

"This time will settle it," said Hunston savagely. "It will be either marriage with me, or——"

He hesitated as if he did not like to pronounce the word.

"Well, go on," she said calmly.

"Death."

"Very good, indeed," said Emily. "Quite melodramatic. You have not forgotten your old accomplishment of threatening a defenceless woman."

"I mean what I say."

"Possibly," she replied with a look of indifference.

Another footstep was heard, and presently a second man entered the room.

But he approached with a polite bow and an air of slight embarrassment.

Emily stared at him with more surprise than she had at Hunston.

"Do my eyes deceive me?" she exclaimed; "or is it——"

"Gus Darrel; at your service, Mrs Harkaway," was the cool answer.

"More surprises," she exclaimed. "Here is my old enemy, Mr. Hunston, and now I see my old—may I say friend?—Lord Darrel."

"By all means. I hope you will never have occasion to regard me as anything else."

Emily smiled upon him.

She saw the advantage of having a friend in Gus Darrel, because his influence would counteract the hostility of Hunston.

In her heart she was afraid of the latter.

During the interview, as far as it had gone, she had not displayed any fear.

But really she felt a great dread of this man, who was all he had described himself to be — drunkard, blackguard, thief, bandit, murderer.

"Will your lordship have the kindness to explain your presence on this shifting scene?" she asked.

"With pleasure. You remember of course my unlucky blow, which settled poor young Cockles?" he asked.

"It is fresh in my memory."

"Well, I could not stand a trial in England, so I came over here by chance, and meeting with Barboni, joined him."

"Why follow up one stupid act by another?"

"Oh, I was desperate, reckless, and did it for the fun of the thing."

"The descent of Avernus is easy," remarked Emily.

"But if I am to descend Mount Avernus in such delightful company as yours, Mrs. Harkaway, I shall not regret it."

"No?"

"Not in the least. But allow me to ask you a question?"

"Certainly."

"What has become of Lily Cockles and her father?"

"Poor Lily?" said Emily feelingly. "Her father died of grief at the death of his son."

"Is the old man dead?" said Lord Darrel, rather touched.

"He is. And Lily was so affected by the double loss of father and brother, that she has been put in a lunatic asylum by her friends."

"Good Heaven! and I am the cause of all this."

He covered his face for a moment with his hands.

"You have much to answer for, my lord," observed Emily.

"I have indeed," he replied, looking up with a haggard expression.

"Did you ever really love Lily?"

"No. I admired her a little, but I

always thought you in every way incomparably her superior."

Hunston jumped up angrily.

"Look here," he said; "if you want to snivel at what you have done, go outside and do it."

"It was only a passing emotion," replied Gus Darrel. "I am not so hardened as you are."

"What business have you here at all?"

"Mrs. Harkaway is as much an acquaintance of mine as yours."

"I don't choose to have fellows poaching upon my preserves," said Hunston.

"Then you must do the other thing, must he not, Mrs. Harkaway?" replied Gus Darrel, laughingly.

"I am sure, my lord, I find you a more agreeable companion than Mr. Hunston," said Emily.

"I am much obliged to you for the compliment."

"Look here, Darrel," said Hunston, all his evil nature coming out of his eyes.

"Well?"

"I must have a word with you. Come outside."

"We shall meet presently, and then you can say what you like."

"No. Now, now!"

"Don't be a fool, my good fellow. I want to talk to Mrs. Harkaway," said Gus Darrel, in his obstinate manner.

"Signors Hunstoni and Darrelli," exclaimed Emily, "those are your new titles, I believe—don't quarrel."

"I have no wish to do anything of the sort," said Darrel. "I never do make a row before ladies. It is bad form. Hunston ought to know better."

With a subdued growl, Hunston sank back again on his seat, and biting his nails glared at each of them in turn.

"What do you want here at all?" he asked in a savage tone.

"I heard that the lovely captive we had taken was Mrs. Harkaway, and I thought I had as much right to pay my respects to her as you."

"I will ask the chief about that."

"You may ask what you like," replied Darrel; "I wanted to assure Mrs. Harkaway that she had one friend amongst us."

"I am sure of that, my lord," answered Emily, with one of her sweetest smiles.

She saw more than ever how important it was to conciliate Gus Darrel.

"Do you think you are more to Barboni than I am?" growled Hunston.

"Anyhow, we occupy the same position in the band."

"No, we don't."

"How do you make that out?"

"I'm first lieutenant and you are second," replied Hunston.

"That makes little difference. I have done as good service as you."

"So you say."

"Well, I take it a man with two arms is better than a fellow with only one."

"Do you taunt me with that?" cried Hunston, his eyes flashing fire.

"I only mention the fact; and I repeat that I hope Mrs. Harkaway will look upon me as a friend."

"I do, indeed, my lord," she replied.

"As for Harkaway, I have always had a respect for him. He was a brother officer in my regiment, and though we snarled at times, I never thought him anything but a fine fellow."

"And I hate him," said Hunston.

"Possibly. There are some minds that can never rise above the dead level of hatred."

"Don't say too much," exclaimed Hunston.

"I have done. You know my sentiments; and if Mrs. Harkaway requires my protection or my services at any time, she can command them."

Emily's eyes danced with delight.

She felt certain now that Darrel admired her beauty.

It was fortunate that it was so.

She could play off one against the other, and Darrel would be an effectual barrier against the persecution of Hunston.

Nothing could have happened better.

CHAPTER XXX.

THE QUARREL IN THE CAVE.

HUNSTON was now thoroughly aroused.

He could see that Darrel meant to step between him and his plans.

His idea was to revenge himself upon Jack by carrying off his wife, and making her his wife by force.

Barboni had been very adverse to this.

The brigand chief had sense enough to tell that there was a great deal of danger in abducting Emily.

It would make the war between him and the four friends more bitter than ever.

But Hunston had been a good servant, and he claimed Emily as his reward.

He did not know that Darrel was acquainted with her.

All he knew of his lordship was that he had killed his man in England, and was obliged to fly from justice.

There were men of nearly every nation who had enrolled themselves with Barboni.

Each had his history.

It was a tale of crime.

Some offence, either murder, robbery, arson, or something disgraceful against the laws of their country.

"You seem to be very thin-skinned," said Hunston; "but it strikes me you are a murderer."

"I did kill a man by an unfortunate blow," replied Darrel, "and I'm sorry for it."

"That shows you're a sneak."

"Shall I tell you why I am sorry?" asked Darrel, quietly.

"Because your conscience smites you, as the Bible people say, I suppose."

"You're wrong," replied Darrel. "I am only sorry because it has brought me in contact with such a howling snob as you are."

Hunston sprang up, and clenched his one fist.

"By Jove! if I had two hands I'd mark you for that," he cried.

"But you haven't, my lad," answered Gus Darrel.

"I've got a dagger, though, and that will let the daylight into you."

He drew a dagger from his waist belt, and rushed upon Darrel, who was unarmed.

With a scream, Emily threw herself between them.

She feared that Hunston would kill her friend and protector.

If Darrel loved her, she knew that he was a gentleman, and would not take any unfair advantage of her, while Hunston was so unscrupulous that her virtue would be at his mercy.

"You shall not hurt him," she exclaimed, pushing back the dagger.

"Do you take his part? That seals his fate," replied Hunston, savagely.

He threw Emily roughly on one side, and again rushed upon Gus Darrel, who had taken up a chair to defend himself.

Emily piled scream upon scream, until the hollow cavern echoed with her voice.

Suddenly a tall form marched rapidly into the room.

With a sharp blow he drove Hunston back.

"Put up your dagger," he exclaimed; "I am master here."

It was Barboni.

Such was the extraordinary influence of this remarkable man over all with whom he came in contact, that Hunston, bully and blackguard as he was, shrank away, cowed and abashed.

"What is the meaning of this?" he asked, in English.

"Hunston wanted to knife me, or perform some other equally agreeable process on my person," replied Gus Darrel.

"I will have no fighting here," said Barboni. "Is the woman the cause?"

"Yes, she is," answered Hunston.

"Then I forbid either of you to enter these apartments again, without my express permission, on pain of death."

"You know what you promised me," said Hunston.

"Silence! Begone! I will talk to you elsewhere."

Hunston hesitated.

"What! do you dispute my commands?" roared the brigand. "By the heavens above us, if you linger another instant, I will send a bullet through your heart, with as little compunction as I would shoot a dog."

Hunston half drew his dagger, and glared fiercely at the bandit. He did not dare to disobey any longer.

He stuck his dagger in his belt once more, and bestowing a vindictive look upon Darrel, strode from the cave.

Turning to Emily, Barboni said—

"Signora, I am deeply grieved to think you should have been annoyed in this manner."

"Don't mention it," replied Emily. "So long as blood is not shed, I do not care."

"You shall not be interrupted again, with my knowledge."

"Oh," said Emily, "I shall be pleased to see Lord Darrel at any time, and even Mr. Hunston, if they will not fight."

"Can you blame me?" asked Gus Darrel.

"No, I don't."

"You are the Helen of this Trojan war; but I will keep Mr. Hunston quiet, never fear."

"Come with me, Darrel," said Barboni. "We have business to transact together."

They bowed politely to Emily, and quitted her apartments.

Traversing the gallery, they passed through the outer cave, which, as usual, was filled with brigands.

The men saluted their chief, in a rough sort of fashion, but not with the heartiness that formerly characterised them.

They had suffered severely in the attack that Jack had made upon them after the ambush, and they had not forgotten the terrible onslaught of Jack and the little coxswain, in the Strada D'Italia, with the iron bars, wrenched from the old railings.

Barboni, who was as sharp as a needle, saw that his popularity was waning amongst them.

Hurrying Darrel into the open air, he took his arm for a stroll through the forest glades.

"You must not have an open quarrel with Hunston," he said.

"I don't want to," replied Darrel, "but I won't let a fellow like that ride over me."

"He is useful to me. The men have confidence in him; and what has happened lately has made them dissatisfied."

"I am sorry for that."

"What is this lady to you?" asked Barboni, turning sharply upon him.

"Nothing particular. I knew her in England, and I like her."

"Is that all?"

Again the searching glance seemed to read him like a book.

"Well, if it comes to that," replied Gus Darrel, "and the lady is to be sacrificed to anyone, she shall be my wife sooner than Hunston's."

"I feared this," said Barboni.

"Why?"

"Hunston is unscrupulous and vindictive, though brave as a lion. Have you remarked that I have been very careful over your life?"

"In what way?"

"Whenever there has been any enterprise of danger on hand, I have sent Hunston in command, not you."

"I would have gone as readily," said Darrel.

"I know it. I am not impeaching your courage, but your life is precious to me," said Barboni.

"How is that? You never knew me before I came over here, and met you by chance in Naples, where you were beating up for recruits."

"Perhaps," said Barboni, "I know more about you than you imagine."

"Have we ever met before?"

"Yes."

"When?" demanded Darrel, in a tone of surprised curiosity.

"In your infancy. I can say no more; some day you may know all."

Barboni seemed affected in a strange manner, and his agitation was not lost upon Gus Darrel.

"I can't understand you," he remarked.

"It is impossible that I can explain further at present," replied the brigand; "all I can say is, that there was more than chance in our meeting—it was fate."

"What connection can there be between you, an Italian brigand, and me, Lord Darrel, a peer of England?"

"That is the mystery," answered Barboni, with a quiet but sad smile.

"Will you not explain it?"

"I have told you it is impossible. Let

it be enough for you that I love you as if you were my—my own son."

The brigand's voice trembled as he spoke.

"Much obliged, I'm sure," said Darrel, twisting his moustache in his old supercilious manner.

"There must be no collision between you and Hunston," continued Barboni, recovering himself and speaking in his usual sharp, decisive way.

"Let him keep away from Mrs. Harkaway then."

"I will manage that as well as I can. It is a pity that I brought her here, though I promised him that I would do so as a reward for his bravery."

"Indeed!"

"It appears that he hates Harkaway, and has been after the lady all his life."

"If he dares to touch a hair of her head," said Darrel angrily, "he shall answer to me for it."

"Still you must not be provoked, and I can have no quarrel between you."

"Which do you like best?"

"You, my dear boy," replied Barboni. "I would sacrifice a thousand Hunstons for you, but——"

"What?" demanded Darrel, as the brigand paused.

"We are in danger. My exploits lately have stirred up the government against us. Harkaway and his friends have sworn to hunt us down."

"They have to do it yet."

"I am not afraid, far from it," said Barboni; "yet we must be watchful and united. We can afford no dissension in our camp."

"As far as I'm concerned, there will be none," replied Gus Darrel.

"That's right. Meet Hunston in a friendly spirit, and let us go hand in hand to success."

They walked in silence under the leafy trees, listening to the humming of the insects under the influence of the morning sun.

"Will you tell me what you knew about me when I was very young?" asked Darrel, suddenly.

"Not now," replied the brigand, who seemed ill at ease.

"I have heard about my father's death," continued Darrel, whose brow was clouded, and lips contracted; "they all tried to keep it from me, but I know that he was murdered."

Barboni turned very white.

"My mother disappeared, and I have some recollection of a foreigner, who was our steward, being mixed up in the affair," continued Gus Darrel.

"It was a sad affair," said Barboni, speaking with difficulty; "I too have heard of it."

"What was it all?"

"My knowledge is very imperfect. Another time we will talk—not now. I have to go to the sybil's cave, and see the wounded in last night's affray."

"Shall I go with you?"

"No. I go alone."

"Do you return soon?"

"To-morrow morning. To-night I shall astonish all Naples, and Barboni's name shall be in every mouth in Europe within the next twenty-four hours."

"That's right; never do things by halves," said Darrel, laughing.

"Promise me you will not provoke Hunston," said Barboni.

"I'll make no promise. If the fellow cheeks me, he will get a bit of my mind to a moral certainty."

"Then I must take him with me," said the brigand chief, after a moment's reflection. "Tell him, please, to follow me to the cave of the sybil, with twenty-five picked men, all armed to the teeth."

"I wish you'd take me," said Darrel.

"Not this time."

"I'm getting quite rusty for want of a little excitement."

"You had some last night," replied Barboni.

"Oh! that was nothing—a mere flea bite. You say you are going to astonish the world to night, and I should like to be in it."

"No," replied Barboni, a second time; "I may not come back alive."

"Is it so desperate as all that?"

"It is indeed."

Gus Darrel looked at him in wondering admiration.

"If I should be captured," said Barboni, "you will open my private desk—you know where it is—and in it you will find papers of interest to yourself."

Darrel gazed at him now in astonishment, mixed with wonder.

"No more at present. Deliver my

orders. You have my blessing," said Barboni.

He wrung Darrel's hand, and rushed away, leaving him much impressed, for he had never seen the brigand so agitated.

It was a glimpse into his inner self.

In spite of his atrocious cruelty and rugged exterior, he had his feelings.

More than that, it was clear that he had a heart.

The enterprise that he had in hand must be of a dangerous nature indeed, thought Darrel, to agitate Barboni in such a manner.

Nor was he wrong.

It was the most audacious scheme that he had yet invented, and dared to carry into execution.

The Contessa Di Malafedi received the *élite* of Naples that evening in her most sumptuous rooms.

General Cialdini and his staff were to be present, and a brilliant gathering was expected.

Barboni had determined to be there too, and to rob everyone in the saloon of the precious stones and money which they might carry about them.

To plunder the English was one thing, to despoil the leaders of fashion in Naples, themselves being Neapolitan, was another.

It was a rash enterprise, and even the author of it had his doubts as to its success.

But he was a remarkable man, and had every confidence in himself, as far as human foresight and daring could protect him.

He walked quickly to the banks of the Volturno, crossed over in a boat he kept concealed for that purpose, and made his way rapidly to the cave of the Cumæan sybil.

Here he was to await the coming of his lieutenant, Hunston, with the band of picked men armed to the teeth.

As for Gus Darrel, he returned to the cave to deliver his orders, and was unable to account for the strange way in which his chief had spoken to him.

He had been so different in his manner to what he usually was.

There was a tenderness in his tone, an almost parental tenderness, which astonished him.

He could not understand this mysterious man at all.

"At all events," he said to himself, "I will protect the pretty Mrs. Harkaway. That villain Hunston shall not have it all his own way."

Providence had raised up a protector for Emily when she least expected it.

So it is in life.

When the clouds gather, or the prospect is most gloomy, an unlooked-for gleam of sunshine darts forth to glad our heavy hearts.

We should never despair.

CHAPTER XXXI.

CAPTURE OF THE BRIGAND CHIEF.

WHEN Jack went to General Cialdini to complain of the abduction of Emily by the brigands, he was received with the courtesy which was always extended to him by the general.

Immediate orders were given to the troops quartered in Naples to scour the country, and intercept the brigands in their retreat if possible.

The police were put on the alert also.

But the Neapolitans did everything in a half-and-half manner.

There was no spirit, no life, no heart about them.

They did not do things as we do them in England—with a slap and a dash.

Jack returned to his home after a fruitless search with the little coxswain.

It was nearly four o'clock in the morning.

They were both knocked up.

Harvey, Hilda, and Tom Carden were all waiting up for them, and thought that Emily had gone to join her husband.

Their alarm was great when they heard what had happened.

"We must get her back," said Carden. "This won't do at all."

"I'm dead-beat," said the coxswain. "What with hunting for brigands, and getting knocked on the head, and fighting with iron bars, I'm regularly licked."

"Go to sleep, little man," observed Carden. "Sleep is good for children."

"I think I'll take your advice," answered Walter Campbell; "and if no one has any objection, I'll pitch on the sofa."

He threw himself down, and was fast asleep in a minute.

Hilda was much concerned at Emily's loss, but she said she had no doubt the brigands would demand a heavy ransom, and she would be returned.

After talking the matter over, all retired to rest.

The next morning they were up early, and Tom Carden came from his hotel to breakfast.

Jack could not eat in his usual hearty manner, for his mind was disturbed by thoughts of his darling wife.

That she was treated with civility by the brigands he did not know.

Neither was he aware that Darrel was with the band, and had determined to protect her against Hunston, of whose presence in Naples he was also ignorant.

Soon after breakfast, the four friends held another brief council, and horses were ordered; they intended to scour the country.

Just as they were about to start, Bigamini made his appearance at the front door.

Monday, who was looking out for the arrival of the horses from the stable, saw him.

He grew very angry.

"Ha," he cried; "you come back. What for you put me in chest? I teach you to come sneaking about um house."

"My good friend," replied Bigamini, "you entirely misunderstand my character."

"Take um hook," said Monday.

"I want to see your master, kind and considerate negro. Ah! if I have a weakness, it is one for converting the heathen from their savage ways."

"Why you call me heathen savage? Me as good as you."

"Quite," replied Bigamini, humbly. "I have always considered a black infinitely superior to a white."

"You chaff me?" asked Monday.

"No, my sable friend, I have always been the friend of your persecuted race. Let me grasp your manly hand, and forget the past."

Monday held back.

"You're not a bad fellow," cried Bigamini, persuasively. "Your heart is in the right place. You will not despise me because I am a miserable Bigamini?"

"Um not want to despise anyone," answered Monday, who was softened by the meekness of the little man's manner.

"What have you to fear from me?" Bigamini went on. "Are you not stronger than me? Could you not eat me if you liked? Shake hands and stand a drink."

"You come in my room and have glass of um wine, if you please."

"That's right; hit 'em up, boys, they're all cocks," cried Bigamini. "I knew we should pal up."

If he had been insolent, Monday would have kicked him out, but as he was meek and civil, he softened towards him.

Leading the way into his pantry, he poured out a tumbler full of wine and ice for his guest.

"That warm um up a bit," said he.

"Thank you," replied Bigamini; "my heart overflows with gratitude. Now let us have a little chat. What's your master going to do?"

"Get back um missis," answered Monday.

"Those brigands are desperate fellows."

"They soon laugh wrong side of um mouth," replied Monday.

Jack's voice was heard in the hall.

"Monday," he said, "what a time the horses are coming round. Where are you?"

Hastily putting the bottle and glass away, Monday answered—

"In um pantry, sare."

Jack came to the little room and looked in.

"What are you doing here?" he asked, as soon as his eyes fell upon Bigamini.

"Come to see my friend, Mr. Monday, sir. Person I esteem very highly, I assure you, sir," answered Bigamini.

"I have my suspicions about you," said Jack, with a frown.

"What have I done, sir?"

"It's my opinion you're a humbug."

Bigamini looked deeply hurt.

"If bigamy and poverty are crimes, sir," he said, "I plead guilty; but if any one had dared to attack my honour when I was a happy Smiffins, I'd have knocked his head off."

He tried to look very fierce, and twisted a little bit of moustache which disfigured his upper lip.

"Just explain how it was that you came here last night, and how you knew the Signora Bianca. I can't help thinking you are mixed up in this affair somehow."

"This is hard, sir," said the little man. "Until I yielded to the force of circumstances and the power of love, which made me a miserable Bigamini, my character would have borne looking at through a powerful microscope."

"That is not an explanation."

"The artist, sir, lodges in the same house with me—that's how I knew her; and if a stranger offers me a ducat in the street to deliver a letter to a certain party, I should be a flat if I refused it."

"A stranger?"

"Yes, sir. I could not tell that he was connected with brigands; and I have come here to-day to tender my most humble apologies."

The man looked sincere, and Jack, who was in a great hurry to be off, did not care to push his examination further.

"Be more careful in future," he said, "and keep your eyes open; you may hear or see something which will be of use to us."

"May I have the proud privilege of accompanying you, sir?"

"When?"

"This morning, in your search for the brigands. Oh! if I could only give it that Barboni hot and strong, I should die happy."

"I don't see what good you can do," replied Jack.

"I can crawl into holes in rocks, sir, and if we find a cave, you can send me in like a dog or a ferret."

"Can you ride?"

"A little, sir. I don't look graceful," replied Bigamini. "You know what ill-natured people say about a tailor on horseback."

"Well," said Jack, with a slight laugh, "you shall go."

Bigamini danced for joy.

"Fancy my being admitted to the proud privilege of brigand-hunting in the distinguished company of Mr. Harkaway and friends!" he exclaimed.

"Cut round to the stable and get a horse. Quick!"

"I'm off, sir, like the arrow from the bow, or, more poetically, like the thunderbolt from the storm cloud. Hurrah! here's 'appiness. Hip, hip——"

"Stop his row," said Jack.

Monday slily put out his foot, and administered a kick to the little man.

"Shut up um mouth," he said, with a grin.

"Mr. Monday, sir," replied Bigamini, rubbing the injured part, "is this friendship, I ask you?"

"Mast' Jack's orders," replied Monday.

Bigamini looked at him, more in sorrow than in anger, gave himself another rub, and slowly quitted the pantry.

He went to the stable, which was not far off, and found Harvey's English coachman and a groom preparing to lead the saddle-horses out of the yard.

"Mr. Harkaway sent me for another horse," he said.

"For you?" asked the coachman.

"Yes. I'm going brigand hunting."

"Then you'd best turn it up, and stop at home. Take my tip, it's straight," answered the coachman.

"I'm not afraid. Give me a fast horse."

"There's Black Prince. He stands sixteen and a half hands, is nearly thoroughbred, kicks like blazes, bolts like old boots, and is a regular crib biter."

"That'll do," said Bigamini.

"What!" said the coachman. "Ain't you nervous?"

"Never was yet, except at the sight of my old woman. I'd rather mount your horse, than see my missis."

The coachman laughed, and muttered to himself——

"If chaps like to break their precious necks, it won't no business of his'n."

The horse with the bad character was saddled, and the others were taken round.

Jack, Carden, Harvey, and the little coxswain mounted, and when they were in the saddle, Bigamini trotted up.

"Which way, sir?" he asked.

"To the sybil's cave, first," said Jack.

"But, I say, you've got on an awkward sort of brute; did they tell you?"

"They said something about his being nasty-tempered, sir."

"He'll throw him," remarked Harvey.

"Get inside, old cock," observed the coxswain.

"And draw the blinds down," said Carden, drily.

"No fear, gents," replied Bigamini. "I can stick on like glue, and hold the reins with one hand and the pommel of the saddle with the other."

"Show us the way, then, and cut out the running," said Jack.

"We don't mean to let the grass grow under our feet," said Harvey.

"Right you are, gen'lemen all," cried Bigamini, who touched his horse with the whip.

The Black Prince put back his ears, uttered a snort, and, striking fire with his iron-shod hoofs, dashed off at a mad gallop.

"Bolted!" ejaculated Carden.

"I thought so," replied Jack. "Let's follow him. Are you ready, you fellows?"

The answer being in the affirmative, they started at a quick trot and soon got clear of the town.

All they could see of Bigamini was a cloud of dust in the distance, and this soon vanished.

His horse, going at racing speed, had taken him out of sight.

The four friends were too much in earnest to waste time in conversation.

As they passed a few lazy Neapolitans, the people regarded them wonderingly.

They thought them mad to go through the severe exercise of riding under a hot sun.

But, hot though it undoubtedly was, they would have gone through fire itself to rescue Emily.

Though they kept up their headlong pace, they could not overtake Bigamini.

Jack felt sorry that he had allowed him to go on such a horse, which was the most vicious beast they had in the stable.

Harvey had bought him because of his speed and cleverness at jumping, intending to get up some steeple chases, and show Naples how the English can win races.

At length the ravine leading to the sybil's cave came in view.

The horses were covered with foam, and their riders were white with dust and streaming with perspiration.

Slackening their speed, they walked their steeds, and Jack said—

"We will search the witch's cave before we go any further."

"Does the old hag sell beer?" asked the little coxswain.

"No."

"That's a pity. I'm regularly baked, and she might do a roaring trade in bitter for half an hour with me alone."

"Same here," replied Harvey.

"Don't you seem to like beer when you can't get it?" remarked Carden.

"Is that a horse," asked Jack, looking down the ravine. "Yes, by Jove! it's the Black Prince. Bigamini has arrived before us, and is cooling himself in the cave, I suppose."

They entered the ravine, feeling glad that the little man had not broken his neck.

Though they had their suspicions about him, they fancied he was more a fool than a knave.

It did not strike them that he had purposely ridden this horse, in order that he might arrive first at the cave.

If Barboni was inside, he could warn him of his danger.

Though a wild and lawless man, the brigand was not devoid of superstition.

He frequently visited the sybil, to consult her as to his fortune.

If she warned him against an enterprise, he would not undertake it.

Suddenly the four friends saw a man come out of the cave.

He looked stealthily up and down the ravine.

The little coxswain had eyes like a lynx, and one glance was enough for him.

"That's Barboni," he exclaimed. "Look! he answers all the descriptions of him; slouched hat, cloak, no beard, and fierce moustache."

"It's not unlike him," replied Jack.

"I tell you it is him. Didn't I and you see him last night when we fought the beggars with the iron railings?"

Jack dug his spurs into his jaded horse's flanks.

"Tally ho!" cried the coxswain. "Hark forrard. Tally ho!"

The others pressed on, and the clattering of the horses' hoofs on the hard, dry road reached the man's ears.

He took one more hurried, startled glance. It was enough. He did not hesitate a moment, but vaulted lightly on the back of Bigamini's horse.

Black Prince, however, had been "pumped out" by the tremendous pace he was ridden at for so many miles.

There was not much going in him.

Neither was there in the horses of those behind him, yet they were fresher, as they had not been pushed at the top of their speed.

Jack felt positive that the coxswain was right, and that the flying man before them was Barboni.

With a hoarse shout of triumph he dashed along.

Away went Barboni with our four friends at his heels.

It was an exciting chase.

Soon the coxswain forged ahead, and got dangerously near to the brigand.

Alarmed at hearing a pursuer so close behind him, he turned in the saddle.

Walter was within a dozen yards of him.

Jack came next, Harvey and Carden being side by side a short distance behind.

He took all this in a glance.

"You'd better give in," shouted the coxswain.

Barboni's reply was to draw a pistol, take deliberate aim, and fire.

But as he pulled the trigger, his tired horse stumbled, and the ball missed its mark. It was not wasted though.

The coxswain's horse, struck in the shoulder, fell in the dust, and shot his rider over his neck.

"Are you hurt ?" asked Jack, as he swept past.

"No," answered Walter, picking himself up.

Barboni's cruel face gleamed with a sparkle of triumph. One enemy was dismounted, if not killed.

Only three remained, and he had struggled with that odds before, and come off victorious.

Jack was satisfied now that he had the famous bandit before him.

He could not mistake that classic face, the thick moustache, the shaven chin, the proud curl of the lip, and the defiant glance of the savage eye.

Barboni urged his sinking horse to its utmost speed, but the poor creature was exhausted.

If he could only reach the banks of the Volturno, he should meet some of his men on their way to Naples, and he would be safe.

Jack now gained upon him.

The thundering of his horse warned Barboni that he was in danger again.

Another hurried look, and again the barrel of the revolver glistened in the sun.

"That's your game, is it ?" said Jack between his clenched teeth. "Two can play at that, my boy."

He too drew a pistol. The game was within range, and both fired at once.

Jack made his horse swerve on one side, and the bullet whistled harmlessly past.

But his ball broke the leg of Black Prince, and he fell down in a heap, plunging helplessly, and raising a cloud of dust.

In a moment, Jack was on the spot.

The dust settled, and revealed a black mass by the side of the horse, lying still and motionless.

This was the brigand, who had fallen from the saddle, to find the road harder than his head, and lie stunned.

"By Jove," cried Jack, " I've hit the brigand."

He took off the horse's curb rein, and making handcuffs of it, fastened Barboni's wrists together.

Then he dragged him to a bank by the river side, where the slight breeze could play upon his face, and waited for Carden and Harvey to come up.

He could scarcely believe in the reality of this splendid capture. It had all happened so quickly and smoothly, without much trouble or loss of life.

What neither the police of Naples nor all the troops under the command of General Cialdini could do, he had effected.

"Bravo! Harkaway," exclaimed Tom Carden, jumping from his horse.

"You've done the trick, I see," said Harvey, following.

"Yes. We have captured Barboni; and now his band will be like a venomous serpent without a head."

At the mention of his name, the brigand opened his eyes and looked around.

CHAPTER XXXII.

"WILL HE DO IT?"

AT the same moment the little coxswain, who had sustained only a few scratches, approached the friends.

"Hullo! old Tommy Dod," he exclaimed; "how do you find yourself, eh? How you was to-morrow, old Schneider?"

"I am a prisoner," answered the brigand, "yet that is no reason why I should be mocked by a boy."

"Can't you stand chaff! Sorry for you, then; you'll have to try."

"Harkaway, the Englishman, has captured me," continued Barboni, "and I expect that courtesy from him which I am at present extending to his wife."

"You admit that you are Barboni?" said Jack.

"I do, and still defy you."

The brigand drew himself up haughtily in the presence of his captors.

"Is my wife alive and well?" asked Jack, eagerly.

"She is."

"Her life is in no danger?"

"None. She is as well treated as circumstances will permit; and if you like to listen to reason, I will make you an offer."

"Name it," cried Jack, whose mind was much relieved by what he had heard.

"I will exchange Mrs. Harkaway for myself. Let me go, and you shall have your wife again."

The offer was very tempting, and Jack had a great mind to accept it.

What was the public execution of the brigand to the delight of clasping his beloved Emily once more in his arms?

Seeing that he was inclined to yield, Tom Carden spoke.

"I have a word to say in this, on public grounds," he exclaimed.

"Leave me to deal with Mr. Harkaway," cried the brigand, biting his lip with annoyance.

"You can say what you like, presently. I only wish to state that it would be madness to trust to your word."

"You need not give me my liberty until I place Mrs. Harkaway in your hands."

"You hear that, Tom?" cried Jack, eagerly.

"We are sure to get Emily, sooner or later," said Carden; "and I say we shall make a mull of it, and be a set of muffs, if we let this scamp go. It is a duty we owe to the public to stick to him like seven leeches."

There was another moment of hesitation, and then Jack's face cleared.

"You are right, Tom. I ought not to think only of myself in this case," he said.

"You agree with me, then?"

"I do. He is not our prisoner; he belongs to the state."

"That's my idea. We'll get Emily by-and-bye," exclaimed Carden; "never fear."

The brigand was silent, as if he would not condescend to beg any further for his liberty.

Jack had made an immense sacrifice, and only he himself knew what it had cost him.

But he had the consolation of feeling that he had done what was right.

Barboni rose and looked grand, even in his captivity.

He was a sort of Samson among the Philistines.

"Mr. Harkaway," he said; "I will not humble myself by arguing the point with you."

"Oh!" replied Jack, a little agitated; "I am willing to listen to you."

"It is your intention to deliver me to the authorities?"

"Certainly."

"Have you reflected?"

"It requires no thinking about. I was a little nervous about my poor wife at first, but directly Carden spoke, I saw he was right."

There was a noise in the distance.

Rub-a-dub-dub, tub-tub, tub-tub.

Tantara, tantara.

"The soldiers!" cried the little coxswain.

It was the drum and bugle of a body of Bersaglieri.

"Too late!" murmured the brigand.

Turning to Jack, he added—

"If anything happens to me, your wife

will die; my death will seal her fate," he said. "But if you hand me over to the soldiers as a prisoner of war, all will be well."

"I shall do so."

"You will not allow them to try me on a drum-head, and shoot me like a dog?"

"No, you will be tried by the courts at Naples; I promise you that," said Jack.

"Then all will be well. I may make terms for the release of Mrs. Harkaway."

"What terms?"

"I cannot talk now. Where shall you be this evening?"

"I am engaged," replied Jack; "the fact is we have all accepted invitations to be at the Contessa Di Malafedi's to-night."

"At the contessa's," repeated the brigand, carelessly.

"Yes."

"I thought you were not very good friends, since the Villanova affair and the scene at the sybil's grotto."

"Nor are we; but all Naples will be there, and to tell you the truth," answered Jack, "I wanted to ask the contessa to use her influence with you."

"With me. There is no connection between us."

"No? I thought there was, and she might obtain my wife's release."

"We will talk the matter over this evening," said Barboni.

"But I have told you I cannot come to your prison to-night."

"I do not want you to."

"Then how shall we meet?"

"At the contessa's. To-night, as the clock strikes twelve, I will be with you at La Malafedi's," answered Barboni, carelessly.

"Are you mad, man alive?" said Jack, staring at him.

"Do I look like it?"

"You will be in the securest dungeon the police can find for you, in a couple of hours' time."

"Never mind that. I will meet you at the contessa's as the clocks are on the stroke of midnight."

Barboni spoke with the certainty of conviction.

"Bet you six to four you don't," said the little coxswain.

"I don't bet with children," replied the brigand; "neither am I addressing my remarks to you."

"It's lucky for you you've got braceleted up," replied Walter, in a tone of deep disgust, "or I'd punch your head for cheek."

"Have you marked me well, Mr. Harkaway?" continued Barboni.

"Yes, I accept your meeting, though I fear there is little chance of your keeping your appointment," answered Jack.

"Time will show."

A little man was seen limping along the road, and as he drew nearer, the coxswain exclaimed—

"Here's that rascal Bigamini; he ought to be locked up too."

Bigamini heard this, and hastened to say—

"That's unkind, sir. I have always been respected as the soul of honour, and when I was a happy Smiffins——"

"How was it Barboni got out of the cave and nipped away almost in time to get off clear?"

"Is that Barboni?" asked Bigamini, straining his eyes at the chief.

"Yes."

"What, the great brigand?"

He drew back in alarm, and stared as if he had never seen him before.

"You don't mean to say he's the awful bandit?" he continued.

"Of course he is. Didn't you give him the tip that we were coming?"

"No, sir—on the honour of a once happy Smiffins, I did not. He can't get loose, sir, can he?"

"Not he."

"Ask him, sir, if I didn't see him in the cave, and if he didn't fall upon me, and we had a tussle in which he shinned me dreadful?"

"If it is of any service to the man," said Barboni, "I can say frankly I do not know him, nor have we met before."

"There! I told you he'd say I was nothing to him," cried Bigamini.

"When I heard a horse stop, and saw a man enter the cave while I was consulting the fortune-teller, I thought he was an enemy," Barboni went on.

"And we had a fight!"

"I simply knocked you down, and may have kicked your carcase out of my way," replied Barboni, with a look of supreme disdain.

EDWIN J. BRETT'S

JACK HARKAWAY AMONG THE BRIGANDS.

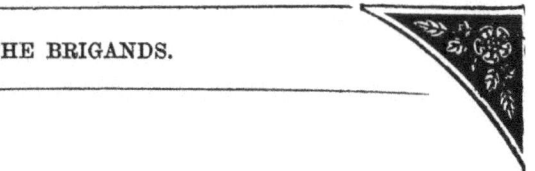

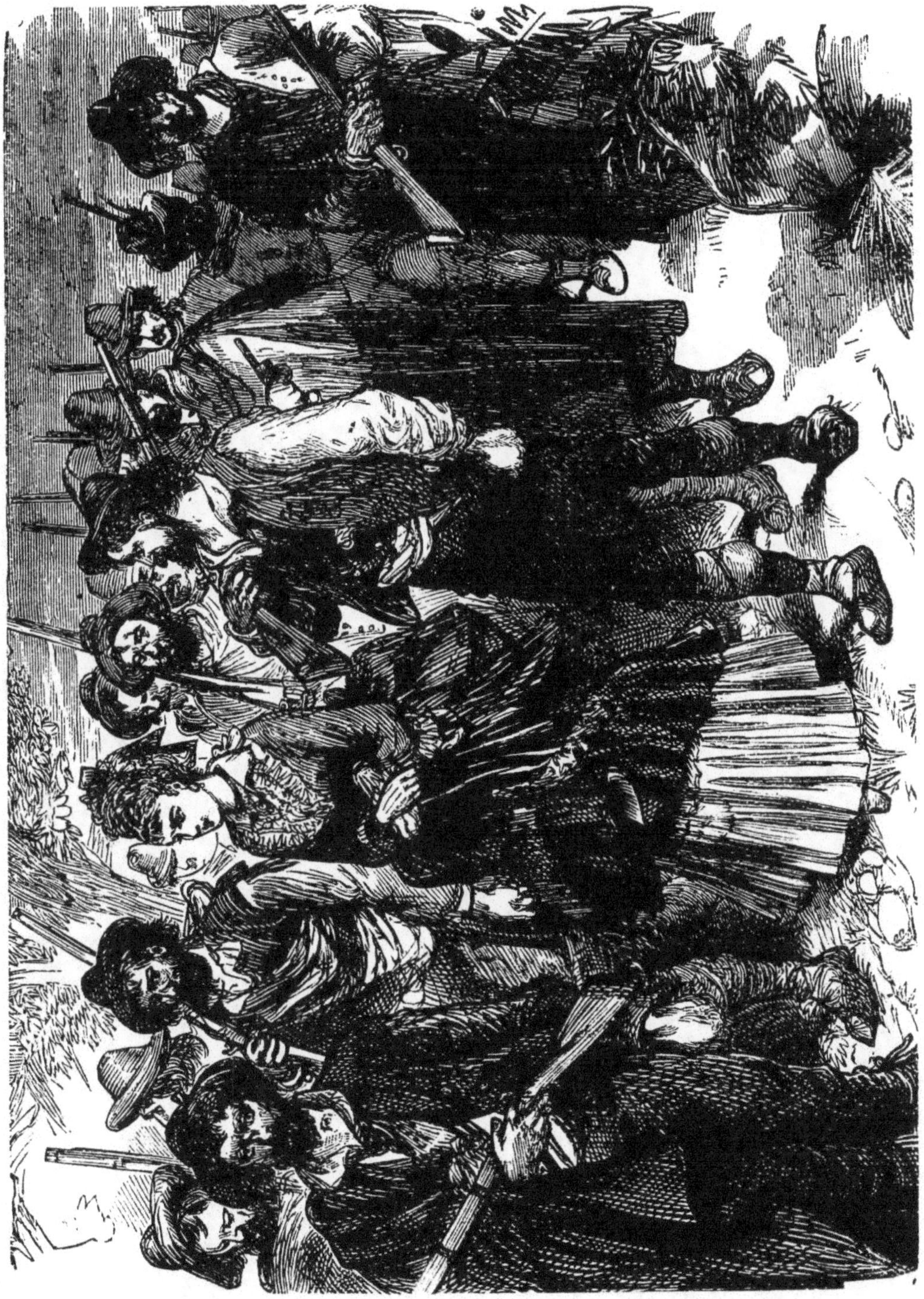

"EMILY WAS CONDUCTED, STRONGLY GUARDED, TO THE ROBBERS' CAVE."

No. 8.

PRICE ONE HALFPENNY

[PUBLISHED EVERY TUESDAY].

" There !" cried Bigamini again. " Who's right now, Mr. Sharpshins ?"

" Don't call me names," said the coxswain, angrily. " I've had to welt you once before, and I can do it again."

" Beg pardon, sir—but you've got such a aggravating way. Keep him off; I'm afraid of brigands."

" He won't hurt you," replied Jack. " I am glad your character is cleared, as I should have tackled you rather hotly, my little man."

" Thank you, Mr. Harkaway; you're a gentleman, sir, and Oxford all over."

" Go and call the soldiers here. You can hear the drum, can't you ?"

" Yes, sir. They've got a foolish way of kicking up a row when they want to catch a weasel asleep," replied Bigamini, with a grin.

The brigand also smiled as Bigamini limped off, pretending that his leg was very stiff and bad where the chief had kicked him, though if he had pulled his trousers up, it would have been seen that he hadn't got a scratch.

" I am no more afraid of a regiment of Italian soldiers," remarked Barboni, " than I am of a flock of sheep."

" They don't seem to be up to much in the way of brigand hunting, if they couldn't catch you," remarked the little coxswain.

" I am not so easily caught," replied Barboni.

" Anyhow, we weren't long over copping you, my hearty."

" You had nothing to do with it. I dropped you quickly enough," said the brigand.

There was a laugh at this, in which Barboni joined.

" He had you there, Walter," observed Carden.

" Let those laugh who win. He is copped—isn't he ?—whether I had a hand in it or not, and I'll bet he wishes himself anywhere else," answered the coxswain.

" Can you dance a hornpipe ?" asked Barboni.

" Yes, against the world."

" And sing songs ?"

" Lots of them—rattlers."

" I'll have you captured and taken alive to my cave," said Barboni.

" Capture me !" repeated the little coxswain, angrily.

" Yes. I want a fool to amuse me when I'm dull."

" Chaff away, old son. It's a case of Jack up the orchard with you, and I don't think you'll have a chance of capturing anyone else."

" You think not ?" said Barboni, with a sneer.

" I don't think—I'm sure of it. The next dance you have anything to do with will be when you're dancing on nothing, with a rope round your neck."

" Thank you," replied the chief. " You are very brave, and extremely gentlemanly to insult a fallen foe."

" I don't call you a foe; you're an enemy to mankind," answered Walter, indignantly; " and I can't get up any romance over a vulgar thief."

Barboni flushed angrily.

" You will repent those words, young man, and regret your insolence," he said.

" I never regret anything I say or do, and I repeat that I wish to have nothing to do with a miserable cut-throat like yourself."

Jack took the little coxswain's arm, and led him on one side.

" Don't get needled, Walter," he said.

" He shouldn't chaff a gentleman," replied Walter.

" But it isn't generous to say anything to him when he's down, let the man's faults be what they may. He's in our power now, and will go to the scaffold, whatever he may say to the contrary."

" That's true enough, and if he wouldn't be so cocky, I should be inclined to pity him," rejoined Walter.

" Well, let him alone, there's a good fellow."

" Oh ! he may go and hunt spiders for what I care," answered the coxswain.

The conversation was interrupted by the approach of the soldiers, who were much excited at the news of the capture of the great Barboni.

He was formally delivered into the charge of the commanding officer, who held himself personally responsible for his safe conduct to Naples.

Soldiers before him, soldiers behind him, soldiers on all sides of him.

Bayonets glistening in the sunshine at the top of loaded rifles.

Twice fifty men ready to shoot him on the least provocation.

On his way to a dungeon and a scaffold, Barboni yet bore himself majestically, and seemed to smile at fate.

"By your right, quick march," said the commanding officer.

The men step out, the arms rattle, and the brigand, looking over his shoulder, says—

"At midnight at the contessa's, Mr. Harkaway."

And Jack nods his head dubiously as he answers—

"I shall be there."

Bigamini walked after the soldiers, listening to the music and keeping step, as if he liked it.

There were but three horses left for the four friends to return on.

"Who'll give me a back?" asked the coxswain.

"I will," replied Tom Carden. "Come here, young one."

Walter approached, and Tom Carden, stooping down, took him by the collar as if he had been a kitten.

A vigorous pull of that strong arm, and the coxswain was hoisted up on the crupper of the horse.

"Thank you," replied Walter, putting his arm round Tom's waist to hold on. "But I say?"

"What?"

"When you do that again, remember there is no occasion to kill me by kindness. I was nearly strangled."

"All right, young one," replied Tom, in a fatherly voice. "Hang on tight."

The three horses started at a fair pace, and soon overtook the soldiers.

Barboni's eye caught Jack's, and there was a merry twinkle in it.

Evidently the brigand did not trouble himself greatly at his position.

Jack was thinking of the audacious promise of Barboni.

He, a captive, had promised to meet him at the contessa's reception that night at twelve o'clock.

It seemed impossible.

"Will he do it?" said Jack to himself.

That question could only be answered as the clock struck the dread hour of midnight.

When they reached Naples, Jack rode at once to the chief of the police and to General Cialdini, to announce the important capture he had made.

He was congratulated on all sides.

The news flew like wildfire through the city.

Excited groups gathered in the cafés, at the Europa, at the street corners, in the Strada Di Toledo, the Corso, and the Villa Reale.

It was the one engrossing topic of conversation.

The evening papers had an account of it, with the usual exaggerations, printed in leaded type.

Jack was the hero of the hour.

An Englishman, as usual, on the Continent, had done what none of the natives could.

But there was a blank in his heart, for, though he had captured Barboni, he had not recovered his darling Emily.

His friends did all they could to cheer him up, and assured him that Emily's restoration to her home was only a question of time.

Hilda nursed and took care of his little child, who was told, when he asked for mamma, that she would be back soon.

Harvey met him on the stairs, and said in an excited voice—

"Who do you think is here?"

"Can't tell. Not Emily!" replied Jack, grasping like a drowning man at a straw.

"You'll never guess."

"I shan't try. Who is it?"

"Don't be grumpy, old man. It's Lily Cockles," answered Harvey.

"When did she come?"

"This afternoon. You know the old dad's dead, and Lily was so affected that they had to put her in a private asylum for a few weeks, because she wanted to kill herself, and join her father and brother, or some sentimental nonsense of that kind."

"Well?"

"She soon got all right when the excitement passed off. All old Cockles' money is hers, and finding herself a wealthy heiress, without a friend in England, she determined to come over to us."

"I am sure Emily would have been delighted to see her," answered Jack. "Where is she?"

"Upstairs. She's a little sad and much cut up about Emily, but as jolly as can be expected under the circumstances," replied Harvey.

" Of course, Hilda will see that she is made comfortable."

" Oh, yes. You can leave all that to Hilda. The two are not strangers, and Lily seems to take wonderfully to her."

" It's a good chance for the little coxswain," said Jack, who, worried as he was with his own private affairs, could not help thinking of his friends.

" He's on like grub already," replied Harvey.

" Is he ?"

" Yes. Awfully hard hit directly he saw her, and Lily is a pretty girl, you know."

" So she is," replied Jack. " Let them spoon. Walter may make a match of it if the brigands don't carry her off."

" We must have another go in at them, and find out their cave," replied Harvey. " I don't think we shall have much trouble now we've got the chief."

" Give me back Emily, and I don't care a rush," answered Jack, dismally.

" What an old croaker you are. Go and dress for dinner. All will come right."

" Would you like Hilda to be among brigands ?"

" No, but I'd make the best of it, and not mope. Barboni told you she was all right, and we've lots to think of. Wonder whether he'll keep his word."

" Who ? Barboni ?"

" Yes. You know he said he'd be at the contessa's to-night," said Harvey.

" It wouldn't surprise me," replied Jack. " I believe he and the contessa row in together."

" So do I. They're in the same swim for a hundred."

They went upstairs and met Walter Campbell on the landing.

" Going to my hotel to dress," he said. " Back soon ; ta-ta."

" Bother the dressing ! We'll excuse you to-day," exclaimed Harvey.

" Couldn't think of it ; you've got company, Miss Lily Cockles, you know. Must cut a shine before ladies."

" Are you always so particular ?"

" When a lady's in the case. Don't care for you men ; but can't sink to the level of the beast, you know," replied the little coxswain.

" Go and beautify yourself," said Jack, smiling ; " Lily is worth catching. She's got lots of tin."

" Has she ?"

" Heaps."

" That doesn't matter ; she's got what I like ever so much more, and that's a pretty face and a nice manner."

" Look out for the tin, my boy," exclaimed Jack ; " that will last longer, if you take care of it, than pretty faces."

" Did you marry for money, Harkaway ?" asked the little coxswain.

" No."

" I thought not. I should not have liked you if you had. There can't be any harm in falling in love and being genuine, can there ?" said Walter.

" Not in the least. A man or a boy can't be a good fellow unless he is genuine," exclaimed Jack. " But what I meant was that if you can love a girl who has a little tin, it is all the jollier for a poor man."

The little coxswain nodded his head as if he quite caught Jack's meaning.

The banisters seemed to him to present the easiest means of getting downstairs, and, getting astride, he slid along, to the great danger of his neck, alighting safe, however, in the hall.

" That kid will run a mucker some day," remarked Harvey, " if he goes sliding down banisters like that."

" Not he ; that sort of youngster never comes to grief," answered Jack.

" He's smart for his age."

" I'd turn him up amongst a hundred boys, and make him favourite against the field," said Jack.

" What I like about him is that there is no nonsense," answered Harvey " He's a regular little brick."

" So he is," exclaimed Jack.

They had now reached the drawing-room door, and while Harvey went up-stairs to dress, Jack entered to make Lily welcome, and assure her how glad he was to see her.

Miss Lily Cockles was paler and thinner than when we saw her last, and had gone through severe trials.

But calmness and resignation had come to her aid.

Hilda received and treated her like a sister.

With our little party at Naples she found what her poor bruised heart wanted above all things.

That was a home.

CHAPTER XXXIII.

THE MEETING AT MIDNIGHT.

BIGAMINI followed the soldiers with other idlers to the prison in which Barboni was placed.

He asked a variety of questions, and gossiped with the guards, ascertaining that the brigand was lodged in a strong cell on the ground floor.

From the prison he hurried to the Contessa Di Malafedi's palazzo.

Here he remained for some time.

As the shades of night began to fall, several men arrived at the door, and were all admitted by Bigamini.

He spoke in a friendly tone to them, and appeared to be on terms of intimacy with most.

Fierce, savage-looking men they were, ooking as if they were capable of committing any atrocity.

At the hour of ten he quitted the palazzo in the Strada Nuovo, and made his way to the prison.

The guard had just been changed.

Under his arm he carried a bundle, and, approaching the porter's lodge, entered it.

The porter recognised him with a nod, and they spoke earnestly together in whispers for some time.

"Come this way," said the porter at last.

He conducted him along a stone passage until they reached the room of the gaoler, whose name was Guiseppe.

"Fine times, Guiseppe," said the porter. "We've caged a big bird at last, amico mio."

"You mean Barboni," exclaimed the gaoler. "Cospetto! we shall have some fun now."

He looked inquiringly at Bigamini.

"A friend of mine," said the porter, "the Prince Di Villanova's valet."

"Ah! the prince shot the heretic Englishman at the Contessa Di Malafedi's ball. I remember."

"Pity he had not killed the heretic. Yet it is this same Englishman—how do you call him?"

"Signor Harkawini, or some such name," put in the gaoler.

"Yes, that is it. Well, he has captured our chief of the brigands."

"Those Inglesi," said Guiseppe, "can never let us alone. Santa Maria! why can't they stop in their own foggy country?"

"That is what I say," replied the porter.

"I expect my master to visit Barboni," said Bigamini. "He sent me on first, and said he should be here, and as I was going to see my old friend Luigi, I brought a bottle of good wine from our cellar."

"Guiseppe will taste it," said the porter.

"You are not far wrong," answered the gaoler. "I have just finished making up my returns, and I shall be glad of a glass."

Bigamini produced a bottle from his bundle, drew the cork, and a glass being forthcoming, the three pledged each other.

"I wish I could get out for half an hour," said Guiseppe, smacking his lips, and adding "rare good wine, this. Per Baccho! that wasn't put in the cellar yesterday."

"My master has as good wine as any one in Italy," replied Bigamini.

"It strikes me you're English," said the gaoler; "your accent has a foreign sound."

"But I'm a good Catholic, and go to mass," answered Bigamini.

"That makes a difference."

"Try another glass," said Bigamini; "it won't hurt you, and if you want to go out to see a pair of black eyes, I'm sure Luigi will take your place."

"That I will," answered the porter; "and it wouldn't be the first time either. Our Guiseppe is a perfect diavolo after the fair sex."

"What would you have a man do?" asked the gaoler with a smile.

"Why, drink to my toast—dark eyes and glossy hair, or the beauties of Naples," said the porter.

Each man emptied his glass.

"Poor Barboni. They say he carried

off the Englishman's wife yesterday," remarked the gaoler.

"Ah !" exclaimed Luigi. "Those Inglesi are devils if you interfere with their women; but go out, *amico mio*, if you have a mind. I'll keep the keys, and mind the place."

"Santo Dio !" answered Guiseppe, "it is just the time when Bianca said she would wait for me outside. You know the pretty artist, Luigi ?"

"You're a lucky fellow," answered the porter. "Go and take advantage of your good fortune."

"I will. The general has been round when the guard was changed, so that there is no danger of my being missed," replied Guiseppe.

He drank another glass of wine, which Bigamini pressed upon him, and taking his hat, left the prison.

His keys were hanging on a nail.

The heavy tramp of the doubled guard could be heard on the stone flags of the prison corridor, leading to Barboni's cell.

When the gaoler was gone, the porter said to Bigamini—

"Now, quick, the reward."

Bigamini placed in his outstretched hand a bag of gold.

"Are you satisfied ?" he asked.

"Perfectly. You have done your part, now I will do mine; follow me. Santissima Virgine! it is strange if two heads like ours cannot arrange a trifle like this."

The porter, taking up the keys, and dangling them on his waist, advanced to the guard, who grounded arms at his approach.

"Let us pass, friend," said he; "we have business in the brigand's cell."

"What business ?" asked the soldier.

"The Prince Di Villanova is with Barboni, and this is his servant."

"I have seen no prince or any other man go into the cell," replied the guard.

"Cospetto !" said Luigi, "how simple you are."

"Why ?"

"How long have you been on duty ?"

"A quarter of an hour, or thereabouts."

"Exactly," said the porter; "you know nothing about it. The prince was admitted before you came on guard. His time was an hour. It is up. I must let him out. Do you see now ?"

"My orders are from the general," replied the soldier.

"What are they ?"

"To let no one pass."

"Without an order, I suppose ?"

"Precisely so."

"But," said Luigi, "the prince is in the cell with the brigand. He came to induce him to give up an English lady he had captured. Surely, the gaoler can go where he likes in the prison ?"

"You are not the gaoler," replied the soldier.

"I am his deputy. He has left me his keys, while he goes for half an hour to see his *bella donna*."

"You should have an order."

Luigi shook the keys.

"Are not these enough ?" he asked. "What more do you want? Do you think I intend to release Barboni ?"

"No, no," laughed the soldier; "you would be clever to do that."

"You know him by sight, of course ?"

"Yes; I was with the detachment to which he was given this morning. He is a man without any beard No one could mistake him."

"Then you are not likely to take the Prince Di Villanova for the brigand ?"

"Not at all; everybody in Naples knows the prince. He wears a beard, and you could not take him for Barboni," answered the soldier.

"Stand on one side, then, and let the prince's valet and me pass," said Luigi.

"Pass," said the soldier, who did not see the use of holding out any longer.

Bigamini and the porter went along the corridor and met the second guard.

"Halt !" he exclaimed, raising his loaded weapon in a threatening manner.

"What's the matter with you ?" asked Luigi.

"Is all well ?" inquired the second guard of the first.

"Si," replied the soldier they had just spoken to.

"Pass," said the guard, lowering his rifle.

The two men hurried on to the end of the corridor, where a door, studded with iron nails, met their gaze.

A capacious keyhole indicated an equally capacious lock, and the porter selected one of the biggest keys in the bunch to open it with.

His effort was successful.

The heavy door at once rolled back on its hinges.

Bigamini was not long inside the cell.

Pushing open the door, he stepped out, followed by a tall, handsome man in evening dress, with a light coat covering him.

"Stand on one side," he said, "and let my master, the Prince Di Villanova, pass."

Luigi the porter fell back.

The guards stopped in their march up and down the corridor.

They seemed doubtful as to what their duty should be.

Bigamini had shut the door of the cell again, locked it, and handed the key to Luigi.

"We saw no prince come in," said one soldier.

"Of course you didn't," answered Bigamini.

"Why shouldn't we?"

"Because he was admitted before the guard was changed, and he came in through the governor's entrance."

"Ah," said the soldiers, "that makes a difference."

"I wish Guiseppe, the gaoler, was here," said Luigi.

"Hold your tongue, fool!" said Bigamini. "Do you want to anger the prince?"

"What has the prince been doing with Barboni?"

"He'd got business with him, or the governor would not have admitted him."

"But——"

"Do you want to lose your berth, and perhaps your life?" asked Bigamini, angrily.

"Lose my situation and my life!" exclaimed the man. "Of course I don't wish that."

"Be quiet, then, and treat the prince properly," said Bigamini.

Villanova smilingly extended a slip of paper.

"My friends," he said, "this is a pass from General Cialdini. Do you require anything further?"

Luigi looked at it.

"That's the general's writing, sure enough," he remarked.

"We only want to do our duty," grumbled a soldier

"Do it then. Present arms, and let the prince pass," said Bigamini.

The soldiers looked at Luigi.

"It's all right," returned the latter. "Present!"

The guard presented arms.

The Prince Di Villanova walked quickly from the strongly-built prison, followed by Bigamini, and preceded by Luigi.

Once in the street he whispered a few hurried words to Bigamini.

At the corner of the street a carriage was waiting.

Getting into this, he was rapidly driven away in the direction of the better part of Naples.

The carriage stopped at the palazzo of the Contessa Di Malafedi.

This was brilliantly illuminated.

Strains of music floated out into the street through the open windows.

The majority of the guests seemed to have arrived, as few carriages were setting down visitors.

Alighting from the carriage, the prince smilingly acknowledged the salutes of the attendants.

He ascended the spacious marble staircase, through a garden of costly exotics and flowering shrubs.

At the entrance to the ballrom, the major-domo said in a loud voice—

"His Highness Francisco Ferdinando Emmanuele, Prince Di Villanova."

Every eye was turned upon the new comer, who, since he shot at Harkaway, had become a celebrity in chatting, gossiping Naples.

A smile of relief seemed to come over the face of the contessa, who was surrounded by a group of officers in uniform.

Conspicuous amongst them was General Cialdini, who from his height and figure, was easily distinguished from his staff.

The contessa held out her hand, saying—

"So pleased to see you. I almost feared circumstances would prevent you from honouring my poor saloon with your company."

"How could I stay away from so much delight and beauty? It would have been equal to ruining one's chance of Paradise," answered the prince.

"Ah, Villanova," said the general, "glad to see you."

"Thanks, your excellency is much too good."

"Of course you have heard the news?" remarked the contessa.

"You mean the capture of Barboni?" he replied.

"Yes."

"Oh! that is old news to me. I have been to see the fellow," said the prince carelessly.

"Indeed?"

"I sent my servant to the general for a pass, which he was good enough to give me, and I exerted my eloquence upon the bandit, to induce him to tell me what he had done with Mrs. Harkaway, whom I hoped to restore to her husband's arms this very night."

"How good of you."

The prince stroked his glossy beard.

"What was the result?" asked the general.

"The wretch received me with sullen indifference, and said he would only talk to Mr. Harkaway himself about that."

"How hardened," said the contessa.

"Why, yes, he seems to have a hide like a rhinoceros, and about as much conscience as a mosquito."

"It is a great satisfaction to me to think that we have him safe after all," observed the general; "he has given me a great deal of trouble."

"They were absurd enough to say that you and the brigand were connected in some mysterious way," said a young nobleman.

"To whom do you allude?" asked the prince.

"The Inglesi."

"Cospetto!" said the prince; "cannot we make some allowance for these English, whose only accomplishments are making steam engines and ships, buying and selling, and eating roast beef?"

There was a general laugh at this.

"For my part," remarked the general, "I knew all along it was an impossibility."

"Thank you," said Villanova, with a smile. "We are not much alike, I flatter myself."

After chatting here, and shaking hands there, he walked up the room.

Near a window were the four friends.

"Look out, Jack," said Harvey.

"What for?"

"There is Villanova, coming towards us."

"Is it? So it is, by Jove!" answered Jack.

Carden looked at the approaching figure with considerable astonishment.

"That knocks my theory on the head," he said.

"What does?" asked the little coxswain.

"Why, don't you see, we've got Barboni under lock and key in the state prison?"

"Yes."

"And here is Villanova; so that Barboni and Villanova can't be one and the same person."

"No, by Jove!" replied Walter Campbell. "Stop a bit, though."

"Why?"

"There's a chimney. I'll put my hand up, and smudge it with soot."

"What for?" asked Carden, puzzled.

"When I shake hands with the prince, I shall black his glove inside, and if Barboni should appear at midnight, and his right hand glove is blacked, it will be a curious thing, won't it?"

"Rather. You've got some ideas in that little pimple of yours, young one," answered Carden, smiling approvingly.

"Some of us ought to have; you haven't got many," answered Walter, with a laugh.

"Don't you be too cocky, young one; you're not too old to lick," rejoined Tom, pretending to be angry.

"Hullo! here's Carden in a wax," cried the little coxswain.

"What's riled the old bear?" grinned Jack.

"I trod on his toes."

"I wonder if some people's ears would stretch if they were pulled," said Tom.

"Yours don't want pulling," replied Walter.

"Why not?"

"They're long and thin already. Got any donkeys in your family?"

"Be off up the chimney. Here's the prince," said Carden, who was getting the worst of the chaff.

Walter disappeared, and blacked the inside of his white kid glove.

When he came back he was just in time to shake hands with the prince.

But his eye was as quick as lightning.

Without pretending to have done so, he had watched Walter Campbell leave the group.

One glance at his glove showed him that the trick had been so far successful.

"There is something on your glove, *amico mio*," he said, "and mine too."

"Is there?" said Walter, in some confusion.

"Is it not odd, Mr. Harkaway, that one cannot touch pitch without being defiled?"

"Oh, I'm sure it was an accident," said Jack, reddening.

"No, no. You distrust me, I see you do. No matter, I will retain this glove. It will gratify you, perhaps, as gentlemen do not spoil their own and other people's gloves for nothing."

Tom drew the little coxswain on one side.

"What a sharp beggar it is," he remarked.

"He's up to snuff, and no flies," answered Walter. "I felt inclined to kick him when he cheeked me, but I was in the wrong. I don't half like it though. What did he call me?"

"Pitch," answered Carden, laughing heartily.

"Hang my sister's cat, I can't stand being called pitch, can I?"

"Poor little man. Isn't it nice to be snubbed, especially when one has such fine ideas?"

"Now, look here, do you want to work me up?"

"I don't think you're quite up to the boiling point yet."

"Yes, I am. I'm boiling over. If I don't sit on the safety valve, I shall burst. No, hang me if I do! I'll have it out with that son of a gun."

Before Carden could prevent him, the little coxswain strode up to the prince with a defiant air.

"Excuse me," he said, "but you made use of an unpleasant expression just now."

Villanova looked at him compassionately.

"Do you mean to apologise?" persisted Walter.

"I never apologise to children," answered the prince. "If they fancy I have hurt their feelings, I give them a few soldi to buy sweet stuff."

Walter Campbell was furious.

Always very hasty, he did not stay to consider that he was the guest of the contessa, and in her ballroom.

"What do you mean by it?" he asked, angrily confronting the prince.

"Mr. Harkaway," said Villanova, "is your little friend at all afflicted here?"

He touched his forehead significantly.

"I am no more mad than you are," replied Walter.

"He is only hasty," said Jack.

"If he belonged to me—but I will say no more. Kindly talk to him, will you?"

The little coxswain faced the prince now.

Without any further warning than "Mind your eye, old cock," he struck out at him.

Villanova stepped back.

The blow hit him with considerable force in the chest.

With admirable good temper, he smiled.

"Mr. Harkaway," he said, "I must beg of you to restrain this boy. I shall not chastise him, as I do not want to be the hero of another scene at the Contessa Di Malafedi's."

"For goodness sake be quiet," said Jack.

"I'm not afraid of him. Let him come on."

"Remember where you are."

"Oh! we've got this part of the room all to ourselves, and we can get behind that screen."

"If you had your deserts, you would be whipped, and put to bed," replied the prince, with a mocking laugh.

"Carden," said Jack, "take the young one away; he's had too much champagne."

"I'm not going to be called names," replied Walter.

Carden interfered, and, seizing the little coxswain's arm, dragged him to a recess near a window.

Harvey followed.

"Don't be an idiot," said Tom. "Do you want to get our names up in Naples as a set of cads?"

"Naples don't keep me," snarled Walter.

"Stand still, I tell you. What, you won't? I shall have to sit on you."

"If you run about wild like this, you will get pretty considerably smashed up," observed Harvey. "Wait for him outside, but never kick up a shindy before ladies."

"All right. I suppose I'm wrong. I'll be quiet. Leave go," answered Walter.

Harvey noticed blood on his knuckles.

"What's the matter with your hand?" he asked.

"Can't tell; barked my fist though. I thought I felt something jolly hard when I hit that cove. It was like striking a lamp-post."

"Curious," said Tom Carden. "It couldn't have been a stud, because the skin is off all round. Wonder if he wears anything underneath?"

Jack meantime was talking to the prince.

"I hope you will pardon my friend," said Jack; "he is a little excitable at times."

"Very much so, I should say," replied the prince.

"Don't take any notice of him."

"I will not. Let us forget him. Flies and gnats are troublesome, but, after all, they are insignificant."

"It wouldn't be well for you if he heard you," answered Jack, "but I don't want a row now. It is close upon twelve, and I have an appointment."

"With whom?"

"That scoundrel Barboni."

"How is that?"

"Oh, out of brag, I suppose, more than anything else, he said this morning, when he was captured, that he would meet me at this ball at midnight."

"Have you told anyone of this?"

"Not a soul."

"No one knows it but you and your friends?" asked the prince.

"No."

"Poor fellow," said Villanova, "I think he will find it rather difficult to keep his word, though I have heard that Barboni never yet broke his promise."

Jack laughed.

"I wish I had a thousand pounds on it," he said.

"On what?"

"On the event."

"How would you bet?" demanded Villanova.

"A level thou. that Barboni is not here this evening as the clock strikes twelve."

"Done with you," said the prince quickly.

"What?" said Jack, in surprise, "do you take the bet?"

"Yes."

"You are sure to lose."

"Perhaps; what matters it if I do? One must have a little excitement this hot weather. If I win, come over to my place to-morrow morning and lunch with me; not that I want the cash, but I should like to have a hearty laugh at you."

"Let those laugh that win," answered Jack.

He took out his watch and looked at it.

It wanted but five minutes to twelve.

"In five minutes," he ejaculated.

"Ah, excuse me," said the prince; "I see the contessa beckoning to me."

With a pleasant smile, and stroking his glossy beard, as was his custom, Villanova glided away.

He was soon lost in the throng.

"Nice fellow when he likes to be," thought Jack. "But he'll drop his coin over Barboni."

CHAPTER XXXIV.

BARBONI KEEPS HIS WORD.

JACK rejoined his companions.

They were at the north end of the room.

The contessa and her guests were chiefly congregated in the centre, and at the top or south end, where the refreshment room was.

On the east side, in the middle, the band was placed in an orchestra or balcony.

Dancing had ceased for a brief while.

and heated couples were promenading the saloon, or struggling for iced drinks.

Neither Hilda nor Lily had come to the ball.

Lily was not very well, and Hilda feared any excitement would do her harm.

Besides this, she was so grieved at Emily's loss that she did not care to appear in public.

Jack touched Walter on the shoulder.

"You've been going it, young one," he exclaimed.

"Why shouldn't I, when that beastly old prince insulted me?" answered the little coxswain.

"You began it by blacking his glove."

"That was only a dodge. He'd better keep his eye peeled, for I shall be on to him like grub when I have the chance."

"He does not like you, old man," said Jack.

"Then he may lump it, for all I care? I'm not going to be called names and treated like a child. But I'll have it out with him some day."

At the end of the room was a screen, though what was behind it could not be seen.

"Shut up about the prince," said Carden. "He's a puzzle to me, and it riles me to think of him. Look at that screen; doesn't it look ghostly in the shadow?"

Ping, ping, ping.

A clock on the mantelpiece began to strike the hour.

"Midnight," replied Jack.

His heart beat a little faster.

"You've gone quite white," exclaimed Harvey.

"Have I?" said Jack.

"Yes, a sheet's a fool to you. Do you expect Barboni?"

"Nine, ten, eleven," counted Jack. "By George! What's that?"

Ere the last stroke of the clock had died away, a sombre form emerged from behind the screen.

The figure was tall and commanding.

A black mask hid the upper part of the face, just revealing dark, flashing eyes and well-cut mouth, about which a sardonic smile was playing, and showing the beardless chin.

On the head was a slouched hat, ornamented with a feather.

The form was shrouded in the ample folds of a long cloak.

"Vi saluta, Barboni!" rang through the room, filling every nook and corner.

Everyone was startled.

A dead silence fell upon the gay and giddy crowd, which could not have been more effectually hushed if their beautiful hostess had suddenly fallen lifeless in their midst.

Advancing fearlessly to Jack, the intruder stopped within a dozen paces of him.

"Mr. Harkaway," he said, "Barboni keeps his word."

General Cialdini and his staff, followed by many of the curious guests, came down the room.

Turning towards them, the brigand waved his hand.

"Back, all of you!" he cried.

There was a sudden halt.

"My business here," continued Barboni, "is with an Englishman. Molest me not. One whistle from me, and the room shall swarm with my men."

The gentlemen looked confounded.

The ladies shrieked.

Some went into hysterics, while many hastily removed and hid their jewellery, remembering that the brigand chief had a fancy for trinkets set with precious stones.

"Mr. Harkaway, if you wish to speak to me, you are at liberty to do so," continued Barboni.

He stood with his arms folded, and cast defiant glances around.

"I have but one question to ask," answered Jack.

"Name it."

"What ransom will you take for my wife?"

The answer came slowly and solemnly.

"None!"

"Do you mean to keep her a prisoner?" asked Jack, aghast.

"Return to England with your companions, and one day after your arrival on British soil, your wife shall rejoin you."

Thus spake the brigand.

"Is that your final resolve?"

"It is."

Jack's heart sank within him.

The little coxswain sprang forward and touched Jack on the arm.

"Are you going to stand this?" he asked.

"What can I do?" returned Jack.

"Shoot the rascal."

"Perhaps he will revenge himself upon Emily."

"He can't blame you if I try to pot him," said Walter.

Several gentlemen had tried to escape from the saloon to summon assistance.

But all the doors were guarded by fierce-looking men in slouched hats.

These were armed to the teeth.

Unfortunately no one had any pistols with him, as these things are not generally taken to balls.

This surprise had not been expected.

Suddenly the little coxswain uttered a cry of joy.

"I've got a pea-shooter!" he exclaimed.

As he spoke, he produced from his coat-tail pocket a revolver.

It had five chambers.

"I'd almost forgotten it," he added, "but I shoved it in at the last moment, thinking we might meet Barboni by a fluke."

General Cialdini was in anything but a happy temper.

"Gentlemen," he said, "advance and capture that fellow."

No one obeyed his summons.

One or two drew their swords, but as Barboni's dagger gleamed in the gaslight, they held back.

"Ten thousand ducats for him, dead or alive!" shouted the general.

This large reward stimulated a few, who for honour alone would not have risked an encounter with the redoubtable chief.

"Hold hard," said Walter Campbell.

The Italian officers looked at him curiously.

"I'm in this," continued the little coxswain. "Let me have my innings."

He levelled his pistol at the brigand.

Every eye was fixed on him intently.

"Are you going to give up Jack's wife?" inquired Walter.

There was no answer.

"I shall count one, two, three," he continued, "and if you don't talk up by that time, it will be all up the Baltic with you."

Barboni's mouth curled with a smile.

"One!" said the little coxswain.

The Italians envied him the possession of the pistol.

"Two!"

"Take a good aim, and kill the villain; you shall have the reward," said General Cialdini.

He was as much excited as anyone else.

"Bother the reward," answered Walter. "It's Jack's wife I want to get back from the thundering thief."

Barboni's arms hung listlessly by his side, and though he held a pistol in each hand, he appeared perfectly indifferent to the result of the shot.

"I've got five lives in this popgun," cried the little coxswain. "So look out, ugly."

Still Barboni made no sign.

He kept his eyes fixed upon the muzzle of the pistol, as if calculating exactly where the bullet was likely to strike.

"Three!"

There was a report.

Barboni just moved his head on one side, about the eighth of an inch, and the bullet swished past, burying itself in the oaken panelling.

"Missed, by jingo! "That's one gone," muttered Walter.

He fired again.

This time, the ball struck the brigand in the breast.

He seemed to stagger a little, but remained perfectly upright.

A third time the little coxswain fired.

The ball lodged in the same place.

The fourth was a miss, owing again to a rapid movement of the head.

The fifth discharge was a hit, and in the region of the heart.

"That shot must have cooked his goose!" exclaimed Walter.

"Yes. He's a settled member," said Harvey.

"Bravo!" cried Tom Carden.

"By Jove! he's not touched," cried Jack as the smoke cleared away.

Barboni was upright and apparently unhurt.

In the presence of all the assembled guests, he took the three bullets which had struck him out of a fold in his cloak.

Tossing them contemptuously to the little coxswain, he cried—

"Take your playthings."

The balls rolled along the polished floor with a dull, heavy sound.

But they did not roll far, as they were considerably indented.

The Italians crossed themselves devoutly.

"He is in league with the fiend," said the majority.

With a polite bow, Barboni said—

"I am sorry, ladies and gentlemen, to have interrupted your festivities, but I felt it a point of honour to keep my appointment with Mr. Harkaway, whom I esteem so highly."

Again the general urged the members of his staff to attack the brigand.

A few attempted to do so.

"Beware !" cried Barboni. "He who comes near me dies."

He levelled his pistols, one in each hand.

"I am tired of childish play," he said; "the comedy is over. I have kept my word. It is for you to say if the tragedy shall begin."

The officers ceased to advance.

"Put up your swords," continued the brigand.

The order was complied with.

"Villain !" cried the general, "you shall pay dearly for this."

"Vi saluta, Barboni !"

The brigand's cry was heard ringing through the saloon once more.

Then he retired behind the screen.

Walter Campbell hurled the pistol after him without effect.

The officers rushed forward and pulled down the screen.

A door was disclosed to view, but it was locked, and defied every effort to open it.

The peculiarly shrill whistle of the brigand chief was heard distinctly.

Those who were looking out of the windows, declared they saw a perfect army of dark forms start out of the flower beds, and from behind trees in the garden.

Barboni did not come unattended.

Naples had a fresh sensation.

News had been very scarce for a long time.

Barboni was a godsend.

The contessa and General Cialdini were trying to put the ladies at their ease.

Carden picked up one of the bullets fired by Walter Campbell and returned by the brigand.

All at once a voice at his elbow said—

"Curiously knocked about, isn't it ?"

Tom Carden looked up, and saw the Prince Di Villanova.

"You !" he ejaculated.

"Why not, *caro mio ?* Where did you expect me to be ? Have I not been an awe-stricken spectator of the visit of that incomprehensible being, Barboni ?"

Carden showed him the bullet.

"What do you think of this ?" he asked.

"What do you ?"

"Barboni wears a coat of strong chain mail. Look, the bullet is almost flat."

"Either that, my dear friend, or he is made of cast iron. I congratulate you on your discovery," replied the prince, with a sort of covert sneer.

He walked away, and was quickly seen in conversation with General Cialdini, and his brilliant staff of officers.

The latter were intensely annoyed at the escape of the brigand.

CHAPTER XXXV.

THE THREE SPOTS OF BLOOD.

IN a short time another attempt was made upon the doors of the ballroom.

They were found to be unguarded.

Every trace of the brigands had disappeared.

They had vanished as if by magic.

Behind the screen was an old disused door communicating by a flight of stairs with the garden.

Jack was the first to discover this.

"By Heaven ! he shall not escape me," he exclaimed.

Followed by the three friends, he dashed down the stairs and searched the garden, but the shrubs and trees concealed nothing.

Crestfallen, he returned to the ballroom.

With the usual light-heartedness of the Neapolitans, the music had again struck up, and the dancers were enjoying themselves.

Ladies ate ices, and fruit plunged in snow, as if nothing had happened.

Gentlemen talked and drank icy cold champagne.

General Cialdini and his staff were the only ones who had gone away.

It was necessary to make inquiries at the gaol, and call out the troops.

Presently the assembly was beaten, and the streets rang with the sound of the drums.

At the prison the gaolers knew nothing whatever.

The cell which had contained Barboni was empty.

It was curious that only one person had seen the Prince of Villanova enter.

This was a servant of the governor, who said he had let him in privately, and opened the door of the cell with his master's key.

Shortly afterwards it was remarked that this man had more money to spare and spend than he had ever had before.

He was frequently seen in conversation with Bigamini.

One morning he was found dead in the street, with a dagger in his heart.

But still no suspicion was attached to the Prince of Villanova, who came and went as freely into Naples as ever.

That he should have been at the prison on the night of Barboni's escape was considered only a singular coincidence.

Everyone had seen him in the ballroom.

Many had talked to him a few minutes after Barboni had thrown back the bullets at the little coxswain and been lost sight of behind the screen.

Finding that all was gaiety once more, the four friends determined to enjoy themselves.

Jack talked to the contessa.

Tom Carden, however, walked about with his arms folded, and sullenly watched the Prince of Villanova.

"This Barboni is becoming quite an interesting creature," said the contessa, fanning herself.

"He's a wonderful fellow," replied Jack. "But I shall give him no rest, for I mean to have my wife back again."

"Ah!" sighed the contessa, "I wish I had someone to love me so dearly."

There was a rustle of muslin behind them, and looking up, they saw Hilda and Miss Lily Cockles.

"How kind of you to come at last. So pleased," said the contessa, extending her well-gloved hand.

"Thanks," answered Hilda. "You are always so good. But do for pity's sake tell us what has happened."

"Nothing; a scene from a theatre, that is all."

"Most alarming reports reached us."

"Oh, about that dear Barboni. It is so amusing. One of your friends tried to shoot him. He laughs at the bullets, and bears a charmed life."

"Is anyone hurt? I feared that something dreadful had happened," said Hilda.

"Fortunately we are all right," answered Jack. "Barboni has escaped from prison, and had the daring insolence to keep an appointment here he made with me."

"I feel so relieved," said Hilda.

"Take a seat by my side," said the contessa.

Hilda introduced Lily, and just as she had done so, a voice exclaimed—

"May I not also have the honour?"

"Oh, certainly. Lily, let me present the Prince of Villanova to you."

The prince bowed, and Lily's pale face flushed as she thought what a handsome man he was.

Soon Harvey came up, and gave his wife a detailed account of the bold act of the dreaded brigand Barboni.

The prince devoted himself to Lily, with whom he seemed much struck.

"Have you been in Naples long, miss?" he asked.

"Not long. A day or two only," she replied.

"The Harkaways are old friends of yours, I presume?"

"No, not very. We met them here last year."

"We," said the prince. "May I ask if you speak of your family?"

"Yes; my father and brother," answered Lily, casting down her eyes.

"They are with you now, I presume?"

"They are dead."

Lily spoke in a solemn voice, and all the light died out of her pretty eyes.

Villanova saw in a moment that he had been betrayed into one of those mistakes which people often stumble into without meaning it.

"Pardon me a thousand times," he said. "I had no idea I should touch such a painful subject."

"Don't be sorry," replied Lily. "I have tried to bear it bravely, and thought I had become resigned, though I shall never forget when my poor brother was —was killed."

"An accident?"

"No; he was murdered!"

The prince positively started, as if the idea of murder was something too terrible for him to dwell upon.

"Ah, me!" cried Lily. "Those were sad days. I did not mean to talk of them any more, but you have made me do so."

"It was entirely unintentional."

"I know it; and now you have heard so much of my history, you may as well know it all."

"It will interest me greatly," replied the prince.

"I fear your Italian politeness induced you to say that," she said, with a half smile.

"On my word it was not that. I have taken an interest in you which I cannot explain, but which I hope sincerely you will forgive."

"Willingly. I am alone in the world now. No one looks after me but my guardians."

"You are rich, then?"

"I have six thousand a year. My only friends are the Harkaways and the Harveys. It is something new for a stranger to take an interest in me, and since Mrs. Harkaway is in the power of the brigands I feel as if I had lost my best friend."

"You were like sisters?"

"We loved each other dearly, and I came over here to stay with her," replied Lily. "Do you think Barboni, as they call him, will hurt her?"

"Would it please you to hear that she is in no danger?" asked the prince, smiling.

"Oh, so much."

"Then believe me, that she is perfectly safe and comfortable, if not happy."

"How can you possibly tell?"

"Because I had an interview this evening with the brigand in his cell, to ask him to release Mrs. Harkaway. Her husband is my friend now, although we once had a little quarrel; and cospetto! one must exert oneself in the cause of friendship."

"How good of you!"

"Barboni told me that he merely kept her as a sort of hostage, and would give her up at once if all the party will leave Naples."

"Will they not?"

"Well, they have some romantic idea that they can capture Barboni, and have vowed to do so," replied the prince.

"I would give the world to see my dear Emily again."

"Perhaps it can be managed. I will—"

Villanova stopped himself suddenly.

"By the way," he continued, in a little confusion, "you were going to tell me all your troubles. Do not, pray, treat me as a stranger."

"I have little to tell your highness," answered Lily.

"That little I shall be pleased to hear."

"My father died soon after my brother was murdered, and so I am alone in the world; that is all."

"Do you know the murderer?"

"Oh, yes."

"Is he not punished?"

"No; he should be, if we were to meet, because, although I once thought him the perfection of manly beauty, I could never respect the man who slew my brother," said Lily.

"Can you not meet?" asked the prince.

"I fear not; we seem to be like two parallel lines, which may run together, but cannot meet."

"What is the name of this man?" inquired Villanova.

"Lord Augustus Darrel."

The prince started again, and this time so violently that his opera hat fell from his hand on to the floor.

"You've dropped your tile, prince," said Jack, picking it up.

"Thanks, *caro mio*," answered the prince, in his soft Italian accent.

Turning to Lily again, he added—

"The scoundrel! Did Darrel really murder your brother? But there is a curse on the race—a deadly curse."

"Let us change the subject, please," said Lily. "It is inexpressibly painful to me."

"With pleasure. Again pardon me."

"Do not mention it."

"May I call at Harkaway's while you are the guest of the English volunteers?" said Villanova.

"Why do you call my friends the English volunteers?" inquired Lily.

"Oh! it is a nickname the Neapolitans have given them because they are doing the work of the police in hunting down Barboni."

"I trust sincerely they will succeed."

"Never, never, never!"

"You speak emphatically," she remarked.

"I do, because I know the man; and I wish they knew Barboni as well as I do."

"It is not an acquaintance to boast of," replied Lily, a little sarcastically.

"'BY JOVE!' CRIED JACK, 'I'VE HIT THE BRIGAND.'"

"Perhaps not, answered the prince, with a shrug of the shoulders; "but what would you have? One cannot always choose one's acquaintance in this world, and believe me, Barboni is not so bad as he is painted."

"The wretch! Don't talk to me about him," replied Lily in disgust.

Tom Carden had been watching the pair for some time.

He came up to Lily, and managed to get between her and the prince.

"You should not talk too much to strangers, Miss Lily," he said.

The prince rose angrily.

"If the lady finds my society disagreeable," he answered, "she can surely tell me so without your intervention."

Carden looked at him.

Suddenly he extended his hand, and, pointing to his shirt front, said—

"Why do you want to quarrel when you seem to be already hurt?"

"Hurt! explain yourself, sir," replied the prince.

"Look at yourself in a glass. Come with me."

Carden drew the prince to the nearest mirror.

If Villanova had started when he heard the name of Darrel, he trembled when he looked at himself in the glass.

What did he see? Three spots of blood.

The marks were distinctly visible on the starched cambric.

Three irregular patches of dry blood.

"Anything wrong?" asked Carden.

"I—I had a fall from my horse to-day," answered Villanova, "and was torn about in a hedge, which I fell into; the wounds have broken out again."

Carden hummed a tune.

"Adio!" cried the prince. "I shall look forward to our next meeting."

"One moment, prince," cried Tom Carden, as he was going away.

"Do not detain me. I did not know these marks were here, and must hurry home."

"How many times did my friend, Walter Campbell, hit the brigand?"

"How should I know?"

"You were in the room," said Carden.

"Yes, yes; three times I think it was."

"And where did the balls strike against his coat of mail?"

"The chest; but why ask such idle questions of me?" said the prince, with a gesture of impatience.

"I only wanted information. The chest is covered by the linen shirt front, you know, and the indentation of the shirt of chain mail underneath that by a bullet would break the skin and cause blood to flow, and——"

"Signor Carden," interrupted the prince, "eight-and-forty hours shall not pass over your head before you bitterly repent these insinuations."

"I am glad you understand what I mean," replied Carden, calmly.

"I know too well what you wish to convey to me, but I tell you the simple truth when I say that I was injured in a fall from my horse; you may believe me or not, as you like."

"I certainly shall exercise my own discretion in doing so."

The prince became livid with rage.

"Santa Maria!" he cried, "you shall answer for this."

He stalked away as he spoke these menacing words.

"There goes a villain, but I'll unearth him yet," muttered Carden, in his sturdy, dogged way.

"I say, Tom," said Jack, "we're going home directly."

"Are you?" returned Carden.

"What's got your temper up, you old bear?"

"You can guess."

"The prince again? I saw you talking to him. You've got your deadly knife into Villanova."

"Barboni, you ought to say," answered Carden.

"Perhaps. That is your particular delusion, you know," said Jack, with a laugh. "But you have not proved it yet, have you?"

"No; but I will, by Jove!"

"You shall have a try to-morrow. I am going to pay Villanova more than I can afford, I'm sorry to say, about a bet."

"What did you bet?" asked Carden.

"Simply that Barboni would not keep his appointment."

"If you will make rash bets, my boy, you must pay," answered Carden.

"It's rather awkward just now. I shall have to borrow it from Harvey," said Jack.

"What's that you want from Harvey?" exclaimed Harvey himself, who walked up in time to catch the last words.

"A thousand pounds, Dick. I know it's a lot of money, but——"

"A lot of humbug," interrupted Harvey. "If you wanted ten or twenty thousand, dear Jack, you should have it."

Jack's eye watered.

"Don't I owe everything to you?" exclaimed Harvey.

"Only a little," replied Jack.

"Didn't you take my part when I was a youngster at school?"

"I tried to."

"And when we were at sea, weren't we pals and shipmates?"

"Rather!"

"And on the desert island, and at Oxford; where I should never have gone if it hadn't been for you."

"I was selfish, Dick, not generous," replied Jack.

"Why?"

"Because I liked you, and couldn't part with you."

"Anyhow, you have stuck to me like a brick all through life, as far as it has gone," answered Harvey.

"And we mean to go on sticking together, Dick."

"Of course we do. I owe my marriage to my darling Hilda to you, and if I have more coin now than you, all I can say is, help yourself."

Jack's eyes got moister than ever.

"Is that straight enough, dear old Jack?" cried Harvey.

"Yes, yes, Dick. I know you'd do a lot for me."

"More than a lot, Jack."

"What do you mean?"

"You should have my life, old fellow, if it would do you any good."

Jack took his hand in his.

The two fists met in one of those grand hearty grasps which, when two men's eyes are looking into each other's, mean so much more than words.

"There's an open cheque for you to-morrow morning," said Harvey. "Fill it up for what you like. I think we understand one another, Jack?"

"You haven't asked me what the bet's about," replied Jack.

"I wouldn't take such a liberty."

"Why?"

"You can bet without asking me, can't you?" said Harvey.

"There is nothing secret about it, though. It was only a thousand with Villanova that Barboni would not keep his appointment."

"If I were you, I wouldn't pay," said Carden.

"Must, dear boy," answered Harvey. "It's a debt of honour.

"That fellow has no honour; he's Barboni."

The young men burst out laughing.

"That was always your idea," said Harvey.

"And it is firmer than ever now."

"It got Jack a shot in the shoulder."

"Did you see the spots of blood?" asked Carden.

"No; what about them?"

Carden related what he had seen on the shirt front of the Prince of Villanova.

"Now I mean to say," he replied, "that those blood marks were produced by Walter Campbell's three shots."

"All rot—excuse me for saying so," replied Harvey.

"'None so blind as those who won't see,'" said Carden. "But you'll all wake up some of these fine mornings, and say I'm right."

CHAPTER XXXVI.

"CAN IT BE ?—NO, IT CAN'T !—YES, IT IS !"

THE cool air blew in through the open windows of the ballroom, laden with a thousand perfumes.

At present the guests did not show any inclination to depart.

"Don't go yet, Jack," said the little coxswain. "This is the jolliest part of the twenty-four hours."

"You'd dance all night, and sleep all day," replied Jack.

"Not a bad plan either, in this hot place.'

" Go and make yourself useful, and send a waiter with some ices—the ladies want some; and, look here, we must go in half-an-hour. There is work to be done to-morrow."

" Brigand hunting ?"

" You've just hit it."

" That's your sort," cried the little coxswain. " I'm on like a shot."

He went off in search of a waiter, and found one with a tray of ices.

" Take those things over there," he said, pointing to Jack's party, " and look sharp, or I pity you."

" Yes, sir," replied the waiter.

" Oh, you're English, are you?"

" Yes, sir."

" Then I need not have wasted my small stock of Italian over you."

" No, sir."

" Don't stand there, yessing and no-sir-ring, or I'll give you a toe-biter, which will make you alter your tune," cried the little coxswain, in his usual overbearing manner.

A sickly smile overspread the face of the waiter, who made no answer.

" Off you go—trot," said Walter.

The waiter shuffled away with the tray.

He was a man past middle age, with a thin, sunburnt face, and an air of long-suffering about him. He wore whiskers, but no beard or moustache. His tail coat was rather the worse for wear, and evidently borrowed, as it did not fit him; a white tie, white stockings, and plush knee-breeches, completed his singular half-and-half sort of livery.

It was clear that he was one of those supernumeraries who are "put on " for the evening, and may be seen at all large parties.

When he reached Jack, he said " Ices, sir?" and then stood staring, as if he had seen a ghost.

" Hand them round, my good fellow," said Jack.

The knees of the waiter seemed to shake and tremble. His tray shook dreadfully, and the ice glasses knocked together as if subjected to a slight shock of earthquake.

" Do you hear ?" said Jack, angrily. " Don't stand staring there like a stuck pig."

The waiter's lips moved, but nothing came from them.

He was trying to speak. His agitation, however, was too much for him.

Again he made an effort.

" Name of Harkaway, sir ?" he asked.

" Yes."

" Commonly called Jack Harkaway, of St. Aldate's, Oxford."

" The same," replied Jack, returning his stare with evident surprise.

The waiter was standing in front of the contessa, and losing all command over himself, he let the tray drop at one end.

About a dozen and a half glasses of delicious cool ices rushed down the inclined plane.

Many landed in the bosom of the contessa.

As she wore a very low dress, the result was not equable to her feelings.

She uttered a piercing shriek.

" Oh, the wretch !" she said. " Turn him out, discharge him. Oh! help! I am freezing to death ! Ugh !"

She shuddered convulsively.

Lily and Hilda rushed to her assistance.

Jack rose and grasped the clumsy attendant by the collar.

" You careless hound !" he said, " I've a jolly good mind and a half to chuck you out of the nearest window."

" Oh, Lord !" said the waiter. " He does not know me. How many more indignities am I to suffer ?"

Something struck Jack as being familiar in the man's voice.

Letting go his hold, he took a good look at him.

" Can it be ?—No, it can't !—Yes, it is !" he stammered.

" Yes, yes," said the man. " In this menial attire—in these cast-off garments of a hired servant, you behold the unfortunate friend of your boyhood, the youthful instructor of your tender mind."

The tray dropped to the ground with a loud bang.

Springing up on his long weedy legs, the waiter extended his bony arms and cast them round Jack's neck.

" Embrace your Mole," he said, in a broken voice.

" By Jove !" said Jack; " wonders will never cease. Who would have thought of seeing you here, Mr. Mole? But I am heartily glad."

" I knew it when I saw you, and felt that I had reached a haven of rest."

Jack gently disengaged his arms.

"Give me your hand, old friend," he said, extending his own.

They met in a cordial grasp.

"Embrace your Mole once more."

"Excuse me, please; it's too hot."

"There was a time—but no matter. Times change, and we change with them."

"What have you been doing?" asked Jack, who could scarcely refrain from laughing at the strange figure he cut.

"My adventures are a complete Odyssey, and it seemed as if misfortune and I were as safe to travel together as that the angles of a triangle are equal to two right angles."

"You went away to be governor of Limbi?"

"I did, but the beasts wanted to eat me."

"To which you naturally objected."

"I did, and came away with my family," replied Mr. Mole.

"Where are they?"

"Our ship was wrecked on the Italian coast, and all perished but myself. My property was lost, and I tramped to Naples a beggar."

"How long have you been here?" said Jack.

"Nearly a month, getting odd jobs occasionally, and to-night I was engaged as a waiter by the major-domo of the contessa, who dressed me up as you see. May the leprosy of Naaman cling to him and his for ever."

"I say, Mr. Mole," cried Jack, "don't be vicious."

"Misfortune has soured me, Harkaway. That major-domo has trampled on my feelings."

"How?"

"In this house there is plenty of good liquor."

"And he wouldn't give you any, I suppose. Quite right, too."

"Hear me. Is it not written 'You shall not muzzle the ox that treadeth out the corn?'" said Mole.

"Yes."

"Well, here have I been toiling all the evening, and had nothing to refresh me but a few brandy cherries some ladies left at the bottom of their glasses."

"It's a hard case. Come and have a bottle of fiz," said Jack.

Mr. Mole seized his hand with both of his.

"Harkaway, you are my friend," he said.

"I hope so."

"You're a fine fellow."

"That is a matter of opinion."

"Embrace your Mole—do."

"Turn it up," answered Jack. "So much of that business won't wash. It looks odd, and your coat's greasy."

"He won't embrace his Mole," said the latter, turning away with a suppressed sob.

Harvey happened to look round, and, seeing Jack in close conversation with a waiter, was astonished.

"Palling up with slaveys," he said. "That's a new game, isn't it?"

"He says he knew you when you were a kid," replied Jack.

"Knew me?"

"Yes; and you were the biggest rip he ever met with."

"It's like his cheek! What does he mean by it?" said Harvey, angrily.

"Come and ask him."

"Do you say you knew me years ago?" he asked, approaching Mole.

"I did, Harvey, and I am sorry to say I never knew any good of you," replied Mr. Mole.

"Why, you thundering old humbug, I've a good mind to kick you."

"I've had more kicks than halfpence since I left Mr. Crawcour's select academy."

"Who is it, Jack?" inquired Harvey, puzzled.

"Thing that burrows in the dark."

"What?"

"Don't you twig?"

"By Jove! it's Mole. I know him now. So you've turned up again, sir," exclaimed Harvey.

"I have."

"This isn't kind of you," said Harvey. "We all thought you were decently drowned at sea, and mourned you as a settled member."

"You mourned me?"

"We wept for you. You shouldn't do such things."

"What things?" asked Mole.

"Coming to life again and startling fellows. It's wrong. Go and die again, do."

"Harvey," said Mr. Mole, "if I thought those were your real sentiments, I would seek——"

"Shake hands, you old duffer. It's only my chaff," interrupted Harvey.

He saw that Mr. Mole was really pained.

"Can't you take a joke?" he added.

"Yes," said Mr. Mole; "but I can't stand being called names, and addressed familiarly. I am poor and in distress, and have lost my all; yet I ought to command your respect."

"You shall have it, sir. To us you will always be the same Mr. Mole, and while we have anything, you shall never want a home or a friend, eh, Jack?"

"Right, Dick. Just what I was going to say."

Mr. Mole's eyes filled with tears.

"My dear boys, God bless you!"

God bless you! was all he could say.

The contessa had gone away in a moist condition, and most of the guests began to take their departure.

Hilda and Lily were ready to go.

Mr. Mole was introduced to them, and they all went home together; apartments being provided for Mole, whom a tailor the next day fitted out with ready-made clothes, such as suited his appearance.

The next day a council of war was held, and it was determined to take a party of soldiers and search again for the brigands. General Cialdini willingly let them have a company.

When Mr. Mole heard of the brigands, and that Emily was held in captivity by them, he became very valorous.

"Lead me against these Amalekites," he said. "Have I not wielded the sword in former times?"

"You shall come with us, sir," replied Jack.

Horses were provided for them, and they were to meet the soldiers, who had been sent on in front, on the other side of the Volturno.

Monday was delighted to see Mr. Mole again, and asked him a multitude of questions about Limbi.

They had spent two hours together before breakfast.

As Mr. Mole got on his horse, he rolled off the other side.

"Hold up, sir," exclaimed Jack.

"It's the sun, Harkaway; I feel a little giddy," answered Mr. Mole.

"You've been in the sun, I think," remarked Jack.

"No, not a drop of anything has passed my lips. No, no, Harkaway; you must make some allowance for my emotion at being amongst old friends again."

Monday appeared with a little cask to be slung over the back.

"Here you are, Mist' Mole," he exclaimed; "catch hold, sare."

"What's that?" asked Jack.

"Only my water cask," replied Mr. Mole.

"Oh! is that all?"

"Yes; on my word, there is nothing more."

Mr. Mole slung the cask over his shoulders, and gathered up the reins.

"I feel as if I should kill brigands to-day," he said; "in fact, several brigands, eh! Mr. Campbell?"

"The more the better," answered the little coxswain.

Beckoning Monday to his side, Jack said in a low tone—

"What's Mole got in that cask?"

"Water, sare."

"If you tell me a lie, I'll break your neck, you old bag of soot."

"You hear him say it am full of um water, sare."

Jack raised his whip.

"Speak the truth, or——"

"Well, it am whisky, sare. He make friends with me, and I give it him out of um pantry," replied Monday.

"All right," said Jack, adding aloud, "now, gentlemen, are you ready?"

The reply being in the affirmative, they started for a brisk ride.

There was bloody work before them, though they did not suspect its near approach.

CHAPTER XXXVII.

CARDEN CHALLENGES THE BRIGAND.

THE little party did not halt until they came to the sybil's cave, where they drew bridle.

A small rill, which trickled down the rocks and, after filling a little basin, disappeared in the earth, enabled them to water their horses.

The poor beasts were much distressed.

Nor were their riders better off.

The heat of the sun was intense, and a draught of the cool, fresh water was as agreeable to them as to their steeds.

Mr. Mole applied his lips to his cask, and drew a deep sigh.

"What have we here?" he asked. "Caves?"

"Yes, and witches," answered Harvey.

"Ah! dear me; I thought witches were an exploded idea. Why not burn a few, as an example to the rest?"

"There is but one," said Jack; "and we suspect her of being an accomplice of the brigands."

"By all means put her to the test."

"We are men, not savages," replied Jack, "and we can't ill-use an old woman."

This response was applauded by the rest of the party.

Leaving the sybil unmolested, they remounted their horses, and cantering on, did not draw rein till they reached the Volturno.

They crossed the rapid river in the ferry-boat, and proceeded to the place where they had appointed to meet the soldiers.

Here they only found a picket.

The officer in command stated that they had fallen in with a band of brigands.

A fight had ensued.

The brigands were beaten back by the soldiers and fled, being pursued to within a short distance of Castel Inferno.

Here they had suddenly vanished as if they had gone into the earth.

The commander was waiting till Mr. Harkaway and his friends came up, not knowing exactly what to do.

Jack pressed forward on hearing this news.

He found the main body of the soldiers lying on their arms, under the shelter of some trees.

The commander at once came up to Jack

"We surprised the rascals, some twenty in number," he said, "and poured in a hot fire."

"That's right," said Jack, rubbing his hands.

"Six fell dead; the remainder fled, and we followed them to this spot."

"What became of them?"

"That is more than I can tell. Per Baccho! these fellows are not like an open enemy; they seemed to sink into the rocks yonder."

"No doubt," said Jack thoughtfully, "they have some caves close at hand. May I offer you some advice?"

"Certainly," answered the officer.

"Throw out some men as sentinels, and keep a good watch."

"I have already done so."

"The scoundrels," cried Jack, "cannot be far off; men don't vanish like smoke."

"Santissima Virgine," cried the officer, "I think they are in league with Satan himself."

"Not they. You will find them as much mortal as yourself, and I hope we shall soon be able to give a good account of them," said Jack.

He rejoined his friends, who had dismounted; their horses cropping the rich grass while they were reclining under the trees, and looking up at the ridge of furze-covered rocks in front.

About a quarter of a mile beyond the rocks rose the gloomy and forbidding towers of Castel Inferno.

"What's the next move?" asked Harvey.

"I am going to visit the prince in the castle."

"Take care he doesn't bag you."

"No danger. I don't fear the prince; it is Barboni from whom treachery may be expected."

"Are we to wait till you come back?" asked Carden.

" Yes ; I won't be long. Keep a look-out for brigands ; they are close at hand," said Jack. " Look well to your arms, or they will be down on you before you know it."

" Cut along," replied Carden.

Jack told his friends all he had heard from the commander of the soldiers.

" It is something to have run them to earth. The place must be thoroughly explored," remarked Harvey.

" When I come back."

" All right ; we'll not be idle while you are gone."

" I shall stick under these trees," said the little coxswain ; " it is so sweltering hot."

" Keep the young one out of danger, Carden," said Jack ; " and watch old Mole."

" Why ?"

" He's got that barrel thing full of whisky."

" The mean beggar ; he's never offered us a drop. I'll be on to him, never fear," said the little coxswain.

Jack explained the object of his absence to the commanding officer, and started on foot for the castle.

No sooner had he gone than Carden said—

" We'll have a lark with Mole."

" I'll help you," answered Harvey.

" Mr. Mole," cried Carden.

" Sir to you," was the answer.

Mr. Mole was lying down at the trunk of a tree, nicely shaded, and enjoying a cigarette.

" Give me a sup out of your water cask."

" Don't disturb me," replied Mole, " there's a good fellow. I'm lying *sub tegmine fagi*, as we used to say at school."

" Don't get up ; I'll fetch the cask, sir."

" I—I don't know where it is."

" Oh ! what a crammer," said Harvey. " It's under your head."

" So it is," said Mole, in apparent surprise.

" Do you mean to say you didn't know that ?"

" I didn't indeed !"

" Humbug !"

" Absence of mind, Harvey. Think of the troubles I've gone through lately, and the responsibility again thrown on my hands of having to look after all you youngsters."

Harvey advanced and took up the cask in spite of Mr. Mole's protests.

" It's empty, Harvey," he said.

" Empty !"

" Yes, put it down again."

" You can't have drunk it all."

" It leaks."

Harvey put the bunghole to his lips.

" Why, hang it all ! it's whisky," he said.

" Nonsense," said Mole, blankly.

" It is, though."

" Bless that fellow Monday," said Mole, with affected indignation.

" Why ?"

" I told him to put water in it, and he's filled it with whisky ; it's too bad. I don't like such practical jokes, and I'll tell him so, too ; he ought not to trifle with a man of my age, in every way his superior."

Carden and Harvey burst out laughing.

" The old un can do it," said Walter Campbell, with a wink.

" I suppose you didn't taste the difference, sir ?" said Harvey.

" No ; I merely sipped it once, and—and there is a mistake somewhere. I'll go and look for brigands."

Mr. Mole was in some confusion, and walked off towards the rocks.

He had not proceeded far before a shot was heard.

Mole rushed back in a hurry, holding his straw hat in his hand.

The bullet had torn part of the brim off.

" They're on us," he cried, wildly. " The battle has begun. Give it them, my brave boys. I will direct your fire. Remember the Pisangs. Up, guards— I mean up, boys, and at 'em."

With this harangue on his lips, he climbed up a tree with some difficulty, and sitting on a bough, surveyed the scene below with his usual complacency.

He had not forgotten to take his whisky cask with him. Applying its bung to his lips every now and then, he continued to shout—

" Give it the wretches—sip—I can see them—gurgle. Shoot every man Jack of them—sip. They'll fly when they see me—suck—I'm the man for brigands— sip. Hurrah for Oxford !—gurgle."

Tom Carden took up the cry,

" Hurrah for Oxford !" he said.

"Give a little one in for Cambridge," said the little coxswain.

"Right you are, my tulip. Hurrah for Cambridge!" said Carden.

"What's to be done?" said Harvey. "There the brigands are, sure enough."

"We've treed them, and it is something to have got at their burrow," said Carden.

"Who'll go in and smoke them out?" asked Harvey.

"Not I," cried the little coxswain. "I'm no mug at a fair. Old Mole's been shot at; and as they are hidden, it is certain death."

"I'll tell you what I'll do," said Carden.

"What, old beans?" inquired Harvey.

"I'll tie a white rag to the end of a stick, and get on that hillock."

"I can't see the use of that."

"Do you think if I challenge the brigand to single combat, he'll come out?"

"Not he."

"I'll try it on, anyhow. Jack's talking to the prince, isn't he?"

"Yes."

"Well, if Barboni comes out and answers my challenge, it follows that the Prince of Villanova and Barboni can't be in two places at once."

"Of course not."

"It will settle the question of identity at once."

"So it will; go in and win, old son," cried Harvey.

Carden quickly tore down a bough, stripped it of leaves and twigs, and fastened a white handkerchief to the end.

Waving it in the air, he climbed up a small hillock.

"I, Tom Carden, captain of the Oxford eight, challenge Barboni to single combat; and let the best man win."

He uttered this in a loud voice.

There was no reply.

The brigands, wherever they were, so far respected the flag as to refrain from firing at him.

"If Barboni refuses this challenge," cried Carden, "I shall brand him as a coward, and I give him fifteen minutes to answer it in."

The challenge was delivered in Italian, and the soldiers uttered a loud hurrah.

Tom sat down leisurely on the hillock,

and, filling his pipe, lighted it with a fusee, and smoked calmly.

At the same time he took out his watch, and contemplated the hands.

"Bet you a bob," said Harvey, "he don't show up."

"Odds he does," replied the little coxswain.

"Bravo, Carden," said Mr. Mole, from his perch; "you're a brave fellow. Oxford for ever."

"Hullo!"

This exclamation was caused by his losing his seat, and falling to the ground.

He was only a little shaken, and picked himself up directly, amidst loud laughter.

"Tight already, sir?" said Harvey.

"No, Harvey, not tight."

"What then?"

"It's a dodge of the rascally brigands; they've greased all the boughs of the trees."

"I'd give them something for it, sir, if I were you."

"So I will," answered Mole, who was made valiant by the whisky.

He advanced recklessly towards the ridge of rocks.

"Haul him back," said Carden; "do you want him to be killed?"

The little coxswain ran after him, and pulled him back.

"Why this violence?" he asked.

"It's dangerous, and we don't want to lose you."

"Bear witness, all of you," said Mr. Mole, "that I am no coward. Harvey is afraid of those brigands, but I am not. I have set him and all of you an example of bravery. Where's my cask?"

He suffered himself to be taken to a safe place, and presently a gentle gurgle came from the bunghole of the cask.

"Brigands!" he said, in contempt. "What are brigands to Pisangs? Ha! ha! we have fought Pisangs, Harvey, with Hunston at their head."

"Yes, sir," replied Harvey; "and we licked them, too."

"We are bound to lick everything. But Hunston was a teaser. The brigands haven't got Hunston."

"It is not very likely."

"Ten minutes gone," said Carden, from his hillock.

"Barboni won't show up," remarked Harvey.

The soldiers roused themselves from the apathy into which the heat of the sun had plunged them.

Sentinels paced slowly up and down, keeping strict guard outside the little camp.

The officers gathered together in a little knot, talked and smoked, looking as if they did not like the duty which had been given them.

They were placed under Jack Harkaway's orders, however, by General Cialdini, and for the day they were obliged to do what he told them.

In their hearts they liked the brigands better than they did the English.

CHAPTER XXXVIII.

THE TELEGRAM.

JACK made his way quickly to the castle in which Prince Villanova resided.

He found the drawbridge down as before, and the same absence of bustle and ostentation.

Passing through the courtyard, he met a servant who at once conducted him to the prince's study.

His highness was reading a newspaper, published in Naples, which gave an account of the escape of Barboni.

He rose instantly, and welcomed Jack in the most cordial manner.

Jack had obtained bank notes for Harvey's cheque, and laid them on the table.

"That will make us quits," he said.

"Oh, yes. I'd quite forgotten our little wager of last night. Many thanks. You will stay a little while with me, will you not?"

"I cannot remain long," said Jack.

"Have you business to attend to?"

"Yes, I am brigand hunting, as usual."

"Per Baccho!" laughed the prince, "you seem to have but one idea in life."

"For the present I have only one, and that is to bring Barboni to justice."

"Forget him for a time. Let us smoke a cigar and drink some iced wine. It is not often I get the privilege of talking to a well-bred, well-read Englishman like yourself."

Jack bowed.

"Have you been in England?" he asked.

"Oh, yes, years ago. By the way, are your friends with you?"

"They are not far off."

"Will you not ask them to honour my poor house with their presence?"

"Thank you; they are otherwise engaged," answered Jack.

He did not say that they were watching for the brigands to appear, and had a force of soldiers with them.

Villanova ordered some wine and cigars to be brought, and he endeavoured to interest Jack in conversation.

While they were thus engaged, we must take a peep into a little room, a short distance from the prince's study.

There sat a man before a plain deal table, the table and the chair constituting the sole furniture of the carpetless apartment.

This man was Bigamini.

Before him, fixed against the bare wall, was a small dial.

On its face were printed the twenty-four letters of the alphabet, like the figures on a clock.

In its centre was a hand or needle, lying motionless.

Bigamini never took his eyes off this dial.

Suddenly there was a sharp noise.

Click! click!

He seized a pen and prepared to write on a piece of paper, which he had before him.

The dial was the face of a telegraphic apparatus.

He was about to read off a telegram.

Quickly the needle flew from one letter to another, Bigamini marking each one, until a sudden click announced that the work was completed.

When the needle had stood still, this was what Bigamini had written down—

"Harkaway's friends and a company of soldiers are blockading entrance to cave. Carden has just challenged Barboni to show himself in fifteen minutes, to fight in single combat. Waiting instructions.   "HUNSTONI."

Bigamini rang a little bell.

Scarcely had its gentle tinkle, tinkle died away when a servant entered.

Folding what he had written, he put it in an envelope.

"Take this," he said, "to your master."

The attendant bowed.

"It admits of no delay."

The servant went away with the missive, and delivered it to the prince.

"A letter," said the latter. "Have I your permission, Mr. Harkaway?"

"Certainly; don't mind me," said Jack.

The prince read the contents of the envelope.

Not a muscle of his countenance moved. He smiled blandly.

"How unfortunate!" he said.

"Why so?" asked Jack.

"It is a letter on business from my lawyer, requiring an immediate reply."

"Answer it, then."

"It may take me a little time."

"Never mind."

"I have to consult documents."

"By all means consult them."

"You are very kind. May I hope that you will be able to amuse yourself for half-an-hour?"

"Oh, yes."

"If you feel bored at the idea. I will put it off," said Villanova.

"I will not hear of such a thing," said Jack.

"Thank you very much. You will find all your favourite English authors on those shelves."

"I shall be all right."

"Is the champagne cup to your liking?"

"Yes."

"And the cigars?"

"Are excellent," replied Jack.

"Then I leave you for a short time, with an easy conscience."

The prince quitted the study, and Jack, taking up a book, began to read.

CHAPTER XXXIX.

THE SINGLE COMBAT.

TOM CARDEN continued to look at his watch with some impatience.

"Time's up," he said, at last.

"The jolly old brigand doesn't mean to show," said the little coxswain.

Suddenly a loud voice was heard.

"Mr. Carden, I am at your service."

This was what it said.

Tom looked in the direction from which the voice proceeded.

Standing in front of a row of bushes was a figure, which everyone instantly recognised as Barboni.

Threescore rifles were levelled at him in a moment.

"Hold!" cried Carden.

The commander of the troops looked towards him.

"I have challenged the brigand to single combat," cried Carden. "Make your men lower their rifles at once; this is treachery; remember we are English-born."

Reluctantly the officer gave the command.

Barboni the brigand spoke again.

"I trust to the good faith of an English gentleman, Mr. Carden," he said.

"You could not trust to anything better," was the reply.

"I am sure I am in good hands with an Oxford man. Here are two swords; will the weapons suit you?"

"They will do as well as anything else," cried Carden.

He walked towards the brigand, who descended the rock, and stood in an open space.

"Back!" said Carden; "let no one come within a hundred yards."

The command was obeyed, with but one exception.

Mr. Mole came up in a tottering manner.

"Just take one sip out of my cask, Carden," he said. "It will enable you to annihilate the brigand."

"If I can't fight without whisky, my dear sir, I can't fight at all," replied Tom.

"That's a shut up for you, sir," said Harvey, as Mr. Mole went back.

"All the better, Harvey; there is more for me; but I thought I would do the generous thing," answered Mr. Mole.

Barboni's lips parted.

The terrible whistle of which we have so often spoken escaped from them.

Instantly the rocks were alive with the forms of brigands, who seemed to have sprung out of the earth.

They outnumbered the soldiers.

"Pardon me," said Barboni, "for this display of my power."

"It was unnecessary, as far as I am concerned," answered Carden.

"I know that. It is not you I fear, but my own countrymen, and you will not blame me for looking after myself."

"Certainly not."

"Choose your weapon, sir."

Barboni handed Carden two swords of equal length. Tom took one.

He bent it over his knee, and found it flexible.

"On guard," cried Barboni; "time presses."

Carden put himself in position, and the swords clashed in the salute.

"Sa! ha!" cried the brigand.

The combatants faced one another, with eyes fixed on each other's movements.

Swiftly flashed the swords, but without any wound being inflicted.

"Ha! I have you there," cried Carden, making a thrust.

But the brigand stepped back, and the sword's point only grazed his shoulder.

It was evident from the first that Barboni was the more accomplished swordsman of the two.

In vain Carden tried to break down his guard.

He could not succeed.

With a dexterity that was marvellous Barboni parried every thrust, and at length, with a twist of the wrist, sent his adversary's sword flying in the air.

A shout arose from the brigands.

Carden stood defenceless before his enemy.

"Strike," he said; "a brave man doesn't fear death."

Barboni courteously lowered his sword.

"It is my right to kill you, since I have conquered," he said.

"Exercise your right; though I could have wished to die by a worthier hand."

"No; you are free to depart."

"Free?" cried Carden, who did not expect this generosity.

"Go, sir," answered Barboni; "and remember that you owe the brigand a life."

"I shall not forget it," said Carden.

He walked back to his friends with a crestfallen air.

The little coxswain had been greatly excited during this affair. His rage knew no bounds when he saw Carden beaten.

"Hi!" he said, "you brigand swell! You mountain robber!"

Barboni turned, and regarded him sternly.

"What do you want with me?" he asked.

"Come and fight me. I'm not afraid of you. Pistols for two and a coffin for one, you know the style of thing."

"I do not fight with children. I am no chicken butcher," replied Barboni.

The little coxswain retired in disgust.

"Hang his cheek!" he muttered. "I should like to paint that ugly mug of his."

Barboni retired behind a knoll, and was joined by Darrelli, who asked for orders.

"Retire with your men to the hills," said Barboni; "you must not let the soldiers suspect the existence of the cave."

"Shall we pour in a volley now?"

"By no means. I do not want to exasperate the troops.

"Lead off your men, throwing them out in order of skirmishers."

"I understand," replied Darrelli.

"If attacked, defend yourselves, and come back here when all pursuit is over."

With these words, Barboni sank through a hole in the rock, which was partly covered with brushwood and grass.

He dropped into a vaulted chamber.

A brigand was awaiting him with a torch.

"Lead on," said Barboni.

He descended half a dozen steps, and entered a subterranean passage, in the devious windings of which he was soon lost to sight.

The brigands, meanwhile, had deployed into the open plain.

This manoeuvre was seen by the commander of the soldiers, who gave instant chase to them.

"Shall we go after them?" asked Harvey.

"Someone must wait for Harkaway," replied Carden.

"Suppose you stay with Mole?"

"Very well. You and Walter can join in the pursuit," answered Carden.

They looked to their arms, and mounting their horses, rode after the soldiers.

A dropping fire was sustained between the two parties, which did little or no damage.

The troops were half-hearted in the pursuit, and all the brigands wanted was to get away.

Carden threw himself on the ground and lighted his pipe, while Mr. Mole, hugging his cask tightly, watched the two bodies of men popping away at one another in the plain below.

"You have missed a splendid opportunity," he remarked. "It was lucky for the brigand he had not me to tackle."

"He knows a trick or two of fencing," replied Carden.

"What you want is to meet skill with skill. Harkaway will tell you that I have slain thousands in battle. You have courage, but no skill. Rowing in a boat does not make a man a soldier."

"Don't worry me, there's a good fellow," said Carden; "I'm rather down in the mouth."

Mr. Mole subsided, and applying himself to his cask, was soon so overcome by heat and whisky that he fell fast asleep.

CHAPTER XL.

THE FOUR FRIENDS MAKE NO PROGRESS.

It seemed to Jack that when the prince returned, he had not been absent more than twenty minutes.

Looking at his watch, he found that the actual time was half an hour.

"Have I kept you waiting?" asked Villanova, with his most pleasant smile.

"Not in the least; the time seems to have slipped away most pleasantly," answered Jack.

"Can I tempt you to stay to dinner?"

"Pray excuse me; my friends are waiting. I was only anxious to get out of your debt."

"Let me walk a little way with you."

"With pleasure."

Jack took another pull at the champagne cup, and putting on his hat, they sallied forth together.

The same stillness was remarkable in the courtyard of the castle.

A stableman was lazily grooming a horse, a gardener carried some vegetables to the kitchen, the fowls and pigeons routed about a manure-heap with the pigs, and the solitude of a country house was everywhere noticeable.

Side by side they crossed some grassy meadows, which led them to the spot where Carden and Mole were awaiting their coming.

At their approach, Carden sprang up.

He looked surprised to see the prince, who extended his hand.

"Excuse me," said Carden, "but I cannot shake you by the hand."

"As you please," replied the prince, stiffly.

"It is as well to be straightforward."

"Certainly."

"I make no secret of my dislike and suspicion of you. I have accused you of certain things, and I live in the hope of tearing the mask from your face."

Villanova shrugged his shoulders.

"What does your friend mean, Mr. Harkaway?" he asked.

"Something has put him out. What is it, old fellow?"

Carden made no reply.

Mole, roused by the sound of voices, woke up, and catching the last words, said—

"I'll answer that question for him. He has been shamefully beaten in a single combat by the brigand chief, who disarmed him, and generously spared his life."

"Is this so?" asked Jack.

"Yes," replied Carden, sulkily.

"Did you challenge Barboni?"

"I did, and we fought, with the result

Mr. Mole has given you. Now let me ask a question."

" By all means."

" Have you and the prince been together all the time ?"

" With the exception of a short while. His highness received a letter from his lawyer, and he went into another room to answer it," said Jack.

Tom Carden looked puzzled.

" I'm blessed if I can make it out," he said.

" Where are Harvey and Campbell ?" inquired Jack.

" Gone with the soldiers after the brigands, who showed in force and retreated. Can't you hear the firing ?"

The sharp, but distant crack of the rifles was heard in the distance.

" I wish those brigands could be exterminated," remarked the prince. " It is extremely unpleasant for me that they should come so near my castle."

" Humbug," muttered Carden, through his clenched teeth.

" To some extent they compromise you," said Jack.

" How ?"

" They are supposed to take refuge on your estate."

" Not with my knowledge or consent, nor do I see where they could hide. I will add this thousand pounds you have given me this morning to the reward the government have offered for the capture of Barboni."

" Bravo !" said Jack; " that is indeed princely."

" Will you tell General Cialdini so with my compliments ?"

" Gladly."

" And now, good bye. I shall look forward to our next meeting," said the prince.

" Is that a friend of yours, Harkaway ?" asked Mr. Mole.

" I consider him so."

Mole rose and with a staggering walk approached the prince.

" Have a suck out of my cask ?" he exclaimed.

" No, thank you, I am not thirsty," replied the prince.

" Not thirsty in this country ? I'm always dry. If you won't drink, embrace your Mole."

He was about to throw his arms round him, when his foot slipped, and he fell on his face.

" It's very odd. What an effect the sun has in this country on me !" he observed. " Bother the sun !"

His cask was by his side.

Drawing it to him, he pressed it to his waistcoat, and murmured fondly—

" Embrace your Mole."

With a careless nod to Carden, Villanova took his leave, and was soon lost to sight among the trees and hillocks.

Harkaway and Carden told Mole to await their return, and strolled arm-in-arm in the direction of the firing.

" My dear Tom," said Jack, " you must see the folly of suspecting the prince by this time."

" I don't," replied Carden.

" Now, listen to reason. How could Villanova, in his castle, know that you had challenged Barboni, and, supposing him to be Barboni, how could he come and fight you and be back again with me in little over a quarter of an hour ?"

" It licks me to make it out," said Carden; " but I've got a deadly knife into that fellow."

" What for ?"

" I believe him to be a brigand in disguise."

They walked some distance in silence.

Before they had got far Harvey and the little coxswain came up at a gallop.

" What luck ?" asked Jack.

" None at all. We have killed a dozen of the beggars, and they have done as much for our side," replied Harvey.

" Where are they now ?"

" They have taken refuge in the hills"

" Won't they show fight ?"

" Not they."

" What of the soldiers ?"

" They've turned it up in disgust and gone home. The captain said it was no use exposing his men's lives in this hill fighting, which would be all in favour of Barboni and his men."

" Perhaps he is right. We had best turn tail too for to-day," said Jack.

" There seems to be no getting at this Barboni," said Harvey, with a tone of vexation.

" It's like fighting a shadow," remarked the little coxswain.

" Because you don't go the right way to work," said Carden.

"How do you mean?" asked all three, in a breath.

"Villanova's the substance, Barboni's the shadow."

"Now, look here," exclaimed Jack; "I'll show you how absurd that is."

He related the fact of his being with the prince all the morning with the exception of a brief space.

"So," he added, "you see Tom's wrong. A man can't be in two places at once, can he?"

"Not likely," answered Harvey.

"And as to the brigands being hidden on the prince's estate, I will say two things," Jack went on.

"What are they?" asked Carden.

"Firstly, would he offer a thousand pounds reward for the capture of himself and his own men?

"Secondly, would the brigands retire to the hills some miles off, if they could burrow in a secret cave close by?"

"I have my own ideas," replied Carden, "and I'll stick to them. It's my opinion that the solution of the problem is close at hand."

"For my part," added Harvey, "I think Barboni is to be hunted down in the mountains over there."

"I fancy he's to be met with in the sybil's cave," remarked the little coxswain.

"I think," said Jack, "that we are on the wrong track, and that his head quarters are at Torre del Greco, at the base of Mount Vesuvius, where several robberies have taken place lately."

"Gentlemen," said Carden, "let us all set out to-morrow morning separately, and pursue our explorations in our own manner."

"Hear, hear!" cried all.

"Let Harvey explore the mountains, Harkaway the base of Vesuvius, Walter Campbell the sybil's cave, and I myself will take the ground about the Prince Di Villanova's castle."

"Right you are," cried Jack. "Let us hope we shall meet again alive, and free from the brigand's treachery."

Carden still continued to unfold his plans.

"No one," said he, "shall be absent in search of the brigand more than five days. If, after the expiration of that time, any one of us is missing, those who have returned shall think something has happened to him, and go in search."

"Agreed, agreed," said everyone.

"I think that's a very sensible proposition," said Mr. Mole, "and as danger may be apprehended in your absence, I will stop at home and mind the ladies."

There was a laugh at this.

After a little more conversation, the party mounted their horses and returned to Naples.

All were fully determined to adopt Carden's plan without delay.

*　　*　　*　　*　　*

The confinement to which she was subjected in the brigand's cave caused Emily to grow pale.

Neither by night nor day was she allowed to breathe the fresh air.

In addition to this, her anxiety respecting her own fate and that of her husband and his friends, was a constant worry to her.

For some time past, as we know, she had been in weak health.

Her captivity rendered her low and nervous.

She drooped like a lily on its stem, when the first frost of winter has touched it with its blighting hand.

Occasionally she saw Barboni, Hunston, and Darrel, who all treated her with the utmost politeness.

Every delicacy of the table she could wish for was brought her.

Iced wines and fruits stood constantly on a table in her prison.

She had all she wanted, but her liberty and the society of Jack.

Shortly after Harkaway's last visit to Castel Inferno, Hunston knocked at the door of the cavern in which she was.

"Come in," she said.

He entered, holding a bunch of rare flowers in his hand.

"Pardon me, Emily," he said, "if I have disturbed you."

"I am your prisoner," she answered, "and I suppose if I objected to your freedom in calling me Emily, it would be of little use."

"Mrs. Harkaway, then."

"As I am Harkaway's wife, and can possibly be no friend of yours," she said, "I think I am entitled to that amount of respect, at all events."

"THE BRIGAND DREW HIMSELF UP HAUGHTILY AND CONFRONTED JACK."

"THE BRIGAND DREW HIMSELF UP HAUGHTILY AND CONFRONTED JACK.'

"It seems only yesterday," exclaimed Hunston, with a sigh, "that we were all children."

"You sigh," exclaimed Emily.

"I have reason to," he answered.

"Are you not happy?"

"No, and I shall never be. I look back upon a misspent life and a career of violence. I may lose my life at any time. I have no friend and no one to smile upon me."

"Whose fault is that?"

"It's Harkaway's," replied Hunston, promptly.

"No, no," said Emily, "that is untrue. You have only yourself to blame."

She did not tell him to go away, because she had been several days alone, and only those who know the misery of solitary confinement, can understand the pleasure there is in talking to somebody.

A prisoner will send for the chaplain of the prison, on any pretext, for the sake of a little conversation, which is denied him with the gaolers or his fellow sufferers.

Even Hunston was better than nobody to talk to.

He might tell her how things were going on, and what Jack was doing.

That Harkaway would leave the brigands alone, she did not expect for a moment.

His efforts would redouble against them since the capture of his wife.

"Well," said Hunston, with a reckless laugh, "we will not talk about a poor devil like myself. While there is wine and brandy to be got, I shall not despair."

"How is my husband?" asked Emily.

"Well enough," answered Hunston. "But he has not routed us out yet."

"He will, sooner or later."

"I can tell you what he will do," said Hunston, with a sardonic grin.

"What?"

"He will join you here soon."

"Join me?"

"Not exactly. You will not be allowed to meet, but the chief has a splendid idea for his capture, which, if it comes off, as I think it will, must place Mr. Harkaway in our power."

Emily trembled.

"You will spare his life?" she said. "You cannot be so brutal as to wish for a death."

Hunston made no answer.

He poured some water into a glass, and placed the flowers he held in his hand in it.

"See what pretty flowers I have brought you," he observed.

"I thank you very much, but never mind the flowers; talk to me about Jack," she replied.

"I would rather talk about anybody else."

"Why?"

"Because I hate him, as you know."

Emily clasped her hands together in an entreating manner.

"Oh! do please tell me, Hunston, that you are still man enough to use your influence to let Jack go if they catch him."

"Not I," he answered, carelessly.

"What has he done, that you should be so hard upon him?"

"You know as well as I do that he has licked me in everything, all my life through. But I am not quite so hard as you think me."

"I thought you—you might be generous, and I am sure Jack will reward you for it."

"I don't want his favours."

"What, then?"

"Your love."

As he spoke, Hunston looked straight in her face, and so ardent was his gaze that her eyes fell as if some wild beast had been staring at her.

"Love me," said Hunston, "and I will take very good care that no harm comes to Jack."

Emily had gone very white at first, but her pallor was succeeded by a deep red flush of indignation and anger.

"Mr. Hunston!" she exclaimed, "you are a low coward and a blackguard, to talk to me in this way! You see I am defenceless, and you insult me."

"Listen to reason, my dear Mrs. Harkaway," he replied, somewhat abashed.

"There is no reason in what you say. It is the old, old story."

"Is it a crime to love you?" he demanded.

"Yes, now that I am another man's wife. You know very well that I dislike you."

"You will not be another man's wife long," he said, with a diabolical smile.

"What do you mean?"

"Harkaway's head will be sent as a present to General Cialdini, and you will be a widow."

"You have to catch him first," answered Emily, repressing her horror and disgust, and trying to be bold.

"That we are sure to do. Our plan is cut and dried. It cannot fail."

"Why?"

"Because the four friends are going to separate, and each one going by himself to hunt for Barboni."

"How do you know this?"

"Our spy, a man named Bigamini, has brought in the information."

"Is Jack coming this way?"

"No; he's going on a wild-goose chase to Torre del Greco."

"Where is that?"

"At the base of Vesuvius, and Barboni is even now making preparations to capture him."

"Very well," said Emily, with the calmness of a true heroine. "Heaven has guarded him up to this time."

"Will you not save him?" asked Hunston.

"He would not wish me to save his life by being false to him."

Hunston gnashed his teeth.

"Think of what you are doing," he said.

"I have thought."

"You can make sure of a happy future. Fly with me to some island in the Mediterranean. I have saved money."

"By what means?" asked Emily, scornfully.

"As lieutenant of this band, I have received a large share of the——"

He hesitated.

"Let me fill up the gap for you. Your money is in reality plunder. I can have no dealings with a thief."

"By Heaven!" said Hunston, angrily, "you will provoke me too far."

"Go; leave me. Never come here gain. Your presence is an insult."

"You shall be mine!" he cried; "if ot by fair means, by foul. As a reward of my services, Barboni has promised you to me."

Emily shrank before his impudent gaze.

At this juncture there was a quick footstep behind him.

Hunston found himself seized by the arm and thrown violently backwards.

Turning angrily, he saw Lord Darrel standing between him and his prey.

"Cowardly hound!" said Darrel. "I came in time to hear what you said, and I tell you it is false. You have no power over this lady, nor does Barboni intend that you should have."

Hunston raised his one arm, and shook his fist threateningly at Darrel.

The blood of both men was up.

"Beware!" he said. "You have come between me and Mrs. Harkaway before, and then I gave you fair warning of what you might expect if you did it again."

"Get out of the vault," said Darrel.

"And leave you here? That is very likely!"

"If you don't go, I shall have to kick you out. No one but a rank cur would insult a lady as you have done."

"Oh, my lord," said Emily, "do not quarrel. Send for the brigand chief. Pray do not fight. My nerves are so weak, I cannot bear a scene."

Hunston drew a pistol from his belt.

Cocking it, he aimed at Darrel.

"Be off," he said, "or I fire."

Darrel was also armed, and he lost no time in imitating Hunston's example.

"Two can play at that game," he said, between his clenched teeth.

Emily, half fainting with terror, sank upon a rude couch.

Hunston pulled the trigger, but such was his rage and agitation that the bullet whistled harmlessly over Darrel's head.

The latter was about to return his fire, when he lowered his arm.

His face was towards the entrance to the vault, while Hunston had his back against it.

He had seen a tall, commanding form enter hurriedly.

The next instant Hunston's pistol was dashed from his grasp, and Barboni confronted him.

"Leave this chamber, both of you," he exclaimed, imperiously, "and never enter it again on pain of death."

"You promised me that I——" began Hunston.

"Not a word. I will talk to you afterwards. Must I lose my best men through a foolish quarrel? Away to the outer cave, Hunstoni, and take command of a band waiting to stop travellers on the Appian Road."

Hunston darted a look of implacable hatred at Darrel, and slouched unwillingly away.

"Madam," said Barboni, addressing Emily in that low, thrilling tone he knew so well how to adopt when talking to women.

Emily rose from the rude couch, and answered him with a look.

"Your pardon for again being annoyed by one of my officers."

"It is willingly granted," replied Emily, "for I do not believe it is with your permission that Mr. Hunston persecutes me with his attentions."

"Cospetto! you may say that with truth. But the dogs will exceed orders sometimes. Rest assured it shall not be repeated with my sanction."

Emily bowed in grateful acknowledgment of this promise.

She would have begged him to spare Jack's life should he fall into his hands, but she knew the uselessness of appealing to such a flinty heart.

"Darrelli," said Barboni, "you will accompany me. I have much to say to you."

Gus Darrel held out his hand to Emily, but she did not take it.

She remembered that it was red with the blood of poor Lieutenant Cockles.

Though he had rendered her a service, she could not treat him as a friend.

Somewhat hurt at this studied coldness, he followed the brigand into another vaulted apartment, where a lamp was burning, and they were alone.

"Darrelli," said Barboni, with a grave, preoccupied air, which was unusual with him, "the time has come for an explanation between us."

"What can there be in common between you and I?" asked Darrel, drawing himself up proudly.

"You shall hear. Since Harkaway and his friends have brought us into such notoriety, we hold our lives in our hands."

"That is true; but my motto is a short life and a merry one."

"Whatever happens to me—and I suppose I shall end my life on the scaffold, or die by a bullet—I want you to be happy."

"I do not know that I am miserable," replied Darrel.

"You must take your place in society," said the brigand.

"How can I, since that unlucky blow killed Lieutenant Cockles?"

"I have agents in England who have looked into the case, which is really one of manslaughter. You had words with and struck him; your punishment therefore, will be a nominal one."

"By Jove!" replied Darrel, stroking his moustache, "if I had looked at it in that light, I need not have cut England."

"There was the hand of fate urging you on. We were destined to meet."

"Bosh!" said Darrel, contemptuously.

"You will not say so when you hear all."

"What possible connection can there be between Lord Darrel and Barboni the brigand?"

"I will tell you. In the first place, you are not, legally, Lord Darrel."

"Not Lord Darrel! Who the deuce am I then?" cried Gus Darrel, jumping up from the stool on which he had been sitting.

"My son," answered Barboni, solemnly.

Gus Darrel laughed aloud.

"That's good," he said. "I like that; go on, pile it up."

"Santo Dio! I speak the truth."

"Who are you then?"

"Dominico Ponilippo, the Italian steward, who murdered the late Lord Darrel, and ran away with his widow and his child, leaving my own son in his place."

"Do you mean to say you left me to be brought up as a peer, when I had no right to the honour?"

"I do."

Gus Darrel's countenance fell.

"Tell me all about it," he said.

"Bear patiently with me," answered the brigand; "what I did was for your sake, and had you not given way to your evil passions, and been driven by the force of circumstances to join me in Naples, you would never have known one word of all this."

"If what you say is true——"

"Santa Maria! I swear it."

"Well, well," said Darrel impatiently "you are right; the hand of fate is in this."

He resumed his seat, and biting his lips till the blood came, waited to hear what Barboni had further to reveal.

CHAPTER XLI.

"LUNI."

"YOUR mother died soon after you were born," Barboni resumed, after a short pause.

"I was born in England, of course," said Darrel.

"You were. It was at Lord Darrel's house that your birth took place. His lordship had given me notice to leave. That angered me, and I resolved to have my revenge."

"A terrible one it was," said Gus Darrel.

"Yes, I have ever been a good hater. Well, I placed you in the cot occupied by the young lord who, like yourself, was only a few weeks old. I killed Lord Darrel, and carried off the young lord and his mother."

"Where are they now?"

"Here," answered Barboni. "For years the mother and child have been captives, living on sufferance as it were."

"Have I seen either of them?"

"Yes; the boy we call Luni, or Lunatico, a half-witted fellow, is the child."

"Luni? Can it be possible?" returned Darrel.

"The boy was never sharp, and the kicks and cuffs he has received have not tended to sharpen his intellect."

"Why did you not kill him out of the way?" asked Darrel, brutally.

"Because I once had a strong affection for his mother, Lady Darrel, and her heart and soul are wrapt up in the boy."

"Does he know who he is?"

"No; I have threatened to kill him if she breathes a word to him."

"Where is Lady Darrel?"

"She, too, poor creature, is half mad," replied Barboni, "and has been for years. At night you may have seen her wandering harmlessly about, dressed in white."

"Ah! she's what the men call the 'White Spectre,'" said Darrel, recollecting that he had seen an apparition such as Barboni described.

"Yes. Il Spirito, or the White Spectre, is the name she goes by."

"Does anyone but yourself know anything of this precious history?" asked Darrel, bitterly.

"Only her ladyship."

"What is your object in revealing this terrible secret to me?" said Gus Darrel, more earnestly.

"I love my son," was the steady reply.

"Am I in future to call myself Dominico Ponilippo?"

"No! a thousand times no!" replied Barboni, emphatically. "I want you to return to England, and boldly face your trial for the manslaughter of that young fellow. Nothing will come of it, and you can enjoy the title and estates of the Darrel family."

The young man made no answer.

"Son of a brigand, eh?" he muttered. "Cruel stroke of fortune this. A beggar's brat. Son of an Italian steward. Son of a murderer. Scum! that's what it comes to. Pleasant look-out. Scum, nothing but scum!"

"I never meant you to know it," replied Barboni. "I meant you to be rich and great."

"You were certainly an affectionate father," sneered Darrel.

"Why not?"

"You never saw or looked after me."

"I knew you were in good hands. I watched over you from a distance. You were sent to Eton; from Eton, you went to a private tutor's, and entered a cavalry regiment. Could your prospects have been brighter?"

"You may be proud of me as a son," answered Darrel, "but I'll be hanged if I am of you as a father."

"Leave me then; quit this place at once."

"No, I won't do that either; I'm not a coward, and I'll see you through this affair of yours with Harkaway. Then, if you like to become a respectable man again, I'll see if I can help you."

Barboni got up and wrung Darrel's hand.

The tears rolled down his rugged cheeks, and it was clear that this roughly-expressed kindness of Darrel had touched his heart. It was a heart not usually accessible to tender emotions.

Yet the man of blood and crime had his weak point, and this was his son.

"Thank you, my boy," he said, in a broken voice. "You do not cast me off."

"You have taken me all aback by what you have told me," answered Darrel. "But I will make the best of it."

"Believe me, I sacrificed much for your sake in the past."

"Say no more about it. I would rather never have heard this confession, and we must meet on the old terms before strangers."

"Certainly. To me only are you the brigand's son."

Scarcely had these words left Barboni's lips when a rustling in a corner was heard.

"What's that?" asked Darrel.

Barboni strode to the spot, and removing some matting which had been placed there, revealed the form of a young man.

Darrel approached curiously.

"Come out," he said, giving the crouching figure a kick.

A thin, wretched-looking youth reluctantly got up, and came into the light of the lamp.

"Luni!" exclaimed Barboni. "How came you here?"

"I fell asleep, signor, and only woke up when I heard voices just now," was the reply.

Gus Darrel took a long look at him

He had before him the real Lord Darrel, the heir to the title and estates which he had so long usurped.

Luni had a vacant countenance, a shambling walk, and a startled manner.

His attire was ragged and fantastic, and his lack of intelligence was easily visible.

Gus Darrel gave him a heavy box on the ears.

"Don't tell any lies, you rascal!" he said. "You've been listening."

Luni was as tall as Darrel, but not nearly so thick-set or strong.

They were both of the same age, though no one would have taken the puny, half-starved, trembling, knock-kneed youth to be as old as Darrel.

Instead of returning the blow, he burst into tears.

"Don't hit me," he said; "please don't hit me again, and I'll tell the truth."

Darrel's only reply was to hit him again, and this time with his fist between the eyes.

"Oh, Santissima Virgine!" cried Luni, as he staggered back and fell on the floor.

"Get up," said Gus Darrel, kicking him. "I knew you were listening all along. Get up, or I'll murder you!"

He hated him because he now knew that he was the real Lord Darrel.

Poor, half-witted, ill-treated, starved, and ragged as he was, this outcast was nevertheless a peer of Great Britain.

It was gall and wormwood to Gus Darrel to know this.

His vicious nature made him detest the poor fellow for it.

"Gently," said Barboni, "leave him to me."

He took the youth by the arm, and raised him to his feet.

"Luni," he said.

"Si, signor."

"You know me?"

Luni looked at him in a scared, half-terrified manner.

"Si, signor," he replied.

"Tell me the truth. I have beaten you before, and you know I can do it again. Who sent you in here to spy upon us?"

"She did."

"Who?"

"Il Spirito."

"What have you heard?" asked Barboni.

"I cannot tell. You frighten me too much. I heard something, but I have forgotten; it has gone all away. He hit me so hard. Oh! let me go, please," replied Luni, in a quick, nervous tone.

"Give him to me; I'll make the obstinate beggar speak," said Gus Darrel.

Barboni allowed him to remove him from his grasp.

Holding him by his hair with one hand, Darrel hit him hard, right and left, kicking him to keep him upright when he stumbled.

Luni struggled desperately, and uttered piercing cries.

Then his yells subsided into subdued moans and sobs.

Suddenly a form darkened the doorway, a dagger gleamed in the lamplight, and Gus Darrel's arm dropped useless by his side, while the blood streamed down to the floor.

"Confound it!" he said; "what is this?"

Luni was released, and he ran to the door.

Gus Darrel looked in the direction of Barboni, and saw him standing with his arms folded. Then he turned his gaze on one side.

Now he saw that it was neither Barboni nor Luni who had wounded him.

The blow had been struck by a woman.

She was tall and thin, haggard and woe-begone, her dress a ragged muslin, which clung awkwardly to her gaunt frame, while her tangled hair streamed wildly over her shoulders.

In her eye was a fierce light, akin to madness, and, attenuated though her features were, they still preserved traces of nobility, if not of beauty.

Her hand was upraised, and still held the dagger which had crippled the arm which dealt the cruel blows to Luni.

He shrank back, cowering before this strange apparition.

"What is it?" asked he of the brigand.

"Lady Darrel," replied Barboni.

Looking angrily at the brigand she exclaimed—

"Murderer and assassin! Heaven will not much longer permit you to continue your infamous career."

"Angela," answered Barboni, softly, as he addressed her by her Christian name, "you are excited to-day. Take the lad and leave me with my friend."

"He, too, is a scoundrel; but the lion must have his jackal," said her ladyship, with a sneering laugh.

Luni took advantage of this lull in the storm to crawl away and hide himself behind his mother.

"Send the old hag away," said Darrel, impatiently.

She turned her eyes fiercely upon him.

"Wretched spawn of a vile race," she said, furiously, "your days are numbered. I speak with prophetic voice. My sufferings have given me a second sight, and with your death will come the time when my child's wrongs and my own shall be righted."

Darrel trembled at this denunciation.

Taking Luni by the hand, she smoothed back his hair, kissed his tear-stained face, and led him quickly from the vault.

"That's a relief," exclaimed Darrel, drawing a deep breath.

"She is becoming troublesome," remarked Barboni, with a clouded brow.

Darrel was engaged in binding up the wound that his strange visitor had inflicted. It bled freely and caused him considerable pain.

"You have the remedy in your own hands," he said.

"Yes," replied the brigand. "But I never could make up my mind to offer her any violence."

"Are you usually so scrupulous?"

"I have pitied her, and considered her as harmless as her brat."

"She might be dangerous, for she appears to know too much."

"It is not often that her mind is so clear as to allow her to speak in the way she did just now. Seeing Luni struck, irritated her. In a short time she will have forgotten all about it."

"I should give the pair of them a bullet through the head," replied Darrel.

"No necessity for that; forget that you have seen them," answered Barboni.

In spite of Gus Darrel's efforts, he could not stop the bleeding from his wound.

It was necessary to go into the outer cave for assistance, and the conversation came to an end.

Barboni evinced the greatest anxiety for his welfare, and from that day showed him a tenderness which few would have thought the brigand capable of feeling.

As for Darrel, the revelation gave him food for thought, which was not altogether of a pleasant nature.

He unexpectedly found himself an impostor.

Augustus Lord Darrel was nothing better than the son of Dominico Ponilippo, *alias* Barboni the brigand.

Lady Darrel and her son, the real possessor of the title, were wretched, half-mad captives in the brigand's cave.

Much rather would he that the bewildering confession had never been made.

Lady Darrel had predicted his death.

This he fancied was simply the foolish raving of an angry and excited woman.

The future was black and lowering.

It was with a mind ill at ease, and a faint heart, that he went about his ordinary duties.

He longed for some decisive event to happen, so that he might make some change in his position.

At one time he thought of murdering Lady Darrel and Luni, and afterwards returning to England to take his trial for the manslaughter of Lieutenant Cockles.

At all hazards, he wanted to get away from the brigands, and once more be the rich Lord Darrel.

CHAPTER XLII.

THE WOLF AND THE LAMB.

THE four friends started as they had agreed.

Tom Carden went across the Volturno in the direction of the Prince Di Villanova's property.

Harvey explored the mountains on the right of Castel Inferno.

The little coxswain started for the sybil's cave, while Harkaway went to Torre del Greco to search among the lava and the vines for the mysterious brigand upon whom nobody could put his hand.

Consequently, Hilda and Lily Cockles were alone, with only Mr. Mole and Monday to look after and protect them.

On the morning which saw the departure of the four friends in different directions, the Prince Di Villanova cantered into Naples.

He rode his horse into the stables of the Contessa Di Malafedi.

Bigamini was lounging about the yard.

Directly he saw the prince, he came up with a respectful salutation, and assisted him to dismount.

" What news ?" curtly demanded the prince.

" The four Englishmen have started each in a different direction, to look for Barboni," replied Bigamini.

" Per Baccho !" said the prince, with a smile which showed his white teeth, " some madness has seized them."

" They're like the bundle of sticks," said Bigamini, " when together, all right, but split up, they'll find themselves nowhere."

" Your letter said that Harkaway intended to go to Vesuvius ; is that so ?"

" Your highness is right."

" Good. Take this paper."

He handed the spy a sheet of paper, on which something was written.

" These are your instructions. At the Portici vineyard you will find Hunstoni with six men dressed as labourers."

Bigamini nodded his head.

" Is the contessa within ?" asked the prince.

" No ; she has gone to Sorrento."

" Go. Do your duty, and you shall be rewarded."

The prince waved his hand and strode from the stable yard into the Strada Di Toledo.

He stopped before the palazzo occupied by Jack and Harvey.

In a deep voice he muttered, " Per Dio ! Both your lives shall yet be in my hands."

And as he spoke, a vindictive frown lowered on his brow.

Monday met the prince at the door, and in reply to his inquiries, said that the gentlemen were all out, but he would take his name up to the ladies.

Hilda consented to receive the prince, who was shown into the drawing-room, where she was sitting with Lily.

Mr. Mole had made himself a sort of bed under some orange trees in the garden, and here with his cask, he dozed away the best part of the day.

He had also renewed his friendship with Monday.

The black would give him his armchair in the little pantry, and place before him the most thirst-provoking drinks.

Not that Mr. Mole required any inducement to indulge himself.

In return for Monday's kind attentions, Mole would give him all the news from Limbi.

Tell him of the latest movements of the Pisangs, and all that had happened during his brief governorship of the island.

The prince complimented the ladies on their good looks in his oily Italian style.

To Lily he paid especial attention.

The girl did not absolutely dislike the prince, but she felt afraid of him.

He fascinated her, as a serpent is said to attract any living thing which comes within the influence of its eye.

Hilda asked him to stay to lunch, which he did.

In the afternoon he was again by Lily's side, and she found herself telling him her history.

She seemed as if she had known this strange man all her life.

Hilda had retired to indulge in a siesta, or afternoon sleep, being overcome by the heat.

"So, my little child," said the prince, "you are all alone in the world?"

"Yes," replied Lily, with a sigh.

"You have cause to dislike the family of Darrel?"

"I bear no malice towards Lord Darrel," answered Lily. "But he made a cruel break-up in our happy family."

"You must marry," said the prince.

"Ah," said Lily, this time smiling, "marriage has its cares, and I do not know anyone who would have me."

"Hundreds of men would only be too happy," answered the Prince Di Villanova; "I know one."

"Do you indeed? Who is he?"

"A prince; rich, considered handsome, loving and affectionate."

"Those are great recommendations," she cried; "what is his name?"

"My child," replied Villanova, "pardon this abruptness; I speak of myself. It is——"

Lily looked up, pained and surprised.

"I cannot pardon such a declaration," she said; "you have no right to make it."

"But——"

"We are almost strangers. I have given you no encouragement."

"You do not know the impulsiveness of the Neapolitan nature," answered the prince, not at all disconcerted.

"I must beg you to leave me."

"Presently, amico mio. First of all, I must see this cloud pass away. You will promise me to think over what I have said?"

In spite of herself Lily was constrained to say—

"Yes."

"Come, add to that something."

"What?"

"Say you are not angry with me for expressing my love for the most beautiful girl I have ever seen."

"I forgive you, prince," replied Lily; "though you really must leave me. I will tell Mrs. Harvey. She is my friend. I will be guided——"

"You will tell no one, cara mia," interrupted Villanova. "This is our secret. Promise me."

Once more Lily found herself obeying him.

"Soon we will talk further of this, for it is your destiny to become my wife. Fight against it, struggle as you may, pretty one, you will be the Princess Di Villanova."

He rose, and kissing her hand, which she allowed him to take, went away.

When he was gone she burst into tears.

The strange scene had taken her completely by surprise.

She knew that Walter Campbell loved her.

A girl can always tell when a man is fond of her.

How angry Walter would be if he knew of the prince's conduct.

Certainly she had not pledged herself to Walter, but she liked him better than she did the prince.

Yet she felt that Villanova had such a magic influence over her, that if he were to command her to accept his hand, she would be unable to refuse.

"I must not see him again. I must hide myself," she murmured in terrified accents. "Oh, how I fear that man."

The prince felt perfectly satisfied.

He had established an influence over Lily, which he knew she could not shake off.

With a smile of placid contentment he went into the city and purchased a very valuable diamond bracelet.

This he carried himself to Monday, requesting him to take it to Miss Cockles, with his compliments.

The door of Monday's room was open, and he saw Mr. Mole sitting in the armchair, busily sucking sherry cobblers through a straw.

"A fine day, sir," he said, recognising Mole as a companion of Harkaway and

Carden, on the day of the duel between the latter and Barboni

"It always is fine here," replied Mole.

"Heavenly climate," continued the prince.

"I don't know so much about that," said Mole. "A jolly good yellow fog wouldn't be half bad, by way of a change."

The prince smiled.

"Have a cobbler?" asked Mole.

"Thank you. Will you mix me one?" said Villanova.

"What do you take me for," asked Mole, indignantly, "eh? I am the late governor of the important island of Limbi."

"Indeed!"

"It is evident you don't know me."

"Pardon me, your excellency," said Villanova, repressing a smile.

"That is better. Excellency; I like that. Nothing like giving a man his title. If you want a grog or a cobbler, Monday will attend upon you."

"I will await his return. By the way, you are an old friend of Mr. Harkaway."

"Taught him all he knows," replied Mole.

"Really."

"And that isn't much. The fact is, Mr. Harkaway can do nothing without me. I shall have to catch this brigand fellow for him."

Villanova smiled again.

"From all accounts," he said, "he is not so easily caught."

"I'll back myself to catch him in a given time, sir," said Mole; adding, "where's that Monday?"

"Here um am, sir," replied Monday, entering the pantry.

"Well?" ejaculated Villanova.

"Miss Lily, she send her thanks, sir," said Monday.

The prince nodded his head.

He thought the influence he had established over her would be great enough to induce her to accept his present.

In fact, Lily was afraid to send it back.

"Mix this gentleman a cobbler, Monday," exclaimed Mr. Mole.

Monday compounded the drink, and handed it to the prince.

"Now I will give you a toast," said Mole.

"I will drink it with pleasure."

"Confusion to the brigands."

Villanova drank the toast in silence.

"If they only knew that I'd arrived, they'd cave in at once," continued Mole, throwing himself back in a chair.

There was a pause, during which Mr. Mole applied himself vigorously to his glass.

"People say um Vesuvius going to bust up, sare," remarked Monday.

"We have been expecting an eruption for some days past," replied the prince.

"What is Vesuvius?" said Mole, contemptuously.

"A large volcanic mountain."

"Pooh! pooh! an ant hill, you mean."

"An eruption is a grand sight."

"Bosh! what is it? Something like a schoolboy's squib. You should have been in the Malay Archipelago with me. We had eruptions there, and earthquakes."

"Vesuvius is not to be despised," said the prince.

"Rot! I tell you," answered Mole. "You know nothing about it. I wouldn't go across the street to see your Roman candle at work."

"I don't think you would go very far for anything at present," replied the prince.

"What, sir? Do you defy me? Monday."

"Yes, sare."

"Did not this man insult me?"

"Um not hear him, sare," replied Monday.

"Oh, yes, he did, and I'm not going to stand his cheek. Take him away, Monday, or I shall do him an injury."

Monday showed his gleaming teeth, but did not move.

Mr. Mole attempted to rise; his legs, however, were not obedient.

They trembled to such an extent that he sank back in his chair.

"You may thank your stars," he exclaimed, "that my gout has come on. Monday, turn that person out."

"I wish to save you the trouble of any further talking," answered the prince. "Good day."

Mr. Mole took up a glass, and threw it at Villanova.

It struck him in the back.

"Ha! ha!" he said, with a drunken chuckle, "I had him then, Monday. By my life, I can do it. Ha! ha!"

The prince turned round angrily.

In a corner of the room was a hat box of Jack's.

It was empty.

Taking it up, he came back to Mole and jammed it down over his head.

The bottom was soon crushed through, and Mole's head was invisible.

With a handkerchief, the prince fastened his hands behind him.

Seizing him by the shoulder, he said—

"Come with me."

"Boohoo! I say, Monday. Hallo! give me air. Hoo! hoo! hoo!" gasped Mole, from the depths of the hat box.

"I will teach you how Italian gentlemen punish drunken Englishmen who insult them," continued the prince.

Monday looked on with a grin.

But when the prince dragged Mr. Mole, still bellowing, towards the street door, he thought he ought to interfere.

He had no very great respect for the late governor of Limbi.

Still he liked him, and was his friend to a certain extent.

"Hi, mist' prince," he said, "you let um go, please, sare."

"He has insulted me," said the prince.

"Mast' Jack never speak to you again, sare, if you hurt Mist' Mole."

"I daresay I can survive the infliction."

"Me tell um all about it."

"You are perfectly at liberty to do so."

The prince had by this time gained the street, into the middle of which he dragged the unhappy Mole.

Giving him a kick, he said—

"Remember in future, how to talk to an Italian prince."

Then he strode hastily away.

The force of the kick precipitated Mole on his hands and knees.

He looked so comical, that Monday, who saw there was no further danger of his being hurt, put his hands on his knees and laughed loudly.

Mr. Mole was too tipsy to get up straight.

Every time he tried, he rolled back, and even had he been sober, it was no easy thing to do with his hands tied behind his back.

All he could do, was to crawl hither and thither.

He poked his hat-boxed head, first one way and then the other.

A crowd of people collected.

It tickled the fancy of the Neapolitans immensely.

Roars of laughter broke from the crowd.

"Um never see such funny thing," said Monday to himself. "Ha, ha, ha!"

"Ha, ha, ha!" echoed the throng.

"Um split um side. Ho, ho!" cried Monday.

Mr. Mole was rendered desperate by the laughter of the crowd.

It buzzed in his ears like the falling of water.

With a desperate effort, he dragged one hand out of the handkerchief which bound his wrists.

Then he grasped the hat-box fiercely.

It came off, after doing some damage to his ears.

"Where is the villain who did this?" he cried, holding the hat-box aloft.

No one made any reply.

"The coward dare not show himself," he went on.

Casting the hat-box on the ground, he jumped savagely upon it.

"Thus I pound and crush my enemies," he said.

The next moment he lost his balance, and fell on the top of it.

Redoubled roars of laughter came from the onlookers, who enjoyed this "comico Inglese," as they called him, very much indeed.

Monday now ran forward, and taking Mr. Mole in his arms, carried him into the house.

"I'm orright, my good fren'," said Mr. Mole.

"Come 'long, sare."

"Lemme 'lone—tell you, I'm orright."

"Keep still, sare, and don't kick um so," said Monday.

"Doosed odd, the 'fect of this country," muttered Mole. "Heat of sun so great, that 'bliged to get blacks to carry me."

Monday carried him along a passage into the garden, and safely deposited him on his bed under the orange trees.

He soon fell asleep.

"Him right now," he said. "When um wake up, um want him supper and begin again."

Then the scene in the street with Mole and the hat-box on his head occurred to him, and he went back to his pantry giggling.

"Ole Mole, him good fun!" he exclaimed. "Monday like um Mole. He, he, he! Ho, ho, ho!"

He burst out laughing again till he was obliged to kick his feet on the floor to stop himself.

CHAPTER XLIII.

MR. MOLE GOES ON THE SPREE.

MONDAY was quite right in his forecast of what Mr. Mole would do when he woke up, and wanted to get rid of a very bad headache.

The professor indulged in a profound sleep of three hours.

Then he became alive to the fact that the lovely climate of Naples is marred by the presence of mosquitoes.

He woke up itching dreadfully.

His face, his ankles, and his wrists were specially troublesome.

"Monday," he cried, "I want you, Monday, you black son of a sea cook, where are you?"

It happened that Monday was smoking a cigarette in the garden.

He was not far from the professor.

The evening was drawing to a close.

Over the beautiful and never-to-be-forgotten Bay of Naples, the sun was declining rapidly.

"Who you calling names, sare?" replied Monday.

"You're a nigger," said Mole.

"Same flesh and blood Mast' Mole. Man an' a brother."

"I'm bothered if I'd have you for a brother, or a sister, or a cousin, or an aunt."

"Go on, sare, pile it up."

"Well, you can't get away from the fact that you are a nigger."

"If you keep on 'sulting me, sare, I'll have to beat you with um stick."

Monday, as he spoke, tore down a branch from a tree.

He stripped it of its leaves.

Then he advanced threateningly towards the professor, who had risen to his feet.

The attitude of the black much alarmed him.

"Strike me!" he gasped.

"Yes, sare, if you call me out of um name."

"Beat a professor of languages, a schoolmaster, the governor of an island, the proprietor of a tea garden in China!"

"Why not? If give um too much of um cheek, old 'un."

"Old! There's a snack. Why, I'm as young as Harkaway or Harvey."

"May think so, but you no good. Keep um tongue quiet; shut up um mouth."

"Not to please you, my coloured friend. Go and fetch me a brandy and soda."

"Not if um knows it—unless you 'pologise to me."

"What! I eat humble pie to you."

"Yes, sare; that's what's the matter."

"I never heard of such a thing in my life!" exclaimed Mole. "Why, man alive, you must be out of your senses! I am a professor of languages, and you, poor benighted savage, don't know your A B C."

"Know how to use um stick, though," persisted Monday.

He advanced in a threatening manner.

The branch was raised in the air, and there was an ominous look in the black's eyes.

Mr. Mole saw that he was standing on his dignity, and thoroughly in earnest.

The blood of a prince was in Monday's veins, and he could not tolerate insults from anybody.

It seemed to the professor that he had better come to terms, if he did not want to submit to the humiliation of a thrashing.

He would be like a child in the hands of Monday.

So, after a moment's consideration, he

determined to give in with as good a grace as possible.

"You are very touchy to-day," he exclaimed—"extremely, absurdly sensitive. I did not mean to say anything personally offensive to you, and, as you have taken it seriously, I can only express my regret."

Monday's honour was at once satisfied.

Though quickly irritated, he soon forgave.

"That good enough; we friends again now," cried he. "Take a fin, as the shark said to the man before eating him."

He held out his hand in token of amity.

Mr. Mole grasped it in a cordial manner.

"That's as it should be," he remarked. "Why should we quarrel? In future you must respect my grey hairs, and make allowance for me. Even that impetuous fellow Harkaway would not dare to strike me. If he did, he would have some plain language from yours truly, Isaac Mole."

"Get um drink now."

"Do so, my worthy, if illiterate friend. I like you, and I will tell you what I will do with you. I feel that I want to enjoy myself."

"Me feel that way, too."

"I must have companionship," continued Mole. "In my purse I have fifty pounds in notes and gold."

"That am a nice tidy sum, sare," replied Monday.

"It is not to be sneezed at. Now I invite you to dine with me, and go to the play afterwards. We'll have a rattling good first-class A1 dinner—all the luxuries, regardless of expense."

"Um jolly fine idea that."

"I will treat to everything; in short, we will go on the spree, and be as gay and careless as giddy youth itself."

"That um way to talk. Three cheers for um Mole. Hurrah! fetch um drink, and then we start," cried Monday.

The black liked good eating, and was very fond of music, though, of course, he did not understand much about it.

When he had attended to the wants of the professor, they put on their hats, and sallied forth into the street.

It was a lovely day, and the charming Neapolitan sky never looked bluer, while the bay was an entrancing picture.

Knowing the city tolerably well, Mr. Mole led the way to a noted place for dining in one of the principal streets.

The windows of the large hall, and those of the private rooms, looked out on to the sea.

It was called the Grand Restaurant Carlo.

A refreshing breeze was blowing landward, and mitigated the extreme heat.

Mole had been there before, and walking through the hall, made his way to a staircase leading to the private rooms.

These were charged extra, but, being bent on enjoyment, he did not care for that.

Thinking that he had previously secured a room and ordered his dinner, the waiters took no notice of him.

He ought to have asked for a private apartment, as many people engage one by letter or telegraph the day before.

Each one was numbered, and seeing the door of number five open, and it being empty, Mole, attended by Monday, entered.

It happened that this room had been asked for previously by a lady and gentleman.

The table was laid for two; flowers being on it, and upon a sideboard were various wines in ice coolers.

A waiter passing by saw them come in, and imagining that they were the persons for whom the dinner was prepared, went below to bring it up.

It was within five minutes of the time at which the repast had been ordered.

Not for a moment did he think that there was anything in the nature of a mistake.

Mr. Mole took a chair, and looked at the printed *menu*, or bill of fare.

Monday placed himself opposite.

"Excellent," said the professor; "all the delicacies of the season, I declare. We shall have a feast!"

"That's better than um famine, sare," replied Monday.

"Just touch the bell, please. I am ready to begin; hate waiting. They looked at me as we came in; my distinguished presence impressed them. I am known here. We shall be well treated."

Scarcely had Monday rung the bell than the waiter appeared with oysters.

anchovies, sardines, and thin slices of bread and butter.

Then soups, fish, *entrées*, poultry, joints, sweets, cheese, salad, and wine to follow.

Some light wine was placed on the sideboard, and the waiter poured it into the glasses.

"Eat away, and drink all you can; I'm paying for this!" exclaimed the professor.

"You very good-natured gentleman, sare. You have my thanks from the bottom of um heart," answered Monday.

"This is better than brigand hunting, eh?"

"Um rather think so."

"Harkaway's a fool not to enjoy himself as I do. Ha! ha! Drink up; try some of these oysters."

"Doing very well, sare, on the anchovy fish. Come to um oysters presently."

They continued to eat with a relish, thinking of the nice things that were to follow.

When the soup was put on the table they were rudely interrupted.

Two middle-aged Italians, dressed in the height of fashion, and wearing a profusion of jewellery, made their appearance on the threshold.

They stared first at Mole and Monday, then at the waiter, and finally at the number on the door.

Addressing the waiter, one exclaimed—

"Guiseppe, you know us?"

"Yes, signor," was the reply. "You are among our best and most honoured customers."

"This is number five?"

"Certainly, signor."

"Very well. We ordered dinner at this house, in this particular room. How is it we find others eating it?"

"Some mistake," said the waiter. "The gentlemen came in. I did not know the room was reserved for you."

"Can we have another?"

"All the others are occupied."

"Confound it!" cried the newcomer. "This is nice treatment. So, we are to have no dinner! By heaven! we will have satisfaction of some sort. There is my card."

"And there is mine," said his companion.

Both threw their cards on the table, and twisted their moustaches fiercely.

They looked as if they were perfect fire-eaters.

One card fell before Mole, the other touched Monday's plate.

The first bore the name of Signor Castel, the second that of Signor Marcelli.

Although they looked like gentlemen, the men were two of the most expert cardsharpers and pickpockets in Italy.

They went from city to city, looking out for victims.

France and Germany had suffered from their depredations, while they were not unknown in London.

They spoke various languages fluently, and were just then carrying on their depredations in Naples.

Neither Mole nor Monday had any suspicion of their true character.

They were much alarmed and annoyed at the predicament in which they found themselves.

"Here's um nice kettle of fish," muttered Monday. "Wish um had stopped at home now."

"It's like my luck," groaned Mole. "I never try to enjoy myself, but there is sure to be a row."

Signor Castel walked up to Mole, and tapped him on the shoulder.

The professor trembled as if he were going to immediate execution.

"You are English, I presume," said the Italian, "and your friend an Indian. You ought to know that you cannot with impunity take possession of engaged rooms, and eat other people's dinners."

"I am going to pay for it," replied Mole.

"Bah! I think you are a couple of swindlers and blacklegs."

"Sir! I am Professor Mole, of Oxford University; my friend is a Prince of Limbi, in the Malay Archipelago."

"It is easy to say so."

"I can prove my respectability," continued Mole. "You are cherishing an error."

"It is my opinion," answered Signor Castel, with a smile of incredulity, "that you have no money. The police ought to be sent for."

"That is easily demonstrated," cried Mole, eagerly.

He produced his purse, and exhibited the contents.

All the Italian swindlers wanted to know was how much money he had about him.

"Fifty pounds English," added Mole. "It is enough to pay for ten dinners."

Signor Castel, as he called himself—he had a dozen aliases—changed his tone immediately.

The sight of the gold and notes were quite enough for him.

"Pardon me!" he exclaimed. "I own frankly that I have been labouring under a misapprehension; but do not allow us to lose our dinners. There will be enough for four. I ask you to dine with us. What do you say? Be our guests, eh, Marcelli? We will all sit down together."

"With pleasure," replied Marcelli.

"That would not be fair," said Mole. "By all means, let us make a merry and united party, but permit me to pay."

"I cannot—my pride will not allow it!" cried Castel. "I am rich, sir. Do you want to insult me by insinuating that I cannot pay for a dinner?"

"That won't do at all," Marcelli chimed in.

"By heaven! if I thought he meant it, I'd cut his head off."

"Or shoot him on the spot," said Marcelli.

Mr. Mole began to quake again.

"I didn't mean it that way, gentlemen," he protested. "If you wish to do so, you shall settle the bill."

"That's better!" exclaimed Castel. "Chairs, waiter! Two serviettes. We join these gentlemen. Never mind the preliminaries. We begin with the soup. Pour out the wine. And, hark ye! let everything be of the best, and in sufficient quantity, or we will never enter the house again."

"Si, signor," responded the waiter.

The dinner now began in earnest, and the Italians proved themselves to be very good company.

Both Mole and Monday enjoyed themselves immensely.

Four portions of every dish were served instead of two. The wines were as excellent as they were numerous, and all went well.

Mole, as usual, drank more than was good for him.

Even Monday indulged more freely than he had ever done before.

When the dessert and the Burgundy were placed upon the table, they both felt unusually sleepy.

They struggled against the sensation, laughing heartily at the funny anecdotes told by Castel and Marcelli.

"I will tell you what we will do for a wind up, and to cement the friendship that has so strangely sprung up between us, which I hope will last for a full lifetime," said Castel.

"What is that?" Mole queried.

"We must go to the theatre. I'll start out and get a box before it is too late."

"A splendid idea! I intended to see a play to-night; but, look here, as you are standing the dinner, let me pay for the box at the theatre."

"Nonsense! You shall not."

"I insist. It is my right," cried Mole.

"Well, hang it! if you insist, what can I do, eh, Marcelli?" replied Castel.

"Per Baccho! it is hard," Marcelli replied; "yet you must give in. Mr. Mole is justified on having his turn."

"Very well. I am annoyed, but no matter. Give me your purse, Mr. Mole. It is a grand opera night; the box may be five or six pounds—I know not which. In a few minutes I will be back."

With the simplicity of a child, the professor handed the Italian his purse.

He did not think of taking anything out.

Was he to be outdone in generosity by the two strangers?

Not if he knew it, he said to himself.

Signor Castel rose, put on his overcoat and hat, and went away to purchase a box at the theatre, which would hold four.

When he was gone, Marcelli searched in his pockets for something.

A look of annoyance stole over his countenance.

"Have you lost anything?" Mole inquired.

"It is extremely provoking, but I have left my cigar-case at home," he rejoined. "I was about to offer you some very choice imported weeds from Havana."

"'LOOK AT YOURSELF IN THE GLASS,' SAID CARDEN."

"Do not be put out; we can procure some cigars in the restaurant," replied Mole.

"You would not care for them after mine. There is only one shop in the city, six doors from here, where you can buy them. I will run out and get a couple of dozen."

"Pray do not trouble yourself on our account."

"Oh! I must—I will."

Saying this with an air of determination, Signor Marcelli took up his hat and coat.

He smiled, bowed, and also quitted the apartment.

"What charming fellows!" exclaimed Mole; "so obliging, agreeable, entertaining, and generous to a degree."

"Um little nasty at first, sare," responded Monday. "Soon get all right, though. First-class dinner. I eat till um feel tight as a drum, and almost ready to burst."

"Really, I never had a better repast. It will come to a large figure. We punished the wines as well as the food, which was of the best, and well cooked. I shall cultivate the acquaintance of these gentlemen."

"Very nice people, sare."

"I should think so. Won't Harkaway and Harvey be jealous when I bring them to the house as my friends. All he thinks of are brigands and thieves. I meet with gentlemen."

Mr. Mole spoke proudly.

The waiter brought in coffee, and, at the same time, laid down a silver salver.

On this was the bill for the dinner.

Attracted by curiosity, the professor took it up and smiled as he looked at the total.

"Grand Restaurant Carlo," he read. "Dinners for four, including wines (12 bottles), 200 lire."

"Bless me!" cried Mr. Mole; "a lire is two shillings of our money. That will make twenty pounds. Just five pounds a head."

"Rather glad um not got to pay it, sare?" asked Monday.

"On consideration, I am. It is rather stiff. I did not mean to spend more than a five-pound note."

"That will be 'bout the price of the theatre box."

"Exactly. That I don't mind. It won't hurt me. The fact is, I am rather short of money. At home, I have not more than thirty pounds in my desk, and I shall not get my dividends till next month."

"You better off than me. Um got no money at all, except what Mast' Jack give me to spend," observed Monday.

"All the better for you; it keeps you out of mischief. Being poor, you can't drink," replied Mole, severely.

"How 'bout umself, sare?" Monday asked, with a grin.

"Oh, I'm different from you," Mole said, loftily.

He lighted a cigarette, a box being on the table, and Monday followed his example.

The minutes passed rapidly away.

Half-an-hour elapsed, and Mole began to get rather fidgety about his new friends and his purse.

He knew that the theatre was ten minutes' walk from the restaurant, and Signor Castel might be delayed at the office.

It was singular, however, that Signor Marcelli did not return, as five minutes was more than sufficient for him to buy a few cigars in.

Had he been imposed upon?

It looked very much as if he had.

The thought made him turn cold, as if iced water had been poured down his back.

Fifty pounds was a large sum of money to lose, and how was he to settle the bill, which, as we have stated, amounted to twenty?

It was also humiliating to think that he had been made a fool of.

Occasionally the waiter, Guiseppe, looked in the room in a suspicious kind of manner.

"It is extraordinary," remarked the professor, at length; "the Italians are a long time gone."

"What you give them um purse for?" asked Monday; "that stupid thing to do!"

"You should have warned me before I parted with it."

"If I had you would have jumped down um throat," replied Monday. "I think we are done, sare."

"For mercy's sake, don't say that!" cried Mole.

"Didn't like um look of those gents· What we do now?"

"I can get no money, unless I go home and open my desk."

"The landlord not let um do that."

Monday was quite correct in his surmise.

At that crisis in the entertainment, the proprietor of the restaurant entered the room.

"Excuse me, gentlemen," he exclaimed, "will you oblige me by settling my bill!"

"The other two gentlemen agreed to pay," replied the professor.

The landlord smiled incredulously.

"That won't do," he said. "They ordered a cab, and told the driver to take them to the railway station, as they wanted to catch a train as quickly as they could."

Mr. Mole's arms fell powerless by his side.

"What?" he gasped.

"Come, no acting; pay up, or I'll bring in the police. You don't play this trick on me for nothing. Am I to lose two hundred lire?" shouted the proprietor.

"My good sir, I don't want you to lose a farthing by me," Mole replied.

"Then settle at once."

"I lent the Italian gentleman, Signor Castel, my purse to buy a box at the opera, and—"

"That won't do. You are all four in league together. Guiseppe!"

"Yes, sir?"

"The police. Make haste. I'll lock the rascals up."

"Be not hasty; I am respectable. Let me go home, and I will get you the money. Really, I am a reliable man; my name is Professor Mole, of England. Do not be rash."

The landlord hesitated.

After all, he might be wrong.

He recalled Guiseppe, and asked Mole where he lived.

He was immediately informed.

After some further parley, he consented to accompany the professor and Monday to the house.

A victoria was sent for, and, much to Mole's relief, they started together.

He had been saved the shame of being put in a police cell.

When the house was reached, he took the landlord inside, got the money required, and paid it without a murmur.

The landlord thereupon retired.

Mr. Mole heaved a deep sigh, poured out some brandy, and drank it slowly.

Throwing himself into a chair, Monday burst out into a hearty fit of laughter.

"What are you grinning at, you ugly ape—you baboon?" asked Mole, crossly.

"That um very fine dinner sare, but rather dear at seventy pounds," replied Monday.

"I've been shamefully deceived."

"Nice to have gentleman friend to call on you, sare. Such very nice people."

"Stop your chaff, or I'll never speak to you again."

"Very good box at theatre, sare."

"Look here, do you want to drive me mad? I think I've had enough."

"What Mast' Jack say?" continued Monday.

"You imp of darkness, if you say a word about this adventure to Harkaway, Harvey, or any of the crowd, I'll be your enemy for life. I'll do you one for it," Mole cried.

"It excellent joke, sare; pity to keep it secret; Mast' Jack make fun of you; but I'll keep it quiet, um have all laugh to umself. You want to see Signor Castel."

"I wish the rogue was in the bottomless pit."

"How you like Signor Marcelli, sare? Very good company. You pick up with um gentlefolk. Ha, ha, ha! Ho, ho, ho!"

"Get out. I can't stand it," yelled Mole, tearing his scanty hair. Monday walked away holding his sides.

In high dudgeon the professor lighted a pipe, filled his glass, and reclined on a sofa.

It was a long time before he forgot how he went on the spree, and gave Monday a dinner which cost seventy pounds.

His only consolation was, that Monday told nobody anything about it.

He was saved from the ridicule of Harkaway and his friends.

"HE FIRED, THE BALL STRUCK THE BRIGAND IN THE BREAST."

"'YOU HAVE NOTHING TO FEAR FROM ME,' SAID BARBONI."

Another Coloured Picture for Binding with the Work will be Given with our Next Number.

JACK RAINED A SHOWER OF BLOWS ON THE BRIGAND'S FACE.'

"BIGAMINI HELD UP THE GHASTLY TROPHY."

Another Coloured Picture for Binding with the Work will be Given with our Next Number!

CHAPTER XLIV.

A FRUITLESS CHASE.

THREE or four days slipped by.

They were passed in great anxiety by Hilda, who was fearful that something had happened to her husband.

The Prince di Villanova called every day, and his influence over Lily grew stronger.

Hilda did not fail to notice that something was preying upon her young friend's mind.

On the morning of the fifth day, the ladies were sitting in the drawing-room.

The Venetian blinds were closed to keep out the heat, and two small fountains sent up their cooling spray to the ceiling.

"Tell me, my sweet pet," said Hilda, " what you are thinking of?"

"I dare not," answered Lily.

She had started at the sound of Mrs. Harvey's voice, as if roused from some deep abstraction.

"Dare not!" echoed Hilda.

"He told me not to breathe a syllable to anyone."

"Who?"

Lily was silent.

"There is some mystery in this," pursued Hilda. "You ought not to have any secret from me."

Still Lily preserved a profound silence.

"I see how it is," said Hilda, with a deep sigh. "You are in love."

"I do not know whether it is love. To me it seems more akin to fear," answered Lily.

"This dreadful brigand hunting is enough to kill anyone. My rest is broken at night, and I have little peace by day," returned Hilda.

"It is not that which worries me," said Lily; "though, of course, I sympathise deeply with you?"

"Are you not in love with Walter Campbell?"

"Walter! No—that is, at least—I was not speaking of him!" stammered Lily.

"Who, then? Surely it is not the prince?"

Lily nodded her head.

"I should never have thought it. He is so proud and haughty, not at all calculated to attract a young girl; and Walter, I know, loves you."

"Does he?" asked Lily, simply.

"Yes, indeed. He told Richard so, and, of course, he told me, as married men generally tell their wives everything."

"I do not know how it is," replied Lily. "I must be very weak-minded, and silly, and foolish."

"Why?"

"Because I do believe the prince could make me do anything he told me."

"Indeed?"

"It is true. Did you ever hear of magnetic influence? I feel like something that must fly to him, as if he were a lodestone," said Lily.

"You must fight against it. The little coxswain, as Richard calls him, would break his heart, if you were to marry that stern foreigner."

"He is not stern to me."

"No?"

"No, indeed, he seems so soft and gentle, and his voice has such a charm, it rings in my ears like sweet music, for hours after he is gone," said Lily.

Hilda was about to make some further remark, when the door opened, and Harvey rushed in.

He was covered with dust, and looked wild and excited, while his skin was as brown as a berry, from exposure to the sun.

Hilda threw herself in his arms, with a glad cry.

"Oh, thank Heaven, you have come back!" she cried, while the tears started to her eyes.

"Bless you, my own love," replied Harvey, straining her to his breast, and kissing her tenderly.

He placed her again in the chair from which she had risen, and shaking hands with Lily, looked at himself in the glass.

"Ah, Harvey," said Mr. Mole's voice, at the door. "I heard you had come back. Have you brought the brigand's head with you?"

"'HA, I HAVE YOU THERE,' CRIED CARDEN, MAKING A THRUST."